ROMAN WOLFE'S
ADIRONDACK ORDEAL

Bill Sheehan

iUniverse, Inc.
New York   Bloomington

iUniverse books may be ordered through booksellers or by contacting:

iUniverse
1663 Liberty Drive
Bloomington, IN 47403
www.iuniverse.com
1-800-Authors (1-800-288-4677)

Because of the dynamic nature of the Internet, any Web addresses or links contained in this book may have changed since publication and may no longer be valid. The views expressed in this work are solely those of the author and do not necessarily reflect the views of the publisher, and the publisher hereby disclaims any responsibility for them.

ISBN: 978-1-4401-2135-7 (sc)
ISBN: 978-1-4401-2136-4 (ebook)

Library of Congress Control Number: 2009922905

Printed in the United States of America

iUniverse rev. date: 02/10/09

And they rode upon the earth,
The Four Horsemen of the apocalypse,
And among them we knew their names:
Conquest, Pestilence, War and Death.
But the most feared among them was
He who was fourth and rode the pale horse.

—Book of Revelations

"People sleep peacefully in their beds
at night only because rough men stand
ready to do violence on their behalf."

—George Orwell

"The only thing necessary for the
triumph of evil is for good men to
do nothing."

—Edmund Burke

Previous books written by Bill Sheehan

MARAGOLD IN FOURTH

MARAGOLD IN FIFTH

MARAGOLD IN SIXTH

To Sandra Grace Sheehan and Mara, Todd, Lily and Slone Bonnewell. The people who are at the very important center of my world.

Prologue

WHAT I REMEMBER MOST during my boyhood was the fighting and the resultant bloody noses, black eyes, cuts, abrasions and bruises that were the natural consequences of my frequent physical combat. It wasn't that I was driven to it by a mental aberration, or meanness or a desire to inflict or receive pain. I just couldn't avoid it unless I constantly backed-down and ran away. But I wouldn't back down and I certainly wouldn't run, unless it was *toward*, not *away* from my opponent. Fighting came to be unavoidable, so I stopped trying to avoid it.

I was tall, skinny and had a small-boned, skeletal structure. I guess I looked weak, vulnerable, and ripe for a bully's exciting exploitation and the amusement.

Bullies my own age, but especially older bullies, thought they sensed a fragile insecurity in my wish to avoid a confrontation. Maybe they thought they saw fear and assumed that it was fear of them—instead of my fear of hurting them badly. Maybe it was just the way I looked, tall and skinny, a nerd with black glasses. Maybe it was my clowning, jocular behavior in which I often made fun of myself for laughs. Bullies thought they could tease me, pick on me, and push me around. Actually, all of that could be done, but only to a point. That point, however, was a sharp one, and the distance to that point was a short one. Many bullies regretted trying to stretch that distance and found that they were suddenly feeling the sharp point of my anger.

1

I could be comical and full of laughter, but there's a lightly-sleeping, ferociousness within me, a wild animal ferocity. I was very aware of it and sometimes feared what I may do with it. I've recognized its presence ever since I was a little, snot-nosed kid. I called this fierce, fiery, ferocious feeling, "Wolf," simply because, when I felt this way, my mind conjured up an image of a feral wolf, usually seen only by me, as a white, "pale" wolf. At that time I didn't know why the images were of a wolf, nor why it was white. I wouldn't learn the significance of those two things until I was older.

When I was older and about to have a physical confrontation, I would usually be vaguely aware of a feral, rumbling growl that only I could hear. I'd know, then, that Wolf had taken control of my body. At that moment, all the characteristics of a strong, healthy, cunning wolf were projected onto and into me. I realized early that this *Roamin' Wolf* lived within me, *Roman Wolfe*. This wolf slept lightly, but once awakened, that feral beast wouldn't shy from a fight, sometimes even hoping for the excitement of battle, as well as the smell and taste of blood that accompanied it. Wolf was my combat companion, giving me an unusually intense fierceness. Wolf and I would certainly leave you alone, if you would leave me alone. But pushing me, teasing me and bullying, beyond a certain point, brought out that wolf in me and the necessity for combat, as if it would purge my body of its tiredness, boredom and frustration with bullies. Unfortunately, at times, due to my youth, recklessness and carelessness were also involved with my suddenly ferocious; combative response to bullies. Usually the trouble started with name-calling, then pushing. Unfortunately, my expression showed how bored I was with the bully and made matters worse—my youth certainly wasn't the smartest time in my life.

Roman is an unusual first name, and that was the first thing about me to get laughed at. It set me apart, made me different. To be different when you're young means attracting attention to the abnormality. Perceived abnormality attracts immediate attention, teasing, and dislike. But I kind of liked my name. It conjured up images of the Roman Empire and Roman soldiers who were tough, strong, battle-tested warriors. I explained my own like for my name, but bullies thought it was a pretense, a sham and a glaring point of exposed vulnerability, but they were wrong and I was persistent.

I could joke and laugh like any young boy, and like most average-looking, young boys I was shy with girls, though maybe more so than other boys my age because I knew that most girls sensed something violent and scary about me—the opposite of a bully's perceptions. Girls intuitively sensed a strangeness in me that made them furrow their brows in suspicion at such a skinny boy with such piercing eyes that showed little fear and would change from joyful glee to dark and dangerous hostility in an instant. Also was the fact that my facial expressions must have shown my attraction, caring and concern for girls, yet, I almost always raised up shields, like Roman soldiers' shields, to keep them away and to keep my feelings for them and about them, hidden. In many ways I felt that I was lucky not to be handsome. That trait only attracted attention, which I wanted to avoid. Mostly I was a loner and just wanted to be left alone with my handful of friends, my thoughts and my privacy.

Around male bullies, my shields came down and the eyes behind each shield would be in a focused glare, so narrowly focused that it felt as if spears were emerging from my eyes, aimed directly at the bully. There was also a feeling of recklessness within me. It was a silent, uncaring, reckless attitude about injury that came over me when I or my friends were being teased by bullies. There was an obvious challenge in my fearless eyes, accompanied by a sarcastic grin, that got me into many fights that, perhaps, I could have avoided. Purposefully, my eyes showed no detectable fear. When fear was there, it was minor and well hidden. My lips would usually spread into a grin that, coupled with my staring silence, mocked my adversaries, making them feel foolish, thus assuring a confrontation. But when I did talk to a bully, he usually became a miser with his own words. Before a fight he would speak slowly, deliberately and carefully, as if his words were hard-earned money not to be wasted on trivialities. But mostly, I willingly irritated and infuriated bullies because I absolutely wouldn't back down, or back up, or even side-step away from them.

Sometimes I could change even more radically when threatened, like a warrior disguised inside a jester's costume. I would remain silent, set my jaw rigid and solid like a steel vice, then focus my intensity on the advancing threat. Somehow I knew ahead of time when there would be no acceptable way to avoid combat, when no amount of talk would placate the threat, and when physical confrontation was imminent. Rarely was I wrong—I believe it was Roamin' Wolf's influence. However, that does not mean that I always fought with every bully. A bully, I learned early, was usually cautious about protecting his reputation. Normally, a bully's reputation is gained by fighting smaller, weaker, less skilled opponents. But I purposely tried to give the impression that I didn't care about the size of the bully, his strength or his skills. I tried to show no fear—though I was fearful— and wouldn't back down unless doing so would protect a friend, or if the odds against me looked insurmountable. I did, however, usually leave an opening, a way out for the bully so that he could "save face," keep his reputation in tact, speak some courageously threatening words, and still avoid physical confrontation. I did fight a lot, but many bullies were willing to avoid confrontation, if given a way to save their rugged reputations. Giving them a way to "save face" would keep their reputations intact without working up a sweat, or risking injury, or possibly being defeated and losing that valued reputation.

I used to seriously think about my fights, especially the ones where I got beat up. When I was real young I tried hard to avoid all fighting, not because of fear, but because I knew that I had something in me that could deal-out punishment, as well as take it, and accept it. But it didn't take me long to learn that no matter how many adults said it, and wished it, walking away from a fight usually only accomplished a temporary delay to the fight. The persistent bully—and most are very persistent—could always find me somewhere, sometime and walking or running away only postponed what seemed inevitable to me. So I stood my ground and waited. Also, there was normally no such thing as "quit" in me. The bully might beat me up, but the bully would take a lot of punishment doing it, and that is exactly what kept many bullies at bay, the knowledge that they would take punishment themselves, risk injury and look bad amongst their friends—I knew it, used it to my advantage and avoided some fights that way.

I have to admit, however, that I sometimes wondered about my mental state. Why, for instance, was I the kind of person who usually moved toward danger and not away from it, like 99.9% of the world's population? Maybe I look like a nut, feel like a nut, smell like a nut, taste like a nut and think like a nut. So I guess I was nuts.

My "no quitting" code developed early. I was only about eight years old when I'd been in enough neighborhood and school fights so that even most older boys didn't pick on me or challenge me. It wasn't because I won all my fights either, because I certainly didn't. Rather it was a deep seated need in me not to quit, not to give up, not to walk or run away, and not to surrender even though I was bruised, bloodied, exhausted and every muscle in me ached. The neighborhood toughs learned this lesson when I kept coming at them, taking the punishment stoically and returning it as brutally as I could. I forced myself to do this even with stronger, older boys. Most of the young toughs were not steadfast in their desire to risk injury, and degrade their reputations with a long, time-consuming, battle that would leave both combatants bloody. Even if the bully wins the fight, if he's injured, especially if he's bleeding, his reputation is very much at risk. Then other kids might think: "Damn! He's not as tough as he thinks he is," or "Wow! He's not as tough as I thought he was."

But my ultimate weapon, when I did lose the fight, when I was knocked down and so tired, and sore, or bleeding, that I couldn't continue, was that I'd get up look at my opponent, his jaw hanging open and gasping for air, and say to him, "You win today. Rematch. Tomorrow." And when I saw this opponent the next day, I'd drop whatever I was doing and fight the kid all over again. And if I lost the fight again, I'd stare at my opponent again and utter those same words, "You win today. Rematch. Tomorrow." And true to my word, when I saw the kid the next day, I'd press on with the fight until I had finally won, or until the kid apologized for whatever he said or did to start the fight, or until the bully was so demoralized that he quit and walked away. It got to the point, eventually, where bullies didn't want to fight me because they knew that the fighting wouldn't end. If they beat me up the first time, I would just continue the fight the next day, and the next, and the next, until I beat them or made them quit. My opponents often became demoralized and discouraged by my masochistic persistence, my indomitable determination, my high threshold of pain and the stubborn pride that wouldn't allow me to give up. I had a fierce—and often foolish—determination to keep taking punishment, until it was my turn to do the punishing.

Each fight, win or lose, brought something good because I got better and better with each fight. With each defeat and each victory I learned more about fighting skills, what worked and what didn't, and even more about myself and how others felt or said about me—my friends thought I was a little crazy, weird; my enemies thought I was insane, a mental case. I also learned about my own intense resolve to win, not to quit, and to stand-up for myself in spite of the punishment that I may have to take. I learned that most bullies don't really want to fight, they just want to look big in the eyes of their friends and to bask in their adoration. That meant that their resolve to win almost certainly wasn't nearly as great as my own determination to win. I also learned that my friends might be right, perhaps I was a little crazy and weird when it came to fighting, but I can't deny that my style worked to my advantage.

So by the time I reached high school, my knuckles, wrists, forearms and knees all had multiple, but minor blemishes—that was my opinion of them. My friends, especially the girls, grimaced when they focused on them. To me those injuries were minor *blemishes* but to others, some of those blemishes looked like *scars*. The worst scar was on his upper lip, beneath my nose. That scar came from a very large and angry football player. It happened like this. One of my friends made a snide comment about the loss of a football game and didn't know that a football player was behind him. I saw the football player spin my friend around and cock his large right hand preparing to punch the boy. I pushed my friend out of the way, tried to block the punch, but only deflected its force into my upper lip. The scar ran from my right nostril to the center of his upper lip. It had healed nicely but due to its whiteness it was very noticeable. I broke the nose of the football player with one sudden, hammer-fist to his face. Blood spurted out of the super-jock's nose and poured off his lips and chin, then through both of his cupped hands that he had raised to his face. The sight of his own blood ended the fight immediately. While all the observers were stunned into silence and wide-eyed stares of disbelief, I grabbed my friend by the upper arm and quickly walked away from the scene. I thought, "Damn, that guy is big," as I took a quick look over my shoulder to see if we were being chased.

The gash on my upper lip stood out brightly when I looked into the mirror to shave or to comb my hair. However, the scar didn't appear ugly to me, but rather I took pride in it, especially knowing that I had saved a friend from worse punishment—though I did forcefully tell the dunce to look around and see who's listening before he defames the school football team or one of it players.

The next day, I, almost literally, got the shit kicked out of me by members of the varsity football team, which included Mr. Big Bloody Nose. After I got up off the floor of the locker room, I limped to the sink, looked into the mirror that was above the sink, and washed my dirty, bruised face and arms. I stared into the mirror, again, and saw that I had a fast-growing lump on my forehead, a swollen left eye, a cut lip, a reopened cut under my nose plus abrasions and bruises forming on my arms, neck and face. I washed the blood away and applied pressure with a paper towel until the bleeding stopped. My legs were sore and ached badly, so I knew they were seriously bruised from being kicked. I looked at my nose and grinned—the grin hurt. I felt my nose. When I realized that my nose wasn't broken or bloody, I grinned wider and said to myself, "Screw you guys! And, hey, look, you jerks. I don't have a bloody nose like your big, asshole friend."

While in the nurse's office, I decided that my "no quit" philosophy of fighting wasn't fool proof. As a matter of fact, to challenge Mr. Big Bloody Nose to another fight would mean a fight with those same teammates. If I persisted with a "no quit" fight rule, I'd be getting my ass kicked every day. In this particular case my "no quit" rule wasn't only not *fool proof,* but would *prove* I was a *fool* if I persisted. So, I took my beating without retaliation and considered it a valuable lesson in humility and in intelligent decision-making. But I did always wonder, and never found the answer to: Why Wolf didn't come to me that day. Must have been out to lunch, "wolfing" down his food and too busy to help me, I thought. Maybe Wolf just didn't help when I was acting like a damn idiot.

One morning, while combing my hair, I saw the scar on my upper lip. The memory of how I got it flashed vividly and accurately through my mind. It was like I had taken a video tape of the incident and the whole thing was as clear as if it was just happening. When I put my comb away, I found myself looking down at my knuckles, wrists and forearms. When I focused on a particular scar, immediately the incident appeared in my memory as vividly as if watching a video tape of the fight. But that wasn't all that happened. I also found myself being able to taste parts of the fight, like the blood from a split lip and the dirt and dust that entered my mouth when I was being kicked while on the ground. I recalled smells accurately, too, mostly the smell of sweat, and cologne, and bad breath. I could even feel the fight, the pain, the sore muscles, the heavy breathing from exhaustion. I heard the sound of fists and shoes colliding with flesh. And all of these things had a face, the face of the person who gave me the upper lip scar. Getting beat up by members of the varsity football team seemed a lot less funny now, so I gave it some serious thought. That's when keeping a "fight diary" occurred to him.

I started my "fight diary" and started listing the approximate ages, height, and weight of all the persons that I had a fight with. With care I wrote about how the fight started, what me and my opponent's strengths and weakness were, what the outcome of the fight was and how I could have ended the fight sooner, if I ever fought that person again. I wrote about my injuries, if there were any, and how they were caused and how to prevent them next time. I added as much detail as I could, even when and where the fights occurred. I wrote random thoughts about tastes, smells, soreness, injuries and my personal feelings about the fight. Each entry got more and more meticulous and, what initially started as a strange idea, became one of my most valuable combat preparation tools.

Then, as one thing led to another, in a chain of events, I realized that my scars were like a warrior's tattoos. They were a fleshy record of my battles. At that time, I was self-taught, but soon it occurred to me that that wasn't enough for my growing warrior spirit. I moved on to formal martial arts training and became an avid follower and practitioner of a Japanese form of martial arts, originating on the island of Okinawa—I worked in a restaurant, washing dishes, to pay for the lessons. To me, learning a martial art style was a natural extension of keeping my "fight diary." Martial arts was a way to vastly improve my self-defense knowledge, but also a way to understand my developing warrior spirit and how to control it.

It was at my martial arts dojo (school) that I picked up the nickname "Wolf" because of my fierce competitive sparring style, which my karate friends said made me appear as if I was hungrily stalking my opponent, like a wolf. They also said that my fierce determination to learn and master my chosen style of martial arts gave them the feeling that I was learning karate by devouring it in large chunks, as if I was a starving wolf devouring chunks of meat.

After high school I joined the Marines and almost everything about my little world changed drastically.

/../.-../- - -/...-/./.../.-/-./-../-.--/.../.../././..../././....././-/-./

Chapter 1

★★★★

Haunting Faces

BLOOD AND DEATH. IT was time for both, I informed the psychiatrist, as I spoke to him of some of my experiences in Nam.

The enemy was out there somewhere, waiting for us. I could literally smell them. I could almost always smell them. It was the smell of the food that the Vietnamese ate, a rotten, spoiled, rancid smell that became body odor. The musty vegetation smells of the Vietnam jungles couldn't mask their body odor—they said the same thing about us Americans.

A crescent moon shone in the night, not offering much light. But darkness was my friend, always my ally. It cloaked me as I stalked the enemy, making it so much easier to kill him from behind a veil of darkness. Sometimes the canopy of jungle foliage was so thick that, in the middle of the day, it was like a moonless midnight. That dark, shadowy, gloom was my best friend and the worst of all enemies for my enemy.

A black, odorless stain covers my entire face, neck, arms and hands. I am a black snake in the night, silently slithering through the fetid, sulfurous, jungle vegetation. I am like a black viper crawling over black velvet cloth, undetectable and lethal.

My body is a weapon of silent death, like a viper inching its way through nearly impenetrable thickets of vegetation, and ankle-high, prickly, wait-a-minute vines that impede my movement, but can not stop me. I also ignore the sharp-bladed grasses as they slice into my hands, arms and face. My eyes are constantly searching, my ears homing-in on any unnatural jungle noises. I move very slowly, cautiously, ghost-like, through the tangled undergrowth, bamboo stands, and man-sized elephant grass. Stop. Very watchful and quietly, I part the vegetation in front of me. I search. Listen. Wait patiently. I continue and death crawls toward the enemy; slowly and patiently. I smell his body odor, and something else, cigarette smoke? The Fourth Horseman has come for some of the enemy, one at a time.

I don't see the enemy clearly yet, just a shadow within a shadow, blanketed in darkness. A subtle noise. His uniform must have brushed against a tree or vine. Then a louder noise as his hand slaps at the ever-present mosquitoes. I lock on his position, then remove my blade from its inverted shoulder sheath. I grin as I crawl like a silent fog over the damp ground. Stop. I see the enemy sentry now. I see his dark silhouette, then notice exposed skin on his hands and on the back of his neck.. So careless he is as he slaps another mosquito on his neck, making noise as well as making his hands and arms visible, again. He is facing away from me now, so I don't see his face, but I know it will look fragile and boyish. That's the way most of this small-sized enemy looks, even the mature men. But this sentry is much too careless. Inexperienced, no doubt, because the enemy forces so many teenage boys to fight this war. Age doesn't matter to me though—a young boy's bullet kills just like a man's bullet kills. Death stalks this sentry and soon I'll feel his warm blood gushing over my hands and arms, like warm syrup. My hands and arms will be like a demonic artist's canvas, stained horribly with the blood of this sentry, who, if allowed to live, might kill some of my fellow Americans. I've, regretfully but necessarily, become an artist at taking enemy lives, young or old, if they are a threat to Americans.

I clench my teeth onto the black-coated, Parkerized blade. No moon light will reflect off its deadly steel. I smell the smoke. I slowly raise my head and detect a small, red glow coming from the tip of his cigarette. So foolish of him.

So many ways to kill. It seems so easy now. But not long ago it was so very difficult. Focus, I tell myself. I'm closer, much closer to him now. He still faces away from me, a stroke of luck for me and a faster, painless death for him. Only ten feet away now. Very little light; no sound but insects, especially those ubiquitous mosquitoes. I see that he is a lone sentry instead of a team. He looks unusually short . . . no, he's sitting on a fallen tree trunk.

My teeth bite harder on the back of the blackened blade. I take a slow, deep breath. I allow no clue that death approaches him. Only eight feet away. I'm careful; very patient, moving only inches at a time, but ready to spring at him if I need to. I rarely need to. Just eight feet to the end of his life. I inch forward, closer and closer to him. No noise. No warning.

Six feet away now. I see his small head with short black hair, his frail, spindly neck and body. Such a pale neck. My eyes focus on it intently, like a moth attracted to bright light.

He wears a light-weight uniform that won't hinder my blade's penetration. His Russian designed AK-47 rifle leans up against the fallen tree trunk. His hands are empty, except for a cigarette that still glows red in the darkness, like a beacon. Such carelessness surprises me. I scan the nearby jungle. There are noises from his fellow soldiers, but they are low and muffled, and not too close. This is an NVA (North Vietnamese Army) camp. This is a lone sentry. I kill only lone sentries. No one will hear his life expire, but me.

I'm four feet away from him and he has no sense of my nearness. Very slowly, quietly and carefully I rise to my knees, muscles taut. I spring and lunge one giant step toward him. My cupped left hand, fingers held tightly together, covers both his nose and mouth. I pull his head back towards me. He falls backwards off the tree trunk, off balance, helpless, flailing his arms and legs. Instinctively he reaches up with both of his hands to grab my left hand. That's when my right hand violently drives the blade into his kidney area. He's not strong. He can't pry my hand away from his mouth and nose. His hands drop. His attempted scream dies quietly, muffled against my tightly cupped hand. Shock and internal hemorrhage begin immediately. I twist the ten inch Ka-Bar combat knife forcefully inside the wound, causing severe shock. His body goes limp against me. I withdraw the blade quickly and hear the soft, sucking sound as it exits the fatal wound. He's still alive. My left hand pulls his chin up farther, exposing the entire neck area. I place the blade on the left side of his neck—under his left ear—then slash deeply into his neck, from left to right. The left side carotid artery and the front jugular vein are severed completely.

Blood spurts, like a crimson fountain, out of the carotid artery and jugular vein onto my hands, warming them with sticky wetness. The smell of copper assaults my nose. Streams of blood continue to erupt from the artery, with each of his final heart beats, making a mild hissing noise that quickly grows weaker with each geyser of blood. The severed ends of the carotid artery look like the opening of a full-blown balloon when the air is allowed to gush out, the severed ends vibrating rapidly. Now I clamp my hand over the severed artery to silence what little noise there is.

In wartime, "sympathy" can be a deadly weakness. I silently drag his light body into a thicket to conceal it. I don't want him found until morning. I have more killing to do before the morning sun vanquishes my dark, private world of blood and death. I wipe my hands and knife on my pants, then sheath the blade and crawl onward, stalking the next enemy, ending his life. I'm constantly smelling, seeing, feeling, hearing the enemy and even accidentally tasting his blood when it spurts and sprays into the air. My heightened senses become flooded with blood as it indelibly stains my psyche. By the time daylight chases the darkness away more of the enemy will die and I'll have another night's mission accomplished during the lethal siege at Khe-Sanh.

In the morning, when I'm safely back within our defensive perimeter, I wonder why I joined the Marines. Sometimes I wish that I hadn't. When I'm moody, I often wish that I'd never been to Vietnam and never heard about South Vietnam's guerrilla warfare troops, called VC—Viet Cong—and the NVA—North Vietnam Army, but I was thankful for being alive and able to get on the "Freedom Bird" that flew me back to the States.

The name "Vietcong" is a shortened form of the Vietnamese words "Viet Congsan," meaning "Vietnamese Communists"—It's difficult to remember that your fighting communism because paramount in your mind is "survival." Most of us just called them "VC" or "Charlie" when we were being polite. Since we weren't often polite, we frequently

called them "slope-heads" "slant-eyes," "zips," and "gooks." It was a
way of dehumanizing them, a way of making them sub-human so that
it was easier to kill them. It's very difficult to kill someone, especially
young teenagers, when you sit down and talk to them, eat with them,
or admire them. It's difficult to kill when you know that that person
is someone's father, husband, son, uncle and that they have the full
spectrum of human feelings that you do. So in order to kill them you
have to be very angry and/or think of them as lower, despicable human
forms. I'm not proud of the vile name-calling or the killing. It was a
thoroughly useless war that brought out the worst in almost everyone
who participated. It happened to me.

The NVA had us pinned down for a seventy-seven day siege at
Khe-Sanh during the early months of 1968. We had hardly any sleep.
We were all so afraid of dying that eating was a terrifying experience
because we had to take our hands off our rifles, or whatever weapon
we had. A weapon was like the air; without it we faced certain death.
Our weapons became our gods and saviors. We never went anywhere
without them, and we took care of them as if they were our beloved
children.

During the heat of the day, our heads would literally bake inside
the traditional Kevlar pot helmets. So most or us wore our green
cloth hats, called "boonie hats," or we wore no hat at all. The NVA
loved that. They had snipers on any high ground or in any available
trees with Russian weapons comparable to Uncle Sam's—but usually
better, especially the AK-47 rifle. The NVA snipers could blow your
head right off your neck. It's an awful sight seeing a friend shot like
that. It's like watching a melon being hit with a sledge hammer. Many
Marines died at Khe-Sanh, in many different ways, but a sniper's head-
shot might have been the worst way. Such a head-shot left nothing
but a butchered stump on the dead man's shoulders. It certainly left
an unforgettable image for anyone who witnessed it. But at least it
was immediate death. No pain; just eternal oblivion. You think of
the victim's facial features and you remember his smile or his eyes or
maybe his nose. Then you see him after an NVA sniper puts a rifle
bullet through his head. The bullet penetrates the skull leaving an
entry hole about the size of a nickel, but upon impact and penetration
of the skull, the bullet flattens-out and seems to explode as it gouges

its way through the soft mass of brain tissue. When the misshapen bullet exits, it rips off most of a man's head as it sends shards of hairy bone, a fountain of blood and clumps of brain matter in all directions, usually onto the uniforms of nearby soldiers. When shot like that, the guy is dead before he ever hits the ground. You are forced to become an unwilling witness as a geyser of blood erupts from his neck as he crashes to the ground, his life's blood forming an ever growing pool, like a crimson halo, as his heart keeps pumping blood to the brain which is not there.

I personally witnessed a soldier shot through the forehead by a sniper. The bullet went in at a forty-five degree angle and ripped off three-fourths of his head. I could see straight through his open mouth and out the back of his head. Gruesome.

At first you want to vomit when you see something like that, but after seeing it a few times you get used to it, like a surgeon gets used to cut flesh and the resulting blood flow. Your mind vividly remembers that tortured face, or whatever is left of it, and you can never forget it. You try to lock it up in some dark, secure chamber inside your brain, but, like a determined prisoner, it wants to escape, so it can haunt you. It will. It does.

When the war ends, you bring that "haunting" home. I did. That's why I've started seeing a psychiatrist. I can't seem to escape the images and the pain. They torture me unmercifully. I get deeply sad and sometimes cry unexpectedly. I never thought I'd ever need to go to a psychiatrist, probably like so many people who said they never thought they'd ever write to Dear Abby, but did.

At first, even though I was told that the psychiatrist would help me, I still felt uncomfortable with him. I'm not used to revealing my inner feelings, even to friends, and especially not to a stranger who's a psychiatrist. Our first meeting was awkward. He asked a few simple questions, to lay the ground-work for his later probing. At least, it appeared that way to me. To his simple questions, I gave him short, concise answers, yes or no answers, if possible. I didn't volunteer much information, so after those initial, probing questions were complete, he and I just looked at each other. I suppose that I was to feel uncomfortable by the silence and start talking, but I like silence and hadn't decided yet if I liked him, or even trusted him. When the silence got boring, I looked out the only window in the room, over his desk. It was a cool autumn day, with a sunny, almost cloud-free sky of cobalt blue.

My thoughts were interrupted by his stentorian voice. "You are a very reticent person," he said, then qualified his statement with, "You need to talk to me if I'm to help you."

I looked away from the window, at him, and replied, "I don't really think I'm a reticent person. I'm more of a taciturn person. There's a fine difference between being *reticent* and *taciturn*. Being reticent is being silent because you choose to do so. You can be a very talkative person and still, in some situations, choose to be silent, reticent. I'm more taciturn because I'm silent by nature, I seek solace, quiet. Being silent or quiet is a natural part of me. It's just the way I am and it's not a choice with me. So, yes, I am by nature silent and not prone to being chatty."

"Do you see any advantages in being . . . ah . . . taciturn? Is it a defense mechanism so that you don't reveal too much about yourself?"

"No. Once again, you are talking about a reticent person. A person who doesn't want to reveal information about himself would choose not to talk, or not to talk too much. It's a choice that he's making. A taciturn person, like me, is not making a choice. I don't talk much, not from choice, but because I, by my nature, find comfort in silence or minimal verbal communication. But there is an advantage to being taciturn. Do you know what 'think linking' is?"

"Sounds like hooking thoughts together, but I don't understand what your point is."

"Yeah, hooking or linking thoughts together is basically it. 'Think-linking' is just a concise chain of thoughts that leads to insights, which lead to a valued conclusion. Let's use our topic of silence and talkativeness. Start with the premise: The more a person talks, the more he reveals about himself. Then continue with the "think-links" like this: the more he reveals about himself, the more strengths an weaknesses he reveals. The more weaknesses he reveals, the more he makes himself vulnerable and open to attack. The more vulnerable to attack he is, the weaker his defense will be. The weaker his defense, the more danger he's in. The more danger he's in, the more careful and paranoid he'll act. The more careful and paranoid he is, the more quiet and secretive he'll be. So a careful person is, by necessity, a quiet or silent, introspective person. Thus a taciturn person avoids unnecessary vulnerability, weakness, danger and attack. So a taciturn person is lucky because he avoids vulnerability, weakness, danger and attack due to his *naturally quiet* manner, whereas a reticent person *chooses to be quiet*, to avoid those same four negatives. See what I mean?"

Dr. Shell stared at me and said, "But you don't need to worry about any of those things in my office."

"I know. But my natural silence was making you uncomfortable, so I decided to get us started on the right footing by describing 'think-links,' which is something I like to do in silence. So now you don't have to feel uncomfortable any more. I'll be more talkative now so that you can relax."—I was teasing him.

Dr. Shell's eyes bulged out and he furrowed his brow. I think he knew that he had been had; that I had turned the table on him and did to him what he usually does to his patients. For a moment he remained quiet, just looking at me, question marks appearing in his expressions. And I also think that this bit of silly chicanery broke the ice in our relationship and made us feel more comfortable with each other.

My psychiatrist is an easy-going kind of guy. He sits quietly in his plush, tilt-back, dark-brown leather chair that rests upon wheels. His office is small, but comfortable and nice looking. It's about fifteen by twenty-five feet long, with dark tiled floor and pale green walls. Beside his desk and chair there is another chair and a couch, with the same material and color as his chair. The couch is too soft. My ass sinks right into it, so I sit in the chair. There's a mahogany coffee table in the space between the chair and couch and the doctor's desk. One wall is all mahogany bookshelves, professional books mostly. Two other walls have nature-type pictures. There's a Boston fern on the window sill by his desk; a clock and calendar on the wall over his desk.

He's now very easy to talk to . . . I guess he'd have to be to have a job like that. He has blue eyes and looks as if he's in his mid-forties. He's about five feet nine inches tall and about one-hundred eighty or ninety pounds. He's got a stocky, solid build; could have been a wrestler with a nice, low center of gravity. He has a head of thinning, salt and pepper hair, plus a thick, graying beard and mustache that make him look like the stereotype of a psychiatrist, complete with suit and tie.

What a contrast we both make. We were almost opposites as far as body build, with me being six feet two inches tall, one-hundred eighty-five pounds and thin. I am about fifteen years younger than he is. My hair is dark brown, as well as my eyes. I'm clean shaven. And, since this is an early Saturday morning appointment, I'm not in my usual dress clothes with tie and jacket. Instead, I had on my Timberland, insulated and waterproof boots, a pair of J.C. Penney jeans and a reddish, plaid, flannel shirt. My new blue, nylon jacket was hanging over a chair in the waiting room.

I told the doctor that I see too many haunting, dead faces. I told him that sometimes, in Nam, we didn't have time to evacuate the dead bodies and as we retreated from the enemy, the eyes in those bodies seemed to follow me, like one of those trick paintings. I could feel those eyes desperately pleading with me to help them, to at least bury them, and to tell their wives, girlfriends, and families that they loved them very much. I see those lifeless, open mouths and glazed eyes and think that I actually see their dead, bluish lips moving. It tortures me, I told him. Even if I didn't look back as I retreated from the advancing NVA, I could sense my dead comrades' eyes burning into the back of my neck, especially when I knew that sometimes these NVA and the VC soldiers would carve up the bodies into a hideous sight by plucking out the eyeballs, cutting off lips and noses, and even emasculating the corpses by severing a dead soldier's penis and testes, then place them on the tip of a sharpened pole and driving the other sharpened end of the pole into the ground, between the corpse's legs, as a sign of mockery. Or the genitals were shoved into the soldier's mouth. It's horrifying to know that, sometimes, that type of abomination occurs before the soldier is dead.

I told the doctor that I once found a dead soldier in the jungle. The soldier was naked, lying on his back, across a large, fallen tree. His legs were all shot up. He must have been in a firefight and his buddies couldn't get to him. The VC got hold of him, bayoneted his hands and feet to the tree, then cut off his cock and balls, stuffed them into his mouth and rammed them down his throat. The VC probably stood in front of him laughing as he slowly suffocated on his own manhood.

It was such a horrible sight, a haunting sight, the soldier's eyes wide open, bulging with fear, his lips and cheeks contorted in agony.

Dr. Shell stared a me as though he had been shocked—I guess most of his patients are more the mundane type, with classical or traditional problems that don't disturb him.

I informed the doctor that war makes legal killers of soldiers, me included. But the kind of butchery I had just described to him was beyond my understanding, beyond my acceptance. I told him that I had heard stories of our own guys doing stuff like that, too, including mutilations, rapes, killing women and children and that they were probably true. War, I said to him, turns undisciplined men into horrible beasts, or it lets out the horrible beast that was already there, but hidden.

I also informed the doctor that experiences like this, in Nam, brought out a deeper darkness in my attitude toward life, but that darkness wasn't solely created by my experiences in Nam. I had always seemed to have them, but to a lesser degree. I told him that I felt a darkness within me, a sadness, an expectation and a comfort with the idea of my own death. Since my late teens, I told him, I've felt that I would die prematurely; in particular, before the age of fifty—acutally, no matter how long a person lives, the moment of death is probably still an unwanted surprise. Then I admitted, with a mischievous smile, that I truly hate surprises, so if death came as a surprise, then my death would have to wait, especially since there's not much that surprises me any more. And, if Death asked me when he could take me, I guess I'd have to be sarcastic and say, "Surprise me." I grinned at the doctor who wore a confused expression concerning my sincerity and seriousness. I'm like that, sometimes.

Another rogue thought invaded my brain, compliments of Woody Allen: "I'm not afraid to die," he once said, "I just don't want to be there when it happens."

I continued telling the doctor that I not only see the faces of my dead buddies, I also see the faces of all the NVA and VC enemy soldiers that I'd killed—sometimes what I saw was just the back of their head.

So many of those faces, I said, looked so young. Many of those faces looked like young teenagers. I was killing children, the enemies' children, who were made to fight even at such a young age. Most of the time I couldn't tell the men from the boys. Full grown Vietnamese men are often no taller, and frequently more slender, than American boys. If you see them from the rear, you can't tell if it's a man or a boy. But I won't kid you, though, because killing them wouldn't have made any difference to me. If that boy had a weapon and that weapon was being used to kill American soldiers, then I'd kill the boy. I just wish that children could be kept out of war. Give them a chance to enjoy life, to grow up. Yes, I killed them silently and quickly; no agony, no prolonged suffering and no butchery or torture, unless you consider silently killing with a knife a form of butchery. Some people do think that way, even in war. But I made an effort not to be sadistic, although, even to myself, that statement sounds ironic, hypocritical and a bold-faced lie.

The average age of an American soldier arriving in Vietnam, after boot camp, was 19 years old. They looked like men, tall in stature, even stout, and compared to the Vietnamese men and boys, the Americans were giants.

I was on a roll now and the doctor didn't have to prod me to keep me talking—not too damn taciturn now. I said to him, "Maybe I'm just as bad as the enemy. I don't know. It gets so confusing sometimes. I killed to stay alive, to help my buddies stay alive and to help my country in a cause that I initially thought to be honorable and just. My mind has now put all those dead American faces into a mental album and each night the album opens and I see all those dead faces, their open mouths with moving lips, their dead eyes pleading for their lives, and the corpses' bloody fingers pointing to me in anger, screaming, "Save us, Wolfe! For God's sake, save us!" God? Now there's the ultimate futile, superstitious cry for help."

I confided in the doctor even more when I told him, "Most days I feel more good than bad, but there are those days where I feel more bad than good. On those days the fires of hate burn within me, and there is no cool, waterfall of goodness in sight that will quench those flames whose flickering, scorching fingers want to consume, in a conflagration of wrath, those who cross me. In Nam those flaming fingers of rage were felt almost daily. But now, in civilian life, I finally feel goodness and happiness dominating my daily routines, their origins primarily come from my wife and daughter, and partly from my career, as well as some understanding friends and relatives. Solace, privacy and meditation help, also. It used to be that I very much feared that my past would always ruin the present and then kill my future. But now I'm a husband, a father and a teacher. I like that very much. It has given me much happiness."

Luckily I lived to be honorably discharged from the Marines in late 1968. But sometimes I feel as if the dead soldiers are really the lucky ones. Maybe death is the only way I'll ever be free of their haunting faces.

I was "honorably" discharged. "Can you see the irony in that?" I asked the doctor. "I turned into a legalized killer, then I was told that I was doing the 'honorable' thing for my country. Then I get discharged with honor. What a shitty joke," I said with a slightly raised voice. "Was it honorable to kill? Was it really? Bullshit! I killed not for honor, but to stay alive, and to keep as many of my friends alive as I could. And I certainly wasn't fearless. I was scared of dying. But, I figured that the more of the enemy I killed, the better chance we all had to stay alive, right?"—the doctor just nodded at me. "I would go out into the night to kill the VC and the NVA before they got a chance to kill me and my friends. My survival instincts told me to *kill-or-be-killed*. There is really no 'honor' in killing, just a need, an obligation, a duty to survive so I can kill, again, in order to survive and be able to kill again. I must also face the reality that I killed with particular weapons because I was damn good at it and I knew that it was also a good psychological warfare tactic that would scare the guts out of the enemy.

I seldom limit myself to linear thinking. Weapons don't have to be the things we normally consider as weapons. If you think about it carefully and escape the traditional mind-set, you'll realize that weapons are everywhere and not difficult to find. The metal band of a watch worn over the knuckles will easily tear an opponent's facial flesh. The holed, leather strap of a watch can be used as a whip that will strike the face of an opponent with, not only the watch, but with the buckle. A ball-point pen or a pencil can be used as a dagger to wound someone or, if stabbed into the eye, to kill. A belt, or shoelaces make an impromptu garrote. The lenses from a pair of glasses can be used to slash flesh and even the bows from a pair of glasses can be used like an ice pick. A rubbery, squeeze change-holder can be palmed to make the fist more solid. A rolled magazine or newspaper can be used as a club or an eye-poker. A set of car keys placed so they stick out from between the fingers can easily stab or rake flesh. Credit cards can be used like knives. Steel-toes shoes are excellent shin-bone breakers; stiff leather-soled shoes work well, too. As silly as it sounds, a rock in a sock makes an excellent sling-club—though it can't be used as hurriedly as other spur of the moment weapons. A stick, twig or branch can sometimes be easily grabbed—not to be used as a club but, rather, stabbing at the opponents eyes, a screwdriver or nail are very dangerous weapons. I could go on and on, but you get the idea about weapons being everywhere and, you'll see them, if you can push yourself away from linear thinking.

Then a funny thought occurred to me: I hope, for all the carpenters' sake, that murderers don't start using hammers to kill with because, if that occurs frequently, "hammer control laws" will be next on the agenda of all the "gun control" dolts in America.

I gazed at the floor, then back at the doctor and said, "Killing releases very primitive thoughts and actions. It puts into doubt our pretentious view and ideas about ourselves as refined, civilized, moral and law-abiding citizens. It seems to me that these doubts will occur to someone with a conscience. But why, throughout history, has mankind been so easily led into war, where killing, even mass killing and "ungodly" torture is condoned and considered moral and advantageous? Maybe it's connected to human DNA and has been there since we climbed out of the primordial muck. It must remain superficially dormant until wars, criminal activities or personal tragedies occur, then the ease of men killing each other rears its monstrous head and goes about the business of ending lives. Of course another obvious answer is religion. More people have been killed, and more blood spilled for the cause of religion than all the wars of the past and present. Even in current times more people are dying because of fanatical religious beliefs than from all the diseases in the world—unless you consider religion itself as a disease, which many people do, a psychological disease of the mind. Believe like I do or I'll kill you, bomb you, terrorize you. Religion may be a much better reason for killing than any primitive DNA programming. As Blaise Pascal said, 'Men never do evil so completely and cheerfully as when they do it from religious conviction.'"

"Sadly," I said to Doc, "actually killing someone is a fairly simple task, if you're not trying to conceal it. Taking a life is easy. It's the two 'Cs': conscience and consequences, that are extremely complex and difficult. If you value life, then ending a life will constantly haunt your conscience, much like a ghost haunts a house. Your conscience will very often cause you to punish yourself in much more severe ways than the consequences that may be forced upon you by the verdict of a lawful society's court system."

I paused, in silent thought, then looked out of the window for a few seconds—Doc remained silent, studying me. After less than a minute I continued. "Sometimes it's necessary, but I see no honor in killing, just disappointment, regret and sometimes horror. I cried a lot, in private, and silently," I told him. "Almost every night I cried for the enemy that I killed and for my friends that were killed by the enemy. I felt like a bottomless pit of sadness when I thought of their wives', children's, relative's and friend's pain. No . . . there certainly was no honor, but there was plenty of gut-wrenching irony. Just how important was that Marine base at Khe-Sanh? Was is really worth all those lives lost in that seventy-seven day siege? It must have been a really important base, right? It was so important that all the Marines were ordered to abandon it shortly after the siege ended. After all those lives lost, after all that sacrifice, all of a sudden it was no longer in the vital interest of American military operations. How's that for irony? It was like mass human sacrifice for the temporary ownership of a small plot of land. Just how important could Khe-Sanh have been if it could so quickly and easily be abandoned?" I asked as I looked at the doctor. He said nothing, just gave me a wide-eyed stare. His expression told me that he hadn't heard these kinds of stories before.

"Of course," I added, "the military isn't really known for it's high IQ status. They're the ones that say that they give dead American heroes a '21 gun salute' using only 7 rifles, not 21 rifles—each rifle fired three times. Duh! It's a 21 "shots" salute, not a 21 "gun" salute. Of course, I guess they could be mathematical geniuses and multiply 7 rifles times 3 bullets fired from each rifle and come up with the product of 21. That's the irony of 'military intelligence.' It makes as much sense as over 58,000 American soldiers lives being wasted in Nam, and over 200,000 American soldiers who came home physically and mentally disabled.

"Some of my commanding officers and their commanding officers often seemed to be lost in thought. I didn't let that fool me. It turns out that they were lost in thought simply because it was unfamiliar territory to them. The military is usually a place where mediocre minds are always at peak performance. There are exceptions, of course.

"Similar trains of thought followed. They may be radical, perhaps unpatriotic thoughts, but this is American, right? I can have such thoughts. The Military? In many ways, it's the most glaring, but necessary disfigurement in the structure of any democracy. The military is like a disease, in a nation, that asks it youth, mainly teenagers, to take refuge in the secure confines of man's most primitive, ape-like instincts: kill to survive, kill to promote the superiority of ideas, cultures, traditions, even religious opinions. Kill to prove personal superiority and national power.

"In the military, I was to find that "thinking" and "questioning" or even asking for an explanation were not just frowned upon, but hated with a passion—you simply do not question military authority, your superiors, or your country's national interests. So taking unquestioned orders, obeying them without thought is considered the most honorable thing to do. Taking military orders without thought, is very similar to religion's demand for "blind, unreasoned, faith."

"Respect is not usually "earned" in the military, it's "demanded" of you. Fear of the punishable consequences is the tool used to gain respect . . . but it's a false respect, not a genuine one.

"The officers seem to think they are eloquent, gifted orators—with tenth grade vocabularies. They talk, they give orders and you obey. One would think that most military officers, like most politicians, contrary to Darwin's theory of evolution, evolved from parrots, not simian ancestors. And like parrots, their bird-brains allow them to proudly recite the words of others—their superiors?—they "parrot" their superiors just as those higher ranked superiors "parrot" their own higher ranked superiors—shit always flows downhill and in the military, gravity has an extra strong pull on the bowels.

"My heart aches when I think of all those dead parrots—young enlisted men and women, as well as young officers—who were not old enough, not experienced enough and not thoughtful enough to know better—myself included—but died with honor and courage in such irrationally motivated wars as Korea, Vietnam and Iraq. Most shameful for me, personally, is the fact that, at that very young age, I, too, was a parrot, fooled by politicians, military gurus and biased news coverage, all of whom had nothing to sacrifice except the lives of unknown teenagers from anonymous families, in unheard of regions of America. The most ironic thought of all, however, is that, basically, the military is a recognized and authorized dictatorship that guards our democracy. That thought, like a giant octopus, wraps its tentacles around my testicles and squeezes tightly. I'm probably supposed to feel guilt and shame for my dreadful, unpatriotic thoughts; the thoughts that originate from analytical thinking, answers that come from reasonable questioning, original, not "parroted" ideas, and a complete lack of confidence in people or institutions who use 'blind faith' and 'fear' as the foundations for their beliefs.

"After being discharged I spent a year-and-a-half working and trying to decide what I wanted to do with my life. I was confused and depressed, but I was only having the nightmares once or twice a week. I could handle that all right. After a few months I thought I had myself straightened around, so in the spring of 1970 I decided to go to college using the GI Bill, even though college was still a place where my Purple Heart and Navy Cross medals would be spit upon, if I showed them to anyone.

"Fortunately, I was so damn busy during those four years trying to become a teacher that the horrors of Vietnam were buried deeply within the core of my mind like rotten apple seeds. Sometimes I even fooled myself into thinking that I had put them out of my mind completely. I was very wrong about that. I had simply buried them, and now, like nightmarish vampires, they have risen from their mental grave and taken control of my life, sucking energy out of me, leaving me drained and discouraged. So I needed to visit a psychiatrist, you doctor, to help me find the figurative wooden stake that will kill the horrific memories and my ever-present guilt.

"I'll lay it on the line," I told the doctor. "I go into deep depressions. When these engulfing depressions occur, I almost always think of suicide. Luckily, I think of my wife and daughter, and the pain that my suicide would create for them. That helps me to stop thinking about actually doing it, but it doesn't stop me from thinking about it. You know the funny thing, if there can ever be a funny thing about suicide"—I paused for him to respond, but he didn't, so I continued. "I don't think of using a knife to kill myself. I usually think of some sort of poison, a pill overdose, a bullet in the head, or even exhaust fumes from my truck. I'll tell you something else, Doc. I think I know why I don't think of using my blade to commit suicide. It's because I feel safe when I have my blade with me. It was my razor-edged savior in Vietnam. My blade saved my life, and others, along with my knowledge of karate. To me, my blade is an instrument of life, not death, because it kept me, and others, alive. It's intended to save my life, not take my life, not destroy my life. How's that for symbolic, amateur psychology, Doc?"

He still didn't respond, though his eyes offered sympathy. He wanted me to get it all out into the open, to flush myself of all the crap that had been building up inside of me.

"Doc, sometimes I get confused very easily. I wanted to show my Ka-Bar combat knife to my uncle, so I unbuttoned the shirt button nearest my belly button, then reached up toward my left armpit. I did it so casually, like reaching into a pocket for my car keys? It was so natural for me to do it, even after being away from Vietnam for so long. We were talking about Vietnam and I wanted to show him the instrument that I used most in the jungles. I was anticipating that he'd be interested and excited, but I certainly wasn't thinking straight, or I would have seen the fear in his eyes. Anyway, when I pulled the blade out of my shirt, I looked at it and not at him. Finally when I saw his wide eyes, gaping mouth and heard his heavy breathing, I realized that what I had done looked very much like I was going to attack him. I had no intention of doing that, but he didn't know my intentions. I wasn't thinking normally, clearly. I wasn't thinking how my actions would look to him, any more than I think about breathing.

"I saw my uncle glance at the door, looking for the quickest way to escape, then his eyes were glued to the knife. When it sluggishly dawned on me what my actions looked like, the excitement turned to supreme embarrassment. I realized that he was now afraid of me and what I might do. Hell! He had every right to feel that way. I must have really been in a stupor. Here I was, a person having problems with depression, talking to him about killing, then all of a sudden I pull out a concealed knife from under my shirt. I was a real jackass for not anticipating his fear and alarm at my actions. All I could do then was talk fast; try to explain. So I told him, in my most sincere voice, that I didn't mean to scare him and that I wouldn't hurt him. I did finally convince him that all I was trying to do was show him the blade that I used in Vietnam. When I put the knife away, I could read the tremendous relief on my uncle's face. I'm so used to the blade being there that it was like reaching to take a pen out of my shirt pocket. That's the kind of thing I mean when I say that I get confused easily."

Doc showed me a mild smile and nodded his head, then said, "Boys need their toys?"

When I heard that phrase, I became irritated. I said, "Doc, can I tell you what I think about the phrase you just used: *Boys need their toys?*"

"Sure," Doc responded, then added, "I didn't mean to offend you."

"I was offended. That phrase is mostly used by women as a disparaging remark about the immaturity of men, and I find it very irritating, especially coming from a man. Perhaps it's something that you haven't had the need to give much thought, but I think you should. Women often say that: 'Men are just little boys that still need their toys.' It's irritating to hear you repeat that 'male-bashing,' typically feminine phrase. It's not only insulting, but intellectually childish on the part of females. I've heard it said so many times that it makes me sick to think about the lack of respect that it implicitly implies. The next time you hear someone say that, it almost certainly will be a woman. I usually give a sarcastic reply such as 'Women are just little girls who need their toys, too, and their toys are new clothes, jewelry, make-up and a plethora of bathroom and grooming supplies, all used as a substitute, in adult life, for playing with their childhood dolls.' '*Boys need their toys*' is a rude insult, layered with contempt that no man should allow to go unquestioned or unchallenged. I'm sorry to act as if

I'm reprimanding you, but it's a shameful phrase, whether it's said by a male or a female. Enough said about that.

"I came to you because I realized I was having odd thoughts and dreams, and needed help. Pulling that knife out of my shirt and scaring my uncle is proof of that. It was an odd, unthinking thing to do, but that's one of the reasons I need to see you, Doc. Odd thoughts, odd actions, and the guilt from unforgettable faces that haunt me like pernicious ghosts in the night.

Doc said, "You told me that you were called Wolf by almost all your Marine friends. That's not odd since your last name if Wolfe. I suppose there was another meaning there, right?"

Oh, yeah. Sure. The reference is to the animal wolf. You know, like stalking its prey at night; fierce, silent, cunning and deadly. Just like my karate friends used to call me Wolf.

"OK. Another question. How did you learn how to handle a knife like you did in the jungle?"

I explained that when I went to combat school, I had to learn a lot of soldiering skills, especially survival skills and rifle skills. I was very interested and learned fast in those three months before I was shipped out to Vietnam. But in the final month of combat school we were all asked to choose one particular weapon that we'd like to become an expert with. It could be explosives, pistols, rifles, .50 caliber machine guns, grenade launchers, or any other weapon the army had on hand. They wanted some of the guys to have a specialty in some area of combat. I surprised everyone and chose the Marine Ka-Bar knife, night stalking and silent killing with only a blade, though I also learned how to use a garrote. Come to think of it, I used a silenced .22 caliber pistol once. It had a special advanced silencer called a "hush-puppy." It was called that because it was originally designed to use when silently killing enemy sentry dogs. One night in Nam, I brought it out with me, when I went stalking, to see how it worked on a human sentry. I got within a few feet of the sentry and shot him in the head. A .22 caliber bullet isn't usually powerful enough to exit the skull, so when it enters, the bullet bounces off the inner cranial walls mixing and shredding the brain's gray matter similar to the small steel ball bearing that mixes the paint in a spray-paint can. That sentry died instantly. The problem was, when he fell, his body made a noise as it hit the ground. Some of his fellow soldiers came to investigate, saw that he'd been assassinated, then sprayed the jungle with rifle bullets. I narrowly escaped and vowed not to use that technique again. I'd stick to the knife where I can grab the enemy, kill him, then gently lower his body to the ground and carry it to a hiding place, if possible. No noise. Also, the pistol, with the silencer, was too bulky and awkward to carry.

"To get back to my explanation about boot camp, from then on, I was placed in a small group of soldiers who were taught knife fighting skills, including stalking and the silentl killing of enemy sentries. It was also a psychological warfare tool. In the morning when all or most of the sentries were found dead, with their throats cut, that would terrify the enemy. Then they'd become superstitious, nervous and afraid of the night. Thoughts and fantastic visions of unstoppable phantoms stalking them in the night would keep many an enemy from sleeping. After a few nights without sleep, or at least, disturbed sleep, that enemy would be careless and sluggish, from sleep deprivation. That made him even more prone to being killed by being careless, like making too much noise and giving away his position, smoking at night where the smell and the red glow of the cigarette could be detected. I can't tell you, Doc, how many enemy sentries I found and killed by seeing the red glow of their cigarette and/or the smell of cigarette smoke. Just yawning or stretching would give away their position and make it so much more likely that they would be killed.

"Also, I joined the Marines with a pretty good knowledge of martial arts skills, specifically Isshin Ryu karate. I was already a black belt so the martial arts skills and knife fighting and stalking skills blended together naturally. I ended up being ranked at the top of my class in knife fighting proficiency. The only persons better than I was, were the three instructors, and they each complimented me by telling me that they'd hate to have to fight me—I think they exaggerated, of course, because at that stage of my skills, they were all much better than I was. They said they could probably best me with the knife, but they didn't know if they could defend themselves well with the added complexity of having to fight someone who was also a black belt in martial arts.

"I didn't really consider myself an expert in karate, but, to them, I was an expert by comparison. I was smart enough to know that they were too damn good for me with a knife, but it was nice of them to compliment me."

I was glad to see the Doc smile. Hopefully, it meant that he was feeling at ease and didn't consider me a whacked-out misfit. His eyes and face grew curious and he asked me how I carried the knife under my shirt and how I got it out of my shirt so fast.

I unbuttoned my shirt and showed him the harness that I made so I could carry the knife under my left armpit with the handle hanging downward. I showed him that the harness was very similar to a cop's shoulder holster, but much more compact, slim and light. I buttoned my shirt back up, then demonstrated the process of extracting the knife. I placed my hands on my thighs and relaxed. Abruptly, I unbutton the shirt button closest to my belt, reached into my shirt and unsnapped the handle strap. The handle of the knife fell silently into my hand and I pulled it out of my shirt. Apprehensive about my actions, I immediately replaced the knife into its sheath and buttoned my shirt. Then I told him that in Nam I wore the upside-down knife harness on the outside of my jungle, camouflage uniform, there being no need to conceal it in actual combat.

"I see how that process could really scare someone. It does have a frightening effect, even on me, and I knew what was going to happen," Doc stated.

I noticed a bit of discomfort in the creases of skin around his eyes and mouth. I asked, "Would you prefer that I didn't wear the knife when I visit your office?"

"Yes. Actually, I would appreciate that."

"I won't wear it to my future appointments."

"So, how's your wife feel about the concealed knife?" he asked next.

"Well, she doesn't much care for it, I admit. But she much prefers the knife to a gun. She's kind of wimpy about guns. She says I have to forget about Nam and what I did there, and that the knife is not needed because of my martial arts training. But I like the feel of it there, you know?"

"You wear it all the time?" Doc asked as his forehead frowned.

"Oh. No, I don't. I only wear it when I'm not working and I wouldn't even have had it on today if it hadn't been a Saturday appointment. I never wear it to work, of course. I wanted to, at first, but my wife talked me out of it, thank goodness. She was dead right on that issue. I admit that. It would have been very upsetting to everyone in school, children, adults and parents, if they knew that I had a concealed knife under the left armpit of my shirt, covered by my sport coat. Does make for an unusual vision, doesn't it?" I said with uncomfortable laughter in my voice. "Hell, I'd probably get fired for being a dangerous psycho. Anyway, the knife would only call attention to what I was in the Marines, in Nam, and who'd want to have a teacher like that in their school . . . especially with children?"

"You like teaching?"

"Oh, yeah. I like the kids. Like being around them, helping them grow and learn. It's very satisfying, it really is. They're the future, right? They are our country's most precious resource, those developing minds. I feel like I'm helping to make a better future for all of us when I help my students. I certainly wouldn't want to jeopardize my job as an elementary school teacher. I should tell you, though, that I don't very often get depressed in my classroom, with my students. They take my mind away from the sources of my depression.

"The real problem is that when I get depressed, outside the classroom, it can get intense and last a day or two, and that sort of thing is killing my marriage. I love my wife and daughter very much and I don't want to leave them or get a divorce. But I think I'm headed in that direction unless you can help me. Sometimes the only thing that stands in the way of me committing suicide is my daughter, Grace, and my wife, Samantha. Grace is such a beautiful eight year old girl. She can melt my heart with love just by winking and smiling at me. I adore her and knowing that she loves me helps me a lot. What more could a father ask for, right? And my wife, Sam, is usually patient and understanding, but I know that, sometimes, my behavior gets on her nerves, and rightly so."

The doctor steered the conversation back to Vietnam, back to 1968, during the more than two month siege at Khe-Sanh. He figured that was the beginning, the source and core of my mental pain; the cancer that needed cutting out before it claimed my entire body and life. I think my depression problems came long before Nam, but I said nothing. Any help I could get would be a welcome relief.

It wasn't a pretty story to tell, certainly not for the squeamish. He nodded and his eyes told me to continue. So I started by telling him that, "My whole Marine platoon, and a few others, were besieged by the NVA—North Vietnamese Army. They had us surrounded, with no way out. The ground fire was so heavy that our helicopters couldn't even land long enough to evacuate the dead and wounded. The NVA had us encircled, like being in a noose, and each day they were making that noose smaller and smaller. They were the hangman and we were his victims with the noose around our necks getting tighter and tighter. Eventually, if the NVA kept at it, the trap-door would open under our feet and we'd all die of broken necks and/or strangulation.

"Militarily, the place was nearly indefensible. Whoever selected that spot for the Marine base must have been a military moron. That Marine base was on low land, surrounded by higher ground from which the NVA could shoot down on us and bomb us with mortars at their leisure. Since time immemorial, military strategists have always known that the best defense is always conducted from higher ground so that the enemy has to struggle up hill to get to you. That struggle slows them down making them easier targets, it tires them and makes them careless, it demoralizes them, especially if their first attempt to over-run you are not successful. But some idiot decided to build the base on low ground, surrounded by hills that gave the enemy a great advantage. A lot of guys died because of someone's stupidity.

"After a few weeks, we were low on food, were getting very little sleep, and the corpses kept accumulating with nowhere to put them, except in stacks, like firewood. The smell of the putrefying corpses was nauseating and morale shattering.

Rescue helicopters couldn't come to our aid because of the intense rifle and machine gun attacks on them as they hovered over the camp. So after nearly two months of the siege, I went to the Colonel and suggested that I take a small group of four to six men and that each night we'd sneak close to the enemy defenses and kill sentries with knives, one at a time. I figured that this would cause such intense psychological terror to the NVA that they would either attack in force or retreat. We couldn't hold out much longer, anyway, so either way we had nothing to lose and everything to gain. It was tough getting volunteers, but finally five other Marines realized that we'd all die within a week if we didn't take action. We'd already been pinned down for ten weeks and half our soldiers were dead or wounded already. A Mohawk Indian guy said he volunteered because we couldn't bury the dead bodies and the smell was so bad it was about to suffocate him. He said he might as well go out and kill some commies. You know how that is. Some people hide their fears behind a mask of jokes. He wasn't from my group, but everybody called this Indian, Hawkeye. I never asked if it was his real name or a nickname. He joked a lot, but he was a really tough guy; had the warrior spirit in full bloom just underneath that thin layer of humor.

"We killed the NVA at night and every night for about a week. Unfortunately, all the night stalkers were killed except for me and Hawkeye. One of them was captured alive and was tortured during the night so that we could all hear his screams. Hawkeye and I kept going out at night, anyway, though we had to be extra careful, and sometimes came back after a few hours with no kills—they were wary of us by then. Hawkeye and I had excellent night vision, probably what kept us alive and not the others I think Hawkeye got his name or nickname from that fact. That's just a guess. At the time we weren't close friends, but he's one of the few people that I remember from Nam. He was reliable and had great courage. But mostly I try real hard to forget the names, faces and places . . . and the awful smells that contaminate my mind.

"Humans, unlike animals, seem to have a natural fear of the dark. You ask most people what sense they think is most important and ninety-nine percent will say it's their sense of sight. You take their eye-sight away from them and they get scared and very uncomfortable (me too). That's what night time does to people, it takes their sense of sight away from them and their sense of comfort, security and self-confidence vanishes, also, and that causes them to panic. I don't care how brave most people are during the daytime, at night a vast majority of them are afraid to be in the dark. That's how we terrorized the NVA into not tightening the strangle-hold that they had built around us. They were so scared at night, knowing we were killing them silently and unseen that they became very nervous, jittery, couldn't sleep and, at dusk, carelessly argued about who had sentry duty—I assumed that that was what they were arguing about, since I don't speak Vietnamese.

But I do know that I smiled with great satisfaction. Even more pleasing was the times when they started shooting each other. You know, like a noise in the dark might cause one of them to shoot, or spray bullets at the noise, then one of their own soldiers is dead after having just taken a leak away from the camp. But sometimes those shots, especially the spray of bullets, went out into the jungle and killed an American. At one point the enemy was in such a panic that they were shooting at almost any sound. That's how three of the other volunteers got killed. The other one, like I said, was careless, made too much noise, got caught in the act and was tortured. But the enemy killed three times as many of their own men, from fear and terror. Soon the NVA got smarter and assigned two sentries for each location. Hawkeye and I couldn't stalk and kill successfully when that happened so we came up with another plan. When Hawkeye and couldn't get close to them any more, we threw stones into their camp, which had the effect of terrorizing them even more. But we made sure we were well hidden and protected because then the enemy shot in the direction that they thought the noises came from. One time, though, we threw clusters of rocks at a sentry post and the soldiers in their own camp killed those sentries, thinking that the camp was being attacked by a small group of American Marines.

"Hawkeye and I made it without any serious injuries, but when we killed enemy sentries and came back to camp with blood soaking our clothes, faces and hands, it had an unsettling effect on our own guys. That's one of my problems, Doc. I still feel the warm, sticky blood on my hands, at times, and sometimes when I look at my hands, I even see red and smell the copper odor that blood sometimes has. It looks and smells so real. At times like that my whole body shakes uncontrollably and the tension seems like it will tear me apart."

I realized that my eyes had filled with tears at the memory of my dead comrades, especially those four brave soldiers who died because they followed me out into the night to kill the enemy. I told the Doc that those four guys sacrificed their lives so that the other soldiers could survive that hellish siege. I told him that intense emotions well-up inside of me like a dormant volcano suddenly erupting. I stated that tears often stream down my face whenever I think of them, and as my hands wipe across my face, like windshield wiper blades, to remove the warm wetness, another stream of teardrops quickly takes their place. I get choked up; can't talk. My mouth goes dry, and the lump in my throat seems so big that it will cut off the air to my lungs. I feel a panic as if I'm about to suffocate. I wondered, then, what the doctor saw and felt when he looked into the horrors hidden in my moist eyes.

"God-damn-it!" I shouted—Doc nearly jumped out of his seat. "I'd gladly flush those medals down the toilet to get those guys back, alive. They were the real heroes, you know. Those guys meant so much to me. I see their faces at night, almost every night, and I wake up crying, with my pillowcase damp. I'd literally give an arm or leg if I could have all those guys back, alive and well, and with their families and friends. All I have left of them is bad memories of how they died by following me. I can't even remember their names, but their faces are vivid pictures framed in my mind.

"Doc. Did you ever look into the eyes of a dying man? Have you ever seen the face of a person who dies as you are looking at them?" Doc shook his head to indicate that he hadn't. "Well I'll tell you about it, then. They look numb, terrified, scared; there eyes pleading for help. And just before they die, their pupils grow real large and become somewhat transparent. That's when you see their agony, just before their whole face slackens in death, while their eyes stare at you without hope. You look into their black pupils, like looking into a haunting abyss, and as their eyes glaze over at the moment of death, their agony transfers to you. They don't mean for it to happen that way, it just does. Each time you see that happen, it's like someone placing a large rock into your backpack. If you see a lot of deaths, you carry a lot of dead weight. But it's not your back that breaks, Doc, it's your mind." I paused, then looked at Doc, shrugged my shoulders, and stated, "Guess that's why I'm here, huh?"

Doc nodded his head in the affirmative, then said, "Please continue."

"I went to symbolically visit my dead comrades at the Vietnam Veterans Memorial in Washington, D.C. I saw thousands of names chiseled in the polished, black marble. It's a nice monument designed by Maya Ying Lin; a breathtaking monument to over fifty-eight thousand of our heroes. They certainly were heroes to be proud of and to be remembered.

"The Three Soldiers Statue, by Frederick Hart, is also a superb tribute. Vietnam veterans often refer to this statue as the 'keepers of the names.' Both the 'wall' and the 'statue' are stunning; with their power to elicit intense emotions and memories. Together, they are a monumentally private experience. You've got to see the monument with your own tearful eyes and feel the names with your own broken heart. I doubt that you can walk away from either one without a sense of being overwhelmed, especially if you imagine that you see your own name chiseled into the wall."

I remember asking the doctor to help me save myself from the horrid memories that I had of Nam. I also remember thinking of my dead comrades' eyes as they begged me to help them live. That's when the doctor explained to me that my most primary instincts for survival had controlled my actions in Vietnam. He said that these instincts were clearly the dominant forces controlling my behavior. They forced me to kill in order to stay alive, and they unquestionably overwhelmed any logical or emotional arguments that I may have had about the wrongness of the war and of the killings that I did. While in Vietnam, these "wrongness" arguments were submerged, concealed, and suppressed so that they didn't interfere with the primary instinct for survival. But, now, he said, I am not in a survival situation. Now survival is secondary, almost taken for granted, and my thoughts about the wrongness of the war, and of the killings that I did, have surfaced. Furthermore, he stated that the memories of the killing in Vietnam are so vivid, they can't be submerged, nor concealed any longer by mental subterfuge. Therefore, I have a grand conflict going on inside my head. I needed to kill to stay alive in Vietnam, but now I feel guilty about my participation in that war, and more importantly, I feel a tremendous guilt for having taken so many lives. And since I was an expert who had killed many times, then every person I killed has increased the weight my guilt until I now sat before him, like Atlas trying to hold up the world and finding the load much too heavy to bear. It sounded reasonable, I guess.

The doctor then ejaculated some non-sense about his suspecting that I may have volunteered for all those dangerous hand-to-hand night time combat missions because, subconsciously, I was trying to kill myself. He said it was a disguised way of committing suicide, honorably, on the battlefield He explained that if I was killed during battle, then I would have secretly committed suicide, while being considered a hero by everyone else because of my apparent bravery during a battle with the NVA troops.   However, this subconscious plan didn't work, he said, because I really was an expert in the deadly technique of night time stalking and silent killing. Thus, he said, the enemy never could help me by killing me, thereby helping me to fulfill my own death wish.

I told him that I thought the "suicide" part of his analysis was pure bullshit—though I did think about it, later—but that I wasn't in the mood to argue with him about it. I had survived by killing, by being a better killer than my enemy, by being an expert among amateurs. Hell, if I wanted to commit suicide I could just step into the enemy camp and yell, "Hey! You bunch of assholes! You all look like runt-assed, foul-smelling gooks!"

We looked at each other. I grinned. He didn't. He looked serious, as if searching my face for some answer, some clue. I don't know if he found anything.

He didn't wish to argue either, not now, anyway. He continued by saying that he believed that I may also be suffering from PTSD, which means "post-traumatic stress disorder." PTSD, he said, gets worse with time, not better. He said that I was already demonstrating some of the PTSD major symptoms, the flashbacks; the visual pictures of traumatic combat situations, the nightmares which seriously disturb my ability to sleep and get the rest that my body desperately needs, the alienation, which makes me opposed to some kinds of authority and prevents me from allowing myself to be emotionally close to anyone so that, if they die, it would be as if a stranger died and, thus, only cause me minimal grief. Then he said there's evidence of psychic numbing, which means that, in some ways, my sense of morality was damaged in Vietnam. He explained that I became an emotionless killer, outwardly calm, but inwardly I had lead a life of extreme violence and now tremendous guilt was bearing down on me. He went on to say that Vietnam vets have an abnormally high, but easily understandable suicide rate. Those that don't kill themselves try to lose themselves in an unstable life of wandering. They have an inability to settle down, mentally or physically, they often attempt to drown their guilt and sorrow with alcohol and drugs. One-third of all male, homeless adults living on the streets are Vietnam vets, he added, to my surprise.

To complicate matters, he informed me that he received my blood-test results from the hospital laboratory. Apparently, there's a chemical called "serotonin" that's made in the brain, the lack of which is very closely associated with clinical depression. The laboratory tests he said, indicated that I had an imbalance of this chemical, which is also significantly contributing to the cause of my depression episodes. He went on the say that the other causes for my depression are, naturally, related to my Vietnam experiences and all these things, cumulatively, are seriously affecting my mental health, which in turn, is affecting my relationship with my wife and daughter, and putting extreme stress on my marital and family relationships, as well as with my teaching career. Doc also told me that the cure would take time and that he would need to see me once or twice every week. He said he knew that he could help me, but that I'd have to give him time and try not to be impatient. He advised me that, sometimes, what matters most in sustaining a good relationship, whether it's with him, my family or with my close friends and relatives, is not so much what you *give* to that good relationship as much as what you are willing to *give up* to keep it

I thanked him and told him that whatever he could do for me certainly would be appreciated because I was tired of being chin-deep in my own personal and psychological cesspool. Then I asked him when we could get started. He said that we had already started and now we needed to continue our talks regularly. Because of holidays and other conflicts, it was decided that we wouldn't be able to meet again for a few weeks. Doc made me an appointment for November 30th, then asked me to keep a diary of my moods and feelings so he could read it and we could discuss what had happened during those weeks. I hoped that I could handle my personal problems for that long. I thought positively and told myself that I could make it. But I was quite sure that the mere "power of positive thinking" couldn't correct a chemical imbalance.

Before I left his office, he wrote-out a prescription for me to take two capsules—25 mg each—a day of an anti-depressant medication called Pamelor.

After we said good-bye to each other, I put on my coat and headed to my truck. I'd get the prescription filled on the way home and start taking the pills right away. I felt really good, hope replaced hopelessness It seemed strange to feel that good. Feeling good had become an alien feeling; something I hadn't felt much of lately, but wanted desperately. Perhaps, I thought, there was a light at the end of the tunnel after all.

As I exited the building and walked across the parking lot, I felt my lips stretching into a smile, which is also something that I hadn't been able to do in a very long time.

/../.-../- - -/...-/./- -/.-/.-./.-/-.../- - -/-./-././.- -/./.-../.-../

Chapter 2

★★★★

The Visit

THERE WAS NO SCHOOL on Wednesday, November 11th, due to Veteran's Day. That's always a sad day for me because I remember all my buddies who were either killed, physically maimed, or psychologically injured. The sadness, however, lost some of its severity due to the fact that this day allows my whole family to be together. My wife, Samantha, is also a teacher, and also had the day off. I explained to Grace just what Veteran's Day meant to me, but, being a kid, she was just excited to have a day off from school. It turned out to be a happy family day for the three of us. We played together and went out to lunch together.

Friday-the-thirteenth arrived. After school Sam and I came home as soon as possible so we could get her van loaded with the suitcases that were packed the night before. When the school bus brought Grace home we took care of a few last minute items—like making sure that Grace went to the bathroom since she had a bladder the size of a thimble and usually needed to stop frequently for bathroom breaks—locked the doors and windows, then got into the van and started driving the two and a half hour trip from our home near Rochester, New York, to Chemung, which is near Elmira, New York.

It's usually a boring trip, especially since I've been driving the same route for many years. Although boring, we made it safely to Sam's parent's house. Actually it was a quick, easy trip with no land mines in the road and no mortar or rifle fire to contend with, and only one restroom stop for Grace.

Just before we get to my in-laws' house there's a short stretch of road that goes through a thickly wooded area. The overlapping tree branches form a canopy over the road. The branches, now defoliated, extend out over the top of the road, like a dome. Normally, in summer, this would be a pleasantly shaded drive-through, but Nam changed that for me. It reminded me of the triple canopy jungles in central Nam. With the bare branches, it was also a stark reminder of the defoliating affects that the chemical, Agent Orange, had on the Nam jungles. It's at this stretch of road that Grace likes to sing a song about teddy bears having a picnic in the woods. It's a cute song. Sometimes Sam and I also start singing, and we all have a good laugh just as grandma's and grandpa's house comes into view.

My mother-in-law and father-in-law met us at the door, as they usually do, with beaming smiles. Sam and I carried the two suitcases and an overnight bag into the house while Grace showered her grandparents with hugs and kisses. We all sat down to eat sukiyaki, which my mother-in-law had hot and ready to eat. She knew it's one of my favorite meals, so she served me a large amount, over rice. She's a great lady, so loving and caring, so much so that I feel closer to her than I did to my own long-absent and now deceased mother.

My father-in-law is nice, in his own way, but usually doesn't show any strong emotions. He's kind of grumpy, at times, but on the whole he's a pretty good guy; certainly nicer than my own father was to me.

The big news around the area that day was that there had been an escape from the Elmira Correctional Facility. Not technically an escape from the facility itself, but an escape while being transferred in a State Trooper car to the Attica prison in upstate, western New York. It happened about eleven o'clock in the morning that day; too late to make it into the morning newspapers. It was getting a lot of coverage on the TV and radio, though, in the evening news.My in-laws informed Sam and I that witnesses had seen a powerfully built, fortyish, long-haired, full-bearded and mustached man waving a white handkerchief at the north-bound State Trooper car that was carrying a young prisoner named Lester Gibson. The bearded man was walking south with a much younger, slimmer, clean-shaven, short-haired man. The young man was hopping on one leg as if the other leg was broken or badly hurt. The young man's arm was around the older man's neck, and the older man had his arm around the younger man's waist. Both men's hair was messed up with dirt and blood on their faces, as if they'd had an accident. My father-in-law said that the troopers stopped their car to assist the two men and were caught totally unaware by the ruse. Authorities are guessing that each man had a concealed weapon, and that they used them to quietly take control of the troopers and their car. The Troopers' car was found a couple of hours later, a few miles away, on a seldom used, dirt road.

Police investigators said there were no signs of a struggle between the men and the two troopers. One trooper was found dead with a bullet wound to his chest, and the other trooper was in critical condition at a local hospital with a bullet wound to the stomach. Both troopers were found lying in a ditch, next to their car, which was parked on the shoulder of the dirt road. Passing motorists couldn't see the bodies from either direction because the ditch was so deep. Luckily for the unconscious trooper, one motorist passed the trooper car once on the way up the road and again, about an hour later, on the way back down the road. He became suspicious, got out of his car and looked around. That's how he discovered the bodies. The wounded trooper would have certainly died if his body hadn't been discovered for another couple of hours.

Dad said that the young prisoner was just a kid, only seventeen or eighteen years old. His name is Lester Gibson, but he was gone, of course. Fresh tire tracks were found near the trooper car where another vehicle had peeled-out quickly. All the evidence led the local police officials and local troopers to believe that the escape was carefully planned to assist the young prisoner's escape from police custody.

I finished my sukiyaki over rice and was quite full, so I turned down an offer for more. Grace had finished her meal and had gone into the living room to watch TV after having become thoroughly bored by the story. I was glad she'd left because I'd become curious and wanted to ask a few detailed questions.

Looking at my father-in-law, I asked, "What crime was this Gibson kid being sent to Attica for?" I paused and waited for Dad's reply. He looked at Mom and they both had disgusted looks on their faces as they looked back at Sam and me.

Dad lowered his voice, so Grace wouldn't hear, then leaned across the table a little so that I could hear him whisper. The kitchen light shone off his bald head as he said, "That animal was found guilty of the rape and strangulation death of a ten year old girl."

Sam and I looked at each other, both of us thinking of Grace who was only eight years old. The thought sent a chilling fear up my spine and the muscles in my right hand twitched as it instinctively reached for the blade, in its sheath, located under my left armpit. I stopped my hand in mid-motion. Any loving father would understand my reaction. Then I asked, "Do the police have any leads?"

"Wait a minute," Dad whispered, "I've got more details about this Gibson fellow that they couldn't mention on the TV or radio."

Mom stood up immediately and left the table. As she walked by Sam, Mom tapped her on the shoulder, as if giving Sam a signal to leave the table and follow her into the living room. Sam shrugged politely and stayed seated, eyes glued to her father.

I knew then that Dad's information would be more than the ordinary kind of detailed, repugnant information, so I prepared myself, mentally. Under the table, I placed a reassuring hand on Sam's thigh and squeezed it gently. She placed a hand on top of mine.

Dad wiped his brow, licked his lips, then looked me straight in the eye and said, "Joe told me this stuff. Bobby told him. It's straight from the official files."

Joe is a close friend of Dad's They both worked for, and retired from, the U.S. Post Office in Elmira. Joe's son, Bobby, is an Elmira police officer. Bobby had all the intimate details on Lester Gibson's crimes, even a psychological report indicating that he was a bed-wetter until his early teens.

Dad proceeded, "Christ," he whispered, "Gibson kept the poor girl tied up and blindfolded for nearly a month after he kidnapped her. Kept her in some cabin way out in the woods where there was no one around for miles. The coroner's report said that the poor kid had cuts, scrapes and bruises all over her body. She'd been beaten several times.

Can you believe that? Gibson's a monster, that's what he is. He needs killing is what I say. The girl lost an awful lot of weight. Either she wouldn't eat or she was practically starved to death." Dad paused to shake his head sadly. I noticed how hard Sam was squeezing my hand, rage making her hand on mine feel like a tightening vice.

Dad's gaze traveled from me to Sam. His face blushed red. Anger, I thought. Dad seemed speechless for a few seconds, just looking at his daughter. "It's disgusting," he said as he looked intently at Sam. "Maybe you better leave for this part," he said to Sam.

Sam sat frozen to her chair, rigid, "Tell us," is all she said to her father, as she stared intently at him.

Dad looked back at me, seemingly grateful not to have to look into his own daughter's eyes. From the tone of his hesitant words and the look in his eyes, I could tell that he was about to say something that a father wouldn't want to talk about and would be embarrassed to mention in front of his daughter.

"The coroner's report quotes the medical examiner's report which said that traces of dried semen were found on and in the girl's body. The semen was found . . . " Dad's voice crackled as his throat tightened up. He stopped, cleared his throat and swallowed hard, then continued. "They found dried semen and blood around the girl's virginal and anal areas"—Dad paused again and I knew his next word would be "mouth." Before Dad said the word "mouth," he looked up at me with tears in his eyes, an expression of rage on his face and scarlet skin due to embarrassment. After the pause to collect his thoughts and control his emotions, he looked again at Sam. I knew that he wanted Sam to leave. I turned to Sam, squeezed her thigh and whispered that I would tell her what was said, later. Sam reluctantly rose and went into the living room to be seated with her mom and Grace as they watched TV.

Dad's eyes didn't follow her. He was staring at the table top, directly under his chin. "Thanks for getting her to leave. The medical examiner's report also states that there's no question that the girl was raped, sodomized and forced to have oral and anal sex." His voice was chocked up as he stated, "And that isn't the worst of it. Just before she died, he must have made her . . . " Dad's voice came to a dead stop. His eyes became moist, which is something very unusual because Dad wasn't one to show hardly any emotion at all. I'd never seen him cry. He had to be thinking about Grace. He was choked-up with emotion that he swept his tongue across his parched lips before swallowing hard to remove the emotional lump from his throat. He looked down at the table, again, then continued. "When they found the poor girl, she even had semen around her mouth. It wasn't completely dry yet. They found . . . they found . . . " Dad cleared his throat again. I didn't know why he stopped this time. He'd already told me that the girl was forced to have oral sex. What else could he say about it? I couldn't figure out what made him pause, even with Sam gone from the table. But Dad's next sentence shocked me like I had seldom been shocked before. Dad said, "They found traces of feces in the semen that was around her mouth."

I was jolted into speechlessness at the realization of what must have happened to the poor girl. I could feel my back press hard against the back of my chair and was thankful that Sam wasn't there. My stomach felt queasy. Dad and I stared at each other with mutual looks of horror and disgust. He followed my right hand as I, once again, unconsciously reached for the blade that was tucked under my left armpit, the Marine's ten inch Ka-Bar, the exact one that I carried in Nam.

I whispered, "The humiliation, torture and pain she went through must have been extreme, unbearable," I whispered to Dad.

"He wants killin'. He needs killin'. When he's caught and sent to prison, I surely hope the inmates find out what he did and shank him, after they abuse and humiliate him."

I agreed with Dad, but no words formed and I remained silent. My thoughts were about cutting off his penis, then slashing his belly so he could watch his guts spill onto the floor and die a slow, painful death, while looking in horror at his uncoiling, purplish intestines.

Neither of us spoke for a few seconds as revulsion washed over us like a waterfall of human sewage.

I thought of the physical and mental torture that the poor girl must have gone through. Tears cascaded down my cheeks, plummeting onto my shirt. I looked at Sam, but, thankfully, she was talking to her mom while Grace watched TV. Dad and I both composed ourselves and wiped the tears away.

Dad said, "They were moving the monster from some jail that's down state, near New York City, I think. The Troopers stopped overnight at the Elmira Correctional Prison. The next morning, the troopers were bringing him to Attica, the maximum security prison up near Buffalo."

I hadn't expected Dad to continue, so it surprised me when he said, "The medical examiner also found that the semen samples indicate more than one blood type. There were at least two men, maybe more who abused her."

Then Dad was quiet, so quiet that I could hear Mom talking to Grace about some knitting project that she was working on. I heard the TV, but couldn't make sense of the voices. I looked at Sam and found her staring at me.

Then suddenly Dad started again, still leaning over the table, close to me. He whispered, "The police got an anonymous tip from a hunter who wouldn't identify himself. The cops checked it out and raided the cabin. Young Gibson was just packing things together, getting ready to get away. Christ Almighty!" he stated through clenched teeth. "They just missed saving that girl by only a matter of minutes. Her body wasn't even cold yet. Just a few minutes, probably less than half an hour and she could have been saved from that monster. He just used her, over and over, for his own sadistic sexual pleasure, then strangled her. From what Bobby says, the Gibson kid gave up easily, no struggle, just a taunting smile. Then he confessed. Said he was alone, no one else involved, which we know, now, wasn't true. But the cops couldn't prove otherwise; couldn't even find young Gibson's father and brother. They had disappeared. So Gibson was the only one convicted, even though it's strongly suspected that his father and older brother may have been involved with both the rape and the escape.

"Any solid leads?" I asked.

"Bobby just told Joe that it's suspected that the Gibson kid and his two accomplices, who most certainly are his father and older brother, must have left this area as fast as they could. I guess that's to be expected. Be pretty stupid of them to stick around while the cops are swarming like bees on a honeycomb. The Elmira cops and the State Troopers are notifying all the area police departments to be on the look out for them, although they don't know what kind of vehicle they're driving, nor have they had time to compile full descriptions of the older and younger man that the witnesses saw. They have shown police artist's drawing of the two older Gibsons and a picture of Lester Gibson on TV and have given physical descriptions. They're asking the public to help if any of the Gibsons are seen. Christ! From what they say, I don't think the bastard is big enough to even play in any little league sport, even though, age-wise, Lester's nearly an adult. A tiny, frail-looking fellow, apparently. Kind of effeminate looking."

I felt as if I was becoming a human volcano. It was as if the angry lava was surging from my toes to my head, hot, burning anger. I knew that I would maim, then kill anyone, anyone at all who did that to my daughter or wife. Sam knew me well enough to know that I would do it without even flinching. But I don't think that Mom and Dad knew it. They weren't really aware of the details of my Nam experiences, nor of my visits to the psychiatrist. I think they suspected something, though. They were, perhaps, just too polite to ask for fear of embarrassing me or Sam.

They knew about the knife that I carried. Mom disliked it, Sam tolerated it and Dad understood it. Dad was a World War Two veteran who saw action in Italy. He knew the horrors of war and of killing. I think I understood Dad, too. I believe that he, too, would kill anyone that raped any member of his family. The only difference between us would be the way we would kill. Now Dad would probably stick his double-barreled, twelve gauge shotgun into the guy's mouth and pull the trigger. He's a tough old bird. I'd stand back to back with him any day as we fought the encircling enemy. Now, me? I wouldn't be so generous with giving the rapist such a quick death. As I said before, I'd probably cut the rapist's cock off, hand it to him, then slash his lower belly and let his guts spill onto the floor, at his feet. Or, perhaps, I'd tie him to a chair with his own intestines. Then he could bleed to death slowly with his penis in his hand.

Dad and I moved to the living room, where Grace was laughing loudly at something funny that happened on the TV. We all grinned and smiled with her, thankful that we were all together and safe at grandpa's and grandma's house. There was something warm and secure about their home in the country. The dirt roads and the forests blocked-out the smells, as well as the stress, noises and visions of harried city life.

The sound of Grace's laughter was so beautiful and so comforting that it seemed to trigger a welcomed change in our topic and we started smiling and talking about Dad's birthday. We teased him a little about 'dinosaur hunting trips' and he jokingly told us to get lost and leave him in peace.

I picked up my Spenser novel by Robert B. Parker and started reading. Sam and Mom were talking about Thanksgiving dinner, while dad read his *Outdoor Life* magazine. Grace continued to watch and giggle at her TV show. Sam and Mom were huddled together in leisurely conversation.

But the living room was only peaceful for a few minutes when the TV show was interrupted in order to show a picture and give a physical description of Lester Gibson. Dad was right about Lester Gibson's size. According to the report he was Caucasian, five feet four inches tall, about one-hundred ten or twenty pounds, very slender, small-boned, no facial hair, and had short brown hair. But it was his eyes that first caught my attention. His eyes looked glazed, unfocused, like someone in a rage while on drugs. Those sinister eyes affected his whole facial expression, radiating their evil influence across his entire face, like polluted water poisoning the earth. He looked like a person in constant emotional pain, with an overwhelming need to vent some of that rage by inflicting pain on other people, especially helpless children, since his stature left him lacking the ability to confront adults, even female adults. The report was over in thirty seconds. Grace appeared oblivious to its information and went back to watching her TV show.

Lester looked like a pathetic young man. A cruel and menacing meanness saturated his face and probably originated from early and constant childhood abuse and suffering. He looked like the type of kid that went through life with no real friends except, possibly, the ugly faces of rage, resentment and bitterness. He was the type of kid that even dogs didn't want to play with, unless he was wearing a pork-chop around his neck. A more unkind thought ripped a path through my mind like a bolt of lightening slicing through the sky: Lester was such a lonely kid that his dad probably had to cut holes in his pant's pockets just so Lester would have something to play with. But even that must have eventually gotten "out-of-hand." Black humor.

The look in Lester Gibson's eyes lingered and haunted my thoughts. I thought of the "pucker factor" that those eyes must have caused in the children that Gibson had abused. It was foolish to think that that ten year old girl was the only one whom he had abused, or even the youngest one, for that matter.

In Nam, we Marines used the term "pucker factor" to describe how our asshole sphincter muscles would pucker-up when we got terrified of dying, before, during or after a battle. It's an involuntary body reaction that really does happen. It sounds funny, but you can certainly be very thankful if you've never had to experience it. It only comes when you're scared out of your mind; on the verge of death, or think that you are.

A couple hours later I took my pills while I was in the bathroom. I remember thinking that I'd been taking them for almost a week and I thought that I detected a noticeably positive change in my moods. The doctor said it would take about a week to notice the effect. They made me feel better, less agitated, less nervous. That good feeling gave me hope and I welcomed it because I knew that a man without hope is an emotional cripple.

The next day, Saturday, November 14th, was a beautifully cold, clear, sunny morning. Mom made oatmeal and we poured Dad's homemade maple syrup onto it. There's just no other maple syrup that can match it. I've had Canadian, New York and Vermont maple syrup, and a few others, but they don't even come close in flavor to Dad's homemade syrup. It's absolutely the best maple syrup on this planet, and that's no exaggeration.

After breakfast, while I was shaving, Grace came into the bathroom to watch me. She liked to watch me shave, especially if I gave her a handful of my foamy shaving cream. She was giggling as she played with the shaving cream. I was half watching her and half shaving when she looked up at me and asked, "Daddy, would you take me for a walk in the woods this morning?" Her face was delightfully radiant and alive with color, as if the sun were smiling at me. I could feel the comforting warmth of her smile. Her eyes sparkled with love and admiration for me, a great reward for being a good father.

I almost always took her for walks in the woods when we were at Mom's and Dad's house for the weekend, unless the weather was bad, or unless it was deer hunting season. Then I remembered that this was the weekend before deer hunting season began, so I said, "Sure, Sweetheart. We can go about ten o'clock, especially since it's such a sunny day."

After shaving I read my Spenser novel and at precisely ten o'clock Grace came up to me all excited and said, "Come on, Dad. Come on. It's time to go." She was waving her arms and jumping up and down with excitement as she talked. Her shoulder-length, brown hair was bobbing up and down with the vertical motions of her body, her pearl-white teeth shone brightly between lips that were curved in laughter and excitement. Her brown eyes seemed, once again, to sparkle, like two twinkling, bright stars in the night time sky. I put Spenser away until later. We bundled up warmly because, although there was no snow, we could tell, from Dad's outside thermometer, that the temperature was only slightly above freezing. We got our boots, gloves, coats, scarves and hats on. We were so warm now that we were both desperate to get outside. We shouted to everyone, "See you later alligator!" and departed.

As we stood in the driveway, I said, "Well, Sweetheart, which way should we go? Over the hill to the pond, or down the road to the creek?" I pointed to each place as I named them, my extended arms making me look like a human, Christian cross.

"Let's go to the creek, Daddy," Grace replied. "We can throw stones in it and then go to that old cabin in the woods. Then maybe we can stay in the woods and walk up that hill that we went up before, and leave signs to help us find our way back," she added, excitedly. She liked to pretend that we were adventurers, explorers who were blazing a trail into the wild, untamed forests of Chemung, New York. She sure was cute. Almost every day she added clusters of precious moments and memories to my life.

Grace's cheeks were nearly red, from the chilly air by the time we completed the walk to the creek, but she didn't behave as if she was uncomfortable, so we continued. When we reached the creek I looked through the naked trees and saw no one at the cabin, no car or truck, and no smoke coming out of the chimney. In five years of coming here, I'd only once seen anybody at this old, derelict hunting cabin.

We threw stones into the creek, then we threw rocks into the deeper part of the creek to see who could make the biggest splash. I won because I picked up a large stone that Grace couldn't lift and threw it into the pool. I cheated, but the resulting splash went up about six or eight feet. Grace and I laughed and shouted and when we heard our echo we laughed and shouted even louder to hear our voices answered by the echo of ourselves. Our uninhibited silliness was fun.

Then we had a little-splash contest. I picked up a tiny pebble and threw it into the pool. It splashed up only about two or three inches. Then Grace laughed teasingly at me as she threw a teeny, tiny pebble toward the water. It was so small that I couldn't' even see it going through the air, but I did see the ring of water where it hit, barely making a perceptible splash and watery ring.

Then I picked up a pebble about the size of a grain of sand and threw it towards the water. We watched as it made a tiny splash and rings in the water. "Ha," I said, "my little splash tied yours, so there's no winner."

"Daddy. Wait," Grace said a she bent down to pick up an even tinier pebble. She stood up, looked at me mischievously and threw the pebble towards the water. "See, Daddy," she said with excitement, "Mine beat yours. It hardly splashed at all." She pointed at me, laughed, and stated, "I really got you good that time. I win! You lose!" She laughed louder, then grabbed my hand and pulled me away—I knew, however, that she didn't throw anything into the water. I allowed her to trick me—she was having too much fun for me to argue, even in jest.

She said, "Come on, Daddy. Follow me." She pulled me forward as she headed into the woods from the edge of the dirt road where we had been standing, looking down at the creek. We had gone this way many times before. I followed her and cautioned her not to step into the creek's chilly waters. We followed the winding creek into the woods about two-hundred feet. Then we stopped at another of our well known pools, where, during the spring, we caught crayfish, to Grace's boisterous and laughing delight. I had my back to the cabin, which was only about seventy feet away. We were both squatting next to a pool, concentrating on stirring up the icy water with sticks that we had just picked up. My ears filled with the loud gurgling of the creek water as it tumbled like an acrobat over and around the rocks jutting from its bed. We were protected from what little wind there was, now that we were well into the woods, but I could hear the wind blowing over the tops of the tall trees, making noises that, at nighttime, might have seemed scary to the uninitiated.

The word "scary" set my mind on edge. It provided a spark that flared in my mind. I felt that something was wrong. The hairs on the back of my neck stood out like pine needles. Suddenly I had this awful, but familiar feeling growing rapidly in the pit of my stomach. I felt a cold chill rising up my spine, then settling like a block of ice at the base of my skull. It was as if I was in Nam again and the VC or NVA were closing in on me. Grace was still looking at the water and stirring the pool with her stick when the urge to whirl around and face the danger became so strong that I picked up a rock for a weapon. I was too heavily and securely dressed to reach by blade quickly. I sprang to an upright position and whirled around with my right hand cocked to throw the rock, or use it as a hammer.

Two large men stood no more than twenty feet away from us. Their menacing eyes harbored about as much friendliness as you might expect to see in the eyes of a rabid dog.

"Now that not a very frien'ly greetin'," the older man said.

/-../.-/.-../- - -/...-/./.../.-../.-../.-../-.- -/-.../- - -/-./.-/-./././- -/-/./.-../.-../

Chapter 3

★★★★

The Kidnapping

I COULD HEAR GRACE make a fearful moan behind me. I tossed the rock down as I faced the two men, then gently took Grace's hand and pulled her close to me. Grace stood by my right hip, slightly in back of me, with her left hand clutching the lower back of my coat and her right hand grasping the right side of my coat, near my hip. I could feel her fear. She was trembling while clutching at my coat.

"What yuh be doin' here?" the full-bearded, mustached man said. His stare was malevolent, his voice was a deep bass, with a ferocious quality to it, as if a threatened, full-grown grizzly bear was talking. He was definitely full-grown; a mountain of a man. He appeared to be about six feet eight inches tall, close to three hundred pounds—some of it bulging over his belt; most of it pure muscle—and had eyes that looked as deadly as a shark's. He looked like he was in his mid-forties, radiated an aura of power and unquestioned authority. He also had the strange habit of sucking air through a gap in his front teeth. I assumed that the habit was formed by constantly trying to dislodge food particles from between those brownish-yellow, stained teeth. The color of his teeth was quickly explained when he spit a gob of chewing tobacco juice out of his mouth. His full-beard had brownish drool on it from having just spit tobacco juice. It reminded me of diarrhea. It gave him a disgustingly comical appearance, as if he had just walked off the pages of Roald Dahl's book, *The Twits*.

Standing next to the mountain man was another tall, slimmer, and much younger man—not nearly as tall or as large as the older man. Their eyes, noses, jaws and general facial structure looked similar, also, so I figured that they were father and son. The younger man just stared intently as he stood with both arms akimbo, apparently quite content to let the older man do all the talking while he experimented with a variety of supposedly evil stares and facial expressions—a movie star wanna-be, maybe.

All of a sudden, I realized who both men might be, although I tried not to let it show in my facial expression—I thought the older man fit the description of the full-bearded man whom witnesses said they saw helping a younger man along the roadway just before the two New York State Troopers were shot. I hoped I wasn't correct, but that hope was dashed when I saw part of the bumper of their car behind the cabin, as if the car was intentionally hidden from any roadside view. If they owned the cabin, why would they park the car in back of the cabin instead of at the parking area in front of the cabin? If I was right, then there should be three of them. These two, however, definitely had something to hide. Innocent people don't act so threateningly.

Holy shit, I thought, how was I going to get us out of this mess, especially if they were who I thought they were? I couldn't get to my knives easily—they were under my heavy coat—and if I attack, using karate, one of them could easily grab Grace and the fight would be over all too quickly and easily, simply by threatening to do her harm.. I decided to try to bluff my way out of this predicament.

I smiled as if we were friendly neighbors, then said, "My daughter and I are just out for a walk. We sometimes walk down this creek. We're sorry if we disturbed you with our laughing and shouting. We didn't know anyone was here. We'll just move on so we aren't disturbing you," I continued, while trying to maintain my smile and friendly tone of voice. "We're expected home for lunch pretty soon, anyway. Have a nice day." I gave a good-bye wave of my hand.

Casually, I took Grace's petite hand in mine and started to walk away, toward the road and toward my in-law's house. At the same time, the younger man growled, "Jus' a second! What's the latest news 'round here? We 'aven't 'eard the news in a few days. Is there anything goin' on that we should know 'bout?"

I turned slowly and absorbed the younger man's dimensions more closely. The sound of his voice left no doubt in my mind that he and the older man were father and son and that somewhere in the cabin there would be a third person named Lester Gibson. The younger man was about six feet two inches, my height, but he looked to be about fifteen or twenty pounds heavier than I; about two-hundred pounds. He was about twenty-five years old, a few days growth of beard, that didn't cover long, narrow scars on both cheeks. They looked like knife scars to me. He also chewed tobacco and had the same cheek bulge and stained teeth as the older man. His voice wasn't as deep, a baritone, but was similar to the older man's voice. The younger man also had a rugged, malevolent look about him, just like the older man. Their stares bore down on my shoulders like anvils.

I noticed that Grace's grip on me had loosened, so she must have calmed down a little.

I had to maintain my composure. I figured that if I told them that there was nothing going on that they would know for sure that I was onto them. They at least had a car radio, I guessed, so they would know that there was a manhunt for them. So I said, "Well, the only thing I know about is that some prisoner escaped while being transported to Attica Prison from the Elmira Correctional Facility." I didn't want to give them too much information or they would wonder why I was so stupid as not to suspect them. That would make them immediately suspicious and instantly they'd know that I was lying and that I knew exactly who they were. So I just said, "We are…my daughter and I, from the Rochester area and just down here for the weekend, so I really don't know much about the local news."

I waved to them, again, turned and started walking away with Grace. Every step seemed to take an eternity, like walking slowly over a red-hot bed of coals. I kept Grace in front of me and my back towards the two men.

"Stop!" was the next word that I heard after only having taken a few steps away from them. The word was said with a bass, deep-throated growl, so I knew it was the older man talking. I thought about running. We had a few steps head-start on them. But then I heard a noise that crippled my thoughts of running. And before I turned around, I heard a second, similar noise, like the dull crack of a twig. I turned to look and whatever shred of hope there was for bluffing and running my way out of this situation had evaporated as Grace and I stared into two pistol barrels, both with hammers cocked and trigger fingers slightly squeezing each trigger.

Later, I found out that I was correct in my assessment of them. The older man was Jake Gibson, a habitual trouble-maker with a list of escalating crimes as long as his legs. He appeared to be a man so full of rage and cruelty that it was nearly impossible for him to glean much pleasure from life. And what pleasure he did get was derived by making others unhappy by inflicting pain on them. He reminded me of a super-bully who took pleasure from meanness, cruelty and humiliating others with his arrogance and physical prowess.

Jake's sons were no different. The younger man was Tom Gibson, a notorious bully and enthusiastic fire-starter, who, only a few years ago, tried to set the school principal's car on fire after the principal reprimanded him for his incorrigible bullying behaviors towards his peers. And, like his father, he was well on his way down the path walked by seasoned criminals.

Now I was positive that Lester was hidden inside the cabin. Lester had obviously shown that he, too, was headed down the same path. He just had to be sneakier, more tricky because of his lack of physical prowess—though he seemed to be better educated. At least he didn't talk like a backwoods hick.

If my knowledge of handguns was still accurate, then Jake had a Smith and Wesson .357 magnum pointed at my chest and Tom had his Colt .38 caliber aimed at Grace. Apparently, Jake and Tom had their handguns concealed in their belts, under the front portion of their coats, where they were quite easy to get to.

Jake said, "Unless yuh an' the girlie wants ta die right where yuh be standin', yuh bes' git o'er here right quick."

From the tone of his voice there was no mistaking just how serious he was, so Grace and I walked back to the cabin with them. Just as I had suspected, we met little Lester Gibson; all of about five feet four inches tall and one-hundred ten or twenty pounds of him. Grace held on to me more tightly now. My eyes locked onto Lester. The sight of him stirred up an intense, roiling rage in my guts. He looked to be more like fifteen years old, instead of seventeen or eighteen. He had soft, delicate, effeminate facial features and from these observations, my deduction was that, in school, some of the boys must have teased him by calling him Leslie instead of Lester or, perhaps, Les, and many girls must have rejected him just as quickly. He probably hated girls who teased him more than the boys because a boy didn't have to attract boys to be considered manly, but boys did have to attract girls in order to be considered as having normal masculinity—there are exceptions, of course. Constant rejection from girls would cause a much deeper emotional pain in him—assuming that he's heterosexual. I opined that he also hated himself for not being big and strong-looking like his father and brother. Of course, these are all just hasty first impressions, conjectures and assumptions on my part, but I would bet that he was now a confirmed misogynist. And if I was correct, then all the pain of constant rejection probably caused him to want to punish and control girls and women—to make them feel the pain that they made him feel. And, I thought, he punishes and controls girls and women now, through a supreme act of sexual violence, he rapes them. With his small stature, he probably plays it safe by only raping girls and very small women. It would be much too humiliating to try to rape a woman who ended up over-powering him. Yes, I thought, I had him sized-up, or, in his case, sized-down.

Lester took a posture of cockiness, of supreme arrogance. I figured that he was so full of hot air that it should have mummified him long ago. Actually all three of them were so supremely arrogant and loud that when they opened their mouths, I swear that it looked to me as if they could each swallow their own egotistically swollen heads. All three of them, combined, probably wouldn't amount to one person of average intelligence, inbreeding maybe? Damn! That thought made me think of the 1972 movie *Deliverance*. The three of them could have played perfect hillbilly, semi-retarded, bad guys in that movie. There was something very primitive about them, or maybe "Neanderthal" is a better word to describe their characters, though Jake had a bit of cunning in him that wasn't to be taken lightly. The only redeeming characteristic, that I could think of, for an egotist is that, if you ever have to keep a secret, but are dying to tell someone, tell an egotist because they don't talk about other people, only themselves.

The handguns were still pointed at us as we stood by the dusty table. "Emp'y yur pockets on the table," came an order from Jake. I took the spare change out of my left front pocket, along with the "Annie button" that Grace had given to me.

Annie was a red-headed orphan girl in a movie of the same name, that Grace loved. Sam and I bought her an Annie doll and one day a button came off the doll. Instead of asking me to sew it back on, Grace gave the button to me and said I could keep it for good luck. So I've had it in my pocket for a couple of years, until now.

But when I put the change on the table I retained the Annie button in the bend of my left hand fingers, where those fingers meet the palm, kind of like a magician finger-palming a coin. I took my keys out of my right front pocket, with my right hand, setting them on the table, then, with the same hand, I removed my locking, three inch blade, pocket knife from my right, rear pocket. The pocket knife always remained in a vertical position in the right, rear pocket because I had stitched-up the pocket giving me a two inch vertical space in which the knife rested comfortably. As soon as I put the blade on the table, Lester quickly grabbed it, laughed, opened it up, flashed it around in front of my eyes as if he thought he was Zorro, then closed it and stuck it in his pocket. He smiled defiantly as he did this, his eyes darting to Jake and Tom for approval. I said nothing to him, nor did Jake or Tom. And lastly, I took the wallet out of my left rear pocket, with my left thumb and index finger which allowed me to keep the Annie button under firm control and concealment with the other three fingers being wrapped around it. I placed the wallet on the table

When I was done, Tom approached me from behind and patted my pockets to make sure they were empty. We weren't asked to take off our coats, thank goodness, so my Ka-Bar knife and throwing knife remained undetected. They were our only hope now, just as in Nam the blade would have to be the tool, not only of my survival, but, more importantly to me, the tool of my daughter's survival. I could afford to die, I thought, but I couldn't allow any harm to come to Grace. Images of some of the VC and NVA I killed with a blade flashed through my mind, like a movie shown at a fast-forward speed. I remained calm. I knew what I had to do, I just had to wait for the right time.

Tom picked up the articles that I had put on the table and stuck them inside his coat pocket. Jake mumbled something and Tom tied my hands in front of me. As Tom finished tying my hands, I told him that he had a bad case of halitosis. "What that?" he asked. I wrinkled-up my face for effect. "Oh, sorry, not much education, huh? It means really bad breath." His face reddened, his face show anger, his brow furrowed and then, as I had hoped, he shot a hard right fist into my stomach. I doubled over and fell to the floor on my knees, but not out of excruciating pain, although I pretended to gasp for breath and act hurt. Karate exercises had made my stomach muscles rock-hard. Since I knew that the punch was coming, and prepared for it, Tom's punch had relatively no effect as far as pain goes, however, it did give me an excellent excuse to fall to the floor—as would a punch to my face. This is exactly what I was hoping for. While pretending to struggle to get up slowly, I placed the Annie button behind one of the table legs where it could hardly be noticed, except, I hoped, by the police who would probably use blood hounds that would lead them to this cabin. They would then be very thorough in their search of the cabin for any evidence of our presence. And when they found the Annie button, if they were smart, they would ask Sam some questions about it and the answers would lead them to the fact that we had been kidnapped and that the kidnappers might be the same people as the ones who ambushed the State Troopers. And if, somehow, they could match the cars tread pattern with the same type of car known to be owned by one of the Gibsons, then they would have the positive information they needed to conclude that we were probably kidnapped by the Gibson clan.

When I got up from the floor Jake held a hand out in front of Tom to keep him away from me. Then Jake told me that Grace wouldn't have to be tied-up as long as we both cooperated. I pretended to have trouble catching my breath, but managed to say that we would cooperate.

Lester suggested blindfolding us, but Jake yelled, "Sure, stupid! We goin' ta travel fer four or five hour an' everybody dat passes us is goin' ta see two blin'-folded people in are car. Yeah, dat be jest what we needs ta git attention on us!" Lester bristled at that humiliating reprimand, then turned meek and apologized over and over again. He was a repulsive sight to look at and intensely pathetic to listen to. Actually, all three of them were repulsive looking. Perhaps Jake mated with Sasquatch, I thought—picturing that sexual union almost made me laugh, but our situation was too serious.

Tom wanted me to sit in the back of the car and Grace to sit up front between his father and brother, as a precaution, in case I tried anything. Once he said that to Jake, Grace started crying loudly, saying, "No! No! I want to be with my Daddy. Don't let them do that, Daddy."

I said, to Jake, in a calm voice, "If you want our cooperation you must let Grace sit by me. You can see how frightened she is. She just wants to sit by me. I can keep her quiet for you and we'll cooperate fully with you. Actually, it's to your advantage, too. You'll need to stop for gas and you won't have to worry about us trying to escape or creating a disturbance to attract attention." I paused and stared at Jake to let him see the determination in my eyes. I tried to let some doubt and fear show in my eyes, however, because I didn't want him to detect any threatening, inner strength in me. I'm sure they saw me as a wimp and that was an advantage for me just like it was in my frequent high school fights and a few college confrontations with bullies. It was difficult for me to say, but I added the "clincher" by saying, "Please."

When Jake moved away from me, Tom took out his Colt .38, shoved it roughly under my nose and belched the halitosis-laden words, "You cooperate because if yuh don't I blow yur fuckin' face off." I could feel the coolness of the steel barrel on my upper lip and nose, but somehow I remained calm, just as I had, most times, in Nam, but it was a ferocious calm, like a predator stalking its prey. It kept me alive and always one step ahead of the enemy. I thought, if it worked in Nam then it'll work here. They wouldn't do anything needlessly violent now. But, I also had to remember that they were beasts, madmen, and it would be damned foolish to provoke them in any way. Patience, I thought.

And, as if to play follow-the-leader, Lester had my jack-knife out and opened. He waved it under Grace's nose until Jake ordered, "Put the damn gun an' knife away, boys, an' let the wimp's little girlie sits by 'er daddy. Hates ta admit it, but he be right. But soons we be pas' Sunday Rock, iffen they don' obeys us, then Tom, yuh can 'ave the wimp an' Lester yuh can 'ave the girlie." He stared at me, grinned, then laughed. It was as evil a sounding laugh as I had ever heard, as if it came from the gaseous, flaming bowels of Satan, himself. His eyes continued to stare at me for a few seconds, like drills boring through wood.

I had the overpowering feeling that I'd seen those eyes and heard that laugh before. It was a feeling of déjà vu. Then I remembered the Charles Manson interview I'd seen on television. The camera zoomed in for a close-up shot of Manson's face. I saw the swastika tattoo on his forehead and the pure evil in his eyes. The brutal, maniacal glare in Manson's eyes was the same look I now saw in Jake's eyes, an insane, murderously satanic kind of stare. I felt my flesh getting hot, as if being burned by twin, red-hot pokers.

Later, I was to learn that the *Sunday Rock* reference stood for the Adirondack region, which, in the old days, was considered to be beyond the law, like a wild frontier ruled by the quickest gun, or the best aim, or by the edge of a knife, and mostly ruled by the most powerful, a place where "might was always right." It was a place where Jake could be beyond the laws of contemporary society and have to answer only to the law of nature. And the law of nature was the survival of the fittest. That was the second clue—the first was the fact that Grace and I knew who they were and could lead the police to them—that confirmed the fact that he planned to eventually kill the both of us. His satanic laughter made me feel hot, as if the fiery laughter had come from the bowels of hell.

Grace sat to my left and Tom sat to my right, in the back of the car. Jake started driving with Lester in the passenger seat. About an hour into the trip, as their careless conversation flowed, I learned several pieces of information about where we were headed. First, I learned why they had been at that cabin in the woods, near my in-law's house. They had discovered it a few years back while hunting. It didn't belong to them and they knew that the aged owners were hardly ever around. It was a relatively safe, out of the way place to hide their cache of guns and ammo and supplies, while at the same time appearing to disappear from the local area. Now the cache was safely inside the trunk of the car.

I learned that Jake used to be an Adirondack mountain guide. And since he knew the wild Adirondack area even better than most other guides, he and Tom had gone, the previous summer, into the deep Adirondack wilderness and built a secret cabin near Preston Ponds, which was a remote wilderness, thickly forested and, thus, an extremely isolated area. That was their eventual destination. Jake believed that they could all remain indefinitely safe in that Adirondack wilderness and that they would be beyond the reach of the law; beyond Sunday Rock.

It was mentioned that it would take about three days of canoeing and walking to get there. The cabin by Preston Ponds was already stocked with enough food to last the winter, but Jake didn't seem at all worried about running out of food, probably because he could live off the land easily, even in winter. It was Tom and Lester who seemed worried about enough food. I guessed that they weren't seasoned woodsmen like their father.

We stopped once for gas and I could feel Tom's handgun pressed into the ribs on my right side. Tom and Lester asked Jake to go inside the garage to buy extra food—it was one of those pump-your-own-gas types of gas stations that sold a few items of groceries—but Jake just scowled and said, "No use takin' no chance bein' seen. I jus' pay an' leave quick."

Grace was asleep, leaning against my left shoulder. At the sound of Jake's voice she shivered and burrowed closer to me as if the sound of his voice triggered a fearful response even while she was sleeping. In me, his voice had the same effect as the pain of having bone-marrow cancer. It went deep to the core of a me and created pain that couldn't be reached or tempered. I was sitting directly in back of Jake and could have easily broken his neck, but Grace would be hurt, so I caged those thoughts so they wouldn't escape into action.

When Grace woke up and started to whimper, I was told, by Tom, to "shut her up." I reached over to caress her hair and rub her cheek, then whispered that I loved her very much and that I was going to get us out of this situation safely. Then I whispered very softly that she wasn't to mention to anyone that I had two knives on me. I also told her that crying made these men really mad and that we would be much safer if she could stop crying. Immediately after I asked her to stop crying, she stopped. She was asleep, again, only a few minutes after Jake drove away from the gas station. I stayed awake, listening and observing . . . and plotting.

We left Chemung about 11:00 o'clock in the morning and we were supposed to reach Raquette Lake about five or six in the evening. I learned that Raquette Lake is where Jake lived when he was being a guide. He had a secluded cabin there, but he said that no one there knew about the cabin that he and Tom had built out of logs in the forest by Preston Ponds.

Jake sucked air through his teeth every mile or so and it was irritating to hear it, like sandpaper scraping across a bundle of raw nerves.

He made sure he was driving under the speed limit for fear of being stopped by a cop. But they had already agreed that this trip might be a suicide mission for them. That is, if they had to, they'd shoot-it-out with anyone who got in their way, whether or not it was the cops at a road block or a gas station attendant who recognized them and was foolish enough to try to stop them. For the Gibsons, this was a "do or die" mission, escape to the forest, or die trying. So far, they were having no problems.

We had gone from Chemung to Binghamton on route 17E, from Binghamton to Syracuse on route 81N, and in Syracuse we got on route 90E until we got off at the Verona exit. From there we got on Route 365E. Then we exited to route 12N which took us to route 28N. Finally we traveled route 28N, drove through Old Forge and continued on to Raquette Lake where we arrived at Jake's secluded cabin shortly before six that evening.

I was then untied at gunpoint and allowed to carry Grace into the cabin where, thankfully, she remained sleeping on a cot while the rest of us ate canned stew, with stale bread and bottled water to drink. I rubbed my wrists trying to ease the pain and increase the circulation where the rope had left deep, red abrasions.

Unfortunately the food gave Jake plenty of reason to suck air through his teeth. With food filling the gaps in his teeth, his air-sucking became a frenzied activity that was becoming quite nerve wracking. He got up and went over to a shelf and pulled some green string out of a very small, white, plastic container. I didn't realize what it was until he pulled it between his teeth to clean them. I was, I admit, startled to see that he used dental floss, and mint flavored. How ironic, I thought, that this huge, uncultured ogre would use dental floss. I would have expected a knife blade or toothpick, but not dental floss. Dental floss was part of contemporary, civilized life and Jake's life was stuck in the distant past. But the floss stopped his sucking noises for a while and that was a big relief.

I saved some of the stew meat and put it on a piece of bread. I folded the bread in half and saved it for when Grace woke up. I knew she'd be hungry and wasn't likely to get extra food from any of the Gibsons. Luckily the cabin was cold and I didn't have to worry about the meat spoiling. If we left without breakfast tomorrow, at least Grace would have a little to eat. I thought it was more important for her to sleep and get her rest because tomorrow she would need all the energy and strength that a little girl of only eight years had. It sounded like we were all going on a tiring, lengthy hike into the core of Mother Nature's kingdom, a place where, Jake said, Grace and I were supposed to be killed and buried—did he really mean it, or was it a terrifying scare tactic to gain complete cooperation? The thought of it almost made me reach for my coat zipper so that I could grab my combat knife. But I knew that, with three-to-one odds, especially in the confined area of a car, my chance of a successful escape were very slim. I felt a panic brewing inside of me that I never experienced in Nam. It was almost overpowering. It wasn't caused by the fear of my own death. Hell, due to depressions, I'd wished for that several times in the last year, and almost every week while in Nam—Was the Doc right about a subconscious death wish in me? Primarily this panic was caused by a fear for my daughter's life. I thought of the ten year old girl that Lester had abused, then killed. I thought of what must have happened to her before her death. So it was a panic that I found nearly impossible to control, and, yet, I had to subdue it, dominate it . . . control it, harness it, and transform it into a life-saving energy that would flow down my arms and into my fists, each of which would be tightly clenched around the handle of a blade. And this thought allowed me to finally control the panic.

Later, at bed time, I was tied securely to Grace's metal cot until morning.

I had trouble sleeping. An hour or two had passed before I started feeling drowsy and in all that time, every ten or fifteen minutes, I heard Jake suck air through his teeth, which told me that he was also awake—unless he did it in his sleep, also. I wished I could bash all his teeth out to stop that hideous noise. I felt contempt for that sound and the man, and I wished that I knew what was keeping him awake and what he was thinking. Finally, in the early morning hours, drowsiness commandeered my consciousness, taking control of me and giving me some much needed rest. I hoped that my sleepy, unfocused mind would think of an escape strategy that would give me the winning edge. It often happened with me that a problem's solution came to me once I stopped concentrating on it; when my mind was on something else. I drifted off to sleep with the word *blade* softly ricocheting off the inside of my skull like a soothing, repetitive echo off granite mountain sides.

/-../.-/.-../- - -/...-/./...,/...,/-../- - -/-./.,/-...,/- - -/-./-./.,/.- -/./.-../.-./

Chapter 4

★★★★

Night Images

I WOKE UP WITH sweat dripping down my forehead in spite of the cold. I sat up as well as I could considering that my hands were tied to the upper leg of Grace's metal cot—with two feet of extra rope so I could move a little. I leaned my back against the cot. I could feel the sweat rolling down my forehead, rivulets of ice-water, the salt from the sweat stinging my eyes, some dripping off my nose, and some running down my cheeks. I wiped the sweat off. I noticed that the cabin had cooled off considerably due to the colder night air and letting the fire in the wood stove burn-out.

I closed my eyes, then shook my head to clear the cobwebs. I found myself desperately hoping that this was all a bad dream. I opened my eyes, looked around the room, saw three sleeping shapes and realized that Grace and I were still in deep trouble. Images from Nam burst suddenly in my mind like firecrackers, then exploded out of view as new, terrifying images appeared. I shook my head and squeezed my eyes shut trying to rid myself of those dreadful images. When I opened my eyes, I told myself that I needed to focus on something else. I bit my tongue until I tasted blood. The pain forced the images away and enabled me to focus. Now that my mind was clear, I realized that the blood in my mouth tasted good, very pleasing. That was a strange feeling because the taste of blood made my stomach growl with hunger, as if I was a hungry carnivore . . . Wolf.

I looked at my glow-face watch—if I push in on the stem, the face glows a dim green. It was nearly 4:00 A.M. I thought that within the next hour Jake would be up and we'd be moving out of this cabin and heading for Preston Pond.

The cabin was quiet. I thought about escaping, but certainly not without Grace. Escaping with Grace would make it much more difficult, of course, but there was no possible way that I would leave her alone with any of these monsters, especially Lester—just the thought of doing that made me hate myself and I couldn't have been more deeply guilt-ridden about that despicable thought, even if bullets were guilt and a machine gun had riddled my body beyond recognition. I bit my tongue again to rid myself of that cowardly thought, then refocused. My mind-set concentrated on indomitable courage and determination. Now there was no doubt in my mind that I'd kill any or all of the Gibsons to get Grace and me away from them safely. But that meant I had to be patient; wait for the right time, the right situation. A time, like in Nam, when the wolf in me was roaming, night time was always welcomed, and I embraced it as I would a loyal friend.

My thoughts wandered. Today was Sunday, November 15th. I doubted that the cops had even started to search for us. I remembered some TV cop show where the cops said they couldn't even begin to search for someone until twenty-four hours had passed. Apparently a person wasn't officially missing until a certain amount of time had elapsed. The cops probably wouldn't give our disappearance genuinely serious effort because they wouldn't quickly make the connection between our situation, the prisoner escape and the troopers being shot. On the other hand, with a child missing and possibly kidnapped, the police may take action very quickly, like they do now-a-days with the Amber Alerts. They probably wouldn't realize that the two cases were related until they found the cabin and the Annie button on the cabin floor, the tire tracks and finger prints—if any existed. Then, hopefully, they would see the connection between those discoveries. I hoped that they were at least competent enough to find the Annie button on the floor of the cabin and to mention it to Sam. She would make the connection right away. I'd give almost anything to be in her arms right now. I missed her so much.

I wiped the sweat off my brow, again. I closed my eyes and in the blackness I saw two images as if they had been projected on the insides of my eyelids. The two images were as vivid, colorful and clear as an organism seen through a powerful microscope. I saw Grace's peacefully sleeping face and an image of Sam's tearful face.

But I also sensed something strange, though I couldn't identify it yet. I kept my eyes closed and studied the image more carefully. I pretended that my mind was the zoom-lens on a camera and that I could zoom-out away from my close-up mental picture of them so that I could see the background. I still saw Grace with her eyes closed, only she was farther away from me in this view of her. She was without her glasses as she slept. She looked so peaceful. She was lying in bed wearing a beautiful white dress with bright orange, marigolds embroidered around each short sleeve. Her hair shone brightly as her head sank halfway into a plush, lacy pillow. Her forearms were crossed over her abdomen and her mother was standing over her, head bent, with tears streaming down her cheeks.

Suddenly I though, "Why would Grace be wearing a dress in bed?" I opened my eyes in shock. My body shuddered. "Shit!" my mind screamed at me. I realized that Grace never slept like that. I knew what the images meant, but not why my brain conjured them up. Grace was like a cyclone in bed; always twisting and turning, and usually falling asleep in a fetal position with her knees bent up toward her chest. I should know because I went into her room every night to kiss her on the cheek, whisper that I loved her and to make sure she was covered-up. Sometimes when I kissed her cheek, even with the lightest pressure, she would roll over in bed. I saw the image of Sam, once again, tears tattooing salty paths down her cheeks.

No! That wasn't a bed. It was a coffin that Grace was lying in. The images that I was having belonged to a funeral scene, and this startling realization brought a flood of tears to my eyes. My head was an anvil and a blacksmith was pounding it. I could feel the feral wolf in me trying to rip its way out of the confines of my inner body. My ribs started to hurt, as if they were prison bars that some tremendously strong and angry beast was pushing and bending in order to escape.

It was a familiar feeling, but one that had been long dormant. It's a feeling that has always been there, just beneath the surface of civility, just waiting to be triggered so it could explode out of me, take shape and turn vicious. And the older I got, the more intense that feeling became.

There's a shadowy, sinister place inside of me where no one should trespass. It's an extremely remote place with an air-tight, heavily secured, extra-thick door that shouldn't be opened by anyone but me. But the Gibsons were breaking through that door. They've begun to trespass into a forbidden area and had no inkling of their truly tragic mistake. Now they must face the wrath of the escaped furies in the form of a pale wolf; an untamed, wild, feral and ferocious creature, known to me alone as my *Roamin' Wolf*, the very dark side of Roman Wolfe.

I felt my whole body trembling. I still had my eyes closed as Sam's dramatic image turned away from Grace's coffin and looked straight at me with glassy eyes and both hands wiping away the scalding tears that were streaming from each eye. Her long, auburn hair glistened, as it framed her head. More startling was the brilliant, purple nimbus—Sam's favorite color—that formed an outline around her entire body. Her soft, full lips opened slowly and in slow-motion she screamed to me, with a pause between each word for emphasis, "Bring… her… home… to… me,… Wolf!" She paused to catch her breath, then repeated the same words, again. Then she said, "I… love… you,… Roman. I… love… you,… Grace. Come… home… safely!" Her hands came to her face and covered her eyes as she wept uncontrollably. As this disturbing image faded away, it was replaced by another. I glanced at my precious daughter lying in that beautifully decorated, box of death. It made me want to scream with rage, as my brain felt as if it was boiling.

I opened my eyes suddenly to rid myself of those tragically, haunting images. The tears poured down my cheeks as if a flood gate had been opened. It was atypical of me to be this emotional, so I wondered what the doctor would think. I didn't have my depression medication and I didn't care. I would force myself not to get severely depressed because Grace's life depended on it. Without Grace, life wouldn't offer much meaning for Sam and me. Death for us would have more meaning than life without Grace. No, I thought, depression won't control me now. I must maintain strict control, controlled rage . . . just like in Nam. I felt as if death was hovering very close, so close that I really thought I could smell its putrid flesh. I thought, "If this struggle is to be anything like Nam, then that decaying flesh would be neither Grace's nor mine. I just had to wait for my chance and not be impatient. I had to stay controlled, stay focused and hopeful, then let the pale wolf come to me.

I wiped my tears away and in doing so, it seemed as if my mental cob webs were wiped away too. I stared into the darkness of the cabin. I realized, then, that in my funereal "death image," Sam had called me "Wolf." That was unusual because she always called me, Roman. It was in Nam that she knew I was called Wolf because of my deadly stalking and killing in the night. So, to her, Wolf was a name of violence, blood and death, thus, she never used my code name, Wolf. She disliked that moniker. So then, I asked myself, why would I imagine that she would say it as she screamed? Maybe she just meant to say my last name, "Wolfe," instead of "Wolf." It was a conundrum that I didn't want to waste time on.

Then, unexpectedly, I couldn't help but smile just a little, like a person on a game show who knows the answer before anyone else does. In matters of great danger, it was "Wolf" that was needed, not Roman. "Roman" was the nice, gentle, civilized guy, whereas "Wolf" was feral, strong, cunning and dangerous. Sam was calling for the Wolf in me to surface, to protect Grace and myself. I knew Sam well. I knew how she thought. She might not like the "Wolf" in me because it was synonymous with violence and death, or my Nam nickname, or what I did in Nam, but she knew that it was time for Wolf to rise-up inside of me. She wanted "Roamin' Wolf" to surface. I knew that that's what the image of her screaming meant. So Wolf would surface . . . soon.

Beyond Sunday Rock was the remote wilderness world of the wolf. It wasn't just Jake's untamed, uncivilized world any more. Wolf was now prowling this vast acreage.

The painful pressure behind my ribcage ceased. The beast had escaped; Wolf was free to roam as he had roamed the nights in Nam. Wolf's growl whispered to me, "You and Grace will be home safely for

Thanksgiving." So the dream and the death box were wrong. The dream wasn't a prophesy, just a tool to motivate me.

I had to focus on my right hand in order to stop its slow movement toward the knife under my left arm. It wasn't the right time, nor was it practical, especially with my combat blade hidden under a heavy winter coat. Wolf was a master at stalking and patience, so I waited for a sign or a feeling from him, my alter-ego.

A lighted match extinguished my thoughts and images, banishing the cabin's darkness. Jake lit a kerosene lamp, then slipped on his boots.

I bowed my head, chin resting against my chest, and pretended to be asleep. In a few seconds Jake's bass voice crashed against the cabin walls, as he yelled, "Everybody up! Come on! Git goin an' git yur asses up!"

Grace woke up startled and frightened. I comforted her by speaking calmly and soothingly to her until she relaxed. It didn't take long for everyone to get ready because everyone slept fully dressed.

Tom and Lester got up slowly and slipped on their boots and coats, also. I already had my coat and boots on. I was never given a chance to take them off, which was probably the best thing that could have happened because my coat kept me warm and covered-up both blades nicely. I was only given one blanket which I used to cover-up Grace. And since I had to sleep on the floor, with no blanket, it was good to have my boots on so that my feet wouldn't get as cold as they would have with them off and just my socked feet on the cold wooden floor.

Jake walked over to me with his blade in hand, threateningly. I thought my throat was going to be slit right then and there until I realized that if he had wanted to kill me, he could have done it easily last night. None-the-less, seeing King-Kong in mountain man clothes approaching me with what looked to be a ten inch Bowie knife wasn't a pleasant experience. I turned my eyes downward so he wouldn't glimpse the angry "Wolf" in me. I felt a silent growl rising in my throat, the hair on the back of my neck spike outward, and felt the eerie sensation of my fingernails growing into claws.

The Gibsons thought I was a wimp and that was just fine with me because then I would own the element of surprise when Wolf leaped out at them. In any kind of warfare, surprise is a definite and distinct advantage and of major importance. So, being thought of as a wimp was my second big advantage. The Gibsons were all doltish louts which is an excellent example of why the world has many more "horses asses" than horses—Tom's breath smelled like something that comes out of a horse's ass too.

I flinched as Grace started screaming when she noticed Jake's approaching knife. "Daddy," she yelled, "he's coming!"

Jake stopped when Grace screamed. Then he laughed and pointed his knife at me and said, "Shud up, girlie! If I wan'ed ta kill yur Pa, I'd of done it las' night." He looked at me with scathing eyes and not one shred of respect, a total wimp is all he saw. Jake continued, "You shud 'er up or I be shuttin' 'er up fer good." As he said that, he held the knife up to his neck and made a slashing gesture, then smiled like a crazed and murderous Charlie Manson. Then, as if for emphasis, he burst into a maniacal laugh to purposely scare Grace, as he glared at her. He was having his sadistic fun, as if it was a morning routine of his, like eating cereal—the Gibson's were probably all "cereal-killers." Inappropriate humor at an inappropriate time, I know, but stupid things like that have popped into my head all my life and I can't help it. I expect that I'll die with a joke on my mind.

Grace leaped off the cot and hugged me, burying her face into my neck. I whispered to her, "He's just going to cut these ropes, Sweetheart." She relaxed, slightly.

Jake started sucking air through his front teeth. It sounded like a snake hissing. From the floor, as I looked up at him, I thought that none of the Vietnamese enemy came in a package quite as muscularly big, ugly and murderous as he was. Not even in the special Marine combat training camp had there been such an example of size, pure meanness, brutality and strength. But that was just Roman's thinking. Wolf looked at Jake and confidently smiled inwardly while thinking, "Rip a man's throat out and his size and strength don't matter. Then he's just a large, bloody corpse."

Fighting is much more mental than most people think it is. It's a lot about strategy and attitude, especially attitude. There's an over-used but true saying that: It's not the size of the dog in a fight, but the size of the fight in the dog that matters most. The size of the opponent matters, of course, but what matters more is you, your attitude about winning, surviving. And attitude, in a fight can be measured by the answers to some simple questions that have complex answers for each of us. for example, Can you take punishment as well as give it? How well can you attack and punish. Can you conquer your fear of injury, but injure some one without remorse? How determined are you to beat your opponent? Is your determination to win, more than his? How deep is your "quit zone?" Is it buried in your bone marrow and is rarely used? or is it superficial, lying just below the first layer of skin? Will you quit after a bloody nose or a cut lip? Does the sight of blood, his or yours, make you want to quit, or does the sight of blood motivate you to continue? Do you have an indomitable urge to win, to survive, to have the spirit of a warrior? And, lastly, but just as important, do you know when it's in your best interest to quit or to walk away before a fight starts? Quitting is not losing, its not being defeated, if it's the best thing to do for you or a friend that you're protecting. However, only you know your personal answers to those questions and only you can set the rules and standards that you need to establish a personal guideline for yourself—those rules and standards will be highly individualized and will determine your mind-set for combat.

Fighting is very mental, but the mental part of it has to be established prior to a fight because there's no time to think about the mental aspects of fighting during a fight. You can't debate with yourself during an epic struggle with a larger opponent about whether or not you can go for his eyes so he can't see through the abundant flow of tears that'll flood them, or strike him in the Adam's Apple so he temporarily can't breath, or kick or punch to the groin, or use a martial arts choke hold that'll render him unconscious, or a wrist lock that may break his wrist, or an arm-bar to break the elbow, etc. The debate about all those things must be complete and accepted prior to a fight, then in a fight you just have to act, not think about those issues. Then, your accepted answers become part of your fighting strategy and the rejected answers become limits and, therefore, useless to your fighting strategy. But be careful, because in a life-and-death struggle, you may have to drastically and spontaneously revise those limits, just like: Is the bear Catholic? and Does the Pope shits in the woods? needs a quick revision.

But only supremely egotistical and maniacal sadists like Jake and his spawn would equate brute strength with unrivaled power and cruelty for entertainment purposes, including sadistic murder. So, too, is the fool—and the Gibsons were all fools—who thinks he is invulnerable to attack and injury. As a matter of fact, when I first committed this same grave error, I unceremoniously and humiliatingly got me ass kicked, my face cut and bruised, and my pride violently deflated. Anyone can be beaten on any given day, just as a great football team can be defeated on any given Sunday. It just takes a careless mistake, or an accident, or lack of preparation and practice, or laziness, or simply a more skillful opponent.

I thought about how we were out-numbered in this ordeal, but Wolf's thoughts over-rode my own as he quoted Andrew Jackson, who said: "One man with courage is a majority."

I calmed Grace and put her down next to me. But as Jake bent down over me to cut the ropes that encircled my wrist, she fearfully gasped air into her open mouth, then covered her mouth with both hands, as if to stop a scream.

As Jake was cutting me free, he suddenly turned to Grace and shouted, "Boo!" Grace did scream then. Jake laughed and looked at his sons who were also amused and laughed hilariously. Jake sheathed his knife, bent down and unexpectedly grabbed the front of my coat with his right hand. He lifted me, from my sitting position, straight up into the air until we were eye-to-eye. My feet were dangling above the floor. I didn't resist and stayed calm, though inwardly I was embarrassed and humiliated by being treated like a rag-doll and not being able to do anything about it . . . for now. He wanted to see fear so I showed it to him—but it wasn't hard to do since I did feel fear. He burst into laughter that sounded childish. But there was no doubt that he was a very strong, brutish man.

"Do what yur tol', Wimpy, an' yuh an' yur girlie may jest live ta see 'nother day." Then he had me in both his hands, pulled me close to him and threw me across the room, toward the cabin door.

Grace cried out and that enraged me. It was Wolf that sprang up off the floor, but I kept my eyes down and controlled the urge to fight right then and there as Jake spoke, not really noticing, or, perhaps, not believing that the "wimp" would ever defend himself. "Boys, help me unload the trunk," he said to his sons. Then, pointing at me he said, "An' don' think a runnin' away 'cause yur girlie will die if yuh do, unnerstand?" I nodded affirmatively to him and put a cover on my barrel of humiliation.

I glanced at Grace. She was terrified and trembling. All she wanted right now was to have me hold her, to wrap my arms around her, to make her feel secure, comfortable and safe. I wanted to show her a smile and wink to show that the situation wasn't as bad as it looked, but I couldn't unwrap her from me. She had her arms round my neck and her face buried into the hollow at the side of my neck.

It wasn't easy being both "Roman Wolfe" and "Roamin' Wolf." In Nam I was almost always called Wolf. After Nam, I was Roman, wanting to be just plain Roman, but now I was fluctuating between both. I had to force myself to be Roman when it was advantageous to be docile and calm, and to keep Wolf under control. But when it was advantageous to become Wolf, then "Roman Wolfe" needed to disappear and the "Roamin' Wolf" would spring forth with all its strength, cunning and viciousness.

An image of Sam's lovely face appeared clearly in my mind. It acted as a reminder to me that I made a promise that we would escape and that I'd protect Grace from serious harm.

I knew that I needed to use my brains first, then my martial arts and knife-fighting skills, combined with Wolf's wild, ferocious nature, to produce a concerted, life-saving force that would protect both Grace and I, especially Grace. But I needed a better opportunity.

I felt myself being pushed toward the door as Tom's voice exclaimed, "Come on! Move it, big asshole! You too, little asshole!"

I opened the cabin door and walked towards their car. Tom opened the trunk. It was mostly full of weapons and boxes of ammunition. There were actually only six guns, but the trunk looked like an arsenal. There were two Browning, 12 gauge, pump shotguns, probably for Jake and Tom, and one Ithaca Featherweight, 20 gauge, pump shotgun, probably for Lester's more frail musculature. There were also three high-power, 30-06 caliber rifles, each with a superior quality Leupold scope securely mounted on it. There didn't appear to be enough ammo, however, so I suspected that most of the ammo was already at the Preston Ponds cabin and, most certainly, other firearms as well, especially handguns. The trunk also contained a half-dozen nylon-type backpacks, canned food, can openers, eating utensils, weatherproof wooden matches, compasses, three plush, lightweight sleeping bags, about six wool blankets, and a few other supplies that were grabbed before I had a chance to see them. We brought all these things into the cabin where Jake now had two kerosene lamps lit. I guess we didn't need the car any more.

Jake told me to put a backpack on myself and one on Grace. I helped Grace put hers on. It was adult sized so it hung down to the back of her legs. I adjusted it as much as I could to make it more comfortable for her, but I couldn't do much with the proper, comfortable fit of it.

The Gibsons each carried a shotgun, but in what I thought was a foolish move, Jake handed the three heavy high-power rifles to me and said, as he pointed his sausage-like index finger close to my right eye, "Yuh carry 'em. An' don' yuh lets nothin' bad happen to 'em or yur girlie gits 'er fingers cut off. Unnerstan'?" Immediately, I nodded affirmatively that I understood and was willing to obey him. It didn't take me long to notice that the bolt actions had been removed. They were probably in Jake's backpack. Giving me the rifles to carry told me that they had more rifles at the cabin and were too lazy to carry these rifles themselves, but if I did do something stupid with the rifles, they had more at the cabin. I knew, now, that I had no choice about damaging or losing the rifles. I had to treat them like gold or Grace would be harmed, maybe seriously, maybe even *fatally*. My heart skipped a couple of beats when I thought about that word.

Grace's and my backpack were being filled with cans of food. I could feel the cans being dumped into my backpack, in no particular order. I could feel the edges of the cans' rims digging into my back. Luckily, some lighter supplies were put into Grace's backpack when I suggested that she shouldn't be made to carry too much or it would slow us down. Jake grunted his reluctant approval and some of the supplies were taken out of Grace's pack and placed into my already bulging backpack. The ammo was placed into the Gibsons' packs.

Luckily the three heavy rifles each had slings which made them a lot easier to handle, though they were still going to be quite heavy to carry, especially if we were going on a long hike into the wilderness.

Since a majority of the heavier supplies, such as the canned food, were in my backpack, that left the lighter supplies to be carried in the backpacks of the Gibsons, leaving their hands free to carry their shotguns and perform other woodsmen activities, like picking up wood to build a campfire or checking a compass.

Each of the Gibsons also carried a tightly rolled, lightweight sleeping bag as well as two tightly rolled wool blankets which were all attached to the top of each of their backpacks with nylon straps that appeared to be made for just that purpose.

Jake gruffly ordered Lester to put the car into the garage to hide it. Lester looked a little irritated by the brusque order because he had to take his backpack off to get into the car. His irritation became my pleasure and I smiled, secretly.

The garage was more like a hastily built and enclosed car-port made out of tree poles for the corners supports and rough planking for the roof and sides that covered a dirt floor. It looked sturdy, but very crude. There was a large door, also make of rough planking that hung on very large hinges. After Lester parked the car in the garage, he locked it with a length of chain and a padlock. Apparently, Jake wanted the place to look unoccupied. It would look natural that way because that's the way it normally was, with Jake quite often gone for weeks at a time, either as a guide for groups of hunters, fishermen, or hikers, or when he went on his own extended hunting and fishing trips into the dense Adirondack wilderness.

I looked at Jake and found myself wondering, if there really is a God, what a cruel trick he had played on Jake. Jake was the epitome of the hard, strong, determined, independent, but mostly savage, rogue frontiersman who lived two-hundred years ago. Jake, it seemed to me, was born two-hundred years too late, and if it hadn't been for the survival of the Adirondack Wilderness Preserve, Jake would have perished long ago, like a nineteenth century Texas cowboy in New York City. Modern civilization, with its morality, laws, and technology would have killed him, like a wind-blown seed settling on a slab of concrete where it was unable to survive. Unfortunately, Jake's seed had fallen between the expansion and contraction spaces between two slabs of concrete and, found just enough space and nourishment to grow and survive to the point where he could spread his own seed and produce two sons who would, in turn, spread their own brand of cruelty to all those who were unfortunate enough to come into contact with them.

And nature also played a cruel trick on Jake because his intelligence and human compassion grew in inverse proportion to his huge size. He and his spawn were some of society's most pathological misfits. It was a wonder that they were able to stay out of prison for all these years. Someone once said that only a man of limited intelligence can know himself well. If that is true, then Jake must know himself expertly. Jake Gibson and Tom Gibson had somehow managed to slip through a huge crack in the justice system, though it looked like the justice system and prison had marginally caught up to Lester. It seemed utterly tragic, I thought, that a free, democratic, lawful society, like ours, has so many easily available cracks for criminals, like the Gibsons, to slip through and hide underground. Perhaps that's the price American Democracy has to pay for our plentiful liberties, though it sure seems like we could do a hell-of-a better job than to allow those like the Gibsons to abuse and use the rest of us as their helpless prey.

/-/- - - /-../-../-.../- - - /-./-././.- -/./.-../.-../.../.-/- -./.-././.-/-/- -./..-/-.- -/

Chapter 5

★★★★

Preston Ponds

I PRESSED THE STEM of my watch and the face brightened with a greenish tint. The time was 4:07 A.M. I looked out a window and saw that it was still very dark.

Grace and I stood by the cot as Jake and his sons hunched over a map that was spread across a dusty table. Jake pointed out their route of travel. Being an alert ex-soldier, I listened carefully to every detail that I could hear. That information may be useful while planning our escape, or when traveling after the escape.

Jake was silent for a moment as he concentrated on the map, typically unaware of the air whistling through his teeth. Tom paid close attention to his father, but I could tell that Lester had to struggle just to make it appear as if he was paying attention, or that he even cared about the details of their trip.

While they were checking the map, I took the opportunity to check my coat to make sure it was zipped up, thus concealing the combat and throwing knives—I raised the collar of my coat to further conceal the throwing knife. It was hard for me to believe my luck at still having those weapons. The Gibsons had thoroughly underestimated me.

They considered me to be a wimp who couldn't possibly be dangerous to them, so they never attempted to search me.

I put my right arm around Grace's shoulder as she stood close to my right hip. She was scared, as she should be, but not as much as yesterday. She glanced at me with a faint smile. I winked at her, then put my index finger to my lips to let her know that I didn't want her to talk.

"Okay!" Jake's voice boomed loudly at his sons. "We be walkin' ta the south en' of this Raquette Lake while it be still dark. We stay off the path 'cause we don' wanna be seen."

Jake scratched his beard vigorously as if some infestation had taken root there, then looked at Lester, who was peeking lasciviously at Grace out of the corner of his eyes. "Now, Lester, boy, yuh needs ta listen careful-like 'cause this be mostly fer yuh." Jake pointed at the map. "Yer brother an' me, we has this planned out." Lester looked at the map where Jake was pointing to show that he was paying attention, but in a few seconds he glanced at Grace again and smiled, the kind of smile a hungry coyote would give a rabbit. I pulled Grace protectively against my hip as Jake continued talking.

"Now, when we get ta the lake, we finds us two canoes that Tom an' me hid there las' week. We hopin' it be still dark so's we be in the lake an' out a sight. Then we stay close ta the eas' shore where it be hard ta see us 'cause a the early mornin' shadows from trees. Me an' Tom, we take the lead canoe, wid me bein' in the back an' Tom in front. The skinny wimp there"—Jake pointed at me with a sarcastic, distasteful grin—"be in the middle so's we keeps are eyes on 'im. Lester, now, yuh be in the canoe in back a us wid the girlie. We be goin' real steady, now, so yuh keeps up wid us. We not a-goin' awful fas', but steady, so's there be no slowin' down, unnerstan'? Yuh be in a lighter canoe so's yuh can keep up ta us easy like."

Lester nodded at Jake. His eyes betrayed the fact that he hated taking orders from anyone, especially his father. I guess it made him feel even more inferior than he already felt and, from the looks of him, that must have been a tremendous burden to carry around. The rage showed in the squint of his eyes, the distortion of his lips, as well as his furrowed brow. He paid attention, though, out of fear, like the rest of us.

Jake noticed Lester's reaction, paused to give him a warning stare, then continued, "We be goin north ta the en' a the lake, then we carries are canoes ta Fork Lake—it was really called Forked Lake—an' we always try ta stay in the shade a them trees. Importan' not ta be seen. When we carries the canoes ta Fork Lake, Lester, the wimp be helpin' yuh carry yur canoe. Be sure he be carryin' the front an' yuh carries the back. Yuh two be ahead a us so's we can watch yuh. Then we goes northeas' on Fork Lake, stayin' close ta the shore like I says before. At the en' a the lake, we goin' ta carry them canoes, just like before, ta Long Lake. An' don't yuh gets carried away, like some fuckin', sight-seein' tourist by it bein' all pretty and such. The lake be 'bout fifteen ta twenty mile long an' 'bout one ta three mile wide, dependin' where yuh be at. There be small islands 'long the whole length a the lake. Stay away from those damn things so's yuh don't hit bottom wid the canoe and so's yuh not be seen. The whole fuckin' lake be surround by thick woods. Trees goes right down to the lakeshore. Once we is there, we has good cover. Damn place be real pretty, but yuh pays 'ttention an' be careful all the way. This be no time fer gawkin' at pretty crap. Pay 'ttention. Yuh hear me?" Jake asked as he stared at both of his sons. Two heads bobbed up and down in unison, making the scene look like a bobble-heads, puppet show.

Jake continued his dictatorial monologue, "At en' a Long Lake we hides the canoes 'cause we cain't paddle agains' the river flow. So we needs ta walk up the shore of Col' River—Cold River. We be goin' northeas', ta the moun'ains. That get us ta the cabin near Pres'on Pon'—Preston Pond. Okay boys, yuh has any questions, then spit 'em out now, or forever hold yur peace."

After saying that, Jake held his fist in front of his zipper. He moved his loose-fingered fist up and down a couple of times. It was obvious what he was doing and that he didn't say "peace," but rather, had intended the word to be "piece." I stepped in front of Grace to block her view, but don't know how successful I was, although I doubt that she understood Jake's obscene, hand gesture and subtle, verbal reference.

After Tom and Lester giggled boyishly, Lester asked, "Pa, how long will it take ta get ta the cabin from here?"

That's exactly what I wanted to know and I mentally thanked Lester for asking.

Jake dug at his twig and dirt ladened beard again—lice too? Got Cooties? Then, naturally, he sucked air through his front teeth before he said, "Take 'bout tree days, if there be no problems 'long the way."

Then Jake looked at Tom to see if Tom had any questions. When Tom remained quiet, Jake stated, "Come on, then, an' let's be gittin' out a 'ere."

Jake looked at me and pointed toward the door. I put the slings of the three rifles over my left shoulder and took Grace's left hand into my right hand as we walked out the door. Jake locked the cabin door and led the way, his twelve-gauge shotgun balanced horizontally in his left hand. Tom held his twelve-gauge shotgun like his dad, while Lester held his twenty-gauge shotgun with both hands, as if it were heavy for him.

I knew the shotguns were all loaded because I personally saw them being loaded just before they went to the table to look at the map. I didn't hear or see any of them click-on their safety-levers; didn't even see any of them look at the safety mechanism.

As we walked, under cover of darkness, to Raquette Lake, Grace kept her hand in mine. It wasn't cold enough for gloves, yet, so we each had the gloves in our coat pockets. When I thought about my gloves being in my coat pockets, I was reminded of the food I saved for Grace. I took it out and gave it to her. Her eyes widened with delightful surprise, then she hungrily devoured the food.

I think the warm flesh of our hands made Grace feel more comfortable. She squeezed my hand tightly and forced a smile at me. I said, "I love you," silently, with just lip movements. She read my lips and smiled. Then I winked at her once more and smiled. We weren't allowed to talk, but our eyes and lips communicated our silent messages of love to each other. Then I remembered the importance of my knives, tapped Grace on the shoulder and silently lipped, "Don't talk about my knives." She lips responded silently with, "OK."

We followed Jake into the Adirondack wilderness. As we traveled, my mind became occupied with the realization that throughout my whole childhood, my teens, and adult life, too, I'd lived in New York State, but not once had I ever been to these Adirondack mountains, until now. I'm a nature lover, too, so it seemed very ironic to me. It also seemed ironic that I would even have such thoughts at a time like this. I should be thinking about our escape, but even by dim moonlight only, I could tell that this was a nature lover's paradise, especially in the late fall when the leaves changed to an artist's pallet of bright colors. I had a vivid mental vision of those brightly colored leaves racing and rattling across the ground like multi-colored field mice searching for food and a warm nest. My vision also included the wavering leaves that were still on the trees as they clattered and rattled in the breeze like colorful hands clapping at the musical sounds coming from the forest, an autumn orchestra. When this ordeal was over, I promised myself that I would come back this way, some day, and enjoy it a lot more.

Grace and I didn't like the idea of being separated in different canoes, but there was nothing I could do about it. When I tried to mention it in the cabin, before we left, Jake nearly went ballistic with rage because I questioned his leadership and authority. So I didn't dare mention it again for fear that harm would come to me when Grace needed me most and when I needed to be uninjured for our escape. However, at least Grace was allowed to walk with me while we trekked through the forest and when we portaged with the canoes between lakes. When I had a chance to whisper to her, I told her not to complain about being separated in the canoes or they might also separate us when we were on land.

That's also when she told me that her back hurt because of the heavy supplies in the backpack. The supplies were poking against her back. I told her that when we had to get into the canoes, she should take the backpack off to give her back a rest, and that while the backpack was off she should try to rearrange the contents so they would lie smoothly along her back without any edges poking into her. This strategy seemed to work fairly well, but she was only eight years old and I knew that her back and shoulders must hurt a lot just from the weight of the pack itself, and this, in time, would get worse. She was trying to be brave about it, but when she looked up at me I could see the pain in her eyes, though she tried to hide it.

The first day, November 15th, we covered the distance from Jake's remote cabin, near Raquette Lake, to the northeastern end of Forked

Lake before we stopped for the night. We stopped for short rest breaks along the way. Everyone except Jake looked tired. Grace was especially tired and had been walking on wobbly legs for the last hour or two. I felt terrible because I couldn't carry her. I had an overloaded backpack and three awkward, heavy rifles to carry. My free arm wasn't strong enough to carry her with her backpack loaded with supplies, which was actually a moot point because Grace wanted to hold my free hand. I also couldn't carry her on my shoulders because of the rifle slings that hung there. I felt great distress and shame because she was hurting and I couldn't remedy her situation.

Luckily, it wasn't long before we made camp. Grace and I, with Tom guarding us and ordering us around, collected dry wood, then large slabs of dry moss, in great quantity, from a large, dry ledge of rocks and moist ground. We, also, had to gather large quantities of balsam and spruce boughs. I may be an outdoor lover, but I'm no woodsman. I didn't know what the hell the moss and boughs had to do with a camp, or a campfire. I decided to remain quiet and see how they'd be used.

Tom started the campfire. Lester opened some cans of food and Jake stood about twenty feet from the campfire with the barrel of his shotgun in the crook of his left arm with his right hand around the grip, near the trigger guard. His finger wasn't on the trigger. He stood their looking like Daniel Boone or Davy Crocket, if they were sentries waiting for an Indian attack, and enjoying the anticipation and joy of killing and shedding blood. Jake seemed to blend into the surrounding trees. His height and strength were magnified as Grace and I sat on the ground and looked up at him. It was like sitting on the sidewalk, in New York City, and looking up at the Empire State Building—his head didn't come to that sharp of a point, though. I could feel the vertebrae in my neck squeeze together as I craned my neck upward. Jake stood like a solid, tall, oak tree, habitually sucking air through his front teeth, like wind blowing through the upper tree branches. He waited for the cans of food to get hot and, like a good shepherd, was watchful of his sheep.

We were given one can of food—hash—and a fork to share. When we were done eating, it had become dark. I noticed that the Gibsons each had a sleeping bag and I wondered how Grace and I would have to sleep. But I didn't have to wonder too long because the answer came in the form of two blankets that Jake threw at us. I seriously doubt that we got the blankets out of compassion for our comfort. Jake was smart enough to know that sick or tired hostages don't travel well.

I noticed that they were "wool" blankets. I'd once read that wool was the best kind of cloth for the outdoorsman because it was able to retain body heat whether the blanket was dry or wet. It was late fall now, but it wasn't too cold yet. I thought the temperatures were in the high forties, by day, and were probably about ten degrees colder at night.

Jake started placing some of the thick, dry moss slabs on the ground, about three feet from the fire and projecting outward away from the fire about seven feet long, and about three feet wide. Tom and Lester started doing the same thing. I was starting to learn why Grace and I had to collect so much moss and boughs. They were to be used to prepare make-shift mattresses, nature's mattresses, so-to-speak. The moss was three to four inches thick and springy. They made double layers of it. Then they placed the balsam and spruce boughs over the moss, making sure that the sharp ends of the branches went down into the moss, out of harms way so they wouldn't get jabbed during the night or have their sleeping bags ripped. Then they each placed their sleeping bag over the bed of moss and balsam boughs. I have to admit that I was impressed to see how easy they made it look. In hardly any time at all, they each had a "nature mattress," which looked to me like a guarantee of a comfortable night's sleep . . . for them.

When they were done, Jake looked at me, spit-out some tobacco juice, sucked some air through his teeth, then pointed to the remaining moss and boughs and said, "Yuh kin 'ave what be left, Wimpy. It be up ta yuh how yuh sleeps."

I got up, collected the extra moss and boughs, then arranged them as I had seen them do. There was only enough moss and boughs left for half a "nature mattress," one layer thick, but I did make it about four feet wide. That would allow Grace and me to sleep together, sharing our body heat. I placed one wool blanket over the boughs for us to sleep on and the other blanket would be used to cover us up. I didn't care that the "nature's mattress" wasn't long enough for my legs, as long as I could keep my upper body warm. Luckily, for Grace, if she curled her legs slightly, her whole body would fit on the soft moss mattress and be totally covered by the blanket.

Grace squirmed close to me as we lay between the blankets. In a few minutes she was sound asleep, a sleep promptly induced by her total exhaustion.

I listened to her breathing. It was peaceful and quiet, such a contrast to this whole ordeal, I thought. Tears rolled from the corners of my eyes as I fought for emotional control and tried to quench a hot barrier of fear that I hadn't felt since Nam. I stared at Grace and thought, "A good father is obligated to protect his children, at all costs." The fear that I would fail with that endeavor caused me great distress. A loving father, a dedicated father, a responsible father must protect his progeny, or else, what is there left of him when he dies? An artist leaves his art for the world of the future, a writer leaves his ideas and stories within his books, and a father leaves his children. He knows that his children's lives are more important than himself, and a valuable gift for future society because of their potential to do great things with the loving memory of their father deeply imbedded in their minds. And so the loving father, though deceased, still lives on in the memories and actions of his appreciative and loving children.

Jake, Tom and Lester stayed up and talked in whispers. I couldn't hear most of it so in five minutes I pretended that I was asleep by snoring mildly. They fell for the snoring ploy and weren't as cautiously quiet as they should've been with their whispered, conspiratorial conversation. Or, perhaps, Jake knew that I was faking and didn't care if I overheard our fate. Maybe he figured that we were well beyond Sunday Rock, well out of reach of the laws of civilization where most people have to face the consequences of their criminal actions. Or, perhaps, he wanted me to overhear their conversation because he received as much sadistic pleasure from the terror he created in his victims, letting them know that he was going to kill them, as he did from the actual act of murdering them while they remained helpless to take any counter-measures.

As I thought more about it, I grew more and more to believe that my snoring was fooling Tom and Lester, but not Jake. Perhaps Jake was letting his boys talk louder because he wanted me to clearly hear their plans to kill me. Perhaps he was enjoying himself because he sincerely believed that I was a helpless, pathetic weakling that didn't stand any more chance of successfully opposing him and his boys as a fawn does against a pack of wolves—Wolf growled at me.

Perhaps it was *me* that was underestimating *his* intelligence, being a sucker to the way he looked, talked, behaved and dressed. I thought, "What if, while I concentrated on how I was out-witting him, due to his underestimating me, that I was in danger of underestimating him?" I had to be alert; I couldn't afford any mistakes in my thinking or in my actions. So, I thought, the standard of thinking and planning for our escape plan had to be: Expect the best, but always prepare for the worst. If plan "A" fails, what's plan "B? or is there only plan "A?"

I knew that I was in one-hell-of-a-predicament, though. My mental imagery focused on hell and I could see red-hot coals and flames everywhere, with Jake appearing as a cloven-hoofed, flaming red body, and black-horned Satan. He pointed at me, saying, "I'm gonna kill ya, Wimpy." Then he sucked the flames between his teeth, laughed crazily and exhaled fire. He continued to point at me, his flaming finger flicking up and down slightly, for emphasis, or in mockery, probably both.

I started to wonder if, perhaps, we were all really dead and this life on Earth was the real hell.

A humorous thought crept out of the crevice of my gray matter, like an ant from a crack. I thought, "Damn! I sure wish the Gibsons would stop calling me Wimpy". It irritated and distracted me to no end; made me hungry, too. Being called Wimpy was even worse than Jake's air-sucking. Made me think of the Popeye cartoons with Wimpy always saying, "I'll gladly pay you, Tuesday, for a hamburger, today." Man! Where the hell did that rogue thought come from? But I would gladly pay someone on Tuesday, for a hamburger today. I grinned, shrugged, then listening carefully.

The secretive talk was about their winter supply of food. Jake was saying that they probably didn't have enough canned and dry food to share with Grace and I, and that eating meat every day wasn't a satisfactory option. Also discussed was the fact that, if they needed to move quickly, Grace would slow them down too much. The only reason they let Grace stay with me when we walked was that she would travel faster when walking next to me. Tom suggested, and Lester agreed, that we weren't valuable hostages any more and that since we were beyond Sunday Rock, they should be allowed to kill us here and now . . . in our sleep.

I quietly unzipped my coat, unbuttoned one button on my shirt, reached in and wrapped each of my right hand fingers and thumb around my Ka-Bar combat knife. My thumb is ready to unsnap the handle strap. Once my fingers touched the handle, I felt a surge of both fear and confidence, which I couldn't explain because they were contradictions. But I hoped I wouldn't be forced to use the knife now. I wanted better odds of escaping than I had now.

Tom was almost begging Jake to let him have me. He said he wanted to jump on top of me, pin me to the ground under the blanket and repeatedly stab my body while I was pinned there as helpless as an insect pinned to an entomologist's display board. Furthermore, he said, with clenched teeth, that he wanted to slash my face to a bloody pulp. He was trying to keep his voice to a whisper, but he was so excited about his method of killing me that I could hear every hushed word that he said.

And while he was begging his dad to let him stab me to death, Lester kept repeating, softly, "Let me have the little girl, Pa. Let me have the little girl, Pa."

Lester's voice was a little more subdued than Tom's, but its high-pitched squeal carried easily to my ears and made me grimace in disgust at both the sound and intent of it.

I was ready to throw the blanket off, spring-up and slash the throat of the first one to approach within arms reach. Then I'd kick to the groin of the second—if there was a second attacker close by—then stab to the back of the neck so that the blade severed the spine, or at least cut a major artery. The second victim would be paralyzed with a severed spine or artery, and the first one would stagger around for a few seconds in a death dance with blood spurting from around his fingers where they would be wrapped around his neck desperately trying to stop the gushing flow of blood. In a few more seconds he would pass-out due to lose of blood to the brain and death would follow a few seconds later. Unfortunately, if I made it that far, I'd be dead before I could confront Jake. He'd splatter my guts all over the ground, trees and bushes with his shotgun. Grace would probably be wounded as the shotgun pellets spread out. I didn't want to think of what might happen after that. If I'm really lucky, I thought, Jake will squash their childish, sadistic excitement and stop his sons from being spontaneously foolish. Maybe he could just send his boys into the dark forest so they could masturbate their excitement away.

I thought," Fools talk too much. Cowards are afraid to talk. Wise men listen, and think before they talk". But all men revert to fools and cowards when filled with wine, or full of the hyperbolic joy of their own bloated egos

In any kind of group combat, where one person faces the threat of a group, the single person must always take-out the most dangerous opponent first, or the leader, if they aren't the same person. Take the leader out of action first and fast with semi-deadly or deadly force, depending on how dire the situation is. But the dynamics of this situation meant that Jake would have to be the last one I attacked because he was standing the farthest away from me, with a 12 gauge shotgun. I could use my throwing knife if Jake paused in shock and delayed shooting me, but I seriously doubted that Jake would pause. Also, if I did get the chance, would the throwing knife penetrate his heavy winter coat? I thought not. I'd have to aim to penetrate an eyeball with the blade penetrating the brain, or aim for the neck. It's probably a million to one odds, or worse, for either of those things happening. So trying to get to Jake was nearly impossible without me getting wounded, probably killed. Then Grace would be alone with Jake. The thought repulsed me; made me shiver with cold sweat.

As I lay there, extremely tense, my heart was sledge-hammering the inside of my chest. It felt like a heart attack. Then I heard Jake's voice say, "No, boys, not yet. We needs 'em ta help us carry are supplies an' canoe. It make the work easy on us, right? So's we best be waitin' til we gits ta the cabin. If nobody be on are trail after a few days then we kills 'em near the cabin an' burries 'em there. Be calm boys. Yuh be gittin' yur crack at 'em."

There was a deathly silence and I could feel each of them staring across the campfire at Grace and me. I opened my eyes to imperceptible slits and saw the fire light shining on their faces forming hideous, dancing masks on their madmen's flesh.

In a few minutes I released the blade very slowly, without causing much motion under the blanket. I pretended that I was changing my sleeping position and this motion covered up the movement needed to withdraw my hand from my shirt. Needless to say, I couldn't sleep for most of the night. I wondered if Jake orchestrated this whole scene, played with me so that I wouldn't get much sleep and be tired. Did he really know I was faking sleep? Was he that clever? I wondered. I shouldn't underestimate him.

While two Gibsons slept, one stayed awake and guarded Grace and me, but Lester wasn't one of the two guards, just Jake and Tom. I assumed that Jake didn't trust Lester to stay awake or to stay away from Grace.

I was tempted to make a break for freedom during the night, but the chances of Grace and I making it were too slim. I needed to remain patient and wait for a better opportunity, but it was getting damn difficult to do that.

To my surprise, everyone slept until daybreak on the morning of November 16th. Jake must have felt that he was out of danger now, so he allowed everyone to sleep late before we all were awakened by his stentorian voice. He had the last watch guarding us so he was already up and the fire was full of red hot coals.

It was a cool, clear, fall morning. The forest glistened with icy dew and the colorful leaves on the ground made the ground look like a huge artist's palette of bright colors. Under normal circumstances this would be one of the most beautiful mornings of my life. But, under these particular circumstances, I couldn't linger long about such pleasant thoughts. But the irony of those thoughts floated across my mind like dark clouds before a storm.

If I wasn't an atheist, I'd say that this was truly God's country. And if, some day or some how, I felt that all this Adirondack beauty had something to do with a God, then I'd have to give up my atheism and embrace this golden Adirondack realm as one of God's temples—Not much chance of that happening, though. Then I started to wonder if, perhaps, my desperation was making me senile. This certainly was no time for any mental thesis on the existence or the non-existence of God, especially for an, out-of-the-closet, atheist like me.

Grace was especially quiet as we got a late start, after we ate, packed up and extinguished the fire. Jake was very careful to cover-up the traces of our passage. He buried the fire pit, smoothed the dirt, then littered that dirt with sticks and leaves to make it look as if no one had made a campfire. He left no litter and as we walked away, I couldn't tell that anyone had stayed there overnight, except for the "nature mattresses." The Gibsons just left them there. It seemed kind of stupid to me. Surely, any other woodsman would know what they were. I didn't understand; didn't need to, I guess.

We walked to the canoes at the lake's edge. I walked with Grace and put my hand on her shoulder. She looked up at me and smiled nervously. She tried to hide her growing fear, but couldn't, and I felt agony for her pain and my feeling of helplessness.

As we approached the lake, I noticed that the sun made the smooth surface look like a calm, watery mirror. I stared into that mirror and saw a huge combat blade shimmering on the surface of the lake. It initially startled me, but I soon realized that it was only a mental image; like a mirage, perhaps, but it was a symbol of hope for me; a sign of good luck and it lessened that feeling of helplessness.

We had just gotten into the canoes and were only a few feet from shore when I saw Jake and Tom snap their heads to look back at the tree line near the shore. My eyes followed theirs. I reined my extreme pleasure and only smiled with my eyes.

"Damn! Tom whispered, but not so quietly that I couldn't hear him. "Looked like a damn white wolf, Pa," Tom continued. "Did yuh see it?"

"Saw it. Cain't be no wolf, son. Be a coyote. No wolves be here no more," Jake responded.

Tom looked doubtful; didn't think there was any such thing as a white coyote. Maybe a white coydog—the result of a coyote mating with a domestic, pet dog. But he said nothing. He knew better that to question is father.

The thought of "Roamin' Wolf" near our camp sight made me, "Roman Wolfe," very pleased. A damn good omen that brought a subtle smile to my face. Two good omens in a short period of time. Hope was on the rise.

Long Lake was beautiful, though, technically, it wasn't a lake. At the campfire, the night before, Jake told his sons that it was really the very wide portion of the Raquette River which follows an ancient and very wide, geological fault line.

Long Lake remained a frigid, smooth mirror. There was no wind to create even the tiniest ripples. I could see the billowing cumulus clouds so clearly that they actually appeared to be huge cotton puffs floating on the lake's mirrored surface. The sun shone on this mirror and I basked in it's reflected warmth. The clear, cold water rippled where the paddles entered it and where the canoe cut through it like a large, silent knife. I could see fish below the surface where the clear water was a few degrees warmer. They seemed undisturbed by our presence. I felt like a fishing pole would be a hated object in the midst of Long Lake's serene beauty. The canoes and oars were an intrusion on the calmness of the lake, like the Gibsons being an intrusion on our relatively calm lives.

In early evening, after long hours of paddling, we reached the end of Long Lake, where the canoes were both well hidden under an assortment of boughs. As we stood by the northeastern end of the lake, where Cold River runs south into it, I continued to look in a northeastern direction and saw a wonderfully amazing natural sight, which I later found out was Mount Seward. It ran across the horizon like a serrated knife. It was truly a wonderful, pleasant sight to see. I thought that Grace and I couldn't die here because we had to come back to see this and other sights again, if it didn't bring back too much emotional pain. Grace was by my side, but she only stared at me as I, in turn, stared at the serrated mountain on the skyline, the "cutting edge of nature." It must have been almost impossible for Grace to see any beauty in any of this experience.

I thought, "That's it. The word 'edge.' Mount Seward was like a knife's edge and, like in Nam, it was a symbol of survival. Another good omen." I smiled at Grace, then whispered that we'd be OK. I wanted to give her hope. I needed some, too, especially since I had been thinking of the future, when there was no future, if I didn't focus on getting away from the Gibsons.

A vision of Sam came to me. I thought about how worried she must be. I longed to see her, to hold her, so even the vision of her tearful face was comforting to me. I'd save Grace for her, though I may perish in the process. The thought of my death didn't scare me, just like in Nam. I could feel my body and mind preparing for the final fight as an aberrant thought raced through my brain: Death itself is not scary at all. It's "how" you die that could be scary. All my life I've felt that Death stalked me, walked in my tracks, far behind me, but on my trail. It seemed to me that Death was also walking faster than I was, every year. Was he now about to catch up to me? Death, life's ultimate, unstoppable, irrevocable disease might be named Jake. I forced myself to struggle out of that mental entanglement.

At the campfire, Jake's Adirondack guide knowledge flowed forth as he talked to Tom and Lester about the area. He said, "Some lumberin' done here 'long this here Col' River—Cold River—an' some a its creeks a few year back, but upper parts be mostly not touched. These here Adirondacks 'ave bout ten thousan' square mile a land. That be more than a million acres a land packed wid lakes, ponds, trees, moun'ains an' all sorts a animals. Some of them are deadly if yuh cross 'em. An' don' be fooled by the pretty face. Good ol' Mudder Nature can kill yuh way out here if yuh ain't being' careful, boys, 'specially this here Col' River area dat we be headin' fer, tomarra—tomorrow. The river be 'bout fourteen mile long wid heavy fores' on both sides so's don' yuh go wanderin' off by yerself. This river be a wil' one. Hardly be no people 'round it at all. Not many people wants ta come this far out in dis wil'erness. No cars 'ere, boys. Yuh git here by water like us, or by walkin', which be awful hard 'cause it be damn hard ta walk through thick forest wid backpacks that be catching on tree limbs an' bushes, an' yur feet be trippin' over roots, fall-downs an saplin's. Only other way ta git close be by horse trail. But that ain't likely ta help since horses cain't leave the trail an' go inta the woods. There be some two hun'red mile, or so, a horse trails. Some horse trails be 'long some parts a dis river, so we stays away from 'em, but yuh listens up now, boys, dis here river area be dangerous. It be the only one in New York State that needs a warning. Us guides are always supposed ta tell people that the Adirondack Park Service warns them 'bout dis here area bein' a very remote wil'erness area where yuh kin git yerself lost an' die real easy like. Yuh listenin' careful, boy?" Jake looked at Lester whose eyes were wondering.

Lester snapped his head around. "Yeah, Pa, I heard yuh." Tom nodded and Jake looked satisfied with his son's responses.

My thoughts focused on Jake's semi-literate speech patterns. If Jake got up on stage and talked like that, applause and laughter would loudly ejaculate from the mouths of the entertained audience. The echoes of their pleasure would bounce off the walls and fill the air with vibrations that titillated the eardrums. And Jake would be called a comic genius of unparalleled skill for his ability to mimic a backward, backwoods, poorly-educated, and possibly a hillbilly born as the result of incest.

The tourists that Jake took on trips through the Adirondacks undoubtedly weren't turned-off by his poor speech skills. Perhaps his poor speech even added to the flavor and authenticity of his knowledge and woodsman skills. Actually, many people probably considered it charming that someone like Jake cared enough about his job, as a guide, that he'd spend many hours teaching himself to talk like a genuine, illiterate, early nineteenth century, mountain man. I started to feel sick to my stomach when I thought that Jake's poor language skills may have been the highlight of hundreds of deep woods camping trips for thousands of campers. I could almost picture someone recalling, ten years later, their camping trip with Jake as their guide and saying, "Yes, our camping trip was wonderful and do you remember that unbelievably authentic Adirondack mountain man guide? Wow! He was great. He made me feel like I actually lived a hundred and fifty years ago."

At the end of the day we prepared the camp in plenty of time before night fall. I could tell that the further we got into the isolated Adirondack area, the better Jake felt. His happy facial expression indicated that he was feeling exceptionally well now. He felt safe and secure. This was his true home.

I heard Jake tell Tom and Lester that tomorrow we'd start up Cold River and before nightfall we'd be at the Preston Ponds cabin. They all laughed with anticipatory joy. I could see big, open-mouthed smiles, showing a plethora of badly discolored teeth, missing teeth and plenty of discolored gum. They acted like horny cowboys must have acted when they headed for the whore-house and saloon after a couple of months of driving cattle to market across the lonely, dusty and dangerous western ranges.

Shortly before dark, Jake and Lester went into the woods, leaving Tom, with shotgun in hand and evil in his eyes, to guard us. This seemed like a good time to make an escape, but Tom had his shotgun and his eyes pointing directly at us and he wasn't about to turn either one away from us. There was no mistaking how badly he wanted to kill me. I wondered what sort of perverted fetish he had with wanting to dive on top of me to stab and slash me to death. Was there some sexual connotation to it?—that was a repulsive, nauseating thought. Was being *on top* a sexual reference? Was the stabbing knife a Freudian symbol for a penis? Why not just blow me away with that shotgun, or one of the rifles? I didn't know the answer, but I did know that it would take a team of ten psychiatrists ten years to thoroughly analyze these three psychotic, mental dwarfs, and even then there would probably be serious disagreement about the roots of their psychosis, as well as how to treat it.

Jake and Lester disappeared quickly into the thickly wooded area. I didn't know their purpose until about an hour later when they appeared, almost as suddenly as they had disappeared, with their arms full of firewood. It seemed strange, though, that it would take an hour to collect an armload of wood in this densely wooded area where firewood was so plentiful, especially in late fall with no snow on the ground. Also, I thought, "Why collect firewood at night when it's so much easier to do it in the daylight? Jake obviously felt safe, so why not stop while there's still enough light to see and collect the firewood? Not only that, but they usually forced Grace and I to do that job. It was too unusual, so it made me suspicious. I decided that they were up to something, but I didn't know what the hell it was . . . not yet.

/../.-../- - -/...-/./.-../- - -/.-./../-.../..-/.-../.-../- - -/-.-./.-./

Chapter 6

★★★★

The Cabin

TOM AND JAKE, ONCE again, took turns guarding Grace and I during the night. Grace seemed to have gotten the rest she needed to regain most of her depleted strength, though I didn't think she had the stamina for much more of this kind of very rough hiking. At least she was able to sleep through the whole night without once waking up. I wish I could say the same for myself. A foggy haze seemed to have wrapped itself around my brain, like a blanket of gauze, from lack of sleep.

The following morning, November 17th (my father's-in-law birthday) we got a late start after a breakfast of warmed, canned hash—again—that was burned and had little taste to it. Lester had been given the chore of warming the cans by the fire. He placed them too close and neglected to watch carefully—Jake and Tom shook their heads in disgust, but said nothing to Lester, but their eyes conveyed their message of displeasure to him. When you're hungry—we certainly were—you'll eat just about anything, even if it tastes like burned toast. Grace and I considered ourselves lucky to get enough food to sustain us. But, Jake knew that in order for us to travel fast, a long distance, carrying supplies, we needed food for energy. If we were deprived of food it would only slow him down, which made it advantageous for him to feed us, but I don't think he understood the meaning of the words "balanced meal" and "nutrition."

We departed Long Lake around mid-morning and walked northward on the east side of Cold River. Cold River ran south into Long Lake so we couldn't use the canoes to travel upstream against a swift current. That really slowed us down, especially since Jake would stay away from any possible trails where we might be seen. He tended to stay in the dense woods where we couldn't see very far ahead due to the density of the tree trunks, limbs and bushes that came close to the edge of the river. However, we were lucky that it was fall. If it had been late spring or summer, the lush, verdant vegetation and leaves would have prevented our seeing more than ten or fifteen feet ahead of us, almost like Nam's dense jungles. But there was, realistically, very little chance of us being spotted, even without concealing vegetation, because I heard Jake repeatedly inform his sons that this was an extremely remote area, very isolated. Jake was taking no chances, though, so he also stayed away from clearings where aircraft might be able to see us—I hadn't heard any aircraft at all, not even distant ones, since we left Raquette Lake.

We stopped to eat a late afternoon lunch of beef jerky. No campfire was built. Jake didn't want to take the time that it would take to clear a space, dig a shallow hole, start the fire, cook, clean up, cover the coals and ashes, then camouflage it with dirt, leaves and branches to make the area look as if no one had been there. He wanted to eat fast and get moving quickly.

Grace sat close to me, her jaw muscles straining to bite, then chew the leather-tough strip of jerky. It was like trying to bite and chew the sole of a shoe; about as tasty, too.

Jake passed a clear, plastic bag to his sons. They reached in and pulled out a handful of what looked like peanuts, bits of chocolate, raisins and oat cereal. Grace and I were not offered any as they noisily appeased their gluttonous appetites. They kept the bag for themselves, hoarding it greedily, as if it was a bag of gold nuggets amongst a trio of poor prospectors. I could see Grace's disappointment radiating from the hatred in her eyes. I tapped her on the shoulder so she'd look at me. I didn't want the Gibsons to see her hatred for them because they might take her away from me. I whispered to her; asked her not to stare at them. She obeyed by looking at the ground. I knew she was hungry, especially for quick energy food like the Gibsons were eating now. I'd beg them for some, to give to Grace, if I thought it would do any good, but I knew it wouldn't, especially when I saw Lester and Tom smiling over their shoulders at us as they enjoyed their moment of adolescent teasing. I thought I heard Grace's stomach growl from hunger. Maybe it was my stomach or, perhaps, Wolf's.

I placed the three rifles carefully against a tree trunk. I knew that I could be ruthlessly killed if I mishandled them, or worse, Grace could be threatened; perhaps abused. It was a huge relief, however, getting those rifles off my aching shoulders while we stopped for lunch. When we were walking, and one shoulder got sore, I'd switch the rifle slings to the other shoulder. But, now both shoulder muscles ached. Even my heavy winter coat, for padding, didn't protect my shoulder muscles any more. The rifle slings had dug into each shoulder muscle, rubbing the skin away until they each felt raw, bruised. They also stung from the salt of my perspiration. I'd be glad to get to the cabin so I wouldn't have to carry them any more.

I kept my left arm around Grace's shoulder while I ate the rest of the dry, leather-like jerky with my right hand. Grace and I strained to smile at each other, but we didn't speak. One of the Gibsons usually stopped us from talking aloud during the daytime, but our whispered communications weren't usually interrupted. Grace was too scared and tired to say much, anyway, and probably what she did want to say had to remain unspoken until bedtime when she could lie close to me and we could whisper to each other. But, as often happened, by bedtime she was usually too exhausted to say much, or to listen for very long. For those reasons, we didn't do much talking unless I felt it was absolutely necessary, like giving her some words of encouragement and praise, or some advice.

But through my anger and fear I could still see and enjoy the splendor of these forests. It was indeed odd to be able to do that with life-threatening danger as a constant companion. Grace only saw the ugliness and I could understand that. For me, the trees stood tall, like watchful sentinels, ever vigilant protectors of this wilderness beauty. I studied the trees for a while and saw that we were in the midst of some maples, beech, elm and birch trees. Among the conifers were red spruce and white pine, which I found later were the symbols of the north woods. I saw a playful and frisky red squirrel jumping back and forth, from limb to limb and from tree to tree. The squirrel was so cheerful and frolicsome that it made me smile. Grace saw where I was looking, so she looked, too. We both saw the white at the same time. Beyond the squirrels, almost out of viewing range, a white object moved slowly. Grace looked up at me; I shrugged me shoulders as if I hadn't see it. When she and I looked again, it had vanished . . . Wolf.

We reached the Preston Ponds cabin about an hour before dark—that must have been why Jake wanted lunch to be an "eat and run" activity. He wanted to reach the cabin before dark. A fire was made in the cabin's stone and clay fireplace to warm its chilly interior. I thought that the smoke rising out of the chimney and into the air would be like a signal flag to show where we were, if anyone was searching for us. But then I realized that the cabin was built right in the midst of a copse of the thick evergreen forest. That meant that the smoke coming out of the chimney had to rise slowly through the heavily laden branches of tall pine trees. And as the smoke rose, the pine tree limbs and abundant needles would disperse the smoke to such an extent that it couldn't be detected by any search and rescue aircraft. The smoke would simply rise through the tops of the tall pine trees and be released as frail, diluted wisps which were almost immediately obliterated by even the slightest of breezes that sailed over the tree tops.

There were no windows in the cabin, though I saw sections of the walls marked, probably to show where windows would eventually be cut in the spring. The fireplace and plenty of candles served as the only light sources. The cabin was almost totally in the shade of the trees, except when the sun was directly overhead. I figured that there must be flashlights and oil lamps, but I didn't see any in plain sight. But they had to be present because this log cabin was basically a wooden cave, dark and dreary, with a dirt floor that had been pounded so hard that it felt like concrete.

There was one table made out of split logs, similar to a rough-looking picnic table. There were four chairs and four bunk beds, two bunk beds built into the wall on each side of the fireplace. I guessed that Grace and I were lucky to share the fourth bunk bed, though I wondered why it was built, until I thought that when building one bed, you might just as well build both. And if the fourth bunk bed wasn't used by someone, then it could very conveniently serve as a shelf.

There was plenty of firewood already cut, stacked and seasoned. I saw it on the way into the cabin. It was stacked up against the weather-protected side of the cabin. Cans of food were everywhere, on shelves built into the interior side of the cabin. Jake really had this all planned out and executed extremely well. I didn't take comfort in this thought, however, but I was well aware that to defeat an enemy you had to study them, learn about them so you could find their strengths and weaknesses, think like them and imagine walking in their shoes. Finding their weaknesses puts you on the path to victory or, in our case, a successful escape. But I found that thought to be more threatening than comforting, especially when I looked into Grace's very young and innocent brown eyes.

Jake dumped about six cans of chunky beef soup into a cast-iron pot, heated it up over the fire and we all ate hot soup. Then we prepared for bed, even though the cabin had only warmed-up a few degrees. Jake and Tom took off their coats. They both still had thick, warm-looking shirts on. Lester, however, looked cold even with his coat still on. Jake and Tom looked at Grace and me curiously. I had told Grace to keep her coat on, just like I did. I couldn't chance taking off my coat and exposing the knives that were under my shirt. Those knives were our major hope and my element of surprise. They must be kept secret at all costs, until just the right moment. But that moment had to be soon because keeping my coat on all the time would eventually raise serious suspicion, especially when the cabin became comfortably warm. I knew that I couldn't keep my coat on too long, but for the moment I made up the excuse that Grace and I were still cold because we weren't used to this rough outdoor life, like they were. I pointed to Lester and said, "See. He's still cold, too." Jake looked at Tom and they both laughed, but they accepted what I said, then looked away from us, one of them faintly whispering the derogatory word, "Wimpy."

I had to act soon, tonight or tomorrow morning. I thought of two proverbs that were in opposition to each other: "He who hesitates is lost"—don't hesitate before you act—and, "Look before you leap—hesitate before you act. Action and inaction. At present, however I couldn't leap, nor could I hesitate for very long. I had to rely on the "Roamin' Wolf" in me to do whatever it takes to get Grace out of harm's way.

Tom kept glancing at us, as we sat on the bottom bunk. It didn't take long for him to say, "Yooh, asshole! You can take yur coat off now," he teased. He surprised me because I thought that that issue had just been settled—the bad apple doesn't fall far from the rotten tree.

Apparently he didn't think much of my excuse for keeping our coats on. "We ain't gonna steal it from yuh. Ain't even worth the effort. Cheap coat." Then he burst into sarcastic laughter that ejaculated through his crooked and discolored teeth. Lester followed suit.

Grace cringed because the laughing sounds exploding from his mouth were more like the vicious snarls of a ravenous lion tearing apart its prey.

The coat wasn't cheap, though it may have looked cheap. It was nylon stuffed with something to trap the warm body heat. However, it was best for fall weather and might not be good enough in the biting chill and blowing snows of an Adirondack winter season. This thought nearly put me in a panic. We had to get out of this mess before it snowed, before the winds howled their frigid anger and touched their icy fingers to all of us warm-blooded creatures, and, also, before the temperatures dropped to serious, frostbite levels. Neither Grace nor I were appropriately dressed for the rugged Adirondack winter weather, or for the rough terrain.

Fear started to penetrate my confidence. I was becoming damn frustrated with myself for vacillating between the twin devils of fear and panic and the twin gods of self-confidence and strength. But before I could berate myself too severely, a mental picture of a wolf took shape . . . a pale wolf—doesn't Death ride a *pale* horse in the mythical, biblical Book of Revelation? Strange that I would think of that, especially since I consider the bible an ages old book of multi-authored fiction. The growling image of the pale wolf broke me out of my daydream, it's lips drawn back to show pink gum and deadly fangs. It was an image that I'd seen hundreds of times before, in Nam, but Wolf wasn't white back then. Back then Wolf was black. I wondered why it had changed color. Was it a double meaning? Was a *pale wolf* similar to the biblical *pale horse*? Death was the master of the pale horse, so, is the wolf's master also Death? Then that would be me. I'm Death? But isn't white also associated with goodness, as in *good versus evil*? So, did that mean that Wolf and I represent Death, that we had to kill the Gibsons, and that in this particular case *Death* would be a *good* thing? Holy shit! Was that just a convoluted rationalization? Shit! I don't know why I'm thinking of this crap at a time like this. I should only have one thought, one goal, one all-consuming duty, saving Grace. I would do whatever it took to save Grace, so screw the *death* and *goodness* crap, screw the *good* versus *evil* bullshit, and screw the law. Grace's survival was all that mattered to me, now.

I calmly looked at Tom and replied, "Grace and I are still chilled from the long, cold trip to get here. That's why we still have our coats on. If we get sick we'll just be an added burden to you, so keeping our coats on helps all of us. We aren't used to the rough weather and the rough traveling, as I told you a little while ago."

Actually, I knew that the Gibsons didn't give a shit about any of that. To them, we didn't need warm coats and it didn't matter if we were sick or healthy because they didn't intend to let us live very long. To them, we were just a burden, just animals waiting to be slaughtered, after they had some sadistic pleasure. Jake whispered to Tom and Tom said no more about my coat. The Gibsons sat at the table grinning at us arrogantly, like children who think they have a secret that no one else can possibly figure out.

Grace was exhausted so we sat on the bottom bunk bed, with our coats on. We huddled together since the cabin was still cold, and covered our legs with our two wool blankets. While we were sitting on the bunk bed I noticed that, instead of springs in the bottom of the bunk beds, there were spaced, taut ropes running the length and width of the wooden frames—in a checker-board pattern. The mattress appeared and felt as if it was nothing more than a huge, canvas sack stuffed with dried moss and dry grass. I was skeptical about its comfort, until I thought of what our beds were like (fairly comfortable) on the way to this cabin.

Soon we laid on the bunk to get some sleep. Lester immediately looked at us and said, while laughing haughtily, "They're just a couple a candy asses, Tom. The wimp there an' his very sweet little girlie."

Then, in a menacing voice, he added," Come here, little girlie, an' I'll keep you warm. I surely will."

Lester reached into his pocket and took out the three inch folding knife that he took from me at Raquette Lake. The perverted miscreant then waved the opened blade toward Grace and beckoned her, in a teasing, licentious tone of voice, to come to him. I kept my eyes riveted on him while Grace buried her terrorized face into my shoulder. I could feel her body shudder with fear. The razor sharp blade in Lester's hand sparkled like liquid silver from the reflected light of the fireplace, as well as light from the candles that were sitting on the crude table and in the corners of the cabin. Barely controlled rage surged through me as I desperately tried not to glare at him, for two reasons: one, my stare might intimidate him and might show Jake and Tom that I wasn't the "ultimate wimp" that they thought I was; two, Grace needed me to comfort her, to make her feel safe, to stroke her hair, to whisper soothingly words to her, to reassure her and give her hope.

Suddenly Jake's massive open paw flashed out and smacked Lester across the back of his head, raising tufts of hair to form faux-cowlicks as his head jerked forward from the unexpected blow. "Knock it off, son. Not now. Yuh hush-up an' be patient," he said, his harsh words pouring out of the hole in his grizzled beard, and his eyes radiating sparks of admonition.

Lester glared at his father, then quickly looked meekly at the cabin floor. Then his head rose as he stared with bitter hatred and clenched teeth towards me, as if I was to blame for what he said, the consequences of his own words, and of his father's stern rebuke.

I closed my eyes to indicate that I was going to sleep, waited a few seconds, then opened them just a slit so I could see all of them sitting together.

In my imagination I could see Wolf pacing around that evil trio, with his eyes reflecting yellow light from the fire, his lips drawn back over wet and glistening, white fanged teeth. It was the dance of a hungry, stalking, feral creature seeking the taste of flesh and blood, and knowing it was all within reach. Lester appeared to be the closest, tasty morsel to the hoary wolf's lolling and dripping tongue. But Wolf, following my lead, controlled his fierce rage, subduing it with patience.

Lester continued his staring faux-bravado, not knowing just how close he was to his own bloody and violent death.

I could, however, see the festering cowardice in Lester's eyes and face; the hesitancy to take action, the grand lack of self-assurance and the subtle way he leaned backward, on his heels, as if to take flight and run away. He wouldn't approach Grace with me in the way, and his father and brother were making no attempt to assist him . . . not now, anyway. I rolled on my side, turning my back to them and drew Grace closer to me. I whispered into her ear, "Daddy loves you. I'll take you home to Mommy, Grandpa and Grandma for Thanksgiving," But Grace didn't relax, rather she burrowed her head into my neck and shoulder as if she were diving down a hole to safety. She was trembling with fear, anxiety and stress. Her arms and legs were alive with short, jerky movement; she couldn't settle down. After about ten or fifteen minutes her breathing became more regular and soothing, indicative of sleep. I hoped that she would be carried off on the dream laden wings of sleep, to a pleasant and safe place, which would probably be into her mother's arms.

As the cabin became quiet, and the Gibsons were left to their own thoughts, I wondered if the police were on our trail. I hoped that they were. I wondered how my in-laws and Sam were doing. I wondered if Sam had called my sister, nephews and niece to give them the bad news. I wondered if Sam had called my school principal so he could get a substitute teacher for me. I wondered who the substitute teacher was. I wondered if I'd ever see my classroom, students, colleagues, relatives and friends again. I wondered what went through their minds when they heard about our being kidnapped. I wondered a lot and guessed a lot, but I thought I did know five things: One, I knew that I couldn't count on any supernatural assistance. No amount of prayers would get us out of this mess. No fairy tale, superhero would come and rescue us; Two, I was on my own and I alone had to be the one to take action to save myself and Grace; Three, I didn't feel nearly as confident as I had in Nam. Fear of dying in Nam didn't bother me—though *how* I would die did. Dying in Nam was no big deal to me because it would end my mental pain and my sense of futility and hopelessness, but now I had much to live for. Mainly, I had Sam and Grace. I felt that Wolf's fierceness hadn't been diluted, just dormant, since I left the jungles of Nam. And, being honest with myself, I knew that my confidence had been shaken and sometimes fear did threaten to paralyze me, which made it hard to plan an escape. But, in mortal combat, over-confidence usually leads to unexpected death. I couldn't afford to be over-confident, nor could I afford to panic. I also knew that here, in the Adirondacks, with my daughter and me against three pre-Neanderthal savages, I wasn't as certain of my abilities, until my visions of "Roamin' Wolf" began to appear, as they had appeared almost every night in Nam. Those visions, plus my own combat skills, strengthened me and gave me hope for our survival. When the right time came, like in Nam, Wolf would have to run the show. His specialty was controlled violence, not random violence. I was Roman Wolfe with a "roamin' wolf" inside my mind, just waiting to be set free to do what it does with expertise . . . mete out sudden, violent death. Roamin' Wolf was made for the brutal violence of combat, for "do or die" situations, but I, Roman Wolfe, was Wolf's General. I gave the orders, the commands that called Roamin' Wolf into action. So the fourth thing I knew was that I needed to be thinking clearly, be alert, be decisive, but patient, and then call upon Roamin' Wolf's full arsenal of savage power at just the right time.

I thought, "What was it that Lord Fisher had once said about war?" Yes, I remember now. He said, in so many words, that the essence of war is violence and moderation in war is imbecility. And, may I add, "moderation" in war leads to certain defeat. That, of course, is how we lost the Vietnam War. We lost mostly because of our politician's and the president's use of "moderation," which equates to their own "imbecility." You don't win a war by not giving your best effort, by holding back, by being afraid to use your power, by being sissies in a land of savages. Therefore, the fifth thing that I knew was what Roamin' Wolf's violence could accomplish when it co-existed with my own martial arts skills. Wolf and Wolfe working together, with no inclination towards "moderation," would enable Grace and I to survive this ordeal. That was my belief; my lifeline for survival. So why did I still have doubts? It was a maddening thought; one that frustrated me.

Beliefs? They are formed in manifold ways, solidified by experience and serious thoughts. But once formed, primary beliefs are like an unmoving, unaltered island, while most other things in life flow and change with the changing currents that must flow around the island of primary beliefs.

I concentrated on gaining mental clarity. If Roamin' Wolf was the warrior and I, Roman Wolfe, was the General, as in Nam, then doubt and fear would have to be pushed aside. Who would have ever guessed that in the midst of all this Adirondack splendor, a very intimate and personal war was about to break out. I smiled and Roamin' Wolf's image snarled back at me. The friendly snarl was a great comfort to me, but not comfort enough to allow me to sleep.

Grace was asleep. As she slept, her body shook in disturbed spasms. She wasn't sleeping as peacefully as I had hoped. I listened, again, to the Gibsons' post-dinner conversation. Most of it was irrelevant, braggart, bullshit, but the part about Jake and Tom going out tomorrow morning to see if anyone had followed us and to set some animal traps, as well as to do some hunting for fresh meat, was interesting. Interesting because that would leave only Lester in the cabin to guard us. Then I could make my move to escape. Damn wonderful, I thought. We have to get out before the snow and frigid weather locked us into a tomb of ice, heavy snow fall, blustery winds and sub-zero temperatures.

Jake, Tom and Lester each checked and unloaded their shotguns. Jake double-checked Lester's shotgun. Then they leaned the empty rifles and shotguns near Jake's bunk bed, against the log wall. Jake went outside and put the ammunition someplace. He's real cautious, I thought. Not as stupid as he looks either. "Know your prey," Wolf growled to me.

Like I said, Jake took the lower bunk bed that was across the room from the one Grace and I slept on.

A thought suddenly burst into my mind, like an air bubble rising to the surface of the water, then popping. I knew that Tom would want to take the bunk bed that was above Grace and I. Lester needed to have his rape victims submissively under him in order to feel powerful and in control and Tom needed that same sort of feeling. He needed to have his victims pinned under him so he could stab and slash with his Bowie knife. This made him feel supremely powerful and in complete control, just like Lester, only Tom's actions were not related to rape, although just as sadistic and lethal. I wondered, again, how he got those scars on both of his cheeks. Were they deep scratches from female fingernails?

I thought, "Too many men denigrate or even brutalize women. Perhaps some men needed to feel physically more powerful that women because subconsciously they feel inferior and use their greater muscle mass to enforce their needed superiority. However, for the convenience and privilege of being able to piss while standing up, and usually being endowed with greater muscle mass, men get to labor harder, fight wars and die younger. Women, on the other hand, get to relax and think while they piss sitting down, so they get to be more thoughtful, safer, more relaxed and live longer. They are normally superior emotionally and intellectually, too. They also tend to be more sensible and reasonable. As if they weren't superior enough, they get to create life. Women are the creators of girls who, themselves will become women who can create life and of the boys who will become men. But those men are simply the guardians of the women and the lives that women can create. The only reason that women don't rule the world is that the world is still such a violent place, where the archaic proposition that "might is right" is still entrenched in the DNA of most men, myself included." I laughed at myself for this train of thought, then Tom's voice brought me back to the present.

"I'll take the bunk bed over the wimp and his girlie," Tom said, huskily. He grabbed his sleeping bag and blanket, then tossed them onto the bunk bed above Grace and I. I smiled to myself. Wolf says, "Know your prey," but more appropriate for me was, "Know your enemy," and I did know my enemy fairly well. They were easy to read.

That left Lester with the bunk bed above his dad. Before Lester got up into his bunk bed, Jake asked him to place several chunks of wood on the fire, which he did, then everyone settled into their bunk. Nobody was on guard duty. Was that a trick, or trap, or carelessness? I waited and wondered.

Then Jake growled, "I be a real light sleeper, Wimp. Yuh makes a move fer that door an' I gut yur girlie right befo' yur eyes. Yuh unnerstan'?"

"Yes. I understand perfectly," I said in my best hesitant, trembling voice, wanting to reinforce the "wimp" image in order to use it to my advantage later on. The 'wimp' had a few surprises planned for them. I was glad that Grace wasn't awake to hear Jake's threat.

I could feel the top bunk jiggling gently from Tom's laughter. I held Grace and kissed her softly on the cheek. I whispered, "Daddy loves you," then pressed my head into the pillow, staring, sleeplessly into the bottom of the top bunk's mattress. "Checkers, anyone?" I thought as I looked up at the checkered pattern of the ropes that served as bed springs.

I thought of the next day being November 18th. Good thing I had my watch with the year-long battery and the day and date indicators or I'd surely lose track of the date and time.

Tomorrow, November 18th, I thought, again. That meant that today was my father's-in-law birthday. Not a good day for a happy birthday, this year, I thought.

In my mind I could see Sam's face as she sat in tears at her mom's and dad's kitchen table. I could also see Mom's and Dad's sad faces clearly, just as I saw images of my sister, brother-in-law, nephews and niece. Their names drifted across my mind like cumulous clouds: Fran, Larry, Mark, Tony, Mike and Lori. Seeing their names was comforting to me.

Just before I drifted off to sleep, I wondered exactly how old Dad would be. I knew he was in his seventies, but not his exact age. Then I thought about being home for Thanksgiving, eating one of Mom's marvelous Thanksgiving dinners of turkey and ham, gravy, homemade dinner rolls, mashed potatoes, corn, cranberries, lettuce salad, pumpkin pie and a few other homemade goodies that always made Mom's Thanksgiving dinners so very special. My mouth watered as my mind wandered, and I thought that I should have said that I knew six things, not five. The sixth thing I knew was that the damn dinner soup didn't fill me. I was hungry for a jumbo bacon, cheese hamburger. I thought, "I'd gladly pay someone Tuesday for a hamburger today."

I dreamed about sitting next to Sam and Grace at Mom's and Dad's large dining room table, feeling happy, safe and comfortable, as I stuffed my face with warm, delicious food and exchanged warm, friendly glances and conversations with relatives and friends.

/../.-../- - -/....-/./..-./.-./.-/-./..-./.-./.-/.-./-.-./..../

Chapter 7

★★★★

Whispering Death

WHEN I AWOKE THE next morning, November 18th, I was somewhat surprised and disappointed with myself for how soundly I had slept. I told myself that, if I could get to sleep, to should sleep lightly, for Grace's sake. But that didn't happen. When I finally did fall asleep my body must have been so exhausted that it went into hibernation.

Then I remembered my silly, unexplainable dream, one of the most puzzling and confusing dreams that I've ever had. I dreamed that I flew with my legs straddling the spine of a giant book. The red front and back covers served as wings, the white pages hung down like a bird's torso and legs. I soared over the earth enjoying the earth's splendor, but then the pages that hung downward started dropping their black words, thousands at a time sliding off the pages, like bird-droppings, leaving a distinct ebony colored trail upon the earth. A few minutes later I landed the book, checked the pages and found all of them to be blank. I back-tracked the ebony trail and scooped up all the words, pushing them into my shirt, making the front of my shirt puff outward like a fat man's belly. Then I flew to a nearby lake, landed on the sandy beach, basked in the sunshine for awhile, then reassembled the words in the book by scooping them out of my shirt and pouring them between the pages, randomly. When I finished, the pages were full of organized words just like any normal book, but the story was totally different: different characters, different plot, different setting, different problems and different resolutions. It was as if I'd used most of the original book's words—some words worked there way down my pant legs and spilled onto the ground and were not used—to magically author a completely different and original novel. I didn't notice the original title of the book, nor did I see the new title of the re-worded book, though I did remember that the title on the spine of the original book was black while the title on the spine of the altered book was gold. As I strained over this conundrum, the new book spoke to me. It requested that I take another ride. I mounted the spine, soared to the highest mountain top and began to read the book that I'd magically authored with those magic, randomly selected and rearranged words.

The three main female characters came to vivid life for me. Sandra, Mara and Grace were their names, but the only familiar name was Grace. "Who were those other two characters? I wondered" They came to vibrant life in my dream, but it was as if that life was a past life, something that I knew and experienced, but had somehow forgotten. I had to ask myself, "How could I have possibly forgotten such caring, loving, memorable and remarkable people?" Was it a silly dream or a vision of a past life? Somehow, for some unknown reason, I felt as if I knew them, and yet I didn't, except for a girl with the same name as Grace. It was a mildly disturbing mystery that seemed to have a tight hold on me for a minute or two, then vanished.

As if reading my mind, the winged book flew above the clouds to some unknown region of the world that it called home. It was a library sitting on the very top of a high, snow-covered mountain, I know not where. I woke up then. I never did solved the meaning and mystery of that crazy dream.

Grace was still sleeping, her exhaustion kidnapping her physical and mental energy just as the Gibsons had kidnapped her body. I didn't know if it was light outside and didn't want to chance using the light in my watch to see what time it was. The cabin was dimly lit by the beginnings of a fire in the fire place. Dark shadows occupied the cabin's four corners as if dark and evil wraiths lurked there. I could hear the wood popping in the fireplace as the fire grew larger. When my eyes adjusted, the cabin seemed to brighten a little. I could hear the burning wood popping louder now, as if someone had thrown popcorn kernels into it. I guessed that the fire hadn't been started too long before I awoke.

I didn't want anyone to know that I was awake so I didn't attempt to look at my watch or turn my head or body to look—the fireplace was in the direction that was over my right shoulder—but I assumed that it was Jake who started the fire shortly before he awakened his sons. I thought that Jake had formed a decades old habit of rising early and getting his day started, just as he did when we were at his other Adirondack cabin.

I had been sleeping on my back with my head facing left, towards Grace and the cabin wall. Now, trying to be unnoticed, I slowly turned my head, to the right, towards the fireplace and the opposite cabin wall. I saw three shapes: small, tall and huge. Tom must have gotten down from the top bunk extremely quietly, or I had slept so soundly that I didn't feel or hear him descend from the top bunk. The realization, that I did, in fact, sleep so soundly, scared me. I had to be alert, sleeping lightly to protect Grace, yet during the night I had put us both in danger by sleeping much too soundly—I must have slept like a damn log if Tom could get down from his upper bunk and me not hear or feel his movement. Again, disappointment washed over me like a waterfall, giving me a cold chill.

The thought of him doing that, while I slept soundly, didn't sit well with me. It wouldn't have happened to Wolf. I knew that for certain. But Wolf wasn't in control . . . yet, and, so far, I couldn't set my figurative mongoose loose amongst the Gibsons: Jake, the cobra, Tom, the rattle shake, and Lester, the garden snake.

It was the conspiratorial whispering and Lester's loud giggling that caught my attention—and what must have awakened me. They must have thought that they were engaged in clever repartee as they huddled together. Jake did most of the whispering, but with Tom and Lester adding bits and pieces to Jake's ramblings. I saw Tom's and Lester's cupped hands go to their mouths, immediately followed by more muffled laughter. But not normal, joyful laughter. Rather, it seemed diabolical, as if Satan and his two minions were trying to quiet the sound of their cruel mirth before it echoed off the fiery halls of hell and alerted their next victims.

As they conspired, I thought about their ignorance and realized that the difference between intelligence and ignorance is simply that intelligence is finite, whereas ignorance is infinite. The proof lies with the Gibsons and all the doltish rubes like them. I couldn't imagine the Gibsons having any normal, genuine friendships. One can't expect genuine friendship and loyalty to survive amongst the poisonous tentacles of treachery and sadistic brutality.

Tom started to side-step and peek out at me from behind Jake's shoulder—Jake's back was toward me. I closed my eyes quickly, keeping my face muscles lax, and breathed softly as if I were still asleep. When I heard the continued whispering, I opened one eye slightly. Tom had returned to his former position in the family huddle. Although Jake's back was toward me, I saw his right hand go to his throat with only his index finger protruding from his fist. Then he made a slow, horizontal motion, a slash, across his Adam's Apple, with that index finger. "Tomorrow?" Tom asked in a whisper of joyful surprise. Jake's head bobbed up and down, affirmatively, a couple of times as Tom and Lester displayed their satanic smiles. Then Jake used that same index finger and held it perpendicular across his lips, combined with a *shhh* sound to have his boys be quiet.

My heart skipped a beat, lost its natural rhythm, and I felt like I was short of breath and suffocating. I heard a growl within me. It calmed me and allowed me to breathe normally, again. Wolf was still riding shotgun on my mental stagecoach. Yeah, Wolf, I thought, and where the hell were you last night. An internal growl was the only response.

As I clandestinely watched the Gibsons, I thought, "If there really was a God, like a Christian God, and if people were created in the image of God, then that God must be just as evil as He is good. Anything that had something to do with creating these three amoral maniacs, and the millions who are similar, or worse than them, had to, at the moment of their creation, been something truly unholy and a fiendishly evil mechanic of the universe." I speculated that, if there was a God he could never live on Earth. He'd be too embarrassed by His fatal mistakes and afraid of what He had created

Suddenly I realized that I was condemning myself, also, Wasn't I a murderous maniac in Nam? Perhaps that could be debated either way. Things are seldom as simple as they first appear to be. It always came back to the same postulate for me. The proven existence of God is not only unknown, scientifically, but, also, unknowable without crippling logic by striking it fatally with the baseball bat of blind faith. Perhaps that postulate isn't as simple as it appears to be either, but "blind faith"—which is a synonym for unreasonable or illogical faith—was the alternative, and that was too ridiculous for me to consider, especially in my present situation. Then I remembered what Benjamin Franklin stated about faith: "The way to see by faith is to shut the eyes of reason."

I knew that Jake's gesturing meant death for me, certainly, and probably for Grace, Tears formed in the corners of both my eyes. Then, in sadness and desperation, I wished that there actually was an all-good God who could come and at least save Grace. But, as usual, that fantasy vanished quickly from my mind, false hopes and false Gods couldn't help me, never did, never will. Feelings of weakness, helplessness, panic and doubt sometimes bring on useless thoughts like that.

My eyes moistened with emotion. I closed my eyes, but made no attempt at wiping the tears away. I didn't want to move; I needed to listen. My right eye's tear dripped off and landed on the mattress— there was no pillow—while the left eye's tear rolled down toward my nose, stopped momentarily at the junction of my nose and my cheek, then slowly ran down the crease of my nose to the left nostril. It continued to the left corner of my mouth and then down under my chin, leaving a warm trail of salty moisture on my flesh. I stopped any further tears from emerging while at the same time I felt myself going through a slow metamorphosis. The wolf was starting to emerge from its long slumber. My emotions hardened and commanded Wolf to remain silent and still. It obeyed. No time for tears and self-pity. The Gibsons thought I was a wimp, but I, and my "roamin' wolf," knew better. I felt strength and confidence slap away panic and doubt as I nearly laughed aloud at the irony of myself as a wimp. But it was good camouflage.

Then I tasted something coppery . . . blood. There was the taste of blood in my mouth. I wondered why? Must be something to do with Wolf. When I glanced at the Gibsons, I had a tremendous, unnatural urge to bite their neck and rip their throats out. I closed my eyes to block out the vision that would be the consequence of that feral urge.

Suddenly, while my eyes were closed, I felt a heaviness crushing my chest and stomach, while my arms were both pinned under the two wool blankets. When I snapped my eyes open, I saw that Tom had quietly approached the bunk bed and was pinning Grace and I down. I could only move my head and neck, my arms were trapped. I felt as if I were in a straight-jacket. I felt Grace squirming in panic, trying to free herself, screaming. As my eyes focused I saw Tom's scarred face grinning at me, real close, almost nose to nose, his foul, fetid breath, was like sewage pouring over my face. I struggled momentarily, then stopped as I felt the point of his blade stick into the soft, fleshy area below my Adam's Apple.

Grace continued screaming and thrashing, trying desperately to free herself.

The pressure of Tom's body on top of me made my throwing knife press deeply into my upper spine. I was thankful that it was sheathed. I could see Tom grinning as he lightly brought the cutting edge of his Bowie knife up in the air, then down, diagonally across my right cheek.

Grace managed to free her head, then stared in horror at Tom's knife. Her screaming intensified when she saw the blood flowing down my cheek. Her voice seemed far away, as if coming from the far end of a long tunnel. Her screaming continued as I felt the warm, moist droplets of my own blood running down my right cheek. The sound of Grace's screaming was only slightly interrupted by the loud laughter of all three Gibsons. I stared at Tom's laughing face as he removed his blade edge from my cheek and held it out in front of my eyes, about a foot away. The knife was like Jake's, more like a large butcher knife than a typical skinning knife used by hunters.

Then the crazed dolt started licking my blood from his knife, relishing it, lapping it up like a mad dog as he smiled demonically at the two of us.

Grace's screaming turned into crying and the tears flowed in abundance from her horror-stuck eyes. I thought, The most dangerous, cruel, heartless, amoral, unethical killer on the planet Earth was a creature that a mythical God supposedly created in his own image . . . man. And, at this moment, that's what I was, and if I could have, I would have killed Tom without mercy or a shred of compassion and certainly not an atom of sympathy. Perhaps I'm not all that different, just a slight DNA variation on the same Gibson-type theme, with a killer's impulses, a killer's knowledge and a killer's abilities—I wonder if there's a specific gene that controls the urge to kill?

I knew, of course, that Tom's actions were meant to terrorize me and Grace. Unfortunately, it had the desired effect on Grace. How could it not; she was only a little girl. But I had seen and even perpetrated much more ghastly horrors than what Tom had just done—when vital information was needed from the enemy to save American lives. No, the desired effect to terrorize me didn't work. It strengthened me. It made my "Roamin Wolf" more alert, tense, ready to spring and rip Tom's throat out, crushing his tender Adam's Apple as the gushing, and the spurting blood, from his severed carotid artery, formed a red geyser that arched, then splashed, to the ground near his feet. It was a horribly, bestial image, but totally satisfying in these circumstances.

I stared at Tom's grinning face, pretending to be helpless, terrified, acting like the wimp that he expected, as he held the blade closer to my face, after having just licked all the blood off of it. He pulled his face away from mine slowly, but continued to hold his blade about a foot from my eyes. We looked into each other's eyes as Grace's crying was reduced to helpless whimpering.

Grace put her left arm around my neck and buried her face into the soft area where my left shoulder and neck meet. Her crying became muffled and I could feel the slick wetness of her tears.

Tom pulled his knife away, turned it over and I saw some blood that he had missed. He licked it off as he had before, then said, "Pa taught me this trick." He pointed to the scars on his own cheeks with his left hand, his crazed Charlie Manson eyes glowing with hatred and near madness.

"Pa says if yuh want someone to obey yuh, yuh got to make 'im fearful of yuh. An' what better way to make someone fearful than pinning him down, holding a knife to his throat, then slicing his cheek so he thinks about what else could be done to 'em, real easy like. An' he feels the fear every time he be seein' or feelin' that scar. An' if yuh don't think he fears yuh enough, well then, naturally yuh cut 'im again, only deeper. An' if he don't obey, or he does something wrong, yuh just give him another slice . . . or maybe you do it to his kin." Tom looked evilly at Grace. She pressed herself against me to feel some sort of security, security that I had failed to provide for her.

Tom continued, "I know how it works 'cause Pa done it to me four times, so I know how its works. Yuh be scarred now, Wimpy. An' yuh will do what yur told, won't yuh?"

Damn! That's incredible. He's even talking like his dad, but not quite as bad, I thought.

I responded quickly, keeping Wolf in check. "Yes. I will do anything you say. I'll try not to do anything wrong." I spoke in my meekest voice. After I answered him, he smiled, then he sat up on the bunk. I could feel the pressure of his weight lessen on my chest. I took a deep breath, then tried to comfort Grace with a grin and a hug, though it was difficult to grin for more than a couple seconds because of my rage. Trying to smile made sharp pains in the back of my neck and head.

I could feel Grace trembling with fear. I hugged her closer, then whispered, "We'll get away. I have a plan." I hoped that I was correct. She needed hope and I offered it readily, but hoping that I wasn't giving her false-hope. Lying isn't always bad, no matter how many times fools tell you that it is. It doesn't take an explanation to know that that's true, it just takes common-sense thought and a minimum of reasoning.

Tom stood up all the way, as Jake and Lester came over to the bunk. They chuckled like Neanderthals; Jake more so than any of them. He must have been proud of what he perceived as Tom's bravery and toughness and, perhaps, even his comparable, mountain man speech pattern.

I wondered how a father could slice his son's cheeks with a blade just to teach him to fear and obey. I thought, even my doctor would go crazy if he had these three for patients. How did they slip through the cracks of a sane society? Know your enemy, I thought, again.

Apparently I didn't know my enemy as well as I thought I did because I would never have expected any father to treat his son like that, not even Jake. But I was learning about my enemies, and each thing I learned about them prepared me to defeat them by knowing how they thought and predicting what they'd do and how they'd act. I was learning fast by asking myself constant questions, then searching for answers. That's important to me. People expect teachers to be geniuses; have all the answers. But, in my opinion, it's not knowing all the answers that would make a smart teacher, or any person, it's knowing the right questions to ask of his students, questions that will lead them to the answers. Telling students the answers will make them smart enough to pass the tests, but asking the right questions that motivate students to search for the answers will last a life time. And, in many cases, the teacher learns right along with the student. The teacher should be used as a valuable resource like an encyclopedia, dictionary, thesaurus and not as a depository for all the answers.

I could feel myself push Wolf away, temporarily, so I could be a dutiful father to Grace. This quick, smooth transformation pleased me because I now realized that I possessed the concentrated control to change from "Roamin' Wolf" to Roman Wolfe whenever the occasion called for that change, like two cooperating, identical twins taking turns at completing the same job, each doing the part of that job that he is best suited for, or, perhaps, Wolf and I were more like Jekyll and Hyde. I don't know.

I drew Grace closer to me, stroked her hair and kissed her forehead. These actions assuaged her screaming and crying, but my heart—a loving father's heart—was punctured with pain and my head ached as if a stroke was inevitable.

Jake said, "Me an' me boy, here,"—he placed his right hand on Tom's shoulder—has ta go out an' do some huntin' an' fishin' after breakfas'. Lester, here, he be guardin' yuh." Now Jake placed his left hand on Lester's shoulder and stood between his two sons, smiling. This made his large body look like an unbalanced cross, with his right arm only slightly bent down onto Tom's shoulder, but his left arm bent way down to reach Lester's much lower shoulder.

He continued to talk to me, "An' I espects yuh ta be behavin' yerself. Yuh be tied up ta the bed, a course, and yur girlie"—he removed both hands from his son's shoulders and pointed to Grace with his right index finger—"she don' needs ta be tied up if'n yuh don' cause any trouble fer Lester"—Jake tipped his head towards Lester. "Does we have a deal?"

I removed the blankets from Grace and I, thankful to escape their heat and confinement, sat up in the bunk bed with my feet touching the floor. I placed Grace on my lap, her arms still around my neck and her head against my chest, and said, "Yes. We have a deal," I lied, knowing that in matters of life and death, lies can often save lives or extend them, at least.

But it wasn't me that I felt smiling. It was something inside of me, a wolfish grin, so to speak. My outward face was frozen in sadness and determination to survive, with Grace uninjured.

This might be the best chance for our escape as the weakest member of the Gibsons would be left to guard us, and Grace wouldn't be tied up. It seemed like *now or never*. This looked like the perfect opportunity for our escape. I just had to act meek, weak and wimpy— the image they wanted to believe—until both "Roamin' Wolf" and Roman Wolfe attacked.

I felt my left cheek, where I had been cut. The cut was scabbed over with dried blood and felt crusty. I could tell that it wasn't a severe cut. It would probably only leave a faint scar, if any at all. It felt like a superficial, thin line of rough sand paper to my touch, but it still triggered a deep-seated anger that smoldered inside of me, an anger that had been dormant since I was prowling in the jungles of South Vietnam . . . when Roamin' Wolf and Roman Wolfe were nearly one and the same.

Then I wondered why Tom hadn't cut me more deeply, as his dad had apparently cut him. Not enough practice, perhaps? Tom was only a novice with a blade, while, unknown to them, I was a wizard with a blade. I had learned the more sophisticated knife-fighting techniques from a friend who was a hand-to-hand combat instructor for the Navy Seals—I didn't want to be in the Special Forces, originally, but if I had to join one and had a choice, it would be the Navy Seals. My Seal friend taught me how to do seemingly miraculous things with a combat knife, as if it were a magic wand in a wizard's hand. Presto, slash, flash, gushing blood, death.

The fireplace hadn't thoroughly warmed-up the cabin yet, which was great for Grace and I because it gave us the perfect excuse to keep our coats on during breakfast. We were both starved due to the lack of a filling dinner the night before. Canned potatoes and canned meat mixed together and fried in a cast iron frying pan in the fireplace wasn't my idea of an acceptable breakfast either, but my stomach felt empty, and so must Grace's. We ate what we were given, which wasn't much. At least we were given something to keep our strength up. All through the meal I noticed Lester taking what he thought were secret glimpses at Grace, then smiling with a lewd twinkle in his eyes. He'd quickly look down at his tin plate while chewing his food, swallow, then smile as if he were getting away with something mischievous.

Grace and I finished before the others—we weren't given as much to eat. Jake and Tom ate enough for ten, so it took them longer to finish. Lester didn't eat much more than Grace and I, but then he was only a tiny little shit.

We sat quietly, my arm around Grace's waist. I looked into her eyes, the sadness and fear almost defeated me, but I could feel the growing feral strength of Wolf inside of me. I smiled at Grace, trying to give her hope, but she was unable to smile back, her fear being too great. Then I felt the pressure of both my blades pressing against the flesh under my left armpit and below the nape of my neck. That gave me the feeling of hope and the comforting warmth that came from it.

I saw Jake's arm rise from the table, his dirty right index finger point to our bunk as he said, "Over ta yur bunk, mister."

"Mister?" I thought. "What happened to Wimpy?" Then, I'm not sure why, I said, "My name's Roman and this is my daughter, Grace."

"Don' care 'bout that!" Jake snarled. "Wimpy an' Girlie is good 'nough fer me an' me boys. Now git over ta yur bunk an' sits yur asses down."

Grace and I obediently walked over to the bottom bunk bed and sat on it. Then I was told to sit by the end bed post, the bottom of which was buried into the ground while the top was securely attached to a thick roof beam. Tom then came and tied my feet together at the ankles. "Nice cowboy boots," he said as he grinned up at me. "Hey, Pa," Tom said, "Wimpy, here, thinks he be a cowboy. Ain't that a hoot, Pa? I do like 'is boots."

"He mus' be one a does tall, skinny, sissy cowboys, huh?" Jake laughed with his sons, then sucked air through his teeth so hard that it sounded like a whistle. That irritating sound echoed in my ears and made me want to reach out for Tom's head, grab his hair with one hand, grab his chin with the other hand, then suddenly and violently twist to break his neck. I wanted to do it so badly, that I felt as if my muscles were getting ready to do it without my permission. It took a focused effort to stop myself. It would only get us both killed immediately. I wrapped an iron fist around my emotions and waited for my opportunity to escape with Grace.

Jake said, "I bets yuh wish does boots was yers, huh, Tom?"

"Yeah, Pa. Sure do look good," Tom replied as he smiled up at his dad, then began tying my wrists in back of me. Tom wound the rope around my wrists and started the knot, but Jake grabbed the ropes and pulled with force, pulling the knots so tightly that they dug into my skin, cutting off the flow of blood to my fingers and abrading the skin under the rope.

I could sense the searing heat of the pale wolf stirring within me as I wondered if the ropes were tied so tightly because they were never intended to come off.

Jake checked the ropes and knots, was satisfied, then pulled the rope, and my arms along with it, to the bunk bed post giving me only three or four feet of slack so I could sit in the middle of the bunk, but couldn't move away from it very far. As I sat there, I realized that the ropes tying my ankles were not nearly as tight as the one around my wrists. Also, the rope tying my ankles went around my cowboy boots. I thought I could take the boots off to free my feet, if I had time and the opportunity.

My thoughts drifted to the superficial cut on my cheek as well as the ropes binding my ankles and wrists. Tom had only cut my cheek superficially, and didn't tie my ankles as tightly as he could have. That made me wonder if Tom simply wasn't as ruthless as his father, even though he pretended to be. If so, then his act was a lot better than Lester's, but Tom's actions gave him away. I wondered if, maybe, there was some small kernel of decency within him that he was loath to admit or show outright. Did it show in the superficial cut that could have been so much deeper and the tied ankles which could have been so much tighter? Not that he was a kind, considerate, young gentleman, just not as severely warped and ruthless as he pretended and that his dad expected him to be. Tom might have turned out a lot better if he didn't have such a bad model and mentor in his father, and if he wasn't so desperate to please Jake by being just like him. But I doubt that his life was redeemable.

Grace sat next to me as I was being tied. When the ropes were tied, she slid over to me and put her head on my shoulder. She sat there frozen in her own icy fear and there was nothing I could say to her at the moment that could comfort her. She just stared at my hands and feet with pearls of tears occasionally running from her nose and eyes. I didn't know how much more of this she could take. Too much prolonged fear was debilitating and she had just about reached her limit.

"Now yuh behaves yerself, Girlie, and' yuh listens ta what Lester, here, tells yuh. Yuh unnerstan' that?" Jake's voice growled at Grace and she shrank back against me, the fear stiffening her eight year old body. She tried to answer Jake, but her lips parted only slightly as her voice died inside her throat. I could hear her swallow hard as she grabbed my coat and pulled herself into me.

Jake bellowed, "Well, Girlie, does yuh 'ear me? Answer me!"

I opened my mouth to answer for her but she spoke up in a very low, hesitant, trembling and terrified voice, like a mouse in the jaws of a cat. She cleared her throat and responded, "Yes sir, Mr. Gibson. I hear you."

"Essellent," Jake beamed, obviously proud of the "sir," or the "Mr." or both. Then his mouth hissed as he sucked air through his teeth. It was as if a hissing snake lived in his mouth. He must have had some meat jammed between his teeth.

Tom's eyes bore into mine. I could feel his hatred. It was palpable, the kind of boiling hatred that brews when a maniac needs to prove something. Tom was learning his lessons all too well. Tom was using me as a tool to prove to his dad that he was tough and mean, and every bit as vicious as his old man, in order to finally earn his dad's respect. I could see, in his eyes, the need to kill me in order to be like Jake and to have Jake treat him like an equal. Equally mad, I thought, in the mental health sense of the word, *mad*.

Then I noticed Lester's gaze boring into Grace. It was no secret what Lester had planned for her, but it was a secret what the Roamin' Wolf had in store for him if he tried to touch her.

During that private thought, Grace held me tightly, not saying a word, just looking down toward my roped feet as she trembled. I was thankful for this because she didn't see Lester's probing eyes searching her young body.

Jake and Tom got dressed warmly, took their shotguns in hand, then walked outside to get their ammunition and go hunting. However, only a few seconds after they departed, the door opened and Jake came back inside the cabin. Jake walked to the gun rack to check the padlock on the three high powered rifles. He grinned at me and said, "Cain't never be too careful," and walked back to the door, where he paused. He ordered Lester to put his coat on, to grab his shotgun and to step outside. Apparently he wanted to talk to him without us hearing what he had to say, and he wanted to make sure that Lester's shotgun was properly loaded and properly functioning so Lester would have it when guarding us.

There being no windows in the cabin, and the door being closed, meant that no one could see Grace and I either. That was careless of Jake; something I had not expected, but was mighty good luck for us.

/- -/.-/.-./-.-/..-./.-././-./-.-/.....///.././...../-/./.-./.-./.././..-./../-.-./

Chapter 8

★★★★

Escape

MY ALERTNESS OVERWHELMED ME like an overdose of a "stay awake" drug when I, once again, willed Wolf to enter my mind—two heads are better than one. I could feel the blood surge into my brain and muscles, like a military, special-forces, combat unit put on maximum alert. My mind, and Wolf's, raced through strategies, paused, then became crystal clear, no lingering doubts concerning what to do next, just a determined, precise plan of action. I felt a surge of strength, a strength beyond my lean, six feet two inches, one hundred eight-five pound frame. It was Wolf's strength, plus the determined, action-oriented, decisive strength of a disciplined warrior, a hunter, an assassin. As I remained submerged in Wolf's persona, I couldn't help but marvel at the two merged personalities that now inhabited my body. I was thankful that, at this moment, the warrior and Wolf were inseparable partners.

I sniffed the air. My fur—hair—tingled at the roots and I felt a sudden urge to be on my hands and knees, like a wolf.

"Grace," I whispered with my lips touching her ear—Grace thought she detected a change in my voice and an animal smell to my breath—"quickly reached down my back, just inside my collar, unsnap the strap, took the knife out of the sheath and put it into my hands. Quickly, now," I spoke with an urgent emphasis on the word 'quickly.'

"The knife, Daddy?" Grace whispered in a confused sounding voice.

"Yes, Sweetheart, my throwing knife. You've seen me practice with throwing knives in the cellar. I carry one of them inside my back collar. No more questions. Get it quickly and put it into my hands before anyone comes back. The point is very sharp. Be careful, but hurry," I said, even more urgently.

I leaned forward and Grace reached down the back of my neck as she thought: "I didn't know Daddy carried a knife here."

I stared at the cabin door, nervously, desperately hoping that Grace could get the knife to me before anyone re-entered the cabin and caught her.

Suddenly, and with great relief, I felt the warmth and smoothness of the metal. The warmth of my back had made the knife feel almost hot. The blade was smooth, hard, double-edged, as sharp as a razor and as dangerously pointed as a dagger. It was one, long, smooth instrument of death; a poor man's bullet. I kept all my knives just as sharp as I had in Vietnam. When I was in the jungle for extended periods of time, I shaved with my knives.

The edges on throwing knifes aren't typically sharpened because it's the point that is of paramount importance. But I knew that I may need to use it like a combat knife, in emergencies, so I always honed it very carefully until it was razor sharp on each edge, about three inches up from the point.

It is extremely difficult to quickly judge distances so that the point would stick straight into an object. More than likely, in actual combat use, the perfect distance for the spinning knife to enter point first wouldn't exist. In that case, the forcefully thrown blade would strike with one edge parallel to the object. If that object was human flesh, then the razor sharp edges would slash deeply into the flesh, although not as lethally deep as the point would have penetrated. Although this type of wound, caused by the edge of the knife, wasn't usually fatal, it could be a tremendous psychological blow to the victim due to the length of the wound and the amount of blood that would pour from it, especially if it severed a large, superficial vein or veins.

"Grace," I whispered, "I think that something bad is going to happen. I think Lester is going to"—

The cabin door opened before I had a chance to finish. Lester closed the door and whistled merrily as he casually walked to the table with his loaded 20 gauge shotgun. He sat down and smiled smugly at Grace. His hubris was at a peak. He had such a cocky, arrogant and confident smile plastered to his face that I wondered what Jake had said to him. Wolf and I stared intently back at him, trying to divert his attention, but Lester only had eyes for Grace.

When Lester's eyes did shift to me, the contact was only momentary. He looked away quickly, which was a sign of weakness, anxiety, and false confidence. As if he knew that he had showed weakness, Lester's arrogant smile evaporated and his eyes started blinking rapidly, as if defending himself against Wolf's intense glare. Lester's eyes then shifted to look around the room. I could see the self-doubt wash over him like high tide over low land; his hubris dissolving, like a sugar cube in water.

It was approximately 7:00 A.M. when Jake and Tom left the cabin. I couldn't see my watch, it being on my left wrist, behind my back. But I was aware of the approximate time from having checked my watch prior to being tied up.

Lester checked and double checked his weapon. Either he was being extra cautious, or he didn't know enough about shotguns to know what the hell he was doing . . . maybe both. Of course, maybe he knew exactly what he was doing—I told myself that I shouldn't underestimate him as he, Jake and Tom were underestimating me. Perhaps all that clicking on and off of the trigger safety mechanism was his way of intimidating me. And, in all honesty, I must admit that it worked. But it was more irritating than intimidating, like Jake's teeth sucking habit. I guessed that this may be the Little Shit's way of letting me know who was in charge; who had the power.

But, looking at him closely, it was difficult to see him as the person *in charge*. He looked too frail, weak and puny, with feminine, delicate facial features, yet I could see in his eyes that he reveled in the masculine power that he was now experiencing. His eyes were like those of a half-starved animal—I didn't want to say *half-starved wolf* and Wolf knew it. I heard his growl in my inner ear—who finally sights the prey that will serve as its long-sought-after dinner. There was an intense hunger in Lester's eyes, but not for food, and I half expected to see him drooling while he, once again, stared at Grace. A few seconds later, he spoke.

"They won't be back 'til around noon, maybe later, so we might as well get to know each other better. What's your name?" he said, looking at me.

"Roman Wolfe," I answered, laconically, wanting to tell him that kids address me as 'Mr. Wolfe,' but that would only make our situation worse. Lester's speech, grammar and pronunciation was so much better than Jake's and Tom's—he must have had more schooling, maybe even speech-therapy.

"Roman," Lester repeated, with a curious expression, followed by "Wolfe," then another curious expression. "Roman? Like Roman soldiers?"

"Yes. I'm named after the capital of Italy, Rome," I replied.

"Funny name. How'd yuh get it?"

"When my parents got married, they spent their honeymoon in Rome. They believed that I was conceived there. So when I was born, they named me Roman, which, in Latin, means 'a person from Rome,'" I explained.

"An' Wolfe? Sounds dangerous," Lester said, with a sarcastic twist to his lips.

"Yeah. Dangerous," I replied, wanting to show him just how dangerous I could be. "My great grandparents thought so, too. They changed the name when they immigrated to America from Germany. To make the name less offensive to American sensibilities, they changed their original name from Wolfanger, like an 'angry wolf,' to Wolfe. It's Wolf with an '*e*' at the end. I don't know why they added the '*e*' at the end. It's W-O-L-F-E," I spelled, emphasizing the final letter "E."

"Wow! Even more dangerous. Angry wolf, huh? Guess yuh really are a scary guy You ever feel like an angry wolf?" Lester asked, with furrowed brow, mocking eyes and a teasingly, sarcastic smile full of crooked, yellowish teeth.

"You have no idea," I answered cryptically.

"Wow! You must be one awesome and dangerous mystery." Lester replied, with another smile that was too insincere to reach his eyes.

"You haven't a clue," I stated.

"You said that already, Wimpy. Oh! Sorry. It must be 'Mr. Wolfe,' with an 'E,' right?"

"Yeah, kids address me as 'Mr. Wolfe,'" I replied with unconcealed disdain—which was a mistake that I knew I should not have committed.

"I'm no damn kid, Asswipe!" he yelled.

I covered my previous mistake by saying, "I apologize. I shouldn't have said that. You're a man, not a kid. Sorry."

The apology appeased his anger, thankfully, and he continued with his questions.

"And your daughter?. What's 'er name?"

"My daughter's name is Grace," I stated, feeling my blood getting hotter with anger.

"Pretty girl. Bet she's real smart, too, huh?" Lester stated.

I nodded my head as I replied, "Yes." I was barely able to keep a calm face while listening to his ludicrous attempts to be deviously sincere and genuine.

"How old are you, Grace?" Lester asked.

Grace looked at me as if to ask permission to respond. I nodded to her.

"I'll be nine soon," Grace said.

Lester smiled and said as a joke, "Amazing Grace. You any relation to her?"

I guess he thought he was being cute and clever, but Grace didn't smile. She just said, "No," then looked at me, then down at the floor.

Lester and I stared at each other for a moment, but didn't speak—I tried not to show my contempt for him. During all the previous, idle chit-chat I had been trying desperately to cut the rope with the throwing knife, but it was much more difficult than I had expected. My wrists were bound so tightly as to prevent almost any movement and my fingers were getting numb and tingly from the poor blood circulation. I curled my fingers and placed the knife edge on the rope, but I could hardly apply any pressure to the blade. Indeed, it was difficult enough just trying to bend my wrists and fingers, but I was glad for the delay that Lester's questions offered.

Unexpectedly, Lester's eyes sparkled with new-found confidence. It surprised me. His frozen stare cracked into a smile that appeared as cold as a snowman's smile. Then the smile melted, but his eyes remained cold, ominous, like the tip of an iceberg, warning of the unseen danger below it. He said to Grace, "Come over here, Grace," as he clicked on the safety button, then set the shotgun down on the table.

"I want to stay by my daddy," Grace said with a tremble of fear in her voice.

"You can go right back to your daddy. Just come here for a minute, okay?" he said, pretending to be polite, calm and friendly.

I could feel Wolf snarling, baring his teeth, and the feeling was so real that I thought I actually felt my own lips parting and my own teeth growing pointed and elongated, canine fashion. My heart rate soared as I frantically kept cutting at the rope. The razor edge was making more progress now; I could feel some severed strands. I kept cutting, but with an impatience that was hard to control. Beads of sweat were forming under and on my arms, then they started rolling downward hitting each strand of hair they met, making me feel like insects were crawling all over my arms. I felt sweat trickling down my spine. My forearm muscles bunched up, my tendons grew taut and my bent wrists burned and ached, begging for relief from the cramped straining and poor circulation and the abrasions caused by the coarse rope.

The cabin grew so quiet that I was afraid that the sound of the knife cutting the rope would be heard. Tension was building in all of us, like a taut banjo wire stretched to its limit and ready to snap. Lester's face got redder and his fingers were white as they tightly gripped the edge of the table where he sat. His teeth were clenched and his lips were slowly separating to show his yellowish teeth as he was about to roar with impatient anger. It was inappropriate for our situation but I couldn't stop myself from thinking how excited a dentist would be to see the three Gibsons, with their crooked, yellowish-brown teeth, walk into his office. In the dentist's eyes the yellow teeth would look like gold nuggets.

Grace moved closer to me, her fear evident in her rapid breathing and her fidgeting actions. Her eyes caught mine, trapped them in a gaze of helplessness, but all I could do was keep rubbing the blade against the rope and wait until it was severed.

It's humiliating, embarrassing, traumatic and shameful for a father not to be able to help his daughter in a moment of utterly, desperate need. I would have screamed with rage, but it wouldn't extricate me from my bindings, so why waste the effort. Actually, my screaming would probably excite him even more—sadism and masochism working as partners within his addled brain. My wrists and fingers burned from the exertion. I knew that my wrists were rubbed raw and were bleeding from the abrasions caused by the tightness and coarseness of the rope. And, yet, all I could do at the moment was whisper to Grace, "Stay close to me."

Lester sounded like his father as he shattered the silence, causing Grace and I both to flinch. "God damn yuh, cunt! Get yur sweet, little ass over 'ere now or I'll blow yur daddy's funkin' head off!" Lester stretched out the word *now* for exaggerated effect. Spittle erupted from his gaping mouth.

Grace threw her arms around my neck and the resulting jolt made the knife slip off the rope and cut my wrist. I felt the sharp sting of it, but doubted that it was serious. My first thought was that the blood might make my wrists and the rope slick enough for me to slip out of the binding, but that quickly turned out to be a false hope. The rope was too tight.

Lester picked up the shotgun, clicked off the safety button, then pointed it at Grace, then more calmly said to me, "Tell 'er to get 'er sweet ass over 'ere or yer guts will become wall paper."—When he got mad his speech became more like his dad's and brother's.

"Daddy, Daddy, please help me," Grace cried softly as she buried her face in my neck.

"Grace," I said, urgently, "get on the bunk bed and crawl behind me, fast."

When Grace did that, Lester threatened to kill both of us.

"I seriously doubt that," I yelled. "Your father will kill you if you shoot us. He's that kind of man and you know it." I sure hoped my bluff was right. It was a damn, risky gamble.

Then the little asshole did something that I didn't anticipate. He rushed over at me and slammed the butt of the gun into my head before I could try to kick him. I was semi-conscious, but, in a few seconds, when my head cleared, Lester had Grace.

Lester was laughing hysterically and inattentive. It was one of the hardest things I ever had to do when I got Grace's attention and mouthed the words, "I need more time to cut the rope."

I saw her tremble, then she looked at me like a child would look at a fallen, shattered, and destroyed super-hero who is no longer invulnerable. I guess that's what I was right then. I was a big, brave, ruthless killer of the enemy in the jungles of Vietnam, now reduced to a helpless wimp in the forests of the Adirondack Mountains. I felt the ultimate in disgusting shame and humiliation, as if I was volunteering my daughter for the purposes of sexual molestation. My guts knotted, my stomach churned and I nearly vomited. My head throbbed as if there was an ice-pick driven into it. My rampaging guilt almost caused me to lose eye contact with Grace. Then I heard the growl of Wolf. It forced me to focus, and I continued, with new energy, applying pressure to the blade. I felt more frayed, severed strands of the rope, but didn't have good enough feeling in my fingers to know how far I'd cut into the rope.

Grace's sad, disappointed, almost catatonic-looking, tear-filled eyes broke from mine as she turned to look at Lester.

With Grace standing in front of him, Lester grinned while saying, "I needs a little pussy to play with. Know what I mean?" he stated, rhetorically. "No? Then I'll be teachin' yuh." Another cruel grin spread across his face like that of a man who's holding a royal flush in a high-stakes poker game. But it wasn't the smile I remembered most; it was those crazed, Charlie Manson eyes, similar to black, powder-burned, bullet holes.

I heard Grace sniffle and saw her wipe her sleeve across her runny nose.

My fingers were working furiously, my face hot with rage as I tried to buy time by roaring, "What's the matter, Shorty? Are you puny and weak like you're mommy? You're short and weak like your mommy instead of big and strong like your daddy and brother, aren't you? Is that why you hate women? You're too weak even to subdue normal women aren't you, you little bastard! That's why little girls become easy prey for you, isn't it?—I kept cutting the rope. You feel really big and strong hurting little girls who can't fight back, don't you? You're an animal that needs killing, you son-of-a-bitch! What do you say, Shorty? Am I right about you being so disgustingly pathetic? I'm right on the money, right?"

A quiet pause as he looked at Grace. Then, "Yeah, Asshole!" he screamed furiously, out of control, his face turned red, his arms pumping, "I am a animal. I'm the animal that's gonna rape yur little girlie right in front a yur big, fuckin' eyes. Pa says yur dead, anyway, as soon as they git back. He's going to let me rape her then, anyway, but I decided ta do it now. An' Tom, he gets to kill yuh any way he likes. Fuck it! Why should I be waitin' till they git back? I make my own decisions, not them. So, Mr. Roman Wolfe, with a 'e,' while I fuck yur daughter, I'll be happily listening ta yuh screamin' at me." His voice grew more calm. "Makes it better for me that way, yuh know? You screaming an' her crying and thrashing around. It'll all make me come sooner an', who knows, Mr. Wimpy, I may even do it again, you know, like having a second helping of tasty dessert. An' for more fun, I may even blow your fuckin' head off an' make her lick the blood and brains off the wall." His exaggerated calmness was disturbingly haunting as it filled every inch of space in the cabin, like water that fills every corner of an aquarium.

Abruptly, he began laughing like a mad-man. He continued his orders, but he was no longer calm. He shrieked at Grace, "Come 'ere, bitch!" I felt a ringing in my ears like one gets with high blood pressure, or from uncontrollable rage. My heart raced out of control; almost exploding out of my heaving chest. I felt short of breath and started panting, but didn't stop cutting the rope. Keep cutting, keep cutting, I told myself.

Though I felt out of breath, my fingers were working feverishly, dragging the blade back and forth across the strands of rope. I thought I felt many more frayed ends, but I figured that I was only about half way through the rope. I felt panic, as if a whale were trying to swallow me, but I kept cutting.

I kept dragging the blade across the rope, back and forth, back and forth, as my bleeding, abraded wrists ached and my fingers danced with painful muscle spasms, causing me to almost drop the knife. The blood flow must have stopped because I didn't feel any sticky wetness now.

Lester clicked on the shotgun's safety button, leaned the shotgun against the table, then buried his fingers into Grace's hair and dragged her closer to the table.

"Take off all yur clothes . . . 'cept yur panties," he barked. Grace's eyes flashed with terror and for the first time I think she knew what Lester was going to do to her. She turned her head, her terrorized eyes pleading with me for help. I was always there to help her before. She needed me desperately now, more than ever before, but I couldn't move . . . not yet. I couldn't help her, yet. It was terrifying for her and agony for me, as my stomach tightened up into a painful knot and my guts coiled tightly and moved about like a sack full of angry snakes.

Tears of outrage soaked my eyes as Lester slapped Grace repeatedly while yelling, "Take off yur clothes! Get 'em off now, God damn it!"

Grace turned her head away from me, slowly unzipped her coat and let it fall to the floor. She was in shock, her movements were in slow-motion. Her cheeks were as red as ripe strawberries from being slapped repeatedly.

I needed a little more time—I could feel more and more frayed rope. I hoped Grace would continue to undress very slowly, pause, stop, delay, give me the extra time that I desperately needed. My vision was blurred with tears. I sensed that Grace wasn't really undressing slowly to give me extra time. It was happening for another reason. My innocent and precious little girl stood there in a state of lethargic shock and terror. Her tears rolled down her cheeks, then off her chin like rain drops off a roof.

My throat emitted a growl. My teeth involuntarily snapped as if I were biting air. My ears were so sensitive that I could actually hear each strand of rope separate as I cut through it. I could smell my own dried blood and feel the burning heat of my abraded wrists. It was all due to Wolf's presence. Wolf's strength and fierceness were supporting me as my painfully, bloody wrists found new strength—I had cut myself again in my fervor to cut through the rope. I didn't care how badly I cut myself. I had to free myself quickly to save Grace from Lester's intentions.

Wolf was emerging. My skin itched like a bushy beard itches, my teeth ached and felt as if they had grown longer, and my muscles felt like taut springs ready to snap. All my human senses became hyper-sensitive.

I worked feverishly at the rope. I felt and heard strand after strand give way faster and faster. Sweat dripped down my forehead, burning my eyes. I squinted and blinked rapidly to rid the salty sting, but my mind remained focused on the object of my rage. If looks could really kill, Lester would have been dead already.

Faster and faster I worked . . . I cut myself once more, but paid no attention to the pain. I kept cutting and cutting and felt the amount of severed rope grow larger.

I expected Lester to tear into Grace's clothes, to rip them from her body. It totally surprised me when he didn't. He just stood there, smiling at Grace, then at me, as Grace lethargically removed her shirt, then her pants, boots and then her socks. I thought: "Lester must frequent strip-clubs and gets erotic pleasure from clothing being slowly removed, one piece at time; bare flesh exposed, little by little, titillating and teasing.

Lester's extreme joy was a direct measure of the extent of his depravity. Then I admonished myself for thinking like a dunce, then thought: "Of course he wouldn't attempt to rip off Grace's clothes." He wanted Grace and the other girls he'd raped, to feel the added humiliation that came from assisting him to rape them. He wanted his victims to feel that they had assisted him in his act of abominable, abusive violence, by making them take off their own clothes. That would make it seem as if they were preparing themselves for him, thus, sharing in the act of violence, which, in a sense, made them a partner to the crime against themselves and would later increase their mental anguish ten-fold. If this was a conscious effort on Lester's part, then he was a worse fiend than I had previously thought, and more cunning, too. None-the-less, the fiend's strategy would give me more time..

Wolf's strength doubled my own strength and now the knife was making fast progress. I guessed that nine-tenths of the rope had been cut through, but it was hard to concentrate as I saw my innocent little girl take off her pants slowly, and then her shirt. Lester stared at her like some vile animal ready to pounce as she stood in front of him wearing only her panties . . . and a flowing veil of tears.

I tried to yell at Lester to distract him, but he paid no attention to me, though I heard him snicker. His total concentration was on Grace as he soothingly said, "That's a good girl. You've done a good job helping me. I see you have your pretty panties on, Honey. That's good 'cause I wanna cut them off myself." After saying that, Lester slipped into a childish giggle, then waited for Grace's reaction.

Grace stood in front of Lester, seemingly semi-conscious, motionless and in shock, frozen in terror.

My wrists ached so badly I could hardly move them and my fingers had gone almost completely numb, but I thought I could feel a good-sized lump of frayed rope. I desperately wanted to pull apart the remaining strands, but I didn't have the strength. I continued cutting.

Grace now stood in front of Lester naked, except for her panties. She turned her head to look at me. Her lips trembled out of control as tears continued to steam steadily out of both eyes.

I heard Lester laughing. The rage within me made my head feel like it would explode.

Lester looked at me and said, "Ready for the sex show, Mr. Wolfe, with an 'e'?

Then I heard a howl, that was so loud and anger-filled that it shook the roof; fill every corner of the cabin. It was me screaming at Lester, begging Lester to stop, to hurt me instead, to punish me, not Grace.

"But I am hurting you," Lester said arrogantly as he laughed, taunting me in my helplessness.

Grace's eyes were begging one last time for me to save her. She spoke almost inaudibly, "Papa. I love you." she said in a terrified monotone. Then she looked away from me and entered what looked like a state of catatonic, motionless silence. Her face showed no emotion, like the open-eyed stare of a dead person. No more crying, no sniffling, no whimpering, just wide-open, staring eyes and stiff, immobile body . . . corpse-like.

Lester grabbed her under the arms and lifted her onto the end of the table; her legs hanging down toward the floor.

Lester pushed her farther back onto the table, then grabbed her ankles roughly and pushed her feet up close to her buttocks while staring between her legs.

Lester turned toward me with a taunting smile as he undid his belt, let his pants drop to the floor and pushed down his underwear.

I kept cutting, pulling and grunting, straining and cutting more as I howled epithets of rage and disgust at him. I could feel that I was extremely close to cutting through the rope. My wrists ached terribly, but I forced them to continue as I thought, "I'm too late. I'm too late."

Lester's small body made his erection look large by contrast. It was gorged with blood and stood straight up, stiffly erect. He held it like a trophy as he looked at me and laughed again, then turned around and stood silently before Grace. He had small, round buttocks, milky white, like flour dough; no hair. The long, thin slashes of white scar tissue on each of his buttocks stood out immediately, reminding me of the scars on Tom's face.

Lester spoke slowly, softly, and gently, as if talking to his favorite pet. "You need to be punished, you know, 'cause girls and women hate me, treat me bad and tease me about being short an' weak an' ugly. They have always done that to me. The girls in school, they always teased me. Women and girls, look at me with disgust, like I was some awful disease. My mom, she made me this way, you know. All women are cruel bitches. So I must punish you for that. Yur all God-damn whores, anyway, so yur only getting what you deserve."

He took his time, dragging out the time to increase my mental pain, before commencing with the physical pain for Grace. The open pocket knife was on the edge of the table. He picked it up then reached for the elastic band of Grace's panties. He grinned, looked directly at Grace and said, "This is yur punishment fer hurting me, Honey. Now yuh will feel my size and strength inside of you," he shouted. He took his rigid, blood-gorged penis in his right hand and tipped it slightly downward, away from his stomach and toward Grace. He stepped closer to her, saying, "Now, Honey, you'll—"

Lester suddenly flinched and stopped talking in mid-sentence. He felt a slight twinge of pain, like a pin-prick, on his ultra-sensitive penis. He looked down to see the cause of the pain and saw his body's crimson fluid spurting from the stump of his severed penis. He dropped the pocket knife and looked at his right hand which still held the severed, bloody and flaccid remains of his manhood.

Blood was flowing outward like a fountain from the severed stump as he stared at his blood-soaked penis. As he lifted his penis up toward his disbelieving eyes, blood flowed from his hand, down his forearm, then dripped rapidly from his elbow as if it were a leaky faucet. His eyes glazed over as he stared in shock at his severed penis. Then his fingers opened slowly and he dropped his penis to the floor. It fell into the pool of blood at his feet and splashed droplets of blood across his boots, pants and underwear. Lester stared down at the large amount of blood slowly spreading across the floor, like spilled syrup. He said, as if in a trance, "My prick. What happened?" He stared at his severed, limp, lifeless and shriveled sexual organ, which looked like a shriveled hot dog after being left too long in a microwave. Only then did he think to turn around and see me standing there, staring at him, with my throwing knife held at his eye level.

Grace didn't move through the whole encounter. She looked deaf and catatonic as she stared at the ceiling. Thankfully she was in a dazed stupor, leaving her unaware of whatever was going on around her—perhaps, she wouldn't remember any of this awful, degrading, and humiliating experience, amnesia. Before she closed her eyes, I saw that her pupils were dilated, unfocused; a sign of being unaware of her surroundings.

"If you don't want to bleed to death, you better squeeze what's left of your penis to stop the blood flow. You lose any more blood and you'll pass-out, and then bleed to death," I advised him, with a sardonic, vengeful smile.

Lester grabbed himself and pinched off the blood flow, then started crying hysterically. Then he screamed, "Please! For God's sake, please help me! Do something! Please help me! I don't want to die! Not like this! Please!"

I checked to make sure the safety was on, then placed the shotgun on the bench-like seat that was built into the table, like a one-piece, outdoor picnic table.

I looked at Lester's pale face and said, "You're a disgusting animal, a human monster and you got what you deserved! It should have been done to you a long time ago. It won't help the girls you've already raped and scared for life, but you'll never do it again, that's for damn sure! And you actually have the nerve to call God for help? If there really were an omnipotent, omniscient, all-good God, mutant, human perversions like you, wouldn't exist. You'll get no help from me, so beg to your mythical God and see what results you get."

Lester continued squeezing the stump of his penis and shuffled away from the table with very short, unsteady steps due to his pants and underwear being down around his ankles and because the lose of blood may have been making him dizzy. He shuffled his feet, nearly stumbled, but made it to his dad's lower bunk bed, then sat down, still clutching himself and bleeding on Jake's bed.

Grace was still in a trauma induced trance and not aware of her surroundings. She had closed her eyes. Her skin was cold and clammy. I knew that she was in shock and that I should leave her lying down and raise her feet up to get more blood to her heart and brain, but I didn't have the time. We had to escape. We had to do it immediately, so I dressed her quickly, then picked her up, and hugged her. She moaned but I couldn't understand her, at first. Then she said, as if she was talking in her sleep, "Daddy. Oh, Daddy, I love you. Please take me home. I want to be with Mommy."

I ignored Lester, who was also in a lethargic shock. I put Grace on the picnic table seat, then put her coat on. She didn't move. I told her that we must escape quickly, before Jake and Tom got back. Then I told her not to look at Lester. She didn't react so I didn't know if she understood anything that I had just said.

What I did know was that I wouldn't waste time helping Lester. He was on his own. Jake and Tom would be back soon to help him. And helping him would delay their attempt to track us down and recapture us. It was to our advantage to leave him as he is. Besides, I thought, those who show no mercy, get no mercy—an unchristian-like stance, but then, by now, you know where I stand on that issue.

I saw Grace move. She turned her head and blinked her eyes as if to shake the fog out of them—a good sign of recovery, I hoped. She looked past me, then suddenly screamed, "Daddy, look out! He's got a knife!"

I, as Roman Wolfe, now, spun around and saw Lester approaching with my pocket knife raised over his head to stab me. Instinct caused me to lash out with a powerful karate front kick to Lester's groin. He had the bleeding almost completely stopped until I kicked him solidly. The knife in Lester's hand immediately fell to the floor, on his knees, as he doubled-over in excruciating pain, then screamed. He slid to his knees, still moaning in pain. I saw the bloody stain increase in size on the front of his pants, indicating that blood once again flowed steadily from his severed penis. His upper body fell forward. He braced himself with his hands, so now he was on all fours. Soon he toppled over onto the floor and lost consciousness. Neither Wolf nor I cared, though Wolf felt delighted by the sight and smell of his blood. I picked up my pocket knife, wiped the blood off onto Lester's pants, closed it, and placed it into my back pocket. I was thankful that Lester had pulled up his pants before Grace saw him.

Grace was more alert now and able to walk. Quickly we hunted for supplies to take with us on our escape. I told Grace to look for matches and a small metal cup or bowl. While she was doing that, I searched the food shelves and what I found might be more valuable to us: a compass. Now I wouldn't have to use primitive methods of finding direction, though following the river seemed easy enough. I found a canteen, tin cup and several containers of dental floss. I took the canteen and cup and a few containers of dental floss to use as string.

I still had a difficult time thinking of Jake as a dental floss kind of person. It seemed hilariously ironic, Like Attila the Hun worrying about oral hygiene. But I was happy to have found it because string has so many uses, especially in "survival" situations.

Grace found a lot of match boxes, the wooden kind, with blue tips. I told her to put two boxes on the table by the candle that I had just found. Then we found a metal cup and bowl, some venison jerky, dried soups and several packages of what I was later to learn was called "gorp."

Gorp is usually a combination of pieces of hard chocolate, nuts (any kind), dried fruit (usually raisins) and grains, like cereals. This was the stuff Jake, Tom and Lester were secretly eating as we hiked to Preston Ponds. I learned, after our ordeal, that hiking the Adirondacks causes the human body to use two to four times as many calories as a sedentary person and, thus, a hiker needs quickly-assimilated, readily-accessible, high-energy food. The gorp met all those criteria, plus, it tasted good. It looked like a terrific, easy, no-preparation meal, so I grabbed ten, pre-mixed, zippered, plastic sandwich bags full of the gorp mixture. Then, on second thought, I grabbed the remaining four bags of it, as I remembered that this was the stuff that Jake, Tom and Lester were eating, and didn't offer us any on our long hike to this cabin. Why, then, should I leave any for them? I thought. Besides, if they wanted to mix some gorp to take as they followed us, it would delay them that much more.

I placed the compass into my left shirt pocket and everything else into one of the nylon, waterproof backpacks that we used on our trip to the cabin. The backpack reminded me of my Nam rucksack, same thing, basically, and the same purpose, just a little bigger and had a different name.

I walked to the table, lit a candle and tipped it so the hot wax flowed into the small cereal bowl that Grace had found. When I had enough melted wax, I put the candle down and asked Grace, with her gloves on, to hold the bowl, with one hand, and the candle in the other. I directed her to hold the candle flame under the bowl of melted wax in order to stop the wax from cooling and solidifying. She looked puzzled, so I told her that by dipping the match heads into the hot wax so that the wax went past the match-heads, a little way up the wooden shaft, I could basically waterproof the matches so that wetness wouldn't prevent them from lighting. I did a bunch of the matches this way and put some in my pants pocket, then put the remainder inside the backpack. with the bowl and candle.

In my desperate hurry for supplies, I made the mistake of not paying attention to Lester, after he'd toppled over unconscious. Only Wolf's highly sensitive ears heard the clicking sound of Lester pushing the shotgun's safety mechanism off and, thus, I was alerted to my nearly fatal error. When I felt Wolf's warning growl, I lunged and grabbed Grace, pulling her to the floor with me as the shotgun blast went over our heads. The deer slug embedded itself into a log in the cabin wall, sending splinters sailing through the air.

We were really lucky. If bird-shot or buck-shot had been used, Lester might have gotten me—my body was protecting Grace. Jake must have let Lester get his own shells and Lester chose the deer slugs over the bird-shot. At close quarters, the large, spreading pattern of the bird-shot was much better than one small slug—but over the short distance between Lester and I when he fired the shotgun, that pattern would have only opened to about a foot or two, still very deadly. But Lester's misfortune was our good luck.

"You bastard!" he screamed as he swayed on unsteady feet. He tried to pump another shell into the chamber, his blood-soaked hand slipping down the pump handle as if it were coated with oil.

I was so distracted that I hadn't been aware of him moving around after he had fainted. What was I doing, I asked myself. I'm being too careless. Thank goodness for Wolf's warning.

I saw that Lester was very weak and very unsteady. He rocked back and forth on his heels, trying to keep his balance. I reached down my back shirt collar, quickly withdrew my throwing knife, gripped it's handle firmly, then stood up quickly and cocked my right arm. Just like Nolan Ryan, in his prime, throwing a blazing fast ball, the knife, like a silver bullet, was airborne.

I stood frozen in place, knowing the blade would reach its destination before Lester could pump, aim and fire his shotgun again. He didn't see the blade coming at him due to his concentration on the shotgun. That silver blade was a streaking javelin; a silver blur, with a vapor trail, like a comet, as it streaked across the short distance in an instant.

The blade slammed into Lester's upper left chest area; slightly left of the sternum. The speed of the blade drove it about six inches into his chest cavity. The sound of its penetration was like the sound of a spade shovel plunged into soft earth, a scraping, sandpaper kind of noise. The blade must have hit a bone first, then slipped between the chest bones, puncturing Lester's heart like an ice-pick violently driven into a basketball.

I had a vision of what happened to Lester's heart as the blade pierced its muscular wall, the blood erupting from the large puncture and blood flooding his chest cavity. Lester dropped the shotgun to the floor, hitting his toes, but he felt nothing. He wouldn't feel anything ever again. He looked at me for just a second, eyes wide with surprise, jaw agape, then looked down at the deadly silver sliver protruding from his chest. I knew he was dead even as he stood there on wobbly legs. He put his right hand around the remaining four inches of the protruding handle of the blade and somehow found the strength to pull it out. I guess it wasn't difficult or painful; not for a dead man.

The blade seemed to slide out too easily, his own blood acting as a lubricant. I heard the typical sucking sound that occurs when a blade is quickly removed from such a deep wound. He stared at the blade as his blood dripped off the double edges, then looked at me again, momentarily, with lifeless eyes that seemed to turn black suddenly, like turning the light off in a windowless room.

There was very little blood until the blade was withdrawn from the wound. But once the blade was pulled out, the lethal, red puncture bled profusely. When Grace saw the blood she gagged, then vomited. I turned her head and buried her face in my left hip.

The front of Lester's shirt was saturated with blood. His eyes rolled upward, his knees both weakened and his body crashed straight downward, like those expertly demolished tall buildings that you sometimes see on TV news reports. Even billowing dust from the floor rose up in a cloud from the downward crash of his body, much like the dust and dirt billowing out from under a demolished building.

He lay chest down, his right cheek pressed against the dirt floor. His eyes remained open, seemingly staring at the shriveled remains of his blood-stained penis which lay only a couple of feet in front of his deathly gaze. A fitting end for the "cock-sucker," I thought. I told Grace not to look, walked over to Lester's bunk to remove his blanket, kicked the severed penis toward Lester—it struck him in the face— very poetic—then I covered his body, and penis, with the blanket.

I sat Grace at the table, facing away from the body. Then I concentrated on preparing for our long journey to escape Jake and Tom. I'd wasted too much time already. I grabbed Lester's sleeping bag and our two wool blankets, rolled them tightly and strapped them to the top of my backpack with the straps that were provided. I loaded everything else into the backpack. With my blade I shredded Tom's and Jake's blankets, sleeping bags and backpacks. I threw the extra boxes of wooden matches into the fire and watched them flare up. Jake and

Tom would follow us, of course, but not very comfortably. I would have taken an extra sleeping bag but it was added weight. I didn't want to carry it in my hand. One hand would hold Lester's shotgun and the other hand would be holding onto Grace. The backpack straps were too short to accommodate the extra sleeping bag, anyway, so we would have to make do with the one sleeping bag and two blankets. I didn't want to burden Grace with something to carry.

Grace was whimpering, with her head down on the table and her arms wrapped around her head, like a child playing a game called "seven-up."

She's such a sensitive girl, I thought. I wondered if the pain would ever heal for her. I wanted to comfort her, but we had to move quickly. It was nearly 9:00 A.M. We could be three or four hours ahead of Jake and Tom by the time they arrived back at the cabin and found Lester, that is, if they hadn't heard the shot from Lester's shotgun and didn't come back sooner. But I seriously doubted that they would have heard the shot, the blast being mostly contained within the cabin, with logs and snow acting as excellent insulation, providing sound-proofing, plus there were no windows that would let sound escape.

I picked up Lester's shotgun and placed it on the table with the backpack. The shotgun made me think of the rifles. They were locked-up on the wall gun rack. My thoughts raced back to Nam and images of men with their heads nearly blown off their necks by enemy sniper-fire sped through my mind like film running at fast-forward speed.

I heard myself mumble, "They won't get a chance to pick us off at long range, not with these rifles." I walked to the fireplace and picked up the wood-splitting sledge hammer, then walked to the gun rack and smashed the sledge-hammer into each rifle barrel so that the barrels were each bent at angles that made them useless. I smashed the scopes, too. It was a shame to destroy such excellent tools, but doing so meant a greater chance for our survival, so it was necessary.

I told Grace to stay close to me as I quickly went outside to look for where Jake had hidden their cache of rifle and shotgun ammunition. I believed that they were in the well-constructed, padlocked wooden box next to the wood pile that was stacked up against the cabin. I went into the house, got the sledge hammer, came back out to the box and smashed the lock off the box. I took some of Lester's 20 gauge shot shells and slug shells and placed them into my coat pockets. Then I picked up the wooden ammo box. It seemed light, must be the adrenaline in me, I thought, or I was still operating on the combined strength of Wolf and me. I carried the box to the nearby pond, set it on the shore, pushed it into the water, where it floated temporarily, then with a long, dead branch that lay nearby, I pushed it as far as I could into the pond. It floated towards the center of the pond and slowly filled with water and sank. Now Jake's and Tom's shotguns would only have the shotgun shells and/or slugs that they brought with them. That knowledge made me feel good, but certainly not comfortable. It would only take two shotgun shells or shotgun slugs to kill us, if they got close. I also knew that Jake and Tom would be excellent marksmen with shotguns and with rifles. Luckily they didn't bring their rifles with them, just their shotguns. The rifles were now inoperable, which meant that the rifle ammunition was also useless, so I didn't bother throwing it into the lake. Now, with their shotguns, they'd have to get close, and to get close they'd have to catch up to us. I thought I heard a pleasing growl from Wolf when I mentioned the word *close*.

I used the sledge hammer to break a hole into their row boat then pushed it out into the pond, also. It went out farther than the box and sank. Now, if Jake and Tom wanted to try to retrieve the wet bullets, they'd have to wade out into freezing water to get to the ammunition storage box. I walked back to the cabin with Grace in tow.

I would have burned down the whole cabin if it wouldn't have been a signal for the two Gibsons to hurry back to see what caused the smoke. The blaze might have attracted attention and sped up our rescue, but it was too risky and I decided against it.

I looked at the ground, spotted a smooth gray, flat rock about the size of a silver dollar. I pick it up, brushed it off and placed it into my back pocket. It would remain warm and dry there until I needed it to strike a match on, then start a fire, if I felt it was safe for us to have a fire.

I put the backpack on, grabbed the shotgun and told Grace that we had to go . . . fast. I hugged and kissed her moist, cold cheek and told her that Jake and Tom would kill us if they caught up to us, so we'd have to travel real fast, especially now that we wouldn't have the extra time that we would've had if Jake and Tom had to delay chasing us in order to help Lester. I also told her it would be difficult for the both of us, but especially her, and that she had to try real hard to keep moving so we could get home to Mommy.

As I mentioned the word *Mommy* her eyes dried and sparkled, and her lips bent at the corners into a faint smile. We both thought of her Mom for a second. We both needed her and loved her very much.

We ran. As we ran away from the cabin, through the thick forest, I wondered if the cops had found the Annie button and Jake's Raquette Lake cabin.

I let the thoughts of a quick rescue evaporate from my mind, but one mental vision remained. It was a full body, clear mental image of Sam facing me with both her hands outstretched, palms-up and her fingers beckoning Grace and I to come to her. Tears were running down Sam's cheeks and her lips were moving, as if speaking, but I heard nothing. I concentrated on her lips as the blurred images of trees floated past my head and shoulders. I remembered how soft, delicate and sweet Sam's lips were to kiss. In the vision, her lips were still moving. I tried, again, to read their movements. They seemed to be pleading for me—or was it Wolf, or both of us—to save Grace and myself, and to get home quickly and safely.

I had a strange feeling about that because, although she was aware of my feeling about the Wolf inside me, Sam rarely made reference to Wolf, and never spoke to or about Wolf, like I did. Wolf was a part of Nam, a very cruel and vicious part of me that she knew about but refused to accept and didn't want to talk about. With time, she probably thought Wolf would go away, vanish, like a ghost in a snowstorm. She firmly believed that my visits to the doctor would eventually rid me of that defect that had aided me to survive in Nam. I thought that she was wrong, but didn't say so.

The vision persisted as I ran. I thought I could see her lips making a kissing, circular shape, like the lip movement that it would take to say the initial sound of the word *Wolf*. Was this just my imagination? The thought shocked me as I ran hand-in-hand with Grace through the naked trees, over the autumn carpet of multi-color leaves, on this somewhat overcast and chilly day. And, strangely, I had the feeling that I was running through an area of the Nam jungle that was bare due to the defoliating effects of the Agent Orange chemical, instead of running through the bare hardwood and evergreen forest in this section of the Adirondack mountains.

Again I wondered if I was mistaken about what I thought the mental image of Sam was saying. Then Wolf spoke to me, referring to Sam, and said, "No. You're not wrong, Roman. Sam needs me now, too. I have waited a long time for her to accept me and I'll do as she asks." Then the warmth from Wolf's smile comforted me like sipping blackberry brandy by the fireplace on a very cold and snowy winter night.

We ran.

/-/- - -/-./-.- -/..-./.-./.-/-./-.-./..../../.../--./.-./././.-/-/

Chapter 9
★★★★
Running Wolfe

SOMETIMES I PULLED ON Grace's mittened hand because she couldn't keep up with me. I felt bad about tugging on her, but I had no choice. We were literally running for our lives. I had to push myself to keep going, but I was used to that. What I wasn't used to is forcing an eight year old girl, whom I loved dearly, to keep going in spite of her exhaustion.

We were slowly jogging in a southwesterly direction. I knew, from the position of the sun and my general knowledge of New York State geography, that we had to have traveled in a northeasterly direction to get from Chemung to the Adirondacks. When we left Raquette Lake, the sun also told me that we constantly went in a northeasterly direction all the way to Preston Ponds. Therefore, I know that we had to travel in the opposite direction, which, of course, was southwesterly. The compass confirmed my reasoning.

Grace tripped over an exposed tree root and fell down hard when her hand slipped out of mine. I was aware of her labored breathing, as well as my own. I certainly wasn't in as good shape as I had been in Nam, so after I helped Grace up from the ground, we stopped jogging and walked at a fast pace so she could catch her breath. I couldn't push her any more. She was too exhausted and weak. She tripped easily because her legs were wobbly from over-stressed muscles. When the sun was high in the sky I planned to stop for a few minutes to rest and to eat some gorp. Grace was so exhausted she almost refused to eat until I convinced her that she'd get worse, much more quickly, if she didn't eat and get the energy that her muscles needed to be able to continue on our long journey.

Nagging doubts pierced me, like poisonous darts. Would I really be able to save us? Were Wolf and I really as good at survival as I had remembered, or were my memories just a lot of pumped-up hot air, imagination, exaggeration and egotistical self-deception?

We sat on a "blowdown" until our hearts stopped racing. I rested the shotgun against the fallen tree and took off my backpack. My neck and shoulder muscles ached from the weight of the backpack, just as they had in Nam. Each of us drank from the canteen and swallowed hard, gasping for air after each long swallow. We rolled our tongues around inside our dry mouths to spread the cool, refreshing moisture. We drank most of the water in the canteen in order to stay hydrated.

Dry-mouth wasn't a good sign because a person in good shape can breath through his nose, even when fatigued. But an out-of-shape person has to open his mouth to breath so he can suck, into his lungs, as much air as possible. That kind of fatigued, exhausted breathing dried out the mouth, leaving it as dry as desert sand, and feeling much like sandpaper.

Grace had a hard time, of course, keeping up the pace, even with fast walking. I had to slow my pace for her. With the backpack sapping extra strength from me, I couldn't carry Grace very far without being totally exhausted myself. I couldn't let that happen; I needed to act and think clearly, so I needed to avoid total exhaustion. Unfortunately, I couldn't risk trying to carry Grace, not right now, anyway.

The gorp helped increase the saliva flow enough to keep our mouths moist. And the gorp wasn't only a high energy food, it also had excellent flavor, sweet like eating a candy bar. The mixture of nuts, chocolate chips, raisins and grains (in the form of an oat breakfast cereal) blended wonderfully, making it very tasty, providing quick energy and activating the mouth's salivary glands. I'd never had it before, although it looked a lot like the stuff that my elementary school used to serve in tiny cups to the children. It was a delightful surprise to my palate, and I was glad that I had taken all the remaining bags of it so that Jake and Tom would be deprived of its convenience and energy content.

We were desperate, running for our lives and burning a lot of calories. The gorp would help us replenish those calories so we could continue as rapidly as possible.

Moving through the thick forest with exposed roots and fallen branches to trip over, bushes to snag our clothing, fallen trees to climb over, or go around, and low branches to duck under, all tended to make traveling through this Adirondack forest a difficult task, especially with a full backpack and no established path to follow. Thus, we were forced to take a serpentine route, constantly dodging around trees, exposed tree roots, bushes and boulders.

Grace's face was taking on a haggard appearance, although she was trying to be brave. She said, "We can't rest for very long, can we Daddy?" Her breath was coming out in ragged gushes as she looked at me with a forced and labored smile.

"No, Sweetheart, we can't," I said. "Only about five or ten minutes." I gave her a hug, kissed her and told her that I loved her. It didn't re-invigorate her, but she said that her legs felt better after I massaged them to relieve her muscle stress. As I massaged and Grace rested, I thought of the Marine survival reminder: IAO (Improvise, Adapt, Overcome). I would do my very best to IAO.

My thoughts drifted. I was her paladin against the gargoyle faces of evil that were almost certainly tracking us by now. I could feel the turmoil of a battle going on inside of me. I was fighting the tendency to become as skeptical of my and Wolf's survival abilities as I was towards religion. It's times like these that religious blind-faith and thoughtful skepticism are put to their true test. It's severely tragic, heartbreaking, helpless times like these that can turn atheists to prayers. But blind-faith never had a rational appeal for me, and any shred of uncertainty, that religious blind-faith was valid, was forced out of me long before Nam. Blind-faith was just that, *blind*, but I chose the *see*, to think rationally and not believe in glorified illusions, superstitions and spiritual fantasies originating from voluntary self-deceptions— the intellectual dishonesty and deception involved with maintaining a unreasoned belief in a God has to be huge. That reminds me of something that both Mark Twain and Will Rodgers once said. It's not an exact quote, but they both said something to the effect that: It's not what you know that hurts you, it's what you think you know that just ain't so.

It's like a child's blind, unreasoned faith that there is actually a real person who makes toys all year long, at the North Pole, then once a year he flies in his sleigh, that's pulled by reindeer, so he can force his fat body down narrow chimneys to leave toys for all "good" children. And Santa does this for billions of children over the entire world, during the few hours of the darkness of just one night. The child accepts all this with blind-faith because he knows that his parents wouldn't lie to him. After all, why shouldn't the child totally accept and believe this fantasy? Isn't it his trusted parents that always emphasize to him that being *honest* is extremely important to them? Now take that child's blind-faith, that this fantasy is absolutely true, and transpose it with the Santa Claus myth and you'll have the adult version of a child's, unreasoned, illogical, blind-faith, where Santa is now God and this adult version of Santa can do many more miraculous things than Santa. So most adults also believe in Santa Claus, only they changed the name to God and accept the myth with blind-faith that's unquestioned and unquestionable, unreasonable and the result of grossly false logic—isn't it a "devilish" coincidence that the letters in the word "Santa," when rearranged, spell "Satan?"

Basically, I thought, what will save us is my actions, my rational thoughts and ideas, my skills, my survival tenacity, and, perhaps, some luck. But depending on unsupported blind-faith, a God delusion, with faulty reasoning, myth and fantasy, will get us killed.

And, if there was a Christian God, I surmised, He has always been extremely hard on the poor—Napoleon stated that, "Religion is what keeps the poor from murdering the rich—hard on the sick, hard on the mentally ill, hard on the police, hard on firemen, hard on soldiers, hard on parents and teachers. Damn! might just as well say He's a "hard-on." Blasphemous! I smiled, then the word "Jesus" popped into my mind and immediately, I asked myself, "If Jesus is supposed to be Jewish, then how come he has a Mexican name?" Sacrilegious? Of course not. How does one commit sacrilege against a institutionalized and cultural myth? You can't do that any more than you can commit sacrilege against Mickey Mouse.

Also, when I hear someone get excited or angry and state, "Jesus H. Christ!" I wonder, What's the "H." stand for? Does it stand for "Homophobic?"

I refocused. I must admit that it did worry me that my confidence seemed to be sinking in the quicksand of my own fatigue and self-doubts. That feeling weakened me in the sense that it put a strain on my decisions, yet, at the same time, that same feeling strengthened me because I felt that I was being honest with myself, and that, like in Nam, I could overcome the doubts and fears that haunted my thoughts and sapped my self-confidence. In the distant, primitive parts of my mind I felt that if I kept pushing, if I kept trying, if I never gave up, then, as in Nam, Grace and I would triumph over all the odds that were mounting against our survival and rescue. So, mentally, I moved on with a feeling of new-found strength.

Grace lifted her head from my shoulder, looked at me with a stern and saddened expression—her lips were slightly parted and her breathing was almost normal. Grace looked down at her hands in her lap. She paused before she spoke, as if she wasn't sure she wanted to say what she was thinking. But then she looked back up, directly into my eyes, and said, "Daddy, will you have to go to jail for killing that mean man?"

We looked deeply into each other's eyes—I hoped that she didn't see the ominous shadows that inhabited a dark portion of my mind. Her eyes were filling with tears. The tears continued, settled on her puffy, lower eyelid, then tumbled onto her cheek, leaving a trail of moisture on her dry, dirty skin.

I tried to be honest, yet hopeful, with her. "No, Grace, I won't have to go to jail because the law says that a person can kill another person if the other person is trying to kill him, or a member of his family." I tried to keep it simple.

I hoped I was correct, but I wasn't sure because I didn't have as much faith in the law as I used to have. It seemed that, now-a-days, the laws were set up to protect the guilty and hinder the innocent from obtaining a full measure of justice. There were too many miscarriages of justice, too many technicalities allowing criminals back onto the streets, and just too much crime that "the law" couldn't deal with. But, to hell with that, I thought, right now I just needed to reassure Grace; to give her confidence and hope. I would worry about the law after we were safely reunited with Grace's mom and grandparents.

"Are you going to try to kill those other men, Daddy? If they catch up to us?" Grace said as fear and pain rolled from her eyes as if they were riding on each teardrop that now streamed down both of her cheeks.

I wanted to say, "Damn right I'll kill those bastards!" but that wouldn't calm Grace and I needed to think of her needs right now, not my anger. So I replied, "If they catch us, Grace, they will kill us." I paused. I forced myself to look in her eyes and not turn away from her gaze. I owed her my honesty, even if it was the cruel truth. I wondered about my own strength and I doubted my ability, again. Would my own daughter see me as a killer? Would she ever forgive me or love me again, if she witnessed me killing two more men? Would she be afraid of me? I feared the lose of her love. Then Wolf growled in my head, a growl of encouragement.

I wasn't the same man that I was in Nam, that night-stalking killer of the enemy. I tried to forget those days—mostly the nights. I tried to resolve the nightmarish guilt with logic. I killed because it was my duty to do so for my country. It seemed like a good idea to do it for self-preservation, also.

Plenty of times, in Nam, I heard guys whispering to one another about how dangerous I was. It was flattering at first, but grew stale, boring and irritating after a short time. What makes a man dangerous? Is it an expert knowledge of a mixture of martial arts styles? An expert with certain lethal weapons? Large muscles and stature? A cold heart that's insulated by a lack of conscience? Rage, anger, revenge or vengeance? You take one or more of those traits and give them to a man who's a little crazy and not afraid to die, or a man that doesn't care if he dies, or a man who wants to die, then you have a dangerous man, a very dangerous man and, perhaps, the ultimate dangerous man. I shook my head to clear the bullshit out of it. I didn't know what brought me to those thoughts. I just needed to refocus and stop thinking of Nam.

After Nam, I tried not to be physically aggressive, and I tried not to use my karate combat skills—but I kept my knives close, like best friends. Everything had worked nicely until our abduction. Fate? To me, fate has a subtle and insidious religious connotation. Was our abduction fated to happen, like a predetermined even in our lives? If so, then who would schedule our fate, then make sure it occurred when and where it was predetermined to happen? If there was such a thing as fate, then who was the master of our fate, the master planner? God? So, if no God, then no fate, then no fated abduction. The abduction was just a highly unlikely, random event that settled on our lives like the marble that falls into any one of the spinning black or red numbers that are on a casino's roulette table.

I decided to rest for five more minutes. My mind drifted to my view of the core of religious faith: intellectual dishonesty. It had already been proven to me that I was lied to about Santa Claus, the Easter Bunny, the Tooth Fairy and many other adult perpetuated religious, semi-religious, or just mundane untruths, as well as grandly exaggerated fantasies, myths and legends, so why not lie about the ultimate fantasy, religion? What I had the hardest time figuring out—and still do—is why adults, with all their maturely developed, rational powers intact, still believe in the God fantasy. In everyday life, if they are skeptical about something, they'll argue about it and ask for proof in order to convince them. However, they appear to be afraid of being skeptical about their parent's religion—which usually becomes theirs—and don't dare ask for proof, don't even need proof—what's good enough for mom and dad is good enough for them. All of a sudden religious heritage and blind-faith are good enough for them, no questions asked. Maybe it's because, if they didn't accept their parent's religion, they have to think of their parents a silly liars.

When I was a child, I found it difficult to think while in church. Years later I thought I had the answer. How can a skeptic, a thinker, be analytical and use deductive reasoning skills in such a climate? To be religious, one has to enter a church willing to accept "blind-faith" in fantasies and be willing to temporarily suspend their ability to reason and be logical.

As I was growing up, I was occasionally dragged off to church. There I heard priests spout many ridiculous superstitious, as well as unproved opinions and childish platitudes. It made me wonder just how useful are priests, preachers, reverends and ministers? Can they really do more than *lay* people? Sorry, sometimes my mind slips into a George Carlin mode.

I remember being punished after one fervent priestly sermon when Father Dacy said that the Pope didn't think that using surrogate mothers to have children for someone else, was appropriate. The crowded pews should have been a cacophony of laughter. Exactly how did Father Dacy think that Jesus was said to have been born? Didn't he know that, supposedly, the Virgin Mary was the surrogate mother of Jesus? Laughter was mandated by Father Dacy's unreasoned foolishness—I was the only one to laugh. The laughter was worth the punishment.

Even as a pre-adolescent, with immature reasoning skills, much of what I heard in church, or during religious conversations by grandparents, parents, aunts, uncles, cousins, friends and neighbors, had a loud and false ring to it. One gem that comes to me now is: God won't give you more than you can successfully deal with. But my addendum to that is: Unless you die of something that you can't deal with. What's my proof? Just listen to your neighbors, friends, relatives; read the newspaper, and magazines, listen to the TV and radio. There you'll hear, read or see stories about millions of people who experience unimaginable tragedy and death. Do you suppose those people were given much more than they could deal with? Of course they were, and inane religious platitudes won't, and didn't, help or save them.

Damn it! I'm wandering and shouldn't be, I chastised myself. I should put all that stuff out of my mind now and focus on Grace. Grace is what mattered beyond all else. She must survive to be with her mom, grandparents, other relatives and friends. I'd die before I'd let those two remaining Gibsons lay a hand on her. My death didn't matter to me. It hadn't for a long time. It's Grace who mattered most. Her welfare was of utmost importance to me. I must get Grace back to her mother . . . at all costs, even if that cost meant sacrificing my life. But, like I said, I'm OK with that.

I looked at Grace and, for a moment, didn't know what to say to her. She was so utterly precious to me; a product of the mixture of her mother's genes and mine, our parental gold mine and treasure chest. How do I tell my own sweet, innocent flesh and blood that, in addition to being an atheist, I was a highly skilled and highly feared killer in a war and that I would, once again, assume that role of an assassin. And once back into that persona, there would be no hesitation and certainly no guilt associated with it, not when the killing was done to protect Grace. Wolf and I would blend, like in Nam, and a killer instinct would become paramount in my actions towards any enemy who tried to hurt my precious daughter in any way, at any time.

Grace was patiently waiting for my response. I could feel the words burn as they flowed over my tongue and lips like acid-water. What I was thinking was, "Sometimes, the right and best thing to do is to kill your enemy, if you believe that you have no other choice. And, if your enemy follows the rule of 'kill-or-be-killed,' then, to survive, you must also kill-or-be-killed. You must be more lethal than your enemy, with your weapon and your mind." Then I thought that, perhaps that would be too vague or too harsh for an eight year old. So I looked at Grace, spoke softly and bluntly as I stated, "Yes, Grace, if I have to kill them in order to save our lives, that's what I'll do." Grace didn't reply. She lowered her head and I could no longer see her expression. She didn't give me a hint of what she was thinking, but a lowered head was not a happy head, except in church.

I was still hot and sweating under my coat. When I inquired if Grace was too hot, she said that she was. We unzipped our outer clothing to let the excess heat and moisture out. When I thought of the moisture, I realized that we needed to replenish the moisture in our bodies. I suggested that we get water from the Cold River. We walked to the shore and I filled our canteen, then we drank our fill. I refilled the canteen.

I told Grace that we had to get moving, that we couldn't afford to sit and chat any longer—our ten minute rest period had already stretched to fifteen minutes. But I still needed to say something else to Grace. I said, "If the time comes for me to fight those men, will you promise me that you will close your eyes, or look away and not watch what's happening. Would you please promise me that?"—What father wants his child to see how brutal and savage he can really be; to see what lies dormant under the façade of a civilized, educated maturity.

"Why do you want me to do that, Daddy? Maybe I can help you."

"If I get hurt"—I didn't want to say 'killed' because that would scare her—"I don't want you to see it happen and if I hurt those men, I don't want you to watch me do it. You saw too much already, back at the cabin. There'll be blood and I know how much the sight of blood upsets you."

"They're bad men. I want to see you beat them up. Punch them hard, Daddy."

Grace spoke with unusually intense anger and that surprised me because she was normally very gentle and very sensitive to other people's needs and problems. I kept my voice calm. "Yes, they're bad men, Sweetheart, and they should be punished. And I wish I didn't have to try to kill them. But if you see them die, you may never be able to forget their faces and that memory will always be scary for you. More importantly, Grace, I don't want you to see me do it. I don't want you to see the beast in me. I'm positive that it would be an ugly sight; a sight I don't want you to see or remember." The word *beast* settled on my lips and, like a heavy anchor pulling downward, I could feel my lower jaw falling until I had an open-mouthed, surprised look on my face. Then I closed my mouth, and before Grace had a chance to talk I had this strange feeling that I had used too strong a word to describe Wolf and our unique interactions. In my thoughts, I apologized to Wolf.

I stood and stated, "Come, Grace. We have to get moving." I reached out for her hand, she took it and I pulled her to her feet.

"What's the beast in you?" she asked, to my apprehension and shame.

As we walked quickly, I responded. "A beast is something like a fierce, violent and dangerous animal. A beast is like a difficult to control monster that likes to fight, to injure, to kill, to shed blood. Sometimes, Sweetheart, I think that there's one locked up inside of me"—a growling noise filled my ears as if I had insulted Wolf, again. Then I added, "But it doesn't have to be a bad thing, if a person can control that violence and fierceness that's inside of him. There's a wildness, a fierceness inside of me that helps me survive, keeps me alive, like it did in the war. It's a savage feeling I don't let loose unless I'm in a fight or protecting people I love. It's a feeling that I call 'Wolf' simply because, when I feel that wildness, that violence that's ready to explode out of me, I see a white wolf. To me, it's a real wolf; a friend, not just a silly, powerless vision. Those savage feelings that I get make me feel that, somehow, I have a wolf's spirit in me. I don't want you to see me fight those men because then you'll see that beast, that wolf in me, and it might make you think of your daddy as a beast; a killer, someone whose a brutal savage. I don't want you to ever be afraid of me, Grace. I would never hurt you. Do you understand?"

"Yeah. I guess so," she said, but she was distracted and stumbled over a fallen tree branch, hands first.. I grabbed her arm and pulled her back upright, then wiped the dirt and decaying leaves off her palms.

"Can you jog for awhile?" I asked. "We need to get as far away from the cabin as we can."

"Okay," she stated, reluctantly, though she seemed to understand the importance of my request.

After a few minutes of jogging, I could hear Grace's labored breathing. I said, "Grace, when the fight comes, and I hope it doesn't, you'll see me change suddenly. I may not look or sound or act like your daddy, you know, like what you're used to seeing. That's when that wolf feeling will take charge and I'll sound, look and act fierce. But please remember, Wolf would never hurt you any more than I would hurt you.

"You never told me scary stuff like this before, Daddy. Does Mommy know?"

"Yeah, Grace, she knows," I said with a note of sadness in my voice.

"The thing inside of you is called Wolf and our last name is Wolfe?" Grace stated through her increasingly labored breathing.

"Yeah. There's always been that "name" connection. But the war was what really started me thinking about my connection with a wolf. It happened in the Vietnam War. I killed a lot of enemy soldiers there, Grace. And that fierce feeling that I got when I silently snuck up on them just appeared and it felt to me like a wolf. I kept getting images of a wolf. When I snuck out at night, I felt like a wolf; I seemed to have the strong senses of a wolf. A vision of a wolf was constantly in the back of my mind. It usually appears, but not always, as a white wolf, a pale wolf. In the bible, there's a part where a pale horse represents Death because the rider is Death. The pale wolf that I see and feel is more like a symbol for a partnership in Death. And Grace, I don't mean the fun of killing, or criminal and gang types of killing. It's killing for your country, killing to survive or to protect other people—"

Grace interrupted to ask me, "How come we don't have a bible at home?"

The question surprised me. My mind went blank. "Well," I started, "it's not an important book to me, but if your mom or you want a bible in the house, it's ok with me. You should talk to your mom about it, if you want to."

"Ok," she replied, then, "Sorry I interrupted you. You were talking about a feeling that reminded you of a wolf."

"Yeah. OK. So it didn't take long for me to give that wolf a name, though. My last name is Wolfe and the feeling and image reminded me of a wolf, so I called the pale wolf, Wolf. Just about everyone in Nam called me 'Wolf,' too

I'm trying to control Wolf's feelings so I don't hurt anyone unnecessarily or unlawfully. The doctor I've been seeing is helping me with my strong feelings of guilt, sadness and depression, especially the depression. But even though I've told you all this, I think it will still be very scary to see me fighting those two men . . . if it comes to that. That's why I want you to promise me that you won't watch, okay?"

"Okay. I'll try, Daddy," she said, hurriedly, then gasped for breath and said, "Can we walk now? I can hardly breathe."

"Sure, Grace." We slowed to a walk so Grace could catch her breath.

After a minute of heavy breathing, Grace stated, "What's depression?"

I didn't want to go into this kind of stuff with her, but I was stuck. It was best to be truthful with her. "It's a very sad feeling, Grace. Not ordinary sadness, but great sadness where a person feels unneeded, useless and a better life seems hopeless. Some depressed people have thoughts of suicide and some actually do kill themselves."

"How could you feel like that when you have Mommy and me?"

"I don't know, Grace. When I'm very depressed, very sad, I don't get to pick and choose how I feel. I don't get to choose to be reasonable, or fair or smart. I don't get to choose to feel that I can be hopeful, or that I'm a good person. I only get to feel what the depression brings to me, how it makes me feel and think."

"I hope the doctor can fix it, Daddy."

"He will, Grace."—Well, that was a 'hopeful' comment.

I picked up our pace so that we were walking quickly . . . as quickly as one can walk on a tree studded, rough, serpentine route that was more like a skiing slalom race where the racers have to ski between poles (trees) stuck into the snow and do it at top speed.

"Is that wolf, the part of you that fights, protecting me and Mommy, too?" Grace smiled up at me as she said that, her eyes searching into mine. She seemed at that moment so much smarter than her eight years. I was proud of her. She was my gift to the world. She was so much like her mother. She was a gift that I wouldn't allow to be harmed . . . not while there was life in my body.

"Yes," I responded, "Wolf as a protector. But my Wolf has human characteristics, too, like being able to communicate his thoughts to me, just as I can pass my thoughts to him without talking. My inner Wolf has some human qualities."

"How can that be?" she said.

"Well . . . Wolf lives in my mind, and that's just the way he exists for me. There's a special word for something like Wolf. The word is *anthropomorphic*. It means to give human qualities or characteristics to a living thing that's not human. That's the way Wolf exists within my mind. He's anthropomorphic. You understand?"

"A little, I guess. Sounds kind of crazy though," she said, then smiled up at me.

"Yeah. It is kind of crazy. I'll admit that." We both laughed.

"Does Wolf ever come out? You know, like so he can be seen by other people?"

"Rarely, but yes, sometimes that happens . . . ah, but I don't know how it happens; I can't explain it."

"If Wolf protects people, then Wolf can't be bad, right, Daddy? He's our friend. He must be your closest friend, since he lives in your head." Grace giggled, then said, "Get it, Daddy? Lives inside of you so he's your *closest* friend." The giggles continued through her raspy breathing. I joined her in more laughter.

"You're just too funny, kiddo. But Wolf is also like an advisor as well as a protector. He can be bad to other people while being good to us. What I mean is, he can hurt or advise me to hurt other people in order to protect myself, or to protect other people. So, I guess I'd have to say that Wolf is both good and bad, just as most people are both good and bad. He's anthropomorphic that way, too."

"You really see him in your mind and sometimes out of your mind?" She asked, innocently.

"Yes," I said with a laugh because she use the words 'out of your mind,' not realizing what she had said, or the implications of it.

"You can talk to Wolf and Wolf can talk to you, right?"

"Yes."

"Wolf protects you and gives you advice?"

"Yes," I repeated.

"And Wolf is your very closest friend?"

"Yeah," I said with rising curiosity.

"If someone didn't believe you, Papa, could you prove that Wolf is real?"

"You know, I don't think I could, Sweetheart."

"So Wolf is like a God?"

I was so stunned that I stopped walking, frozen in my tracks. Grace looked surprised, not knowing that she had asked me a shocking question. She thought it was no big deal. She was just curious, but I was filled with wide-eyed, slack-jawed amazement as I stared at her.

Suddenly I felt a loud echo inside my head, as if Wolf were standing at the very top of Mt. Marcy, the highest elevation in New York State—5,344 feet into the clouds—howling joyously. That sound temporarily made me smile outwardly and forget our dangerous predicament. I had thought of Wolf as a beast, but he really wasn't, not to me or the people I loved. He was, in fact, my protector, our protector, my *closest* friend, as Grace put it, and it took a child to make me understand that better. Wolf was 'good' from our point of view, but 'bad' from the enemy's point of view. Out of the mouth of babes, I thought. What an absolutely wonderful daughter I have. She had said, "So Wolf is like a God?" to which I had no answer.

Though she was now breathing heavily, I told Grace that we must walk faster. She didn't hesitate, but for a child of eight, walking fast to keep up with her dad was the same as jogging slowly. But she was being a trouper about it.

Before we picked up our pace, we drank our fill from the canteen. We headed for the river to fill the canteen. On the way I heard, then saw, some ravens. I couldn't help but think of Edgar Allan Poe's poem, and his stories filled with sadness and death. The sight of those ravens sent an ominous chill up my spine, as I thought of their funereal-like image, with their all-black plumage looking like dark, evil cloaks, and making their somber noises.

Actually, I knew from reading, that ravens were considered to be highly intelligent birds whose black pigment allowed them to absorb solar energy. Their intelligence and flexibility have allowed them to adapt to and survive in the more hostile and ever-changing environmental conditions that they find in this more modern, crowded and polluted world.

As Grace and I reached the riverbank the ravens flew away, the Doppler-effect causing their cawing sounds to diminish in intensity as their distance away from us increased. That was fine with me. It was a relief, like evil specters slowly withdrawing from my life. I couldn't help thinking, though, that Poe made an excellent choice when he selected the raven for his spooky poem. I also figured that he was wrong about his claim that the saddest thing in life is the death of a beautiful woman. I thought that the death of an innocent child was even more sad and that it's a million times worse if it's your own child—I don't think Poe had any children. Perhaps that's why he didn't think like I do.

I looked at Grace, still thinking of Poe, then turned away from her quickly so she wouldn't see the tears welling up in my eyes.

I quickened our pace for a short distance when I heard the gurgling of water. I turned toward the sound, then continued to the river bank. The land sloped downward steeply for about ten or fifteen feet. At the top of the river bank I removed the backpack and set the barrel of the shotgun down on top of it to keep dirt, twigs, fallen leaves and anything else away from the barrel and the action mechanisms.

Grace and I got down the slope rather easily by bracing ourselves against the trees that went to the river's edge. Also, on the way down, I held Grace's hand as we proceeded slowly and carefully down the slope. It was mostly controlled sliding that got us there. We'd done this many times before while exploring in the woods at Grandma's and Grandpa's house, in rural Chemung, N.Y.

I filled the cup for Grace to take a drink and, as frigid as it was, she drank all of it. I filled another cup and told her to drink it even if she felt full because her body would need to replace the water that was lost due to our strenuous traveling pace—not as strenuous for me, but very strenuous for Grace. She got "brain freeze" from the cold water, but it didn't last long.

I quickly gulped down two cups of water to make sure I kept my own body hydrated. The frigid water sent a sharp pain to my brain, also, but my mouth was delighted as the cold liquid passed over my tongue and down my parched throat, coating each with cool, refreshing moisture. Then I used the cup to fill the canteen with more water. I poured slowly so as not to get the outside of the canteen too wet with ice-cold water which would make it inconvenient to carry comfortably. As long as I had the tin cup to fill the canteen, I wouldn't have to dunk the canteen into the water to fill it. That's why I was very glad that I'd grabbed the cup as we left the cabin. I should have used it before when I filled the canteen—too much on my mind, I guess. Plus, near panic made me forget I had it. I hooked the canteen and cup to my belt and we started back up the steep slope.

Grace was ahead of me so I could push her as we climbed up the slope. Our feet slid on the loose ground and gravel of the steep slope. We grabbed saplings, exposed roots, tree trunks, anything to help us pull ourselves up the embankment. I pushed on Grace's rear end to help her up the slope. Grace was at the top and things were going well, then disaster happened.

Grace lost her footing and started sliding backwards. She would have slid into me in another two or three feet and I would have caught her, but instinctively she grabbed the backpack strap that was hanging slightly over the slope. The front sight of the shotgun apparently snagged on the backpack and when Grace pulled the strap, the backpack came tumbling over the edge of the embankment . . . so did the shotgun.

Grace fell backward into my arms as I leaned my back against a stout sapling that I had just used to pull myself forward. I got a secure hold on Grace with my right arm and with a pure reflex action I reached out with my left hand and luckily grabbed one of the backpack straps . . . but the shotgun went cart-wheeling, end-over-end, down the slope, hitting heavily on a boulder, then bouncing into the air, as if off of a trampoline, then flew out into the frigid, clear water of the Cold River.

I held Grace and the backpack tightly. Grace and I remained immobile in our precarious position. Then I felt Grace's body shake against mine as she burst into tears. "I'm sorry, Daddy," she whimpered. "I didn't mean it. I was slipping and falling back, so I grabbed something. Please don't be mad at me."

"I'm not mad at you, Grace. It was an accident," I said as I pulled her closer to me and hugged her tightly, more of a secure caress than anything else. I looked over my shoulder and saw the shotgun lying in its frigid, clear, watery grave.

Seeing the shotgun lying in the icy water was a jolt to my sense of security. I wanted to scream, but didn't. I felt panicky as my heart raced and the scream of frustration kept building inside my throat. I controlled the frustration so Grace wouldn't feel devastated.

As Grace was crying, my thought was statically fixed on the importance of that shotgun to our escape. I experienced such a gut-wrenching and helpless feeling of disappointment that my muscles started to slacken and I had to tighten my grip on the backpack strap, and Grace, before the supreme disaster took place, me reduced to an idiot by my frustration.

When I calmed down, I thought: Shit! There's nothing I can do about it now. I couldn't prevent it; sure as hell didn't anticipate it. Can't retrieve it. I'll get wet in the process and need to build a fire to get warm and to dry my wet pant legs and hands. I looked at the shotgun again, with much regret. I thought: "Even if I could retrieve it from the icy water, it probably wouldn't be of any use to us." The barrel had smashed against a boulder and looked bent—though it could look that way due to the refraction of light in the water—which would cause it to explode if I tried to fire it. Even if that wasn't true, and I could retrieve it, the moving parts would be frozen, the shells would be wet and useless. Retrieving it, building a fire to dry it and myself would take too much time. We didn't have that time to waste. We needed to move, fast.

Grace saw me staring at the water. She was crying heavily against my chest. Forget the shotgun, I thought. I would get along without it, I would improvise, adapt and overcome (IAO). Pay attention to Grace, I told myself. I said, "I don't need the shotgun, Sweetheart. No need to cry. I know it was an accident. There's no need to blame yourself—I wanted to shift the blame to me so she wouldn't feel so terrible. It could have happened to me, too. Actually, I think it was my fault. I shouldn't have rested the shotgun barrel on the backpack. That was careless of me. But we'll be fine, Sweetheart, you'll see. It's all over and done with now. It was an accident so let's forget about it and continue our journey. We've delayed too long already. We need to go quickly. Jake and Tom are gaining on us. Let's concentrate on getting far away."

I tossed the backpack up and over the embankment, then pushed Grace to the same place. I pulled myself up to Grace, slipped the backpack straps over my shoulders and we quickly started walking away. I gave Grace a reassuring pat on the top of her head and as I lowered my right hand, she grabbed it with her left and we walked hand-in-hand, as I gradually increased our pace.

As we walked, I shifted the backpack to a more comfortable position by raising my shoulders, then shifting my weight right or left until I got the backpack to settle where I wanted it.

I heard the ravens cawing and that irritated me because they seemed to be laughing at me, as if they knew that the shotgun was much more important to our survival than I had led Grace to believe. But then I heard a soothing growl and my cheek felt wet as if Wolf licked it like a pet dog would do to its owner. I chuckled at my paranoia, then grinned about the wet feeling on my cheek. I knew it wasn't really wet; it was just Wolf reassuring me, like the reassuring pat on the head that I gave Grace. I raised my hand to my cheek, anyway, and when I rubbed it, it didn't feel like skin at all. It felt like wet animal fur. I said a silent, "Thank you" to Wolf.

We walked quickly and silently. Grace was breathing heavily, again, which made it difficult for her to talk. During this quiet time, I thought, "The shotgun wasn't my choice of weapons anyway. My kind of fighting was CQC—close quarters combat—within arm's reach, of the enemy, or closer." When I'm that close my head—for head butts—hands, fingers, elbows, knees and legs were all dangerous, vicious and punishing weapons. The secret to winning a one-on-one fight is CQC. If someone throws a punch or a kick, you should move forward to block it or, if hit, shake off the effects of it, but you seldom retreat, retreat is defeat. The enemy expects you to back up, retreat, and continue long range fighting at least at distances that are within and arm's reach.. So I, usually, suddenly and surprisingly move in close at the very first opportunity. A head butt or an elbow to the face has a far greater impact than a fist. Up close, fingers can reach the eyes and throat, knees will punish far greater than karate kicks that use shin bones. The natural inclination is to defensively move away. Fight that inclination and move in, crowd him, jam him, destroy him. That's my mantra. You won't be able to avoid taking some punishment, but *move in*. Use all your body's weapons, even teeth if necessary and, most of the time, you'll win by quickly dishing out much greater punishment than you'll take. I heard an affirmative growl of agreement from Wolf.

I was about to remove the shotgun shells from my pocket and throw them into the river. Then I remembered that, if I needed to start an extra fast fire, I could cut the shells open and use the gun powder to create a fast, hot burn which would start a fire very quickly. I let the shells fall back into my pocket.

We were away from the accident area quickly. With Grace's mittened hand still within mine, I started to jog with her, slowly. It was nearly 12:30 P.M. and I wanted to put more time and distance between the Gibsons and us. Grace kept pace with my slow jog the best she could. She stumbled a few times, but I pulled-up on her hand and saved her from crashing onto the cold ground. More importantly, she didn't complain, though her mouth was open, her breathing was labored and her legs were getting weaker.

We didn't talk much because talking used up energy and made it harder to breath. I concentrated on moving southwesterly. However, I did tell Grace, at one point, that if she ever got lost in the woods, that she should always remember to follow a stream or a river because streams always flow downhill and sooner or later they will take her to people that can help her.

I hoped, again, that the cops had found the Annie button and that they were on our trail. I wanted to be saved, of course, but my paramount concern was for the safety of Grace. She is my flesh and blood. I knew that I couldn't ask for the help of a mythical God. I also knew that, like so many times in Nam, more than likely, no one was going to come to my rescue. Not that they didn't want to, just that they usually couldn't, for one reason or another. That meant that our survival probably depended on me alone—I heard a dissatisfied growl, so I must include Wolf. I forced myself to stop thinking of outside help. That kind of thinking would only hinder my attempts to save Grace and myself. It was Roman and Wolf that would have to do the saving. We had always gotten the job done in Nam, so why not in the Adirondack Mountains, too? The solution was my responsibility. Our survival depended on my decisions and my judgment. That's the way it had to be and that's the way I had to focus my mind and all my effort.

Grace was breathing too heavily and starting to stagger on weakened legs. I knew that she was giving her very best effort to do her share, but she was so young, her stride so short and her stamina nearly drained, so I had to slow down and walk.

Grace immediately sighed with great relief and took a few deep, lung-filling breaths. When she walked, I could tell that her leg muscles were nearly exhausted, making her stumbled easily. Her right hand gripped her side and massaged the skin over the painful 'stitch' caused by prolonged exertion. My heart ached for her, so I bent down and scooped her up into my arms and carried her. Without the shotgun, my arms were free. She went limp with grateful relief. I kept walking as fast as I could.

As the afternoon wore on, and the temperature remained frigid, I worried about hypothermia. When your core body temperature falls because of exposure to continuous coldness, you lose your ability to think clearly. You get tired, lazy and want to sit or lie down to rest. This condition catches many people off guard, making it even more dangerous because then they can't take precautionary actions. In cold weather, like this, a person could freeze to death at night.

However, I didn't think we were in danger, not yet. It was cold, though, and as night came, it would get even colder in spite of the fire that I intended to build.

After a half hour or so, my arms ached and I had to put Grace down to walk. I had to be careful of Grace's health, so now, every hour that we walked, I took a five minute break. And after the break I tried to carry Grace for another five minutes.

Wolf had an acute instinct for danger, yet he had not given me any warnings. Because of that, I was sure that Jake and Tom wouldn't be able to catch up to us tonight. We'd made pretty good time even with the five minute rest breaks that we took every hour that we traveled after we ate our lunch.

I wasn't worried about getting lost, just getting caught. I was glad there was no snow on the ground, yet, and I was elated that we had a river to follow instead of always having to check the compass. A compass is good for "straight line" travel, but not when you have to travel a very serpentine route, as we had to do, with constant directional changes to avoid trees, bushes, fall-downs, rock out-crops, large boulders and other path-blockers.

It made me think about how the new guys in Nam got lost so easily. I remember once reading a report that said that the almost natural inclination of people in deep forests to roam about in circles is an unexplained phenomena, and that scientists aren't sure why people tend to walk in circles when lost. We sure were in deep woods now . . . and "deep shit," too.

I could remember how some of those new recruits were so cocky and over-confident upon arrival in Nam. But in the jungle it was remarkable how quickly most of those cocky, over-confident and fairly, well-conditioned teenagers lost that arrogant, self-assurance when they were lost in a dark double and triple canopied jungle; a place where the sun was blocked out and the afternoons were like night time and the nights were so pitch-black that you couldn't see very far beyond your own outstretched hand Because of Wolf's incredible instincts and sense of direction, I never had that trouble. I didn't expect to have any trouble in this Adirondack forests either. Then I laughed silently as I wondered if I was being too cocky and over-confident. Can't afford to let that happen.

"Why are you smiling, Daddy," Grace asked.

"Oh," I fibbed, "I was just thinking of how much fun we'll have at Grandma's and Grandpa's house for Thanksgiving." I didn't want to have a conversation. We both needed to conserve our energy, although, by the way she was walking, I didn't think Grace had much energy left. Grace forced herself forward, sometimes dragging a foot. But we continued even though I knew that her legs ached and that the temperature was getting colder.

Suddenly I had an over-powering urge to hug Grace, to tell her that I loved her more than anything in this world. I also had great sympathy for her pain and discomfort, so, once again, caught up in my emotion of love for her, I bend down and swept her off her feet. I carried her against my chest to give her legs and lungs a rest. Her cheeks were rosy red, cute, but cold. I pulled her head towards me so she could rest it on my shoulder. I knew I could only do this for a few minutes, but Grace needed the rest in order to catch her second-wind—I hoped that was possible for her, in the short time that I could carry her. As I held her and kept walking, I whispered, "I love you more than anything in the world, Grace." She snuggled closer to me and I hugged her tightly, then released the pressure.

After about ten strenuous minutes we came to another blow-down tree and it gave me an idea. I put Grace back down on the ground, shook the cramps out of my arms, and told her to walk forward with me and to put a lot of pressure on each step that she took. We both walked forward, heavily, for about fifty feet and then I told Grace to stop and stand still. She looked up at me curiously. I told her to walk backwards and to place her feet back into her tracks until we got back to the blowdown. I held her hand to steady her and we both back-tracked inside our own previous tracks. When we reached the blowdown, we stood still and I explained my actions and reasoning to Grace.

"Sweetheart," I stated, "You know that the Gibsons are following us. They are woodsmen and can track us easily. They push the leaves aside and see our tracks, and if they're really good, like Jake probably is, they can look at the impression on the fallen leaves and tell that we have walked over them. But you and I will leave a dead trail for them. That's a trail that goes nowhere because it appears to end suddenly. We walked forward, then backtracked to this fallen tree. Now I'll climb onto this blowdown and lift you up to me. Then you and I will walk the length of this bare tree, which looks to be about sixty or seventy feet long. We'll step over all the branches, carefully. Then we'll get down as easily and as lightly as we can, trying not to make obvious tracks. We'll walk flat footed, not pressing our heels into the ground, which leaves marks that are easy to follow. Then we'll walk off in a totally different direction. After about a mile, we'll circle around and continue in the same direction as we were going before. This tactic should confuse the Gibsons and cause them to waste time. You see, the Gibsons think I'm a wimp, an ignorant weakling, and they won't expect this trick from me. It'll only take us five minutes to do it, but, if we're lucky, it'll take them fifteen, maybe twenty, minutes to figure out that we've done and we'll be just that much farther ahead of them. They'll, of course find our trail, but they'll be confused and start wondering why we, all of a sudden, are going in an unexpected direction. If they stopped to think about it, or if the puzzle causes them to walk instead of run, or walk slowly instead of fast, then we will be gaining time on them. Understand?"

Grace smiled as she looked up at me and said, "You're not a wimp, Daddy. You know karate real good."

"Yeah, you're right, but they don't know that. They don't know that I have my knives either. Nor do they know how good I am with them. So we have surprise as our big advantage. They just think I'm a pathetic wimp who knows nothing about how to survive in the woods. That's why I'm so sure this trick'll fool them. They'll be over-confident and careless, so they'll fall for this trick . . . I think."

Grace smiled as I slid off the end of the tree. I picked her up and decided to carry her. I walked gently and carefully, flat-footed, on the soles of my boots, for about a hundred yards in the wrong direction, then I put Grace down. We jogged as we circled around to get back to the river and proceeded southwesterly.

After jogging a half mile, we slowed to a fast walk. It was the middle of the afternoon. When Grace caught her breath, she said, "Daddy, I'm really tired and hungry, When can we stop for a rest?"

I could see that she was still out of breath and this ordeal was extremely difficult for her. But I was so proud of her for giving her best effort, though I couldn't help wondering how long she could last at the pace that we were traveling.

"It's a little after three o'clock now, Sweetheart," I said affectionately, as I looked at my watch. "We'll be able to stop in an hour or two, just before it gets dark. But until then we need to walk as quickly as we can and you can eat the gorp as we walk, OK? I could use some, too," I stated, as we both reached into our jacket pocket to get a gorp bag that we had both placed there after lunch.

I said, "When we stop, I'll build a fire by the river and I'll fix you a package of dried soup that I found in the cabin. All I have to do is mix it with hot water. You'll like it and it'll warm you up. Then I'll show you a special way of keeping warm at night, so you'll get a good nights sleep even when the night temperature keeps getting colder and colder. OK?" Grace gave a tired but affirmative nod of her head and looked at me curiously. She must have been wondering how she'd stay warm on a frigid night.

We kept walking and eating gorp, but near dusk we stopped to build a campfire and rest. I put my arm around Grace and called her attention to the western sky, where the sun was setting behind the horizon, while casting a beautiful crimson glow onto the bottoms of milky white, cumulus clouds. It made those clouds look like pure, white snow that's piled on top of red campfire coals.

Prior to building our campfire, however, we both went off in opposite directions to relieve our bladders. When finished, we both picked up dry sticks and tinder for the campfire. We met again at the spot I had indicated for our camp, a small, level clearing covered with a thick mattress of brightly colored autumn leaves. Grace slumped to the ground, exhausted as a few of the brightly colored leaves crinkled under her weight. She looked as if she were sitting on a huge artist's pallet. Looking at her, I wished I had a painting of her just like that.

/--/../-.-/./..-./.-./././-./-.-./.....//../../...//..-./..-/-./-./-.-/

Chapter 10

★★★★
Nightfall

"THIS LOOKS LIKE A good place to camp tonight," I said to Grace.

She nodded her head up and down, too exhausted to speak.

"Sit down by that tree, Sweetheart, and I'll get things ready."

Grace dragged herself, head hanging so low that her chin pressed against her chest, to the tree that I'd pointed at and sat down like a dropped sack of potatoes. As she sat, her back pressed against the tree, her head continued to press against her chest and all four appendages immediately went limp. She looked like a marionette with all its strings cut. I heard her ragged breathing. I assumed that her ragged breathing was caused by her chin poking into her chest and the way her neck was bent. My assumption was confirmed when she tilted her head back, closed her eyes, then opened her mouth slightly to take unimpaired, deep breaths. I could see the arteries on both sides of her neck pulsating to the rhythm of her heart beat. I knew the rest would do her good, but I also knew that we wouldn't be able to make good time tomorrow.

I paused to take into account my own condition. Since Nam, I hadn't kept myself in top shape. I guess the part of my forgetting about Nam also included forgetting the rigors of physical fitness since the latter always reminded me of the former.

So, the fact was that we would both be sore and stiff-muscled in the early morning and our muscles would rebel against our activities. How we reacted mentally was yet to be seen. I knew, however, that physical fatigue and mental fatigue were often sad partners Thus it would be an extra tiring day, and being tired physically, as well as mentally, usually meant grumpiness and impatience. But, guess what? When death stalks you, your mind stays alert; an alert mind overrules physical fatigue and you'll "run-till-you-drop." Nam proved that to me . . . but would that platitude hold true for a child, for Grace?

Of course, we'd have to push ourselves to our known limits in order to escape, and, if necessary, we'd have to redefine "our limits"—the notion that one can "push themselves beyond their limits is illogical." If it's your 'limit' then you can't go beyond it, and if you do go beyond it, then it really wasn't your limit—in order to keep pushing ourselves as much as it takes to escape this ordeal. I would have to force myself, and Grace. It will be cruel to treat Grace that way, but it will be a necessary cruelty.

Running for my life wasn't my style, unless against insurmountable odds. If it wasn't for my need to protect Grace, at all costs, I'd be stalking Jake and Tom, instead of them stalking us. Jake and Tom had no idea that they were screwing around with a Jekyll and Hyde personality; Roman and Wolf, respectively. I'm not the reclusive, secretive, intellectual that Jekyll was, nor am I the feral, stalking, lawless killer that Hyde was, but sometimes it seemed that way. Wolf is much more like Hyde than I am like Jekyll. Wolf is somewhat like Hyde with a conscience, and that conscience came from and blended into me. It was how I controlled Wolf. It was what turned Wolf into a weapon of survival for me, in Nam, and now for Grace and me, as we ran from peril and struggled to survive.

There is no doubt that Wolf is vicious, cunning, strong and fast. But Wolf is the silent, hidden part of me that I use to protect myself, and the people I love or care about, in times of dire necessity, in an emergency. He's the "inhuman" part of me, so to speak.

Everyone has certain parts of themselves that they want to hide, I thought, but the important thing was to make sure that the relatively good side is the dominant side, the one in control. In the classic story of good versus evil, Jekyll couldn't control Hyde, but, luckily, I can control Wolf.

Personality aberrations are interesting. We as individuals, who form societies and unite into countries that inhabit the world, are not as civilized as we would like to believe. We disguise our uncivilized attributes behind masks of laws, manners and politeness. We are all capable of viciousness, we are all capable of killing, but we are not all capable of admitting the existence of our darker sides. And who might know the human personality better than Sigmund Freud? In his day, he was the unchallenged master of human personality via his newly formed techniques that became know by the word "psychoanalysis." What did Freud think of mankind? He said, "I have found little that is good about human beings. In my experience most of them are trash." We lie to ourselves every day, not wanting to admit that our basic instincts are savage-like, cruel, blood-thirsty. Thus the need for man-made laws and man-created religions that build a wall between our civilized façades and our uncivilized, primal instincts. I'm not saying it's a bad remedy to control our baser, savage instincts, but I am saying that it's true, though I doubt that one in a thousand would ever admit it. Only when some tragic, life-and-death emergency situation occurs, and they do something violent, perhaps even kill a person, will the doubters finally recognize the truth about themselves and what they are truly capable of doing. War certainly doesn't bring out the very best in "human nature."

I cleared my mind and refocused on myself, Roman Wolfe, and my alter ego, Roamin' Wolf. I knew that I projected onto and into Wolf a conscience that enabled Wolf to see beyond his feral, savage nature and have compassion for those who were weaker and helpless. It is a compassion that doesn't totally focus on my own survival, but on the protection and survival of those who need protection, whether it be from a bully on a school playground or from the anonymous enemy in a war combat zone. My desire and willingness to protect weaker friends showed itself in elementary school, where I reluctantly became acquainted with bullies.

I let Grace sleep as I hurriedly made the Dakota Fire Holes, then walked around the campsite clearing it of surface rocks and fallen branches. I also gathered moss for bedding and plenty of dry firewood and kindling. I started the fire in the Dakota Fire Hole. As I did this, I glanced often at Grace in repose, my great concern for her obvious in the straining creases on my forehead and around my eyes.

If you could read my mind, you'd understand me a lot better. I certainly didn't seek to harm or kill indiscriminately. I wasn't blood-thirsty, like some stereotypes of a wolf, or even like a rogue soldier, but in a "kill or be killed" confrontation, especially one involving close quarters combat, it wouldn't at all be wise to bet against me.

I could feel the presence of Wolf prowling back and forth, like a zoo animal in its cage. Of course, Wolf's cage was my mind, where he kept me alert to my surroundings and attuned to noises that might signal danger. The pressure I felt in my mind was the pressure of Wolf's white paws as he paced back and forth over the soft, spongy, gray-matter of my brain.

I stood with an armful of firewood and remained immobile, my thoughts concentrating on a strange, mental feeling. At first it was a gentle and vague thought that smoothly poked its way up to consciousness, like an air bubble rising to the surface of a body of water. I became apprehensive because, as the thought developed and gradually became more clear, I didn't like it. It brought discomfort with it, yet it was a thought that needed to be prodded, needed more thought so the details became clear. A voice in my head said: *Close quarters combat may not settle this ordeal because Jake and Tom are armed with shotguns, which meant that, for them, close quarters combat wasn't necessary.* But immediately Wolf's voice growled a rejoinder that asked: *Would they really want to immediately kill you and Grace? Wouldn't their sadistic nature require them to have their victims close to them so they could enjoy your terror up close? More than likely they wouldn't want to shoot either of you. To satisfy their sadism, they would want to be close and "close" meant the possibility of close quarters combat.* I smiled delightfully.

"So," I thought, "given the right opportunity, Grace and I could be blown away from a relatively safe distance, one that was out of reach of Wolf, my martial arts and combat knife skills." But considering their sadistic personalities, that probably won't happen. They'd want to capture us so they could torture us, for fun. That thought really agitated me, but being agitated kept me hyper-alert and washed away any minute particle of over-confidence that may have been germinating within me. Then, a thought that had always been present, but always pushed so far back in my mind that it was almost hidden, came to the forefront: Wolf may have to become more active. Grace and I may not be able to run much longer—I could, but probably not Grace. She was exhausted, her energy depleted, her muscles on the verge of collapse. My heart cried tears of blood for her physical and mental pain and discomfort. Was this ordeal to be like Nam with me and Wolf prowling, stalking, then killing the unsuspecting enemy before that enemy had a chance to launch an attack? I stared at Grace during this sobering and frightening thought.

I forced myself to refocus on our immediate situation. Grace and I were about one hundred feet from the Cold River. I had to hurry before darkness set in. I picked up another armload of dry firewood, then searched for five dead, but sturdy branches that would assist me in building a quick lean-to for a shelter, in case of snow. It took a couple of trips, but I located five long branches that were each about eight feet long, then two shorter ones that were about four feet each.

I was reluctantly forced to use one of my knives to dig two narrow holes in the ground, about seven feet apart. My knives were my only weapons, now, and I didn't want to dull or chip a blade on nearly-frozen ground or on a sub-surface rock. Therefore I used my pocket knife. I looked around and found a sturdy stick and shaved the end with my combat blade so that the end of the stick was now pointed. It would make a very good dirt-punch and digging tool and only took five minutes to prepare. I also dug about a foot deep, a foot wide, and a four feet long trench in the ground near the center of the side of the lean-to that Grace would be sleeping on.

Now the narrow holes, seven feet apart. The first inch of ground was almost frozen, so digging the holes with my stick would be a tough job. I didn't want to expend a lot of energy like I had done on the trench. Therefore, I carefully used my pocket knife to cut circular, one inch diameter and one inch thick pieces of dirt off the top of the ground where each hole would be. Then, to make the two holes deeper, I used the pointed stick-punch. I inserted the stick-punch into the shallow holes and pounded the top of the punch to drive it down into the softer dirt. I did the same for the other hole. Each hole only needed to be about six or eight inches deep, so it didn't take long to do that job. When I had finished digging the two holes, I placed each shorter branch into each hole so they were straight up and down, then packed the dirt back in around the buried portion of the branch. I made deep, "V" shaped cuts into the upper part of these shorter branches, about two inches down from the tops. I then cut off two pieces of dental floss, each about two feet long and two more pieces each about a foot long.. I made a loop in each of the two feet lengths of floss by tying the ends together, then used the one foot lengths to attach the loops to the "V" shaped cuts. When I finished tying the loops to the upper pole's loops I grabbed three of the five, eight-feet long poles. The first pole I pushed into the loops that were hanging down from each of the four feet poles so it looked like a rectangle with a piece missing— the ground piece. Then I took the other two, eight-feet poles and slipped them into the floss loops so they slanted backwards away from the other three poles. Lastly, I place the other two, eight-feet poles equidistant between the first two, slanted eight-feet poles. When all this was done, my lean-to looked like two, attached right-triangles with the short, upright side being nearly four feet high, the slanting eight feet branches being the hypotenuse and the ground being the base that formed the right angle.

There wasn't much of a breeze within the tree cover, but there was a little, so I built the lean-to so that the wind would strike the slanting roof, which, when covered with a thick layer of pine tree branches, would shield Grace and me from the wind-chill factor.

I looked at Grace, again. She was still sound asleep, her head leaning down to her shoulder and her back up against the tree. I knew I'd have to wake her up when I was done because we needed to eat before we slept. I thought: "Our bodies needed nourishment so that we will be better prepared to get up early and move out quickly. That way Jake and Tom wouldn't gain too much time on us while we were sleeping. They would leave their camp at dawn, or before, but we would wait until dawn so Grace could see where she was walking."

I cut a couple dozen, long pine tree branches off the plentiful, nearby trees, then used the floss to tie them perpendicularly across the four, eight-feet sections of the lean-to—so they didn't fall through. When I couldn't see through the layer of pine branches, I was nearly done.   I quickly found four, long, dead branches and laid them equidistant on top of the pine tree branches to keep the pine branches from dislodging or shifting from their positions. Now the lean-to was complete and only took about twenty minutes of hurried work.

Building a lean-to is the secret to staying warmer on cold nights. It was protection from wind, rain and snow. It was one of the things I was referring to earlier when I told Grace that I'd show her the secret to keeping warm outdoors on a frigid night. It's extra work, but keeping warm and dry is of life-saving importance.

I noticed that the light was fading sooner than I had anticipated, so I quickly looked for four flat rocks that were approximately one foot long, about six to nine inches wide and a couple of inches thick. I intended to heat them with the campfire. These heated rocks would be the most important factor of all for keeping Grace warm until morning.

I stayed well away from the river in my search for these rocks because river rocks often have trapped moisture in them and when heated, the moisture turns to steam, which creates tremendous pressure inside the rocks, which causes the rocks to explode, spraying dangerous, stony shrapnel into the faces of those persons who are sitting around the campfire. I found the dry rocks that I needed.

Next, I scurried to gather as many dry leaves and moss as I could and placed them on my side of the lean-to so the wind wouldn't blow them away. Then, quickly, I cleared an area of ground about three feet in front of the opening to the lean-to and prepared to build a regular, above ground campfire. I wanted a clear area, free of flammable objects because I didn't want to start a forest fire, although, on second thought, I figured that, maybe I'd get help faster if I did just that. But I immediately discarded that line of reasoning. It was a bad idea and I didn't have time to waste on bad ideas.

I sure was glad not to have to try and make a bow drill like the Native Americans used in order to start a friction fire. I pulled two of the waxed matches out of my pocket and placed them on the ground. The ground was still rather dry and, knowing this made me appreciate the fact that, although the sky had been overcast all day, it hadn't rained. But I was even more appreciative of the fact that it hadn't snowed yet either, nor had the weather turned bitter cold. I knew it would happen soon, however, but I hoped that Grace and I would be back to civilization by then. I wasn't really a woodsman. I just liked reading about survival situations, and much of the information I read stuck in my mind. Now I was using some of that dormant knowledge.

Of course Nam was a survival situation of a different sort. Supplies were dropped to us from helicopters so we didn't have to worry about building fires, or hunting for our food, or what to wear, or where we'd be sleeping. Our needs were taken care of by the omnipresent helicopters, but out here, in the Adirondacks Grace and I were on our own. Whatever we brought with us is all we had and if we needed more, then we had to find it in nature, or make it from nature's materials. We simply didn't have the time to do any of that. I was also extremely thankful for our good fortune in finding the bags of gorp.

I built a special, Native American fire called the Dakota Fire Holes. It takes a little more work than simply building a fire on top of the ground, but it has definite advantages, especially if the ground surface is wet or nearly frozen. The extra work is worth it because the Dakota Fire Holes have an efficient consumption of fuel that greatly reduces the amount of firewood needed to cook a meal—it produces hotter fires with less wood—boil water, or to keep warm. This type of fire is like having a wood stove, using the ground as a level and stable platform for cooking food—four green branches laid over the hole can be used as a grill for cooking. Also, at night, the firelight itself is hidden in the hole, plus the fire does not give off as much smoke since the fire burns hotter and more efficiently than an above ground fire. Furthermore, all the heat is directed upward, not sideways for three hundred and sixty degrees around, as it would be with an above ground fire.

To build it, I first had to dig two holes in the ground about a foot apart and, also, about a foot deep. When I finished that, I dug a small hole, like a short, small tunnel, connecting the bottoms of the two holes. One hole serves as an airway for the fire—the hole that is closest to the direction the wind is coming from. The other hole is for the fire. These Dakota Fire Holes work so well and are so efficient because, as the fire burns, the hot air that's created travels up through the fire hole, which, in turn, creates a suction-type of draft that forces air down the other hole and through the tunnel directly into the base of the fire, sort of like the bellows in a blacksmith's shop.

With both holes completed I got up and walked to a copse of trees to collect tinder and various larger sizes of firewood. I needed to collect a good supply of firewood before I started the kindling—you can't very well build the fire, then have to run around collecting wood for it. I peeled off sections of the paper-like bark from some birch trees. This bark can be peeled off quite easily, using a knife or sharp-edged stone, and has combustible, natural oils in it. Then I crumpled the paper-like bark so the fibers started to show and the bark started to shred. I added dry grass and very tiny twigs that I located under pine trees, where the umbrella shape of the lower branches keeps them dry. I placed this ball of tinder into the fire hole. Then I took out the dry, smooth, flat rock from my back pocket, picked up one match and struck the waxed head against the stone. The tip of the match broke off and ignited at the same time. The flaming tip jumped to the ground like a comet leaping across the night sky. It landed on the cold ground and died immediately, after a brief sizzling sound.

I took the second match in hand and, not putting as much downward pressure on it, I struck it across the face of the stone. It burst into flame, and as the flame journeyed up the wooden shaft, I carefully placed it into the ball of tinder. The tinder caught fire easily and the twigs were in flames almost instantly. Then all I had to do is add thicker, dry twigs, then thicker, dry branches—they have to be short to fit the diameter of the hole.

As I placed thicker pieces of wood into the fire hole, I thought about some of the information about survival that I'd never used, but had remembered. I could have used the toilet paper for the tinder, if I couldn't find dry tinder. I even remembered about using punk for tinder. Punk is wood that's so thoroughly decayed, dry and crumbly and, supposedly, makes easily ignited tinder. And punk can be found dry even on rainy days by searching the hollow sections of fallen, rotten trees. Another unexpected source of tinder, I thought, was abandoned bird's nests with their intertwined bunch of dried twigs which will usually ignite quickly. Bird's nests are often easy to find in the short saplings, especially in the winter when the tree branches are bare, though climbing is sometimes necessary to retrieve some nests.

I walked to the river and filled our canteens, then filled the aluminum cup three-fourths full of water, poured some dried soup mixture into the cup and placed the cup next to some red-hot coals over the fire.—the cup rested on very green, small sapling sections that, when placed over the fire hole, make them look like a grill. I also grabbed the four large, flat, rocks and placed them half hanging over the lip of the fire hole, to be heated and used later.

The fire was a comforting sight. Its warmth was welcomed and it also pushed away the night's blackness and the nighttime's damp chill that will soon engulf the both of us, like having a damp blanket wrapped around you on a very cold night.

Of course, those were *my* thoughts, not those of Wolf. Wolf was seldom cold. Wolf and I saw the night as a loyal and trusted ally, but I got cold and Wolf didn't. Wolf and I thought there was no better time to meet one's enemy than in the *dead of night*. The darkness wrapped itself around us like a dark cloak of comfort, unless, for me, it was one of those damp, chilly nights that could chill me to the bone, though, if I had to, I could mentally block out the cold, like John Madden. He was the long ago coach of the Oakland Raiders professional football team. He prowled the sidelines on a cold December Sunday coaching his football team while wearing a short-sleeve shirt, yet he looked comfortable and never shivered—at least not when the camera was on him.

It was time to wake up Grace. I walked to her, shook her, but she didn't want to wake-up. I didn't blame her, but I knew she had to eat, even though her body was screaming for rest. She woke up after a few minutes of my prodding and coaxing. After she got over being angry at me for waking her, she hugged me tightly. We sat on the unrolled sleeping bags which were on the ground next to the fire. Her face was buried in my chest and as she spoke, her words were slightly muffled by my coat.

She said, "Why don't those awful men just let us go? I want Mommy and Grandma and Grandpa, Daddy." Then she cried and I could feel her body shaking against mine. I didn't answer any of her questions. I felt that they were questions that were rhetorical and said out of a deep sense of frustration and fear. Her questions were a way to vent her angry feelings, but didn't require a direct answer. So I quietly sat there stroking her hair gently, comforting her as much as possible; staring out into the night time blackness in a semi-daze. In my mind

I was in Nam, in my heart there was rage and at my core there was Wolf.

I couldn't tell her the truth, that we couldn't move as quickly as Jake and Tom because she simply didn't have the stamina or the strength to move that fast. I knew she was doing the very best that she could, but she was exhausted from that herculean effort. We had to move as fast as Grace could go, but she was slowing down quickly like a long-distance runner approaching the finish line of a race. That meant that we would be constantly losing ground to them. I also didn't tell her that I thought they'd catch up to us about the time that we reached Long Lake, probably tomorrow evening. They'd be extremely volatile and hostile men as they fast-walked and ran as fast as they possible could, with short rest breaks. But, they were grown men, woodsmen, with a lot of stamina for quick, long distance traveling. I was worried, but I didn't let Grace know it, not in my voice, nor in my actions. She hurt enough physically already and I didn't want to add stressful emotional burdens as well. I tried to keep my attitude hopeful and self-confident.

Actually that response worked well for my platoon buddies in Nam, too. Their self-confidence was tied to mine, as their leader, just like the tail of a kite is connected to the kite itself and keeps the kite stable. So, for them, I kept the kite as high and as stable as possible without letting them know or see my own fears and doubts because, then, they would be fearful and doubtful, perhaps making deadly mistakes for themselves and others.

Grace's soup was ready. It was hot and it nourished her as well as it warmed her. The cup was so hot that she had to hold it in mittened hands. I was relieved to see her enjoy the warmth on her fingers and palms as she sipped it slowly so as not to burn her lips and tongue. She offered me some, but I told her I'd make some for myself later—though I would probably just eat some gorp.

The fire's hot coals were radiating comforting heat, but we had to hold our hands and faces close to the fire hole. We could each feel the warmth on our hands and faces. The heat felt good, like the feeling of the sun shining on your face on the first clear, warm, spring day. She drank her soup with a satisfied smile. I suddenly remembered the venison jerky that was in my backpack—a needed change from the gorp. I took some out. It was hard chewing, putting a strain on my jaw muscles, but it didn't taste bad once my saliva softened it. Grace didn't want any of it. The hot soup was having a wonderful drowsy inducing effect on her.

Actually I really wasn't that hungry. Most people who are in a survival situation become overly concerned about what they're going to eat. Yet out of the four necessities for survival: shelter, water, fire and food, food was usually considered the least important. Chances are you can survive for a month or more without eating very much. Water is usually considered the most essential, much more important than food because you can survive only a few days without it, which makes sense since nearly seventy percent of your body is water. However, shelter could be the most critical necessity in survival situations because a person stranded in a hostile environment, without any shelter from the elements, in extreme heat or cold, may not live more than a few hours. In a warm or hot climate, like Nam, shelter was not as important to survival, but in frigid weather, like we were experiencing, shelter was of paramount importance. The circumstances dictated the relative importance of the four necessities for survival, but food was almost always the least important.

Water is of critical importance to every bodily function including an alert thinking process. A person couldn't live without water much longer than a few days, maybe a week at the most, and possibly only a few hours in a very hot, very dry desert climate. The liquids we drink simply do not stay in our bodies for very long and constantly need replenishing. The lack of water not only leads to adverse physical effects but also to adverse mental effects. Dehydration can cause mental depression (leading to body pains, hallucinations, and delusions), poor judgment and reasoning ability, slowed muscle activity and nausea. That's why I keep Grace and I both properly hydrated.

I looked at Grace. Her soup was gone, the cup had fallen out of her hands and was on the ground. She was fast asleep with her head in my lap. I got up, unrolled the sleeping bag, placed her inside it and zipped it up, but left her near the tree. Then I used bendable sapling tongs to place the four, hot rocks into the trench that I had previously dug in the ground, inside of the lean-to. I spaced the four rocks about a foot apart, then I covered the rocks with four to six inches of dirt so that the area was fairly level. I then covered the trench, thinly, with pine needles, leaves and dried weeds. I waited for about fifteen minutes to let the hot rocks steam away the moisture that was in the dirt so that Grace wouldn't be sleeping in an uncomfortable steam bath. Then I walked back to Grace, picked her up, while she was still inside the sleeping bag, walked back to the lean-to and held her as I placed my hand over the trench to feel for too much heat. I could feel the warmth on my palms. The sensation was pleasing, like a hot shower on a cold morning. The warmth of the rocks was heating the dirt and boughs nicely, so I placed Grace on top of the heated trench. I knew that she would sleep warmly all night.

Not much fire light reached her, but some did. I studied her pale face and admired it, as well as her nose, her soft, full lips (which were just like her mom's), her fair, clear complexion, rounded cheekbones, all framed within fine, dark brown hair (like mine). There was strength of character in that eight year old face. She was no ordinary child— every parent has a right to be biased in their opinions of their children. She was very special, she was mine, a part of me. After all, I thought, hadn't she run, jogged and walked quickly with me all day with few complaints and only one break for lunch? Yes, that was a strength that few eight year old girls could possess. I must save her, no matter what, I thought, even if it costs me my own life.

Wolf stirred with agreement inside of me.

I tenderly kissed Grace's cheek and, as I do nearly every night, I whispered in her ear, "Daddy loves you." I looked down at her lovingly as fear festered in my guts. I thought: "When a person becomes a parent, fear attaches itself to them permanently, especially in this age when so many crazies and perverts lurk behind, or in schools, churches, parks, or wherever children congregate. There's so much potential danger in the world that a parent can never be without fear for the well-being of their child or children. And if something terrible did happen to their child, the staggering weight of a ton of sadness, grief and guilt would settle on their shoulders which could only be assuaged by time, and even then, only an ounce of pain a day could be taken away.

I mentioned that dehydration can cause mental depression and decreased mental clarity. That thought jumped into the forefront of my mind, and almost as a reflex action, I bent over to pick the cup off the ground, then started walking toward the river to get more water. When I reached the Cold River and dipped the cup into the water, I had a sudden feeling of panic. I'd left Grace alone. I imagined the worst, of course, so I dashed back to the campfire. The sight of her safely sleeping calmed me. I looked at the empty cup in my hand. The water had all spilled out during my run back to the camp. I scolded myself for going to the river when all I had to do was use the water that was in the canteen. Was my fatigue causing me to lose my mental alertness? My answer was yes . . . and I was angry with myself.

Instead of soup, I drank plenty of water from the canteen, knowing that I could easily fill it tomorrow morning. The water would keep the mental lethargy and depression away. I joked with myself to ease the pressure that I placed on myself. In all seriousness, however, I didn't really have time to be depressed, though I wasn't as mentally sharp as I wanted to be, due to my own fatigue. Can't really nice killers, like me, be happy? Can't fun-loving killers, like me, have a sense of humor? Who was it that said, "Seriousness is the last refuge of deeply, shallow minds?" Jesus Herman Christ! I guess I am getting foggy headed.

I hadn't taken my depression medication and I was in a life threatening situation, but I didn't feel any serious depression, a little dazed from fatigue once in a while, sometimes giddy, but not depressed—hell, I figured that I had plenty of time to get depressed, after I'm dead, and find out that all those anti-God comments that I've made are wrong. Yep, I'm giddy, but at the same time I felt in control . . . mostly. I hoped I wasn't falsely bragging to myself, but I did feel a growing, solid sense of confidence. The problem, however, was that the confidence came and went. One moment I'd feel confident and the next moment I'd be riddled with doubt—manic depressive? My thoughts drifted back and forth like a sail boat in an ever changing wind, but my confidence acted like a rudder that kept me on an even keel, gave me a stable direction and kept me pointed into the troublesome, white-tipped waves that threatened to capsize me.

I closed my eyes and mentally wiped my mind free, like a teacher's freshly erased chalkboard. As my eyes were closed, I asked myself to make a mental picture on that empty chalkboard. As I wondered why I should request such a thing of myself a face slowly took shape, not line-by-line like an artist might sketch or paint a portrait, but the whole face slowly appeared, fuzzy and indistinct at first, then unquestionably distinct and vivid—my face. I saw it as my own face, but it wasn't the way I appeared to others. The image was really a composite of two faces blended together, my human face and Wolf's face. It was like two images, one over-laying the other with my face on top of Wolf's so that my face was much more distinct and predominant than Wolf's. Then I noticed my eyes and, to my surprise, they didn't look like a man's eyes. I realized that they were Wolf's eyes, dark, piercing, searching and wary.

I heard, or thought I heard, a growling voice that said, "Home for Thanksgiving." Immediately following that voice was a distant howling that repeated itself, as if it was echoing off miles of steep canyon walls. Was the howling a real sound coming from the distant forest, or was it a sound created and living totally within my brain?

Abruptly, an image of a fierce-looking, white-wolf replaced the composite image. This wolf looked like it does in some picture books that tell the story of Little Red Riding Hood, its teeth bared, with fierce, piercing eyes and lips pulled back in a feral rictus. I couldn't help but laugh quietly, the face looked comical. I wondered if I should be ashamed of these occasional fantasy, dream-like episodes that I was having. But I did have to admit that they were helpful, no matter what the doctor may say about them, with reference to dealing with reality instead of escaping it. My thoughts unexpectedly shifted again, thoughts that led me to realized that I wasn't trying to escape reality and that I wasn't trying to fool myself. I really did feel confident that I was feeling confident—sorry about that. That feeling of confidence was real. Wolf was a deeply personal, entrenched thought, a vivid concept, a unalterable principle of my survival behavior and that was all very real to me. I smiled as I placed the empty cup back into the backpack.

I was growing tired, but I knew I wouldn't be able to sleep. I kept wondering if Jake and Tom really did stop for the night. They had to stop, I thought, or they'd get lost, or stumble and trip over roots, rocks, or fallen branches. Although that conclusion sounded reasonable, I couldn't relax. Jake and Tom didn't impress me as reasonable men. Also, experience had taught me that conclusions, or solutions, are simply that point at which someone stops thinking. Further thought may have altered or added to that conclusion and made it much better, or more thought could produce a completely different but viable conclusion or solution—a "line" is just a "period" that keeps on thinking. But Jake and Tom didn't seem like the type to give too much thought to the wants and needs of other people. They were very consistent with their behavior and actions. If you knew them for a few days, you'd predict very accurately how they'd think and act because of their consistency—A foolish consistency is the hobgoblin of little minds said Ralph Waldo Emerson. The trouble with persistent consistency, though, is that, by its very definition and nature, it mandates that a persistently consistent person be just as stupid today as he was yesterday and as stupid next year as he is this year. Martial arts training and military training taught me that one step in the path to victory is to *know your enemy*. I know that the Gibsons are very consistent and that's a disadvantage for their "little minds."

I snapped out of my philosophical episode. I had to stay awake, stay alert to danger, just like in Nam.

I stared out into the night. The trees stood out like sentinels surrounding our campsite, tall, black, forbidding, with bare limbs reaching out as if in an attempt to touch us. Then, for some unknown reason, the trees appeared like accumulated columns of towering sins, must be my sins. A weird thought, I admit, but it made me think. I knew my sins were many, too many. But everyone has secrets and sins, some blacker than others. And everyone has their own way of dealing with them. My greater sins weren't just confined to Nam. There are so many things I wished I hadn't said or done, some insignificant to anyone but me, some mortal; unforgettable and, perhaps, unforgivable. Many secrets and sins are the same thing, I thought. But I'm not one to ejaculate them onto the nearest friend or relative, hoping to assuage my guilt. I already knew that my guilt is the consequence of actions that I know are wrong. To be a responsible person means that I must accept responsibility for the consequences of my actions. Since the consequences of some actions is sometimes guilt, then I am responsible for that guilt. In other words, to me at least, guilt must be dealt with responsibly and personally. And how does a former killer deal with guilt responsibly? Well, I certainly don't whine and cry about it to friends, relatives or even strangers in order to make myself feel better.

Such confessions may make me feel better, but the people I tell won't feel better for it. They shouldn't have to bear my secrets or my sins. Telling them and asking them to forgive me or help me deal with it, I think, is cowardly—if you were in pain from a cut, a responsible person would not cut a friend so that he could share the pain. They didn't assist me in the actions that I keep secret or in the sins that I have committed. The guilt is mine alone. I must deal with it without causing more pain and discomfort, instead of spreading it around like some contagious disease, causing misery and pain to friends and relatives. I try to leave them disease-free by handling my own guilt, and I handle my own guilt by trying not to make the same mistakes and trying to be a better person. However, for ordinary shame and guilt, *forgiveness* can be a good, healing salve. I know that there are a plethora of occasions when I need to make sure that I *forgive and forget, before I forget to forgive.*

I laughed at myself when I realized that I had gone back to preaching and philosophizing to myself, as if that was appropriate to my current situation. But, sometimes, one doesn't steer his mind, his mind steers him.

I pushed more wood into the fire and moved over towards a tree to lean my back against it. I thought about how much I missed my reclining chair, how comfortable it was to relax on it as I read one of the Spenser detective novels that I'm so fond of. I remembered the T.V. show, based on Robert B. Parker's books, entitled *Spenser For Hire.* I'd read every single one of those books and was thinking of reading them all over again. I wished that Spenser and Hawk were here with me, but I reminded myself that they were imaginary characters and that they were fun to think about and enjoy. I still had fun comparing Spenser to myself, as Roman, and comparing Hawk to Wolf.

I wondered if Spenser and Hawk weren't just the two sides of Robert B. Parker, Spenser being the logical, moral, humorous side of Parker, while Hawk represented the emotionally hostile, semi-moral, mean side of Parker that was hidden beneath the surface of a calm Spenserian exterior, like me and Wolf. They both have their place, I thought, and if I had to pick between the both of them to help me out of this particular situation, I'd pick Hawk, just like I readily accepted Wolf's assistance in Nam.

It was getting late now. I could hear the noises of prowling animals, the hoots of owls and the branches at the tops of trees clashing into one another due to the strong breezes. I wondered if some of the noises were footsteps, but Wolf would have let me know if there was danger lurking in those night time shadows.

But as a precaution, I put the fire out quickly, especially to lessen the amount of smoke that would be created—smoke can be smelled for quite a distance—and to eliminate night blindness from the firelight.

I checked on Grace. She looked at peace and comfortable, sleeping soundly and warmly on nature's version of an electric blanket. She wouldn't need the fire for warmth. I would endure the cold like a night stalking, roamin' wolf.

The Adirondacks have a lot of black bears. I wondered if one would come crashing into the camp looking for food. I decided to worry if and when that happened, though, I thought that that's not likely to happen since there's no strong-smelling food or garbage to attract them.

I returned to the tree, sat down and rested my back against it, then pulled out my Ka-Bar, military combat knife from under my left arm. Then I pulled up my left shirt sleeve and coat sleeve until they were about six inches above my wrist. I checked my watch. It was almost eleven P.M. I placed the flat of the blade next to my watch face, blade facing toward my left elbow and slid the edge of the blade carefully up my forearm, as if I were shaving. I smiled with great satisfaction when I felt my arm, where the blade had passed. Where the path of the blade had slid through the hair on my arm, it was now as bare and as smooth as a baby's ass. The blade had cut through the hair as cleanly as a razor-sharp scythe cuts through wheat.

I brushed off my arm after placing the blade on my lap. The feel of it, the weight of it, the experiences that I had with it gave me comfort. The Ka-Bar was Parkerized (blackened so that it didn't reflect light). It was a combat knife used in the Armed Forces, especially the Marines and some special forces groups. It was long, sleek, rugged and had good balance. It was a very lethal, up-close combat weapon. I had been well-trained in its use. Specialized combat training and Nam experiences had made me an expert with it.

I held the point of the blade up to the sky. Against the light of the stars I saw its deadly shape. For a few seconds I was mesmerized by its sleek form, like many people are mesmerized by the flames of a fire. I held it tightly and it felt like I was shaking hands with a best friend, then I returned it to its sheath.

I thought about how much I loved nature and smiled at the incongruous fact that I didn't really enjoy camping. I liked hiking, hunting, fishing, but wasn't a fan of tent camping and campfire cooking. Weird, I thought.

The thought of cooking made me think of Sam. I loved her with all my heart, but wasn't very good at showing my feelings. I don't think she ever really understood the extent of my love for her. Sure, she knows I love her, but it's the degree of that love that I don't think she fully comprehends. It's almost like she feels that she may not be good enough for me when, actually, it's exactly the opposite. I am very much like Spenser, in some ways. Spenser would only sleep with Susan (his exclusive inamorata in the books) and I feel that way about Sam. I love her too much to cheat on her. Plus, I consider myself to be basically honest, honorable and trustworthy. Cheating on Sam would force me to change that image of myself, and I don't want to do that. I like being an honorable person who can be trusted in such matters.

I know that I don't show Sam enough how much I love her. I'm not too verbal about my love for her. Plus I know that I'm moody and depressed a lot. I enjoy being alone too much and she probably feels like I'm shutting her out, but I don't mean it to appear that way. When I'm alone, I'm not lonely, I'm at peace, happy contented. I've also been easily distracted lately. My thoughts drift and I appear to be a million miles away, not responding to her, or anyone else's inquiries. I'm not as good a husband as I'd like to be, but I can't help myself. That's who I am. But when I get back, I'll have to talk to Sam, try to make her understand that I do love her and that my silence, moodiness and depression aren't caused by her presence, speech or actions.

I pictured Sam in my mind and very much wanted to hold her, kiss her, but I knew that those feelings would have to wait. Then a thought occurred to me: When Grace and I make it through this ordeal (positive thinking), Sam would have to love the Wolf part of me, too, wouldn't she? I humorously wondered how Sam would react to having a wolf in bed with her, figuratively speaking, of course. My stomach muscles jumped with muted laughter.

/-/..../.-/-./-.-/.../-/- - -/.-../.-/-./.-./-.- -/..-./.-/./.-./-.-./..../

Chapter 11

★★★★

Footsteps

SLEEP DIDN'T FIND ME that night because I spent the late night and early morning hours patrolling the camp area. I was sure that Jake and Tom wouldn't be able to catch up to us during the night, but I didn't want to take a chance on Grace and I being murdered in our sleep. I kept myself alert for most of the night. Actually, Wolf's acute senses were mostly in control. He wouldn't allow me to take any chances. Being tired was a lot better than being dead. The feel of anxiety and fear of impending battle was similar to Nam, but much more intense because I had Grace to protect. Going into battle alone, in a "kill or be killed" situation, with just my own life at stake, is not as frightening as knowing that if I don't prevail, my daughter dies with me . . . and, perhaps, dies painfully. That's the kind of fright that paralyzes the muscles and freezes the brain of a loving father. I couldn't allow that to happen; I wouldn't allow that to happen.

Grace and I would be home for Thanksgiving, I demanded of myself. Then, just prior to 2:00 A.M., I gave myself permission to get a couple hours of pre-dawn sleep. Wolf would be on guard during my short slumber, which turned out to be shorter than expected.

Wolf startled me awake with an serious growl. I cleared my head of grogginess. Footsteps? Did I hear footsteps in the forest? Sound carries more clearly and for a greater distance in the night time air than in day time, especially if there's no foliage to block the sound waves. I thought I detected a dragging sound, like tired feet that weren't being lifted high enough to clear the dead leaves and branches that lay all over the ground. Then I heard crunching, scratching sounds—my vision and hearing were heightened by Wolf. Twigs were being broken and clothing was brushing against bushes. Jake and Tom might be woodsmen, but in the dark their silent, stalking skills apparently were being nullified.

I sprang to my feet and leaned closely against the tree that had served as my back support during my short sleep. My eyes carefully searched the area where I thought the noise was coming from.

Grace and I were vulnerable. I was wrong about the speed with which vengeance had propelled Jake and Tom through the forest. I was near panic, worried sick and feeling grenades going off inside my stomach. My Ka-Bar appeared in my hand as if by magic.

My eyes penetrated the forest's black shadows. I transferred the knife to my left hand and slowly, while concealed by the tree, reached up to my collar and grabbed the throwing knife. I broke out in a sweat knowing that Grace was only a few feet way, sleeping and in danger. Increased panic started to bubble up inside of me, like a boiling geyser. My stomach muscles tightened and my guts twisted into Gordian knots. My chest felt as if it were in a vice as my heart raced almost out of control. The night air was cold, but my face felt hot, flushed, and I couldn't think clearly. I couldn't shake my head in an attempt to clear it of the mental fogginess because movement, especially quick movements, attract attention the most and I didn't want to give my position away. I squeezed my eyelids closed and mentally forced clarity. Finally, a plan of action developed. Because I had the element of surprise, I could probably incapacitate either Jake or Tom with the throwing knife, even though they had shotguns. But then the remaining man would have a tremendous advantage over me since I couldn't both save Grace and dart into the forest to stalk the lone survivor. He would just grab Grace and I'd have to come out into the open to try to save her. I'd have to stand my ground and hope that

Wolf's survival instincts were as good as they were in Nam. Not much of a plan, I thought, but better than dazed panic and inaction.

The faint noises continued to approach. I searched through the underbrush as my chest shook from the force of my battering heart beat. My eyes strained to focus on the origin and direction of the sounds as I willed my heart beat to slow. I felt my eyes widen, like huge saucers. My jaw went slack, then tightened. My arms fell limply to my sides. The sight that I saw was shocking.

I returned my blades to their sheaths, closed my eyes and took deep, lung-filling breaths of air. The sight of those two raccoons slowly foraging for food over the dry autumn leaves was a relief that defies explanation. What a hell of a way to start the early morning hours of November 19th.

For breakfast, I could have eaten my own heart, it was so far up into my throat that it was almost chewable. I wiped the sweat off my forehead with my forearm sleeve. Raccoons, I thought with a grin . . . not men's footsteps. Those damn raccoons, I thought. They scared the shit out of me, figuratively speaking. That scare had an extreme asshole "pucker factor" rating. I felt myself rubbing my face in embarrassment, as if I was washing with a wash cloth. When my hand dropped away from my face, panic was replaced by calm, and the grimace was replaced by an embarrassed smile.

I walked to the lean-to and checked Grace immediately. I could tell that she slept deeply and comfortably during the night because her face looked angelic and peaceful. I hoped that it had an invigorating effect on her because I knew this day would be very difficult. I also knew that her present comfort, warmth and restored energy wouldn't last long. I hoped that she would have the stamina to keep traveling quickly, at least for the morning hours. I lowered myself next to her knowing that I could never sleep after the scare and embarrassment that I had just been through. I lay next to her just resting for a little while, until dawn.

I awakened a couple of hours after dawn, amazed that I had fallen asleep. I woke Grace and we packed our things quickly. As we did that, I told Grace, "We'll have to eat as we walk. We have to get moving quickly because I fell asleep."

I had intended to leave at daybreak, but now the sun was up over the horizon and I berated myself for my carelessness. Wolf must have thought that I needed the rest, and since he sensed no immediate danger he let me sleep. I mentally berated him, too. A recalcitrant growl is the only response that I received from him.

As we were about to leave camp, I picked up a cool chunk of charcoal from the campfire. I stuck it into a corner of my backpack, then kicked as much sod and dirt as I could onto the feeble remains of the campfire. As we walked southwest, along the Cold River, there were flurries in the air. Again, I was very thankful that there was no heavy snowfall because it would severely limit our chances of escaping. Even a light snow would make tracking us so much easier and neither Grace nor I were dressed for windy, bitterly cold or snowy days in this wild, remote Adirondack wilderness. We'd be in serious trouble if there was a snowstorm—of course, so would Jake and Tom, but they'd know how to survive it better than I. By now, however, they really didn't need to track us. They would know that we were heading for the canoes.

"Daddy? Can't we sit while we eat the gorp?" Grace asked.

"No. I'm sorry, Sweetheart, but we need to keep moving as fast as we can. We'll have to eat as we walk because I overslept, but we can stop for a while when it's time for lunch."

Grace's brow wrinkled with concern and I knew that she was thinking that lunch time was a few hours away.

So we both ate our breakfast of gorp as we walked, being extra careful not to trip and spill any of the precious energy-packed food. I was sorry that I couldn't fix us a hot meal for breakfast, especially for Grace. It would have gotten us off to a better start and in a better frame of mind—teachers always say that breakfast is the most important meal of the day for children.

I tried to stay close to the river, where the trees weren't as dense. That way we could walk faster and straighter because we wouldn't be constantly dodging as many trees. It would be nice to travel "as the crow flies," fast and straight, but that wasn't a possibility. The forest made travel very difficult and slow, especially for Grace whose short legs weren't made for a fast pace that included dodging trees, bushes, fall-downs, rocky outcrops, slippery moss, and the constant ups and downs of the wilderness terrain.

We both finished our gorp about the same time and put our bags away. I pulled my gloves back on and Grace pulled on her mittens.

I took Grace by the hand to help her keep pace with me. After a couple of hours walking, then jogging, then walking, again, over the rough terrain, with only very brief "catch your breath" stops, I felt as if I were dragging a heavy bag.

"Grace," I said too impatiently, "I know how hard this is for you, and how tired you are, but we just can't slow down. Please try to keep up with me. Okay Sweetheart?" I immediately regretted showing my impatience.

I knew she was drained, exhausted, discouraged, but I didn't know what else to do. I could carry her for awhile, but that would slow us down almost as much as Grace's tired body slowed us. I thought about hiding her and seeking out my pursuers, but just the idea of that option scared the crap out of me so I dismissed it quickly. I've always had a serious aversion to running away from my enemy, as we were doing now. My tendency is almost always to move forward, into the danger, head on, one-on-one, best man wins. Alone, I'd be stalking Jake and Tom. The hunters would become the hunted. But I had Grace to protect and not many options about how to protect her. I decided that hiding her and going off to hunt the hunters was a terrible option and to take that option would expose my growing panic and unclear thoughts.

I could see the tears well-up in Grace's eyes. I could feel some of her pain and exhaustion and then my own guilt. Discomfort and sadness was etched all over her dirty face. She looked up at me and spoke. "Daddy, I'm trying. I really am. But my legs and feet hurt bad. I can't even breathe good. My chest hurts. Don't be mad at me, please, Daddy."

"I'm not mad at you, Grace. Really, I'm not. Just do your best, OK?"

Grace hugged my leg and nodded her head to me.

My heart broke as she hugged my leg for support. Shit!, I thought, as I severely chastised myself. How can I treat Grace like a soldier. She's only eight years old. So I bent down and picked her up. I'd carry her as far as I could. She desperately needed a break from our rapid pace. We had come a long way, and almost at top walking speed, in order to make up for the lost time from my over-sleeping.

As I walked as fast as possible, Grace remained on my mind. She was a very sensitive child, always has been. I felt guilty about what I had just said to her. Of course she was trying. She was already doing her very best. Hell, most of the guys in Nam couldn't keep up with me, so how's a little girl supposed to do it?. I shook my head feeling like an insensitive ogre.

Grace wrapped her arms tightly around my neck. Her legs wrapped around my waist. I grabbed my left wrist with my right hand so that both my forearms were under her butt to support her.

I walked quickly, but after a couple hundred tree-dodging yards, I was starting to have difficulty with my footing as we progressed over some rough terrain. Getting through or around the thick underbrush was an awkward strain, also. I slowed my pace. My arms and shoulders ached and my lower back felt like a dagger had been plunged into it. The backpack straps bit viciously into my shoulders and the contents poked me. My breath became raspy with fatigue.

After approximately one-hundred more yards I had to put Grace down. She thanked me for the brief rest, but I knew she was a little disappointed that I had put her down so soon. But she looked up at me and smiled with appreciation.

I looked into her eyes and could feel my heart consumed in an intense conflagration of fatherly love. I realized then, as if it were a revelation, that, where there used to be cold in me, she brought warmth and where there used to be darkness, she brought light, where there used to be sadness, she brought happiness. Then a surprising thought occurred to me. Eventually, she was going to be the mother of Sam's and my grandchildren. The sweet smile spread across my face like maple syrup across pancakes and I could taste the sweetness of it.

We walked until the sun peaked over our heads. I noticed that Grace's face was cut and dirty. Her coat and pants were ripped, also.

I felt my own face and checked my clothes. My clothes were basically in the same condition. Duh! What did I expect, a pristine tuxedo after sitting and sleeping on the ground, constantly brushing my bare skin and clothes against tree bark, branches, bushes, vines? I felt silly. Lack of sleep was having adverse affects on me.

After a couple of hours we stopped, sat on a blow-down tree and shared water and more gorp. It gave us a chance to catch our breaths. We didn't talk; only the wind and the crunching noises of our chewing could be heard.

Tiny snow flurries were increasing, but I doubted they would cover the ground even if it flurried all day, the flurries melted as soon as they hit the ground. The clouds were not numerous enough, nor dark enough to carry much snow. But I could feel the cold wind picking up and, as I had expected, Grace shivered and said, "Daddy. I'm getting cold." I was determined not to speak harshly and with impatience to her.

I could easily see that her lips looked bluish. She shivered again, the body's way of burning energy to produce more heat. To produce more heat, the body needs energy and the gorp was our source of energy. Again, I was very thankful for taking the bags of gorp.

I looked around and spotted an area that must have been marshy during spring and summer. There were many dead and dried cat tails there. Those fuzzy, furry cat tails can be slid right off the plant stem. I gathered many of these, pulled them apart until they resembled large puffs of cotton fibers, then I shoved them inside Grace's coat, between her shirt and her inside coat lining, to act as a good insulation. I did this to her chest and stomach areas and for her back as well. I even shoved them down her sleeves—lightly, so as not to hamper her mobility. Then I took out the dental floss and tied her jacket sleeves more tightly around her wrist to prevent as much heat loss as possible. I tied her coat tightly around her hips, also, so the insulation wouldn't fall out. I also tied the bottom of her pants legs tightly to her boots for the same reason—I didn't put puffs of cottony cat tails down her pants legs because it would take too many cat tails and it would consume too much time, plus it would only hamper her mobility and the cloth-like fibers would probably chafe her skin. I remembered something. I took off my backpack and removed the roll of toilet paper. Paper makes a very good insulation material, also. When Grace was through eating her gorp, I wrapped both her hands in toilet paper, then helped her put on her mittens. And, finally, since the most serious heat loss from the whole body comes from the head, I wrapped the top of her head with several layers of toilet paper so that she looked like a hospital patient who had her head bandaged after brain surgery. Then I placed her hat over the layered toilet paper. I was sure that she'd stay a lot warmer now.

"I bet I look like a silly scarecrow, Daddy, but you know what?" she said, "I feel warmer already."

She gave me a hug and I bent down and kissed her cold cheek. I hoped that she would warm up a lot because kissing her on the cheek was like kissing an ice cube. I maintained a positive attitude and replied, "Yes, Sweetheart, you'll stay a lot warmer now. Wait right here as I climb this tree."

I wanted to find out if I could see Jake and Tom and, if I could see them, how far away they were. I didn't waste time wondering if they were following us. I knew that they had to be following us, I just didn't know how far away they were. It wasn't likely that I'd see them, anyway, not through the thick forest, but I needed to try, just for peace-of-mind.

Once up the tree, as high as I could go safely, I looked across the leafless forest valley that I thought we had just passed through only a few hours before. I spotted a slightly open area that I remembered. I stared at it for about five minutes with the tree swaying in the cold breeze and my cheeks stinging from the wind-blown flurries hitting my frosty flesh.

I thought that the Gibsons were either further back than I thought, or they were further ahead than I thought and, believe me, the latter thought wasn't at all comforting.

I decided to wait in the tree for a couple more minutes. I strained to keep the area in focus. The wind caused my eyes to water and distort my vision. I felt a anxiety twisting my guts as I thought of Jake and Tom being closer than I anticipated.

Then, suddenly, I thought I saw movement. I wiped the tears from my eyes and strained them as I focused on that small, open area that we'd passed through only a few hours ago. Sure enough, incredible luck was on my side and I caught a glimpse of two figures, one behind the other and each with a shotgun barrel across his left forearm as their right hands held the grips. Jake and Tom looked doll-sized and the shotguns looked like toothpicks from this distance. They appeared to be slow-jogging with their heads down, not as a protection from the cold wind or the snow flurries, but because they were looking for tracks, or a place where the ground was disturbed, indicating our travel direction and rate of travel—a good woodsman can get a good idea how fast a person is traveling by the distance between the foot prints and the depth of the foot prints—jogging will leave deeper prints that are farther apart, slow walking will leave shallow prints not spaced too far apart and fast walking will be in between those two. But a tracker would have to know how big and how tall a person is to figure that out and they certainly knew how big and how tall I am.

I looked down, to the ground, at Grace and a great sadness burned inside my chest, as if my heart was on fire. A silent, lingering and desperate hope that they weren't after us—which, realistically, I should not have harbored—was ripped from my flesh like a stubborn, rusty nail from a board.

Ever since we left the cabin, I had secretly held on to the hope that Jake and Tom had wisely decided not to follow us toward civilization, but, rather, had decided that they would bury Lester and travel to other parts of this wilderness with as many supplies as they could handle, now that the Preston Ponds cabin wouldn't remain a secret for very long, not once Grace and I reached safety.

But they'd spent too much time secretly building the cabin and laboriously carrying supplies to it. They intended to use the cabin, not abandon it, therefore they must stop us from reaching civilization and exposing their location. I should've known better. It wasn't a realistic option for them not to follow us, catch us and kill us.

I hurried down the tree—ripping my coat in a couple of places— trying not to show my heightened anxiety to Grace..

Jake and Tom wanted the satisfying taste of revenge for my having killed Lester. Their rage was probably just barely controllable, so they were traveling at a steady, rapid pace. We needed to move quickly.

I grabbed Grace's hand, pulled her up from her sitting position, then started out at a quick pace, thinking, "Is it time to stalk the stalkers, attack the attackers, kill the killers?" Then I thought, "Should I tell Grace what I saw?" No, no, I can't do any of that . . . Not yet, Wolf's voice whispered to me. Grace was already afraid enough and I was already surprised at how fear for her well-being was growing inside of me, like a well-fed monster.

In Nam I acted fearless—maybe crazy, numb and stupid, too—after my first couple of kills, but now I felt more panic and fear than I'd felt in the thirteen months of almost constant jungle warfare in Nam. I didn't like vacillating continually between self-confidence and self-doubting fear. Then, thankfully, I heard the fearless growl of Wolf and felt the great strength that he possessed—that my mind possessed? I calmed myself and mentally prepared myself.

Wolf and I would own the night . . . tonight. I thought that my fear and anxiety would lessen. It should have, but it didn't. I wondered if it showed on my face.

We were about three, possibly four hours ahead of the Gibsons, I calculated. They had gained two or three hours on our approximately six hour head start. That meant that they would catch up to us a few hours after we made camp tonight. I needed to stop an hour or two before night time. I had to stop and make camp and prepare for the Gibsons' arrival. Plus, Grace simply couldn't travel through the night in order to stay ahead of the Gibsons. Even if we could travel through the night, we couldn't maintain a lead on them with our pace slowing drastically and their pace being constant and fast. They must know, I thought, that they are very close to us and were pushing themselves even harder than yesterday. They were full of vengeance and rage, as well as all the adrenaline-induced energy that accompanied those traits.

Grace stumbled, staggered and then caught her balance. She looked up at me, as if she had a sixth sense and could feel my fear and know my thoughts. She said, "You saw them, didn't you, Daddy?"

She stared at me as she walked by my side. Her eyes glazed over with a film of tears, her eyes pleading for me to respond in the negative, but trying to be as brave as she possibly could. I wanted to sweep her off her feet, hug her and kiss her and tell her that we were going to make it, that we were safe. And before I realized what I was doing, that's exactly what I did. I didn't know if what I said was a good thing or a bad thing in this situation. It just happened. It was like an emotional imperative. I felt myself smiling . . . and lying to Grace.

"No, Sweetheart, I didn't see them. They must be farther back than I thought they were. Our tricks must have worked and they couldn't find our trail for a long time. And, with you working so hard to travel fast, we must have gotten way ahead of them. I picked her up, held her tightly and put my cheek against hers. At first she was stiff, like a frozen rope, then she relaxed, like a warm rope. I hid my face from her. Yes, I lied to her, but, I rationalized, and said to myself, "Everybody, except newborn infants, lie don't they?" Truth be told, we are all liars—intentionally saying something that we know is not true. Then I thought, "Sometimes lies aren't only good, they are necessary, like telling a dying person what they want to hear so that their dying is more peaceful for them, even though you are sure that you can't do what they want you to do. Rationalization? Maybe, maybe not. You show me any normal person, over the age of one year old, who claims to have never lied and I'll show you a certified liar. Even the bible is full of intellectual dishonesty, lies like virgins giving birth and oceans being parted. Of course, lies do comfort millions of people, giving them a false, but accepted, feeling of security, happiness and a sense of immortality (in heaven), but accepting lies to make your life comfortable, secure and happy is still a lie, deceitfully told to you and willingly accepted by you, at the cost of truth, rational inquiry, scientific facts and common sense logic.

Referring to religion, George Bernard Shaw stated: "The fact that a believer is happier than a skeptic is no more to the point than the fact that a drunken man is happier than a sober one."

I'll admit, however, that not accepting religious lies does make life much harder, more pessimistic, less hopeful because now all the pressure is on you, and you alone, to solve your personal problems and societal entanglements. There's also no solace in praying to a God for assistance and that knowledge can make life less happy, less comforting, less secure. Nonetheless, personally, I prefer rational thought, its questions and its rational answers based on logic and scientific proof. I'm simply not a person who can abandon rational, common sense in order to search in a dark cellar, at midnight, for an imaginary black cat. Chapman Cohen said, "Gods are fragile things, they can be killed by a whiff of science or a dose of common sense."

A growling cacophony filled my inner ears, giving me new strength. It was Wolf's battle cry, a howling challenge to the evil that was approaching us.

As Grace and I moved quickly through the forest, I imagined that the bare branches were saluting us. I saw it as a sign of respect; of encouragement, a good omen, perhaps, especially since, the night before, the trees looked like the Gibson's evil minions surrounding us like a hangman's noose, then pulling that noose tighter and tighter around us.

Sam's face appeared on my mind-screen. She was one of those rare women, with strikingly beautiful, green eyes that made me feel warm, accepted and comfortable. Her sensuous, full lips were always inviting, but it was her green eyes, flecked with gold, that made me smile about their sensuous invitation. The very first time that I kissed her I felt those warm, soft, pliable and accepting lips. It was as if my own lips were being pleasantly melted by hers, as her eyes invited me to come inside and learn her secrets of love and longing for the right man. I was so glad that it was me that got that invitation. I accepted it without hesitation.

Sam's image lingered in my mind. She was waiting for us. Her smile told me that she knew, one way or another, that I would bring Grace home safely. I would. I had to.

I took Grace's hand in mine and we started to jog slowly. As we jogged, my mind drifted to Dante's Divine Comedy, which begins with the words: "In the middle of the journey of our life I came to myself in a dark wood." My mind kept repeating it over and over like an echoing mantra. I certainly was near the middle of my life and I also was in the dark woods, literally, although it was probably meant to be figurative symbolic for "evil." I'm not sure what it meant in the Comedy, maybe approaching death, but as applied to me, I seemed to be discovering myself all over again. I knew, of course, that I wasn't invincible, that I wasn't an emotionless killer, like I felt that I sometimes had been in Nam, that I was a devoted and loving father, as well as a loyal and loving husband, and that Wolf was just the survivalist part of me—some people might say he was my "dark side"—that became an anthropomorphic white wolf. Nor was Wolf a crazy, rabid or blood-thirsty slayer. He was a personal, private illusion, a mental construct of mine, used for the purposes of vigorous self-protection. This anthropomorphic wolf and I both disliked killing—because I'd given Wolf some human characteristics—yet we were practical realists and knew that killing was sometimes necessary to defend one's life and the lives of others. Killing, like lying, is not always a bad thing.

I snapped out of my daydreaming as Grace asked, "Does Mommy think we're dead, Daddy?" Grace keeps asking me probing questions that I don't want to answer, or that I don't know the answers to.

I answered in a fraction of a second, so sure was I of my lie. "No," I said immediately. "Absolutely not, Grace. Mommy won't believe that, no matter what anyone tells her. She will know that we're alive until she sees . . . (I almost said, 'our bodies.') until she has absolute proof, and that won't happen. I won't let it happen. We'll be home with Mommy soon. She's probably sitting home waiting for us, Sweetheart. She knows I'll bring you home. She knows that if anyone can bring you home, safely, it's me. I promise you that I will. We'll be home for Thanksgiving for sure." I spit those words out rapidly, machine-gun style, then gained control of my emotions. I was being economical and judicious with the "truth," I rationalized.

I stopped myself from verbally rambling on. I was thankful that Grace hadn't noticed the doubt in my voice, but I did believe that, with some good luck and great perseverance, that I could get us home. I had the determination to do just that. We walked quickly even though our legs ached and, to my great surprise, I found myself almost saying a prayer from my childhood Catholic up-bringing—that was definitely not a good sign for a "born-again atheist." Something in me—was it the needed comfort, security and happiness that I mentioned before?— wanted to believe in an all-good and all-powerful and omniscient God who could save us, with one sweep of his or her hand. Maybe that's the primary appeal of religion. When anyone feels that they or anyone they know lacks the power to solve a dire, or potentially tragic problem for them, then, in their helplessness, they conjure-up an imaginary being, God, to give them hope; peace of mind.

My brain became inundated with quotations that I'd read in my search for the existence or non-existence of the Christian God. Clarence Darrow, the famous Scopes trial lawyer, said; "I don't believe in God because I don't believe in Mother Goose." The German philosopher,

Nietzsche, said: "Which is it? Is man only a blunder of God, or God only a blunder of man?" Tennyson, the poet, said: "There lives more faith in honest doubt, believe me, than in half the creeds." And Plato got right to the very heart of the issue, saying, "He was a wise man who created God," though I could easily question Plato's use of the word *wise.*

So here I was, a stern doubter; a serious skeptic of religious beliefs. I couldn't appeal to God for help because I was an atheist who simply didn't possess the ability to have an unquestioning blind-faith in what seemed, to me at least, mankind's biggest fairy tale, a fairy tale full on incredible, naked nonsense, illogic, misinterpretations, grand hyperbole, contradictions and sprinkled with impossibilities.

Occam's Razor is a principle of thought that in essence says: "All other things being equal, the simplest solution or answer to a problem is best." In other words, when more than one competing theories are equal in other respects, this principle recommends selecting the theory that introduces the fewest assumptions and postulates, the fewest entities and the fewest complexities. So which is simpler to understand and believe? God or no God? The irony of Occam's Razor is that it was postulated by a Catholic, Franciscan Friar, named William of Ockham—the principle is named after him, though, today, his name is spelled differently.

I wondered, "What is there that could constitute a convincing proof that a God existed, or didn't exist." Perhaps there was no such thing as proof. Perhaps there is just blind-faith (a believer), doubt (an agnostic), and rejection (atheist). In that case, everyone simply makes their own personal, subjective choice. It would be vastly simpler if God would simply present Himself to the world. Sure would eliminate all doubts. Too simple a solution, I guess. Perhaps God doesn't think too highly of William of Ockham.

But I was attempting to be a critical thinker. There is a significant problem between critical, rational thinking and religious, blind-faith thinking. Critical, rational thinking and religious thinking will always clash because critical, rational thinking is all about questions which may never be answered—no valid proof, yet—whereas religious, blind-faith thinking, in large part, is all about the mandated, religious answers that may never be questioned.

My personal values distinctly parallel Christian values because I was brought up in a predominantly Christian country, but amongst Sunday Christians—Monday through Saturday most were the ward of the devil—Is it just a coincidence that the word "evil" is included in the word "devil?" I certainly didn't grow up to consider myself to be an uncivilized heathen. I was, in most respects, just an average person who acts according to his own secular moral code and that moral code coincided quite closely with a traditional Christian moral code. And why shouldn't it. I was raised in an overwhelmingly Christian society. I felt that I behaved in a way that was best for that society in which I lived—not best for the religion of that society, best for that society. I also believed that I was probably more honest and trustworthy than most Christians that I had experiences with, but that certainly didn't make me a Christian. I believed in the secular code, but not that it had to have religious origins or be inundated with mostly meaningless, religious dogma. I couldn't help grinning when I thought of the majority of Christians, especially the supposedly "born again" minions. They're usually triple pains-in-the-asses, their "second" time around. Naturally, by comparison, my being a "born again atheist" made me perfect, the "second time around." I couldn't help laughing at myself.

I was one step into the shallow part of the creek before I snapped out of my meandering philosophical thoughts. I turned around as I felt the sudden tug on my arm. It was Grace trying to stop me from walking farther into the water. She had been yelling to me to stop, but I had been deep in thought and was oblivious to her words. I was holding her hand and almost pulled her into the water. Luckily, I stopped just in time. Creek? I looked around and saw that this was a small creek that flowed into the Cold River, a small tributary. It was a very shallow area of the creek and the water didn't penetrate, nor overflow, my Timberland boots (the kind that used to sit in a container of water, week after week, in many shoe stores, so that the manufacturer could prove how wonderfully waterproof they are).

I knew it wasn't just a feeling, but a fact, that the temperature was getting much colder when I saw the thin, lacey, fragile fingers of ice that were forming along both edges of this shallow creek. The danger, here, wasn't the deepness of the creek, but the coldness of the water. No matter how waterproof, or insulated a boot is, if you dip it in something extremely cold, then the coldness—not the wetness—on the outside of the boot will eventually transfer to the inside of the boot. But I had taken my boot out of the water almost immediately and hoped that the coldness wouldn't transfer to my foot.

I had been worried about cold feet, especially Grace's, but she hadn't complained about cold feet at all. Cold feet would have slowed us down considerably more, I would've had to carry Grace more often and may have had to stop to build a fire to warm her boots and feet.

Slipping and falling into the water would have certainly meant the death of us, since there was no way to survive without a fire, but stopping to build a fire would have allowed the Gibsons to catch us much more quickly. Death was stalking us. Now I knew what it was like.

I rebuked myself, once again, for my mental wandering. Right now I had to focus not on philosophy but on reality. The Gibsons possess a large reservoir of hatred in which they must bathe daily. When they sweat, I thought, they must ooze anger, vengeance and cruelty. Where other people lived for praise, adulation, or love, the Gibsons lived for fear . . . creating fear in others was their pleasure and entertainment. They were the ultimate sadists and an instinctive proof, for me, that their certainly was no "all-good" God.

I had to keep us traveling at a quick pace, until night time, to maintain our dwindling lead on the Gibsons. I needed the darkness of night and the lead that we had to prepare myself and Grace for the Gibsons angry arrival. I had to admit to myself that I could no longer out-distance them. I had to face reality, face facts. Grace had been stumbling more and more and she was totally exhausted, her energy tank was dry. I had to stop and make a stand . . . a bloody stand . . . a kill-or-be-killed last stand.

I thought about the blackness of night and felt good. Darkness was my friend, my ally, just as it had been in Nam. I wore darkness like a cloak, comfortable, yet deadly.

We were both thirsty so I stopped at the edge of the creek and filled the aluminum cup and we each had a drink. I saved the canteen water just in case our travels took us away from the readily available creek or river water. The water was so cold that it gave me a temporary headache. The same thing happened to Grace. Neither of us drank as much water as we should have because of the "brain-freeze." I was worried about dehydration so I emptied the frigid cup of water and refilled it with the warmer—because it was next to my body—canteen water. We each drank our fill, then I refilled the canteen, carefully, with the frigid river water.

As the brain-freeze ceased, I had an idea that would help us gain a little time on Jake and Tom. So I said to Grace, "Sweetheart, I have an idea and I'll need to carry you for a short while, okay?"

It was almost time to stop for the night and set up camp. Grace was very weary and welcomed whole-heartedly the thought of being carried. She extended her arms to me, as her eyes said, "Thank you." I picked her up into my arms in the same manner that I had done before.

We had been headed southwesterly for two days and, I thought that Jake and Tom would never suspect that I would suddenly veer in another direction, especially since they both thought of me as an unknowledgeable wimp. Of course, I thought to myself, after killing Lester and after yesterday's backtracking maneuver, they may not think I'm such a dolt. But I was betting that they felt so strongly that I was a skinny, helpless, asshole, that they were thoroughly convinced that I had been completely lucky to have gotten the jump on Lester and probably accidentally stumbled on the idea of backtracking. Anyway, I felt Grace and I had a good chance of fooling them, again, by using this creek that ran almost at a right angle to the Cold River

So, with Grace in my arms, I walked into the shallow water at the creek's edge, heading east, against the flow of the creek that eventually emptied into the Cold River. Jake and Tom would certainly expect us to have followed the creek in a westerly direction right to the Cold River. And when they followed the creek, one on each side, all the way to the Cold River, without finding any of our departure tracks, then they'd know that I'd fooled them again. They'd backtrack, of course, then go eastward until they found my creek departure tracks upstream, where they hadn't expected us to go. And, whereas I'd have wasted a fifteen minutes performing this maneuver, they might waste two or three times that amount of time to locate our tracks, again. By then they'd be furious and frustrated (I loved the thought), and, I hoped, would still consider me just a damn, lucky fool to have accidentally mislead them . . . again. I was hoping they would be doggedly stupid and follow us.

Wolf growled, but I was too distracted to pay attention.

I was pleased with myself, my confidence was bolstered by this maneuver to gain time, although the danger of our situation normally wouldn't allow me to have such a thought, as I walked up the creek—without a paddle, so to speak

Suddenly, I felt Grace stiffened in my arms as I heard the ugliest, meanest, deep-throated and terrifying growl that I had ever heard. I looked in the same direction as Grace. For a moment all I could do was stare into those crazed eyes and opened mouth. Those eyes were black pits consumed in agony and clouded with a veil of death. The teeth were literally dripping with pinkish, frothy saliva.

/- -./..-/...-/-.-/- - -/...-/.-/.-../../-.-/../...-/.-/- -./.-./././-/-./..-./.-./.././-./-../

Chapter 12

★★★★

Edge of Night

"ABANDON HOPE, ALL YE who enter here," were the words that inexplicably came to my mind. Those words are from Dante's Inferno, a reminder of hell, pain and anguish. What Grace and I saw was terrifying. For me, it was as if all hope had completely drained from my body. I could feel my heartbeat thumping wildly and coupled with Grace's trembling, my whole body shook and caused me to stumble in the shallow creek.

My constant vacillation between self-doubt and hopelessness, and self-assurance and hopefulness was keeping me off balance, both mentally and physically. I hated that feeling and fought desperately against it. I didn't know why it was happening. Nam wasn't like this. In Nam my confidence was stronger and more consistent, nearly unshakeable. Maybe in Nam I was really overconfident and was just lucky not to have been killed by it. Perhaps I was in denial about the true cause of my inconsistency and unusual self-doubt. It had to be Grace, I thought. I was faced with protecting the life of my own child and that scared me, especially when I valued her life more than my own.

I stared at it as the deadly silence surrounded us and threatened to drown us in its ugliness. No squirrels protested loudly against the blue jays that approached their nests, nor did I see squirrels jumping from limb to limb in the trees. No birds were twittering from their lofty perches. The air was so still it smelled stagnant. Silence was an Army General in full command of this area. Silence, in a forest—or jungle—is a grave warning of some disturbance, of some danger whose unseen presence has frightened the animals and birds into a wary, noiseless fear.

I stood motionless, listening and staring with horrified disbelief.

I stumbled on a slippery rock while crossing the creek. I caught my balance and tried to clear my mind, my ears riveted on the crazed animal's growling, while my eyes saw something out of a Stephen King movie. What the hell was I looking at? All I could see was a slow moving lump on the ground. It wasn't moving forward, but twisting, turning, arching it back like a prostrate person dying in agony.

I asked myself, "Is it a timber wolf, coyote, coydog, or was it a fox? No, I thought, not a fox. It's too large and the wrong colors. A wolf? No. Wolves are larger than coyotes and darker in color. Wolves also carry their tails in a very distinctive position, almost horizontally—a mental message from Wolf confirmed that what I was seeing was not one of his species. Also, I noticed that the animal that we were facing was smaller than I would expect of an adult wolf—though I couldn't tell age—and its fur was light in color. Its tail was carried low, near the back legs. So, Grace and I were staring at a discolored, dirty and mangy coyote or coydog . . . a crazed coyote. One with full-blown rabies. It was "mad" in the very worst, psychatric sense of the word.

I knew that rabies is an awful disease that attacks the brain and spinal cord, creating tremendous pain which is radiated throughout the body by the spinal cord. It also slowly ate away at the brain, eventually causing madness and unstoppable viciousness.

My next thoughts raced through my mind like a cluster of comets racing across the night sky. It's strange how thinking sometimes seems as fast as the speed of light, but using words to express those thoughts seems to take forever. Amongst many Native American tribes, the coyote was a spiritual animal, like the wolf but not nearly as powerful. Those Indians thought of the coyote as a Trickster who loved to play pranks on humans. The Indians were fearful, suspicious and leery of the Trickster's presence an believed the Trickster could communicate with all living things, in their own special language, and thus was able to play devious, dangerous and often fatal tricks on people. And what made him especially dangerous to children was that children were naïve and innocent, whereas the Trickster was a charismatic sycophant, a master charmer, posing as a kindly and flattering friend who could easily lure children into tragedy or death by tricking them into doing something or saying something that might have grave consequences.

I faced directly into the snarling face of Trickster as he lifted his head higher and increased the force of his growl.

Slowly I bent down and gently placed Grace's feet on the ground. I released my grip on her as I kept one eye on the ferocious growling that was coming from the slowly moving lump of ragged, matted, filthy fur. Then I realized that I couldn't straighten up because Grace hadn't let go of my neck.

I saw the beast rise as if from a fresh grave, the leaves, dirt and twigs stuck to its matted fur having camouflaged it so well that it could hardly be seen as it blended into the forest ground and surrounding area. But it was standing now, so I had a good look at it.

When the coyote started snarling louder, Grace pleaded, "Daddy, please . . . I'm scared! Chase it away, Daddy!" Her emotions, coupled with tears made her words come out as if she was being choked. Still close to my ear, as I was bent over her, she tearfully begged me to make the ugly beast go away.

I quickly placed my hand over her mouth and whispered, "Don't say anything, no talking, no noise." I said it in a harsh whisper and stern facial gesture that couldn't be misunderstood. I had to keep her quiet so her loud, panicked voice wouldn't trigger an attack.

I pulled her hands free of my coat, then used my straight index finger, placing it perpendicular to my lips, a silent indication for silence. I whispered, "Take out the knife that I gave you. Open it till it locks and stand behind me. Move very slowly." She whimpered, so I had to whisper, "Stop crying. The noise will upset the coyote." She did as she was told, getting the knife and being silent. She did it very slowly as if the fear she felt was a pair of shackles that hindered her movement and was immobilizing her.

My mind was reeling as it tried to process too much information. I stood on the edge of panic, my heart feeling like it would explode at any second. My thoughts slowly became crystal clear as I felt Wolf leap from a hidden crevice in my brain and spread himself, as of by osmosis, to all areas of my body. Immediately, I felt his strength, speed and cunning. Then I felt something in each of my hands, a combat knife in my left hand and the throwing knife in my right hand. I don't remember taking them from there sheaths, but it was the same phenomenon that often happened in Nam. My heart was still racing, but not racing as it had been a short time ago. Wolf was no longer dormant. In my mind, the feral Wolf in me bared its teeth, snapping his jaws viciously.

When my pale Wolf stood with me, there was always hope. In a life-or-death situation, fear wasn't a weakness, but rather a strength because adrenaline surges through your body, producing the instant energy, speed and strength needed for a desperate fight for life. Also, who would know better how to fight a coyote, than a wolf? Wolves are not only more fierce fighters than coyotes, they are also much smarter.

Wolves are often said to be the smartest of all the wild animals. They will not attack a human, even a child, contrary to popular belief, unless cornered, injured, or if they think their young are in danger. They live in an organized society, with strict rules and positions of dominance and work. They also care for their young until their young can take care of themselves. Wolves, like well trained soldiers, or woodsmen, demonstrate complex hunting tactics and understand how to use strategy and cooperation. Wolves have a bad reputation and for hundreds of years may have been the most misunderstood of all the wild animals, simply because they kill the weakest of the animals that man keeps in herds, even though that kind of killing will improve the breeding results of all those herds due to the fact that only the strongest and brightest will survive to breed.

I understood wolves better than most scientist because Wolf was part of me and communicated with me. We lived together in harmony.

The Native American Comanche believed that a wolf had the soul of a man, a fierce, strong, courageous man, a warrior. When a wolf's spirit found such a man it would inhabit his soul and become that man's spiritual leader. Roamin' Wolf, thus, inhabited Roman Wolfe in a symbiotic relationship.

I felt Grace's hand on the back of my leg, the other hand, hopefully, had a knife in it. I could feel her trembling hand, but couldn't attend to her needs. Our lives were at stake and it wasn't just any animal that confronted us, it was a life-threatening, vicious, rabid animal.

In my initial, startling fear, the coyote seemed to grow larger. Fear makes things larger than life; fear tends to make your senses exaggerate what you see and hear. But Wolf and I had no time for that now as we recognized the beast for what it was, a severely diseased killer . . . an extremely dangerous animal that I desperately wanted to walk away from.

But the coyote took a couple more threatening, unstable steps towards us. I wondered if it was injured, in addition to having what, certainly, had to be a full-blown case of rabies. The growling increased in intensity, a deep throated, primal growling accompanied by eyes that resembled red hot coals in a midnight campfire. Its stiff, mangy fur stood straight up, like the spines of a frightened porcupine and pinkish, frothy saliva dripped from its lips and canine fangs, another classic indication of well developed rabies.

I didn't know what the incubation period was for rabies. But I knew how Jake thought. If one of us were bitten, Jake would hold us both captive for the incubation period, then force whichever one of us wasn't bitten to watch the horrible, lingering death that the rabies disease would cause in the other person. If both of us were bitten, Jake would still hold us captive so he could enjoy watching our slow, agonizingly and torturous demise. But he wouldn't enjoy it this way as much because he wouldn't get the ultimate pleasure of watching the healthy person suffer the terrible agony of watching the diseased person's death after the prolonged, advanced stage of the brain and spine-eating, rabies disease.

I stood perfectly still and as I did this, Grace must have realized that she must do the same because I could sense no movement behind me. I raised the throwing knife slowly up to my right ear. Time slowed down as my senses, Wolf's senses, became hyper-sensitive. I could see the rabid coyote better, magnified, as if I was using binoculars. I could see the coyote's matted fur embedded in it's filthy skin and patches of fur missing where it fell out in clumps. I could smell the foul odor of disease, filth and infection, and I could sense that their was still a primitive, crazed strength in this dying beast.

I whispered to Grace to move when I move. We moved sideways, two short steps, trying to exit this area, to get away. The coyote's growling grew more threatening and its teeth started gnashing, so I stopped moving. I would have to use my throwing knife.

The throwing knife accidentally pressed against my ear and it's coldness caused me to be even more alert. My cold fingers gripped the handle of the balanced blade, my wrist and arm ready to snap forward with both power and speed. I held this position, waiting to see what the rabid coyote would do, but hoping that it would walk away. It didn't appear to have that in mind. It's posture was extremely aggressive, confrontational, with its head held low, body leaning forward and back legs bent. The attack posture.

There are probably only a couple of dozen men in the world that can successfully hunt small game with a throwing knife. I was one of those skilled few. But this wasn't small game. This looked like a large sixty to eighty pound coyote, or coydog, and my ten inch, ten ounce throwing knife probably wouldn't stop it in its tracks. But it would start the death process if I could get an accurate hit that had great velocity and deep penetration. The rabid beast was facing us, thus, I had no shot at all at any soft body area. The head was too boney; the blade would bounce off the hard bone. To hit an eye socket would take a miracle and, if a miracle occurred, that boney orifice was probably not big enough to allow the knife to penetrate deeply into the brain—the width of the orifice being smaller than the width of the knife. So a head shot was a thoroughly wasted shot. Plus, even in a slowed, diseased state, the coyote's reflexes might still allow it to move out of the way of the hurled blade. To get a good shot, I needed to have the animal's body turned sideways so I could have a clear shot at the soft rib area, hoping to penetrate between the bones of the rib cage and hit the heart, or a lung, or anything that would immobilize it.

I turned my head slightly and whispered over my right shoulder, "Grace, slowly pick up a rock and throw it as far as you can over my left shoulder. Don't talk. Poke my back just before you throw the rock."

I could hear Grace's rapid breathing and could sense her bending down to pick up a rock.

The animal's growling became more forceful and intense. It stepped forward aggressively, jaws snapping violently. It stopped its forward movement and I saw its back legs flex, again, becoming tense as it prepared to thrust off of them and lunge at me.

The growl of my own internal Wolf rang in my ears. My legs and arms flexed and I felt a surge of animalistic power grow rapidly in my limbs. My sense of touch, sight, hearing and smell were already acute. I could feel Wolf take control of my body, as my mind gave the commands.

My right hand was still cocked to thrust the throwing knife toward the rabid animal. I wished that I had a Bowie-axe type of throwing-knife made by a knife-maker named Harry McEvoy. This particular hunting and throwing knife was thirteen inches long and a full pound of sleek, deadly, and finely sharpened steel. Thrown with force and speed, its sudden and penetrating impact could knock a large dog, like a German Sheppard, right off its feet. This rabid coyote, or coydog, certainly looked like a large dog, but, like I said before, fear has a tendency to exaggerate things.

My senses were synchronized with Wolf's senses. I had Wolf's speed, strength and cunning, but the karate combat skills and knife fighting skills were those that I had been taught by martial arts experts. However, I doubted that martial arts skills would have anything to do with this confrontation.

I was looking with Wolf's eyes and staring at our mortal enemy when I felt Grace poke my back. A couple of seconds later, Wolf's ears detected the noise from the rock as it bounced off the earth, then rolled across the ground, finally crashing into a bush to our left.

Despite her fear and anxiety, Grace had made a nice throw. Nice because it startled the coyote and caused it to wheel around sideways, to its right, to face the sound.

I quickly took aim at its left side rib-cage area and snapped the blade forward with every ounce of strength that my right arm possessed. Not a sound came from the blade as it sliced its way through the cold air like a silent, heat-seeking missile homing in on its target. The coyote didn't have enough time to react defensively until the blade plunged deeply between its ribs and into its chest cavity, with only a couple inches of the handle sticking out of its body. It was nearly a perfect hit, with very deep penetration . . . but not perfect enough.

Incredibly, the coyote spun around, toward me, as if unhurt, like mortally wounded people and animals can do sometimes, it charged, in spite of the deadly, steel sliver that was now deeply imbedded into its left rib cage area. I gave a loud, panicked yell for Grace to say behind me and to use her knife to protect herself. As I yelled, I was acutely aware of switching the combat blade from my left hand to my right hand, then holding it at waist level, slightly out in front of my right hip, with the razor-honed edge facing downward.

Before it even happened, I could envision the beast leaping up into my face and neck area. It was the same sort of vision that I had had so often in Nam when I was able to clearly picture, in my mind, how the enemy would act and react.

Roamin' Wolf and Roman Wolfe were one, like two sides of the same coin, a unity defined by desperate circumstances.

Wolf was keenly aware of how a coyote would think, act and react and those thoughts became my thoughts. Therefore, I could anticipate the coyote's actions and position my body and my blade to counteract that movement, which I did.

The next thing I saw was a blur of fur as the feral beast sprang off its muscular hind legs, from a running start, its jaws agape in a maniacal snarl, its eyes as black as tar, as its frothy fangs sought my throat.

My gloved left hand came up instinctively under the animal's mouth and clamped into its throat securely, like a vice-grip tool—I was thankful for all the finger and forearm strengthening exercises that I had regularly performed in my karate training—as my right hand thrust the deadly blade swiftly upward and deeply into the solar plexus area of the fierce beast. The blade sank about six inches into the solar plexus cavity and then the breast's weight pushed down on the blade and I felt the blade sink to its full length, all the way to the double, protruding finger guards.

The forest seemed to come alive with noise from the thunderously loud and agonized scream that came bursting from Grace's mouth. She screamed with each breath she took, as the weight and momentum of the beast bore down on me, causing me to free-fall backwards on top of her.

As I was toppling backwards I forced the blade to cut deeply from the chest area to the stomach. Then I felt the sharp claws of one of the beast's paws rake across his right cheek. I wasn't yet conscious of any pain, just the warm sensation of blood welling up to the surface of my skin, then feeling the downward flow of a scarlet rivulet. I held onto the beast's throat as the weight of him forced its Adam's Apple deeply into my iron grip. I took advantage of this fortuitous stroke of luck and squeezed the coyote's Adam's Apple more securely and then strained to grip it so tightly that I thought I'd tear a muscle or tendon in one of my fingers or in my wrist. I felt like my grip was a powerful, mechanical clamp that wouldn't let go, like a pair of vice-grips or a C-clamp from my tool box.

I heard the coyote's front and back legs shredding my coat, and I hoped that they would not penetrate my coat and rake my chest and abdomen.

I rolled off Grace forcing the coyote onto the ground beneath me as I continued to squeeze its throat with my straightened, elbow-locked left arm. I continued to twist and slash with the combat blade inside the beast's chest cavity, hoping to slice or puncture the heart and end the struggle immediately. I couldn't cut his throat because my hand was in the way and I wouldn't release the secure grip that I had on his throat. Now totally focused on the coyote, I wasn't aware of Grace's squirming movements.

I withdrew the blade, then thrust it deeply back into the beast's chest cavity, each probing thrust containing my full strength . . . but the maniacal animal continued to struggle, twist, turn and snarl at me as it sought to sink its teeth into any soft, fleshy area that it could reach. Blood and raw, pink flesh were abundantly exposed.

Though staring into the terrifying mow of this rabid coyote, with bloody mutilation and horrific disease only inches away from me, my iron-will and grip, for the moment, was prevailing.

Instinctively, I knew that I had to keep the mouth and teeth of this fiend away from my cut right cheek because the rabies virus it carried in its saliva is passed into another animal, or human, by biting and getting the virus into the other animal's, or human's, bloodstream.

Suddenly and very fearfully, I realized that I was starting to lose my left hand grip on the slick fur of the coyote's throat. I knew that if I lost that grip I would no longer be able to prevent this maniacal monster from biting me and Grace. I had to control its head or it would be almost certain death, though a delayed death sentence—much later, I found out, after our ordeal that rabies has an incubation period of four to six weeks—for Grace and myself.

This frightening thought sent a new surge of energy to my cramping arms and hands and, in desperation, I pushed the blade deeper into the chest cavity by pushing against the animals soft underbelly area. The blade penetrate, so deeply, in fact, that my fist sank into the warm moistness of the animal's internal body cavity. Steam-like vapor rose, like thin wisps of smoke, from the coyote's body as the cold air and the warm, moistness of the animal's internal body joined together. The stench was nauseating. I immediately repositioned the blade and drove it, again, into the animal's left side chest cavity. I heard the animal gasp and realized that I had finally punctured its heart.

Suddenly all the coyote's muscles slackened, like the rubber of a punctured balloon. Its eyes rolled up into its head, its tongue fell out of its mouth and continued to drip bloody saliva. I felt, with relief, the last spasms of its body. Nevertheless, I took this opportunity to quickly withdraw the blade, push upward with my left hand to expose the neck and, as a precaution, I immediately cut the animal's throat.

After I cut its throat, very little blood flowed out because the pump—the heart—that would have forced the blood out of the coyote's arteries was no longer working.

Finally I knew that the coyote was dead. I moved off the coyote and sat next to it, terribly exhausted and breathing heavily. I dropped the combat blade to the ground, then drew deep breaths into my burning lungs. My wrists and fingers ached from the strained effort of choking the wolf and gripping the combat blade. When I tried to open the fingers of either hand, the curved fingers popped as if they were frozen or rusted into those fist-like positions. My head felt like a drum being beaten upon viciously, as if a migraine was developing. I was out of breath and felt dizzy, but aware enough to feel Wolf's presence fade into a safe place in my mind.

I felt an incredibly deep exhaustion, like none that I had ever felt before and I closed my eyes. When I heard a loud noise, I opened my eyes and was startled to see Grace furiously, like a demonic child from some horror movie, repeatedly and violently stabbing the inert coyote's body with her three inch, lock-back, Ka-Bar pocket knife. She vented her rage as she repeatedly stabbed the coyote, saying, in an angry voice, "Die! . . . Die! . . . Die!" Slowly, cautiously and gently I used my aching left arm to take hold of her stabbing right hand at the wrist. I pulled her hand toward me and, using my right hand, gently tried to pry her fingers off the blade handle. But she too had a vice-like grip on the handle that belied her age and strength. It surprised me just how much pressure I had to use to release her fingers from the bloody handle of her knife. Once released, I let the blade drop to the ground, near my combat knife, then pulled her trembling body toward me. I hugged her closely and tenderly for a long while, rubbing her back and whispering soothing words of comfort to her as she melted into me as if I were her security blanket. She didn't talk, didn't cry, didn't move. For awhile, I didn't move either, despite the fact that in some distant crevice of my brain, I could hear Wolf telling me that I was losing time and needed to get moving.

I recovered my strength slowly. I welcomed the added extra strength and endurance that I received from Wolf, but seeing Grace's rage and furious effort at survival gave me added determination to stay focused and to get home for Thanksgiving.

I looked at Grace. Her mittened hands were covered with blood, fur and intestinal gore. She had stabbed the animal so many times, in one small area, that the animal's intestines were not only protruding, like purplish, coiled snakes, they were severed in many places. In her shocked state, she couldn't see the leaking, intestinal gore, nor smell it, but I could and my nose rebelled against its overpowering stench.

I stood, then bent down and picked up Grace. I carried her as I walked a short distance into the forest, where I laid her down, facing away from the coyote, placed my back pack under her legs, to lift them and get more blood to her brain, then covered her with a blanket.

I returned to the dead canine to skin it. I was sorry that it was rabid—the word "rabies" is a Latin word meaning "rage" or "fury"—because I wanted to cook its hind legs over a campfire and eat the meat, but I couldn't take the chance of doing that since I wasn't sure what the consequences would be (Would cooking it kill the rabies?).

I knew the difference between a poison and venom. A poison had to be swallowed to do its damage, but venom must enter the blood stream to do its damage. That's why a healthy person—no ulcers—could drink a cup of rattle snake venom and have no ill effects from it. But I was too damn exhausted to try to think about how the rabies virus acted, though I assumed that, like venom, it must enter the blood stream to do its damage. But I would take no chances. Better hungry than dead or immobilized by sickness, I thought. However, I couldn't help thinking how good the cooked meat would have tasted, especially since the constant diet of gorp and jerky had changed from being very tasty to what was now a boring chore to eat. The thought of roasted meat inundated my mouth with saliva and I spit it out. Unfortunately, my mind pursued the thought and I ended up spitting or swallowing several times before I could focus on something else.

Much later I was to find out that coyotes are now prevalent in the Adirondack mountains because their natural prey, the timber wolves are gone. According to the New York State Conservationist magazine, wolves were extirpated from New York State approximately by the year 1910. This was mostly due to expanding civilization and its resulting conflicts on the wolf's way of life. I also found that coyotes are much more successful at adapting and living close to civilization because, whereas the wolves normally hunt in packs and need bigger game to eat, such as coyote, deer, moose and caribou, coyotes will hunt individually and can survive and proliferate more easily due to the availability of foods, the variety and quality of foods, and the size of the prey that they will eat, such as rodents, fowl, snakes, frogs, toads, carrion and even fruit, which are all plentiful in the Adirondack mountains.

When I finished skinning the coyote, I used the frigid creek water to wash the combat blade, the throwing knife that I pulled out of the coyote's rib cage and the folding pocket knife. I dropped them all into a shallow, clear part of the creek, used a twig to move them around in the water so the current would wash off the blood, gore and fur, then pulled them out using two twigs as tongs. I dried them off with some of the toilet paper that was in my backpack. I cleaned Grace's mittens and my gloves the same way. Once dry, I placed the combat knife and throwing knife back into their sheaths, then walked to Grace and put the pocket knife into her pants pocket. She said not a word, just stared off into space. I picked her up, then carried her to a clearing where I built a fire to warm her. I also pounded four, two-feet long sticks into the ground, close to the fire. I pushed a glove onto each stick to let them dry.

I cut two saplings, each about three feet long and, using my combat blade, I dug holes into the ground—I was now too tired to worry about dulling the blade—far enough to push the sharpened end of the saplings into the ground about four feet apart, in back of the fire, but only about a foot away from the fire. I washed the coyote skin in the creek, then scraped it—I scraped off the blood, fat and gore from the skinned side. I placed the coyote skin between the two saplings so that it hung, fully stretched out, with the fur side away from the fire so that the side where the blood, fat and gore was, could be dried-out by the heat of the fire.

I felt ecstatic when I heard Grace's voice about an hour later. She said, "I'm hungry, Daddy." I grabbed her small, blanketed body and quickly drew her to my chest. I hugged her and she hugged back as she buried her head into my neck and whispered, "I love you, Daddy."

I was afraid she might be mentally incapacitated by the horror of my life an death struggle with the rabid coyote. To survive that incident, and move on, I needed her help and cooperation. If she had gone into emotional shock, I wouldn't be able to get her cooperation, plus I'd have to carry her. We ate handfuls of the gorp, we looked at each other and smiled often. I was so very thankful that she was okay. I could feel Wolf smiling within me. We were both feeling relieved.

As I looked around the area, it seemed vaguely familiar. I shrugged it off as wishful thinking. But the instinctive feeling persisted and I knew that, just as in Nam, I should listen to my instincts and Wolf's growls.

Wolf's growls were intelligible language to me. Those growls spoke to me, rather than being simple unintelligible varieties of noises. Wolf's growls now made me pause and look around more carefully. I thought I recognized a widow-maker—a blown down tree—lying on the ground, just inside of my visual range. Suddenly, a burst of unforeseen hope inflated my chest. I hurriedly put out the fire, picked up the dried gloves and coyote skin, put the gloves on mine and Grace's hands and shoved the coyote skin into my backpack. I placed the backpack onto my back, then scooped up Grace in her blanket and walked toward the widow-maker. It was late afternoon, but not dusk yet, and as I walked closer and closer I could see the blown-down tree much better. I especially noticed the pointed stump—where the trunk had snapped off—with its wooden shards, of various lengths, standing straight up, as if they were wooden, micro missiles preparing to launch skyward. I set Grace down next to the stump so she could lean her back against it. I then walked along the fallen trunk of the tree, hoping that I was right, but with every footstep I vacillated between elation and fear. I circled around to the north-facing side of the fallen tree and saw a flat rock about the size of a silver dollar wedged into the bark of the tree. That rock was right where I had left it, at the end of Long Lake, where the Gibsons had hidden the canoes. It was my marker. This was the tree that Grace and I sat on while we all stopped to eat, after finishing the long, fifteen mile canoe trip. That meant that the lake and the canoes were close.

My head started spinning with joy. I was so exuberant that I felt like screaming just to listen to the elation in the echo. I restrained myself, however, and smacked my right fist into the palm of my open left hand, then smiled with self-satisfaction.

Now, back to reality. I had been withholding so much fear and anxiety from Grace because I was fairly sure that Jake and Tom would catch up to us tonight. Like blood hounds on a fresh trail, they knew they were close, so they might try to travel by moonlight to raid our camp, catch us unaware, and kill the both of us. I had to decide whether to make camp and prepare a surprise, counter-attack, or to travel by moonlight, without rest, which meant taking the chance of tripping and breaking a leg or arm, or having an eye poked out with a sharp, unseen and low-hanging tree branch, or any other accidental injury. Also, I asked myself, "Could Grace travel through the night with only that one hour of sleep?" I seriously doubted that.

But now that I had found my marker, and knew where I was, I didn't have to think of any of that. I knew I could easily paddle the Long Lake in one of the two hidden canoes. Naturally, I would destroy the other canoe so that Jake and Tom couldn't follow us. And since canoe travel would be so much faster than hiking through thick forests, then every paddle of the canoe would increase our lead over the Gibsons, as long as they were still on foot. As a matter of fact, I thought, once they knew that we were traveling in the canoe, and they couldn't use the other canoe to chase us, Jake and Tom would be forced to give up the chase altogether and take their chances avoiding the law by returning to the wilderness.

I could see that daylight would run out on me soon, so I told Grace about the canoes and the news created an instant source of energy in her. We raced, feeling giddy, for about two-hundred yards westward until we saw the lake through the nude arms of a copse of tree limbs. Beyond the copse of trees I recognized the shoreline and, filled with hope and joy, we walked along it to where the canoes were hidden.

I was in such an unrealistically happy mood that I couldn't help getting side-tracked by the beauty of this Adirondack Forest Preserve. I knew that President Teddy Roosevelt had something to do with setting this land aside so Americans, especially New Yorkers, could enjoy it forever, and I silently thanked him for being such an insightfully, great conservationist.

The beauty of these dense forests, azure ponds, crystal lakes and rugged mountains was astounding. There was a unique and harmoniously symbiotic relationship between these elements of the Forest Preserve and all the wildlife that inhabited it. No other Eastern mountain range, of any Forest Preserve, can boast of more plentiful, more remote or dazzlingly beautiful natural elements. It was truly Mother Nature's eastern treasure chest.

Standing on the shore at dusk, I looked out at Long Lake. While holding Grace's hand, I walked quickly toward the canoes, but my eyes were constantly lured to the beautiful lake as I was mesmerized by the peaceful, mirror-like quality of the water, with the various fall, forest colors and shapes. Even the color of the sky was exquisitely reflected in this pristine, liquid mirror.

But, as I broke out of these thoughts and looked at where the canoes had been hidden, I suddenly felt sick, literally sick. All the childish joy and excitement drained from my body, like a cadaver that has been drained of its blood by a mortician. I could feel the cold embrace of devastating and terrible disappointment as I noticed that the life-saving canoes were gone. I was horrified . . . and now I was unable to hide my feelings. My mind shut down and clouded over, shorting-out the electrical and chemical synapses of human thinking. Mentally, I collapsed. I was a robot without a source of power. My brain was unplugged.

Slowly, I emerged from that overwhelming and demoralizing dark cloud and after the initial shock I remembered that on that night that we all camped here, Jake and Lester left the camp to gather firewood, while Tom was left to guard us. I realized, now, that when they had said they were going to get firewood, it was only a ruse. They had been gone for nearly an hour, but I hadn't been overly suspicious of the length of time that they were gone because they both came back with arm-loads of firewood. Of course, now I knew what had actually happened. They had left camp to go hide the canoes in a different spot or, perhaps, they had knocked holes in the canoe bottoms, then floated them out into the lake to let them sink.

Reluctantly, I had to admit that Jake, though in many ways a misfit miscreant, was a good General, a good tactician to have thought of that—the brilliant, Greek military strategist, Aelianus Tacticus (from which the word "tactics" and "tactical" come from) might have smiled upon him.

So, I suddenly realized, that's why they were still following us and not giving up. That's why they seemed so determined that they'd catch us, in spite of our long head-start, in spite of the fact that we'd probably reach the shore of Long Lake before them. They must have figured that Grace would slow me down tremendously and, if that wasn't enough, then the physical and mental shock of not finding the canoes would act as the final blow to our thoughts of a successful escape. They probably figured that that's when I'd finally panic and lose control. But, abruptly, and to the contrary, I felt an inner strength beginning to grow . . . a strength whose source came from the forceful howl of Wolf. That up-lifting and motivating howl filled my mind like an orchestra's music fills a concert hall.

Grace tried to hold back her tears, but couldn't. Her color, energy and hope drained from her small body simultaneously as she collapsed to the ground in a small, sobbing bundle of despair.

I knelt and gathered her limp body into my arms and said, "Don't you worry, Sweetheart. Daddy will still get us out of this mess." As a confirmation of this statement, Wolf's howl, again, echoed off the walls of my mind, like any wolf's howl would echo off the mountains and through the valleys. And, as always, it provided me with an elastic inner strength . . . one that made me bounce back with hope, confidence, self-assurance and a staunch determination to save Grace.

"Grace," I whispered, "We'll make it home safely. I promise, Honey." I hoped that I was correct, and it wasn't a lie if I made it come true.

It was nearly dark and the only choice I had now was to make a camp and try to surprise Jake and Tom, for they would surely catch up to us some time tonight. If my calculations were correct, they would be in the camp, ready to kill us in just a few hours, in the dark, early hours of the next morning, November 20th.

Something caught my attention. I looked at the base of the distant trees and saw a pale wolf. I knew now that it was definitely time to stop running and take the offensive, my and Wolf's, specialty.

/.- -/....//../.-./.-../../.- -/- -/.-/...//.-../.-/-./-./

Chapter 13

★★★★

Edge of Doubt

I DIDN'T HAVE THE choice of attempting to travel through the night. Grace was thoroughly exhausted; on the verge of collapse. We could trek no farther. I had to set up an ambush and, like Nam, I knew that the best ambush would be a normal-looking campsite. I'd start on that soon.

The crescent moon looked like a lighted fingernail and not offering much light compared to a full moon which takes command of the sky and all its heavenly objects. The stars competed with the dim crescent moon for dominance, each of them determined to wrest control from the other and become victorious over the ominous cloak of darkness. But it was of little importance to me, since my night vision has always been unusually acute. No doubt that was a gift from Wolf, the ability to see into the bowels of darkness.

I told Grace to rest. She needed it. I kept busy, though I felt Grace's steady gaze on me.

Grace sat very still, leaning her back against a tree; quietly observing me. Her love and admiration for me seemed boundless and, sometimes unwarranted. However, it made me feel completely happy, satisfied that I was performing well at my fatherly duties, though, when in darker moods, I wondered if I really deserved such admiration. I told her that I loved her and that my love would never end as long as I lived. She responded with a joyful countenance with brilliant, dancing sparkles in her eyes and a grand smile.

A minute later, when I gazed at Grace, her countenance turned sad. I wondered what she was thinking.

Grace was thinking about death. She wondered if she and her dad would really escape. She agonized over the thought of her dad being hurt or killed. She dreaded the thought of either one of them being seriously injured or killed. She wanted them both to live for a long time. Then, as if those thoughts weren't bad enough for an eight year old child, she thought that if they both survived, she'd still lose her dad in the future. Everyone dies and some day her dad would die. What an awful day that would be, she thought . . .and mommy will die, too, was her follow-up thought. Those thoughts depressed her to the point that she had to erase them from her mind, but the deeply sad, residual effects of those thoughts left a painful mask of sadness on her face.

Grace turned toward me and caught me looking at her. She smiled at me, but the smile looked strained and didn't reach her eyes.

Grace was very much aware of my problems with depression. She knew that I'd started seeing a doctor and was taking medication. She'd seen the effects of my depressed moods, sometimes personally, when I would lash out verbally, in anger and frustration. But it didn't affect her love and admiration for me—I was very lucky.

Grace's mom told her that I had been in a war and some bad things happened that I couldn't forget and didn't want to talk about, things that I was not proud of, things that made me feel shameful and guilty. It was pretty hard for me to deal with it, Sam told Grace.

I saw Grace peek at me and wondered what she was thinking.

Grace was thinking: *I'm glad he's my father. He's so brave. I wish I could be that brave. He told me he would gladly die if it would save my life. I don't want him to die. I'm scared. Really scared, but I don't want to get in Daddy's way. Papa's changed. He hates those Gibsons. It's like he has fire in his eyes. It makes him look really mean. I shouldn't think like that. I don't like those thoughts. They scare me, too. He's working so hard to save me. I can't be brave because I'm too scared. Maybe this was what it was like for him in that war. Look how busy he is. He lets me rest while he works hard. I feel good when he's near me. I feel safe. He's my dad. I love him, but I don't know how to help him. It feels good just to look at him. He promised to get us back to mommy. I wonder what mommy's doing and thinking. I have to stop thinking like that. It makes me too sad. I better wipe my tears away so Papa doesn't see them. When I look at Papa, I feel safe. Mommy says that fear does not stop him from doing what needs to be done. I'm not sure what she meant by that. Was mommy talking about war or just regular life? How can fear not stop somebody? Isn't Papa afraid? He looks afraid, sometimes. He worries a lot. I wonder if I can stop being afraid. I don't know how to do it, though. Papa's looking at me. It makes me feel good. What's that white stuff behind Papa? Not snow. It's moving like a walking cloud. Where'd it go? It's gone. Am I seeing things? Must be 'cause I'm tired. Seeing things, I guess. Whatever it was, I feel better, but I don't know why. I know Papa doesn't believe in God, but if there really is a God, I hope he helps us.*

She knew her father didn't believe in God, anyone's God. She didn't understand most of what he said, but he did tell her that, when she was an adult, she'd have to decide for herself. But, to him, it was all frayed threads of legend, myth, exaggeration, contradictions, impossibilities and superstition all weaved into a rug called religion. But it was a rug that was so believable to so many people that they thought it was a magic carpet that would take them to a mythical place in the sky called Heaven. But, did that make him a bad man? Grace knew that he was a good man. He just used different rules of goodness. She thought how he often told her that good atheists are just as good as good Christians—and bad atheists are no worse than bad Christians—who try to guide their lives with religious rules of goodness, honesty, caring and charitable consideration for and towards others. Good atheists are equally as good by following the secular rules of a civilized, orderly and lawful society. Steven Weinberg summarized it best when he said, "Religion is an insult to human dignity. With or without it, you'd have good people doing good things and evil people doing evil things. But for good people to do evil things, it takes religion."

Grace recalled his saying that believing in a God isn't necessary for being a good person and that it also wasn't necessary for explaining the beginning of the universe. He said that religious organizations have just as much criminal activity within them as most other organizations in any society. Religion is not exempt from evil activity, and, in fact, religious doctrine, especially Christian religious doctrine, has been responsible for most of the evil, horrendous, and torturous deeds in the history of mankind. Think for yourself, he often told Grace. Don't let other people do your thinking, especially concerning religion. Be a skeptic, ask questions, demand rational answers before you believe. Think, research, then decided what you believe to be true. If you decided to believe in any particular God, of any particular religion, and you feel that your beliefs are justified, in your own mind, then be religious. If it all appears to be non-sense, then be something else. Belief in God, he said, just like atheistic beliefs should not be a family obligation or tradition, as if it were some inherited physical trait forced onto them by the structure of their DNA. Rather, it should be a thoughtful and responsible choice for adults to make, like choosing to be a Democrat, a Republican, an Independent, or something else. Grace didn't know much about religion, just that it was pretty complex and confusing stuff.

She loved he dad without reservation, accepting his strengths and weaknesses. She observed her dad working. He was tall, of medium build, and unbowed by evil men. He was a man who almost always took the side of the underdogs in life, a man who fought bullies all his life. He was a man who loved her and her mom more than he loved his own life.

After a few minutes of thoughtful rest, Grace bravely got up to help me—she had appeared to be lost in serious thought, but I had no way of knowing what thoughts they were. I didn't want to invade her privacy, so I did not question her. I allowed her to help me instead of resting because I wanted to show her a few things about how to survive in the forest, just in case she survived and I didn't.

"Grace," I said, lovingly, for I knew this night may be a nightmare for both of us, "I want you to watch everything I do so you'll know how to do things to help save us, just in case I get hurt." I couldn't mention the possibility that she and I may be killed. Why scare her any more than she already was?

Suddenly she grabbed my hand in both of her hands, then glanced up at me, saying, "Daddy, you won't die, will you?" She said this with tears filling her eyes and her lips trembling.

My own eyes burst open with sudden shock. "Of course not, Sweetheart. That's not going to happen. But, Grace, you must understand that I'm probably going to have to kill those men before they kill us."

"Shit!" I silently exclaimed to myself. I just got done thinking that I didn't want to scare her any more than she already is, then I start talking about killing. "Damn dummy!" I chastised myself, again. I shook my head, angry with myself, but deep within me I knew I couldn't protect her from the reality of this situation any more, so, reluctantly, I continued.

"Grace, please listen to me." She was looking at the ground, hiding her face. I gently lifted her chin with my left hand so that she was looking into my eyes. "Grace, I love you very much and I want us both to live so we can go back safely to Mommy. But in order to do that, I will have to do things that may seem awful mean and terribly cruel. We can't run any more and we can't hide. It's time for me to fight back, which means that I'll probably have to kill these men. If I don't, they will surely kill us."

"You're not supposed to kill people, are you Daddy?"

I took a deep breath. "Grace, usually killing is bad, but sometimes it's good, especially when it's necessary to save your own life from a bad person who's trying to kill you. But, Sweetheart, it's never heroic or thrilling or exciting, not if you're a good person, anyway." I hesitated to explain my thoughts to her, not knowing if she'd understand, but I felt that I must clarify some things for her. "Grace, when you kill someone, you will feel good if it saves your life, or someone else's life. But later on you feel guilty because you took away the most valuable thing in this whole universe, someone's life. And the fact that he deserved it, and that killing him saved other people's lives, is the only thing that allows you to live with yourself. Killing isn't like you see it on TV, or in the movies. It's much, much uglier than that and if the killer is a good person and kills for a good, lawful reason, he'll probably still view it as an ugly, regrettable action and dislike himself for doing it, even though, if he hadn't done it, he wouldn't be around to feel the guilt or shame that he has to live with."

I paused to let Grace think. Racing through my mind were many different thoughts. One thought was like a fishhook that caught a particular line of my thinking. As I thought of this *kill-or-be-killed* situation, a list of knife fighting books raced through my mind, such as: *KILL OR GET KILLED* by Col. Rex Applegate, *COLD STEEL* by John Styers, *DO OR DIE* by Col. A.J.D. Biddle, and *KNIFE SELF-DEFENSE FOR COMBAT* by Michael D. Echanis. I didn't need to study them any further. I learned what I needed to know from those sources and had practiced for many hours. They were now part of my reflexes and my mind and muscle-memory. I could move with speed and coordination so that my movements appeared to be automatic, blurred and without thought, a partnership between self-preservation, instinct, skill, muscle-memory and sharp reflexes.

I looked down at Grace as she stared up at me, studying me—what could she be thinking? Something made me lift my eyes and look around. Something in the air had changed. The chemistry of the air? The smell? The color? It was something subtle; something a woodsman would notice. Then I spotted it. It was Wolf. I looked into the blanket of darkness that covered the forest and saw Wolf's hazy, white shape. It was a familiar ghostly, pale shape; a shape that I saw often in Nam, but only when I went out to kill the enemy at night. I stared at Wolf who looked back with eyes that turned bright yellow, like the fiery glow of the devil's twin lanterns. Wolf stared back, silently communicating with me. His ghostly body looked as if it was made of fog or, perhaps, white gauze. He was silently drifting from tree to tree. Wolf turned his head away from me, then slowly turned it back to face me and his face had changed to mine. My face on the body of a white wolf. Our eyes locked together, our thoughts mingling and it seemed as if I was talking to myself: "Born for violence, shunned by many, yet desperately needed by many." I was a paladin by nature. I heard a voice. Wolf's voice? Words saying: "You've always known your nature, though it was concealed cunningly, deceptively in a body almost the opposite of what one thinks of as a warrior. You fooled all others, but not me, my brother. You felt the violence, you felt the strength and the power when no one else could see it or feel it. You felt it in your quick reflexes, your unusual speed, your need to assist the underdog and the helpless to fend off bullies. And it was constantly confirmed in clashes with older, stronger boys who couldn't see your hidden strength, then had to pay the price for their blindness when they pushed you into combat. They felt your strength, saw your speed and feared your rage. They thought, when they saw you turn pale, that it was a sign of weakness and fear. They couldn't understand that you had just transformed yourself into me, the pale wolf.

Native Americans saw this transformation as a rare, mystical, magic power, and he who possessed it was shielded from defeat (though not meant literally) and, thus, destined to be a reluctant leader.

I heard a growl, deep throated, menacing, but friendly to me. If Death rode a pale horse, then death was the business of my friend, the pale, roamin' wolf. He wasn't threatening me, just warning me that death was eminent, that the killings weren't far away. Another growl seemed more like laughter, then came the words, "Death is a *breath-taking* experience." I could only shake my head at the "black humor."

Grace was hugging me and did not notice Wolf. I didn't think he let anyone else see him so I didn't have to worry if Grace noticed or not—later I found out that I was wrong. The sight of the pale wolf calmed me. The feeling made me think of a brick of C-4, plastic explosive. I could squeeze it, fold it, twist it, even pound on it and nothing happened to its calmness, but if the calmness is disturbed with an electric current, then that calmness gets replaced with a highly destructive explosion. That's the type of calmness I was feeling now. I was the C-4 and the electric current was Jake and Tom.

Once, in Nam, a scared, young soldier asked me how I could be so calm and why I was so quiet and didn't brag about my stealthy, night time killings. He said he thought it took more courage than anything he'd ever seen or heard of to leave the safety of my position and crawl out, alone, into the jungle, at night, so that I could kill the enemy using only the darkness, stealth and a knife.

The scared kid was thrown out into Nam like so damn many other teenage boys. I talked to him kindly, treated him like a friend and told him that, "You have to know yourself, know what you can do and can't do well, the extremes that you're capable of and what conditions need to exist to provoke you into going to extremes and using deadly skills". I told him that my calmness was only superficial and that it only prevails until something triggers the explosion that catapults me into action. I told him that bragging isn't necessary to know who you are and what you can do and what you believe. "You should already know that," I said, "so why should you need to advertise it by bragging? I have nothing to prove to others, nothing to demonstrate, no need for pats on the back and no desire for verbal applause." I paused in thought, then continued, "If left alone, unprovoked, I can remain calm, smiling, even jocular. Hopefully, I won't be provoked because all it does is scare people around me, especially friends, though I have very few of them, who make the mistake of thinking that they know me quite well. If they only see the calmness in me, then they only know one small part of me and, like naïve weathermen, they entirely miss the darkness, the cloudiness and the storms that thoughts of the enemy builds within me.

"And before you ask, I don't have many friends because I don't want to get too close to the other guys. It hurts too much when they get injured, maimed or killed. I'm quiet because I'm thoughtful. I live inside my head a lot. It's peaceful there. And I'm not as brave as you think I am, nor as courageous. I don't want to die. I want to return home in one piece, not in a body bag and a closed coffin. You might see bravery or courage, but it's really fear that motivates me and makes me determined to survive Nam. A friend told me that *death is a breath-taking experience.* He meant it as a joke, but I've taken it seriously. It's an experience I'm determined to avoid. And if I need to stalk and kill the enemy during the blackness of night, then, in spite of my fear, that's what I'll do. That's what I am doing."

The kid smiled at me, said thanks for talking to him and being friendly to him. After that we talked most evenings, before I crawled beyond our camp to kill the enemy, until he was reassigned about two weeks later. Less than a week after that he was killed when he stepped on a land mine and bled-out minus his two legs. The medics couldn't stop the bleeding. Exsanguination, I think, is the million dollar word for it, death from lose of blood. Anyway, that nice kid died on the dirty, smelly, scorched ground of South Vietnam. If he hadn't been transferred I might have been able to watch over him, but then, if he got killed, his death would have demoralized me like other friend's deaths had done. So, no close friends is best. The death of an acquaintance, or a name on a personnel list, doesn't hurt nearly as much as a close friend's death. When I was informed of the kid's death, I was sad. I walked away and didn't ask for more details. I didn't want to know.

His name was Phillip. I never knew his last name. I did shed tears for him that night. I killed more enemy than usual that night, too, and I didn't just cut their throats, I decapitated them and jammed their heads on sharpened stakes for the enemy to see in the morning.

I ached for that kid. He was only eighteen or nineteen years old, just out of high school, but still just a boy. A teenage boy with a long life ahead of him. A whole world of opportunity. A whole life-time of opportunity. All dead now. Vanquished by presidents, politicians and military leaders. Now he's just bones in a casket that lies in a hole in the ground, like the hole in the hearts of everyone close to him. All their tears will wet the ground around his grave so that the government can send flowers and have them flourish. All for nothing, especially when governmental assholes start a war, send young boys to fight in it, then make rules and regulations that won't allow those boys, and the men who lead them, to win the war. The kid died for nothing, just like more than 58,000 other boys, an incredible, unforgiveable waste of life.

Damn ass-wipes in Washington sending America's babies to war. Old bastards staying nice and safe in their comfortable houses, with their safe and loving families, in safe neighborhoods, going to work in their safe offices, then sending thousands of teenagers to die in a land thousands of miles away from their own safe and loving families and safe neighborhoods. Damn them!

I brought myself back to my present situation and thought that my doctor would be happy. I was fairly calm, even though I hadn't been able to take my medications, and in spite of some nightmarish memories of Nam. I didn't have time to stop by the house and get my pills after becoming a hostage. A smile bent my lips at that personal, but inappropriate bit of humorous sarcasm. This was far from a humorous situation.

I felt Grace pulling on my jacket, saying, "Daddy . . . Daddy . . . Daddy. Are you okay?"

I looked down at her with hope in my eyes. I felt confident again. I smiled warmly at her, thinking, it wasn't going to be an uneven battle, the two Gibsons against Roman Wolfe and Roamin' Wolf. I looked into the forest. The pale wolf was gone, if it had been there in the first place, probably just my imagination. Still, I smiled, feeling surprisingly well.

That feeling of wellness, hopefulness and confidence rushed through me as I knelt on the ground and embraced Grace. I told her that I was fine and that I needed her to be very brave and to trust me. I told her that I certainly wouldn't leave her and that I'd protect her, but that she must do whatever I asked of her as I prepared to deal with Jake and Tom Gibson.

Grace recognized the feelings of hope and confidence that radiated from my voice and eyes, and that, in turn, revived the same feelings in her. She embraced me, wrapping both arms around my neck and rubbing her cheek against mine, then kissing my cheek ever so gently, just like her mom often did.

"Are you feeling good enough to help me," I asked.

"Yes, Papa, I'd like to help you," Grace said, happily.

Then Grace and I got busy. There was no more time for my wasteful, daydreaming. I needed to concentrate on action; violent, deadly action to save Grace . . . and me, though I've always had this strange feeling that death didn't scare me. If my dying saved Grace, I'd actually be very pleased, although dead people can't be pleased. I figured it would be an excellent trade-off, though Sam would be violently upset with me for that line of thought. Damn! I'd rather face Jake and Tom than Sam's wrath. Funny, huh?

It was dark now and we would have to do everything by firelight—as soon as I built the fire—and by moonlight—there was only a crescent moon allowing dim darts of light to shoot through the bare trees. That, combined with my excellent night vision, however, would do nicely. I noticed that the moonlight shone on some larger rocks which were jutting out of the earth, making them look like bone-white, tombstones planted in the ground of the black, shadowy forest. I wondered if Wolf hid behind one of them.

First, I quickly built a teepee fire—I was in too much of a hurry to use the Dakota Fire Hole method—with dry twigs and loosely wadded toilet paper placed at the base, under the twigs that formed a teepee shape. I told Grace that, if she had to build a fire, she could also use strips of white birch bark like we had seen on some trees, yesterday, or she could use dried grasses, or the dry inside of a piece of tree bark.

Then I showed her how to find dried twigs on the ground, at the base of evergreen trees or under bushes where they would be protected from the rain, or even abandoned bird's nests, if they were accessible. But, best of all, I showed her how to break off dead twigs from underneath pine trees, about a foot or two off the ground and still attached to the tree. These were the best fire starters because they were almost always absolutely dry because they were so well protected by the upper branches and didn't touch the wet ground. I showed her how to strike one of the waxed matches on my flat rock to make it light, how to hold the match in cupped hands to protect it from the wind and how to stick it under the base of the teepee of twigs so it ignited the toilet paper, birch bark, grass, fine twigs or whatever was used for kindling. We had various sizes of larger, dead branches ready and soon we had a medium sized fire.

With the fire started, we had warmth and light. I gave the remainder of my waxed matches to Grace; I placed them into her coat pocket along with the flat rock. "Hold these for me," I said with a reassuring smile, "so I don't have to worry about losing them." I checked to make sure she had the pocket knife. She did. She looked at me, suspiciously, but didn't say a word. I could tell from her expression that she knew why I gave her the matches, stone and knife. Though she was silent, she knew what I was doing; what I was preparing her for. Her lips curved downward, misty eyes glowing with reflected fire light, but no falling tears. I'd asked her to be very brave. I'd asked the nearly impossible of her, at such a young age, but she was attempting to obey, though every emotion she had rebelled against her. I asked her to be brave; she was. I assumed she would trust me; she did. I told her I would protect her; I will . . . or die trying.

I added larger pieces of wood to the fire and soon campfire light splashed across our faces with long, flickering fingers of red, yellow, gold and orange. When I looked at the fire, I imagined fiery phantoms dancing wildly at the top of each finger of flame. Grace's eyes, like miniature, circular mirrors, reflected the images of the camp fire.

Soon there were red hot coals, so before I forgot, I placed four flat rocks half-way into the fire so they could get hot. When they were hot, I'd use sapling tongs to pick them up. Grace would be warm tonight, though I doubted that she would get much sleep. It's quite difficult to be brave when you're too scared. I was hoping that her extreme exhaustion would force her to sleep through the night . . . so she would miss the killings.

Wolf howled. Usually he appeared only to me and could be heard only by me—though there were rare exceptions. That was also the way it worked in the killing fields that I walked on in Nam. The howl sent an icy chill up my spine. I looked at my hands and remembered the feel of the dark, sticky blood, remembered feeling it drain from a sentry's body as I held him tightly with a cupped hand over his mouth. Sometimes I saw the flame of life vanish from an enemy's eyes and wondered what it felt like, though I wasn't anxious to find out. I thought about my kills in Nam. It was nothing to be proud of, except that maybe those killings saved American lives and/or prevented other killings of innocent people, including, perhaps, some of the local population.

Killing is a huge burden, unless you're without a conscience and remorselessly sadistic. You don't need to believe in God to feel the guilt, the shame, the regret for having killed someone, even in wartime. But some men are born protectors, born to help the weak and helpless, and in that act of assistance and compassion, they are born to violence, which is quite ironic. I'm one of them. I only kill to protect relatives, friends, or comrades in times of conflict like war. I've killed a lot and by doing so, I've saved many more lives, like the Atomic bombs dropped on Japan during World War II. Thousands of Japanese died from those bombs so that hundreds of thousands could be spared by ending war with Japan. Were those bombs justified? I think they were, just like I think my killing was justified in order to save American lives.

I didn't notice the cold, although the temperature must have dropped into the high teens and would probably drop into the low teens, or lower, as the night progressed. The cold would be a minor issue with me, however, just like the humid inferno of Nam was. I put the cold out of my mind, didn't let it touch me, my intense concentration blocking everything except Grace and surviving the final conflict with the Gibsons.

I remembered the compass. I told her that she should keep it for me, also, because I didn't want to have anything in my pocket that might get in my way, or that might restrict my movements, or have something in my pocket that might make an inopportune noise which might give my position away. I told her that, if she had to do it herself—tears threatened, then retreated like a tide on a beach—all she had to do was follow the lake southward and if, for some reason, she walked too far away from Long Lake, she could travel southwest by lining-up the red needle in the compass with the capital letters SW printed on the compass. I'm not sure she understood this, but I wanted her to have every chance for survival. I told her that if she did wander away from the shore of Long Lake and if the compass got lost or broken, then in the morning, if the sun was out, she was to keep the sun over her left shoulder as she walked. She could then rest when the sun was almost directly overhead between noon and two P.M., and when she resumed her walking, the sun should then be over her right shoulder as she continued to walk.

"Do you understand what I'm saying," I asked. I could see some wetness dripping from her nose. Her eyes, however, were still dry because she was trying so desperately to be brave for me, to control her emotions for me. But the tears had to go someplace, so her nose was the outlet. She sniffled frequently and brushed away the moisture with her sleeve. I knew then that before she could ever fall asleep tonight there would be a bucket of silent tears, shed in private, because I had asked her to be brave. She was such a smart girl. She made the connections. She knew that I wouldn't have needed to ask her to be brave unless I thought that something bad might happen. I just hoped it didn't happen to her. But logical chain-thinking pried its way into my thoughts. For nothing bad to happen to her, I had to survive. For me to survive, I had to kill both Jake and Tom. To kill Jake and Tom, I had to walk in the killing field, again. It wasn't just necessary that I kill tonight, it was absolutely mandatory, if I wanted Grace to survive this terrible ordeal.

My comely daughter stared up at me and said, "Yes, Daddy," and I could hear her voice crackle with growing fear as another droplet of wetness, from her nose, stopped momentarily at her upper lip, then following the contour of her upper lip, rolled leftward until it reached the corner of her mouth and suddenly dropped down to her chin. She took a deep breath, wiped the wetness from her chin and stammered, "I . . . yes . . . I will try to remember everything, Papa."

The sound of the word "Papa" brought a sudden surge of tears to my own eyes. I hugged Grace. I thought about how strange my tears must look to Grace as she was trying to hold back her own tears. I wondered what she thought about it, but didn't have the time to formulate an answer. I did, however, know that Grace only used the word "Papa" when she was extremely happy and excited, or extremely sad and disappointed. There wasn't any doubt as to which occasion this was.

I was trying to be subtle about teaching Grace a few independent survival lessons. It wasn't just "independence" for survival in the forest; independence was preparation for life. That was one of my chief complaints about our modern school system. It didn't breed independence in our youth, it bred conformity, the needs of the group, the collective. As Frederick Nietzsche said, "The surest way to corrupt a youth is to instruct him to hold in higher esteem those who think alike than those who think differently." Now-a-days its practically a social sin to think differently, both in and out of school. I shook myself vigorously, forcing myself back to the present situation.

In order to control our emotions and prepare ourselves, I grabbed Grace's hand gently in mine; squeezed it lovingly. Grace's hand seemed cold, almost lifeless. But then she squeezed my hand with a strong, confident grip that uplifted my spirit and transferred what felt like hopeful rays of warm, comforting energy throughout my body. Then we got busy making our campsite preparations.

I didn't know how much time we would have, so keeping busy was of the utmost importance. We needed to build a lean-to, but in the dark, away from the fire light, we would only stumble around, especially when the clouds started blocking the moonlight. So I decided to make a tent out of one of our large wool blankets. I took out my combat blade and cut three thicker and sturdier saplings that I could see at the periphery of the campfire light. Then, using my knife and a digging stick, I dug two holes in the ground, the first one only a yard away from the fire and the second one five feet directly back from the first one. These saplings were only about four feet off the ground so that the blanket would cover a larger ground area. Grace helped me as much as she could. Actually, she was doing very well now that her mind was on preparations for living instead of thoughts of dying. I noticed that her nose was dry now.

The third sapling, the six feet long one, I lashed securely with dental floss and horizontally to the other two upright poles so that there was about a six inch overhang at each vertical pole. I knew the floss would come in handy.

Then, with Grace's help, I placed one wool blanket over the horizontal pole and, with a rock, I drove short, sharpened stakes, that I had cut previously, into the ground-level edges of the woolen blanket so it was fastened, as securely as possible, to the nearly frozen ground. The open end of the tent that was farthest away from the campfire was then closed off from the wind using thick layers of overlapping pine boughs which, more importantly, negated any possibility of viewing the inside of the tent from that direction. The fire and the general darkness of the forest wouldn't allow someone to see very far into the open, front end of the tent either, especially when the campfire had burned down to coals. With no flames there would be little light.

It was about nine o'clock and we still weren't finished. Grace dragged the backpack, from beside the fire, to the tent and we placed our sleeping bags into the tent. The sleeping bags were longer than the blanket so about a fourth of them stuck out of the tent. This made it look like sleeping bags should really look when they stick out of a makeshift tent that was built a little too short for the long sleeping bags, especially one that would contain a long adult body, mine.

Grace looked a little puzzled at the sleeping bag arrangement. Then she said, "Can you make the hot rocks for me, again, Daddy?"

"Yes, Sweetheart," I replied. "I've already put the rocks near the fire to get them ready for you to sleep on. But we won't be sleeping inside this tent tonight, so we'll have to put the rocks and the balsam boughs, grasses and leaves in a different spot. I'll look around and decide where to put them."

Grace looked at me in an even more confused manner than before and said, "Then why did we do all this work, Daddy?"

"To fool the Gibsons into thinking that we're sleeping inside the tent."

"Why do you want to fool them?"

"Grace, it's difficult to explain because I don't want to scare you any more than you already are. It might also make me look like a bad person doing bad things, so if you still want to know, I'll tell you, but I would rather not."

Grace looked at me with intensity in her eyes. She was curious, just like her mom always was. She needed to know things. Her mom believed that the more she knew, the better decisions she could make and those better decisions would result in a better life for her and us. I agreed.

Grace's eyes were beautiful, like her mom's. I knew what she would say before she even parted her lips. She's certainly her mother's daughter.

"You're not a bad man, Daddy. But I want to know no matter how awful it is, okay?"

"Okay, Sweetheart, but I hope you won't hate me, or become afraid of me if I tell you how I plan to kill Tom and Jake. If I didn't have to do it, I wouldn't, but, in order to save our own lives, I'm sure that I'm going to have to kill them before they kill us. Do you understand what I'm saying?"

"Yes, Papa. I understand. I still want you to tell me."

There was that word "Papa" again. My heart bled in sympathy for her as I prepared to tell my eight year old daughter how I planned to kill, and in so doing, I was telling her that, in Vietnam, I killed many times, over and over, night after night. Would she see me as a vicious, crazed murderer, or forever fear me and my special martial arts and knife-fighting skills? I hoped not. I said, "I think I know what Jake and Tom will both do as they enter our camp tonight. We can't out-run them any more. I'm sure they'll be here tonight, Grace." Then as we ate, I explained to her what I had planned to do.

I got up and found a patch of moss, pulled it up, leaving an indentation in the ground, and waited for the water to fill the indentation. I let the water settle for a minute or two, then, very gently placed the metal cup into the water, being careful not to stir up any more sediment than was necessary. I scooped up half a cup of water for Grace to drink. Then I repeated the procedure until we both had our fill.

Grace was getting extremely tired very quickly and I was glad. I was afraid she wouldn't be able to sleep and would stay awake all night. I hoped she would fall asleep quickly. Sleep would be so good for her—and me, knowing she was safe and out of harm's way. In a few minutes she became so completely exhausted that she walked with a wobble and sometimes staggered.

I also hoped that she'd fall into a deep sleep, quickly, because I needed time to make further preparations, and I needed time to concentrate on martial arts techniques, both defensive and offensive. I also needed time to psyche myself up, to meditate prior to battle, like I used to do for my formal karate katas and for sparring classes. But most of all, I wanted her to sleep so she wouldn't have to witness the senseless brutality of men trying to kill each other. When I defeated them—never go into a fight with a negative attitude—I was afraid that I'd look like an insanely furious creature of death—sometimes I do dream about myself riding a pale horse—to Grace. That's where my fear was planted. What would my daughter think of me? But there couldn't be any thoughts of losing. I will defeat them. I would meditate and see victory in my mind before it even happens. Think positive, do positive and positively win.

Joyfully, I saw Grace drift off to sleep after she sat down, leaning her back against a tree. I picked her up and laid her down on half the blanket then folded over the other half to cover her.

I proceeded about seventy-five feet westward, toward the lake, toward some thick bushes, which were a few feet outside the perimeter of light from the campfire. Those thick bushes would conceal Grace's sleeping area. I went westward because I figured that Tom would approach the campsite from the northern direction and that Jake would circle the camp prior to Tom's entrance and approach the camp from the south in order to prevent an escape into the forest from that direction. The tent was slightly east of the campfire and since either Jake or Tom might easily attack from that directions, I figured that the safest place to hide Grace was to the west of our camp. But even if they came into camp from the west, Grace would be well hidden and unseen in the dark, if she didn't move or talk in her sleep.

I used a thick, sturdy branch to dig a shallow trench on the far side of the thick bushes. Then I gathered dry leaves, dry grasses and the balsam boughs to use as softer, warmer bedding for her to sleep on. The cotton-like, fluffy cat tails inside her coat would also help to keep her warm. She hadn't been cold since I placed them there.

I cut two long, but thin and very flexible saplings. I bent them in a U-shape and picked up a hot rock like a nut in a nutcracker, but with the rock hanging downward. One at a time I carried the hot rocks to the trench and placed them in it until all four hot rocks were safely in the trench. Then I buried the rocks with four to six inches of dirt. I went through the same procedure as when I made this same kind of bed for her before. After the trench was covered, leveled and the moisture was allowed to escape via steam, I collected, then covered the trench area with the warm balsam pine boughs, then added leaves and grass. I transferred Grace to a sleeping bag, then used the blanket to cover the pine boughs, leaves and tufts of dry grass. With that done, I walked back to Grace, picked her up, inside the sleeping bag, carried her to the warm blanket and set her on top. I could feel the warmth from the rocks coming through already.

On top of the sleeping bag, I placed delicate pine boughs, twigs and a fine layer of dirt. The camouflage worked wonderfully. From six feet away I couldn't tell she was there.

I walked back to the campfire, misty-eyed. I looked back at the bushes, toward my precious daughter. The darkness and the bushes totally concealed her. I blocked my emotions and went about my critical, unfinished work.

I picked up the backpack, took a container of floss out of it and placed it into my pocket. I carried the backpack to where Grace was and gently placed it next to her and covered it so it wouldn't be seen. If she needed it, it would be there for her. I wished that I could believe in prayer, but this was no time to be wasting time fooling myself with fantasies. When reality viciously bites you in the ass, there's no use pretending it's a gentle kiss. It was me and only me that could save her, so wasting time with irrational ideas, empty words and soporific platitudes is something I simply couldn't afford to do.

I walked over to the blanket-tent and picked up two of the extra stakes like the ones I used to pound the blanket edges into the ground. I worked quickly, whittling one end off to make the one inch diameter wood into a shorter piece only about four inches long, just about the width of my fist. I whittled one more in the same manner. Then all the way around the middle of each smooth stub of wood I cut a shallow V-shaped groove, about one-eighth of an inch deep. I whittled the ends of each piece of wood so they were blunt. Next, I took out approximately a twelve feet length of dental floss, doubled it over on itself twice so it was four strong strands that were three feet long. I tied the ends together, then securely tied each end into each grove with a series of square knots. Now I had a garrote with two solid, smooth, handles and four strands of tough dental floss that measured between two and two-and-one-half feet long—the double knots used up a few inches of dental floss—between each wooden handle. I held onto each handle of this garrote with my fists together in front of me, then yanked my fists violently apart to test its strength. It felt very secure, solid, and the fineness of the floss wouldn't only strangle, but would also cut into a victim's neck and, maybe, the jugular vein or one of the carotid arteries. So death by strangulation, or death by exsanguination or both would be the result. I preferred strangulation. It's not as messy, nor sticky, nor as unpleasant and sickening as the coppery smell of a large fountain of spraying blood.

However, I hoped I wouldn't have to rely on the garrote. I was hoping my knife would end their lives quickly. But with the large size and strength of both Jake and Tom—the Vietnamese enemy was short and usually very slim, not muscled—major arteries or veins in the neck, arms or legs had to be penetrated, or major organs in the chest cavity. A deep knife wound in the abdominal area would cause death, if unattended, but death would be much slower in taking effect—no major, vital organs—compared to a violent tearing thrust or slash in any area where major arteries or organs are located.

Death with a garrote was a relatively slow process, but I viewed the garrote as a last-resort weapon, in case my blades and martial arts skills failed me, although they had never failed me before. Looking at the garrote, I thought: "Better to be over-prepared than under-prepared."

I felt good knowing the garrote would be in my back pocket, just in case I needed it as a back-up weapon that would be easily accessible, and very deadly—the wooden handles could also be used to slam into the eyes, nose, teeth, Adam's Apple and temple. It was a specialty weapon with a lot of uses that most warriors didn't give the credit it deserved. Maybe it was because the garrote took special handling and a special technique to master. The garrote, once mastered, is such a deadly weapon because once it's wrapped around the victim's neck, the more he struggles, the deeper it cuts into his neck, and the quicker he will bleed-out. Of course, at the same time that it was cutting into the neck, it was also compressing the esophagus and slowly strangling the victim. After the deed was over, it was often hard to tell if the victim died by strangulation or by exsanguination, but that didn't matter, death is what mattered, not the exact cause. The garrote, like the knife was a silent instrument of death that I valued, even if it did cause a comparatively slower death than that of a knife. I held the garrote in my hands as if it were a hundred dollar bill. I caressed it, then smiled and tucked it into my back pocket.

/.…././-./.-./-.- -/- - -/.-./-…/.-/-./-../

Chapter 14

★★★★

Do Not Go Gently

I LOOKED AT MY watch. It reminded me of my wonderful wife, Sam. She had gotten the watch for me a couple of Christmases ago. How I longed to embrace her, to feel the warmth and pleasing scent of her body, to press my lips to hers, to run my fingers through her fragrant, auburn hair. And her eyes? Gorgeous, light green orbs with golden flecks embedded in them.

I closed my eyes. I could see her face smiling at me and the melodic sounds of Roy Orbison singing "Running Scared" in the background. The lyrics to the song reminded me of when we were young lovers. Like Roy said in the song, Sam really did turn away from other guys and walk away with me. Feelings of triumph, joy and enduring love engulfed me. "I will be home soon, Sam," I whispered to my vision of her . . . "very soon, my dear wife."

I opened my eyes and shook myself out of that enjoyable daydream. I knew that I must concentrate all my efforts and all my remaining cunning and strength on the upcoming struggle because this enemy was deadly. Instinctively I knew that Jake wouldn't stop to make camp tonight and try to catch up to us tomorrow afternoon. He'd come at us in the very late night hours or the very early morning hours, probably the latter. I could feel it in my gut. He'd be here in a few hours. He'd push himself and Tom, hoping that we had made camp and had not expected them to be so close. He'd relish a dead of night attack. But what he didn't know was that I preferred the night, especially the "dead-of-night"—I even like the sound of it—with its brotherly darkness and its friendly, black shadows that prowled the darkness with me. That's where I fit in, where I was at home, comfortable with my blade and garrote, a dark, lethal and destructive force, when the situation called for me to be that way.

Yes, I thought with certainty, Jake and Tom would be here soon. I felt a feral chill in the air, a coldness in my spine, as well as a putrid smell, as if Jake was close enough to breathe on me. Jake and Tom would naturally think that they were the substantial threat that lurked in the darkness. However, on this night the superior force that lurked in the night wasn't them, and they would soon be hunted by me and Roamin' Wolf.

I peered into the vast blackness of the forest, in the direction from which Jake and Tom would most likely come. My vision was sharp and focused into the blackness of the forest where I saw the pale wolf prowling, on guard, waiting to warn me of the Gibsons approach by giving a piercing howl. Then Wolf changed until he blended into the chilly darkness, like a white marble slowly changing to black as it rolls across a black velvet cloth.

Something on the ground grabbed my attention. I squatted and reached for it. I held a piece of dried, hardened bark that must have come from a mature, but small tree. The bark looked like it had a 180 degree curve to it that spanned only about three or four inches in width and was about eighteen inches in length. I stared at it as my mind wondered about the possibilities for its use. There was an idea that lingered concealed in my mind, but I couldn't put it into focus. If I stopped straining to think about it, it would probably come to me, I thought, so I stayed busy and very alert, until midnight, with no warning signal from Wolf.

The final preparations inside the tent and around the camp were completed.

I cut in half the fire-dried and thoroughly warm coyote skin. I took off my boots and placed one piece of coyote skin on the ground, the fur side up, then stepped on the center of it with my right foot. The fur felt soft and warm against the sole of my foot. I bent down and used the point of my knife to poke holes into the four corners of the skin, then brought up all four corners against my upper ankle area and tied them securely, making sure that I left plenty of loose coyote skin around my feet. Then I bound all that loose coyote skin to the shape of my foot by wrapping many feet of floss around my feet many times and tied it securely so that the final result was something that looked like an Indian's moccasin. I did the same with the other foot—in Nam, I actually wore hand-made leather moccasins. Why? Because the thick, somewhat stiff soles of boots dig into and crunch objects that are on the ground. They also leave obvious tracks. This usually can't be prevented because the thick soles of the boots don't allow the foot to feel objects on the ground, until it's too late. The noise that boots make as a person walks through a forest—or jungle— can cost a person his life. The American Indians knew that wearing moccasins allowed them to feel objects that are under their feet as they stealth-walked, thus, they could feel the ground with their feet, detect an object that will make noise, then place their foot elsewhere to prevent that noise. I've removed my boots and made crude moccasins for that same reason.

Next, I removed the chunk of charcoal that I had taken from last night's dead campfire and had stored in my backpack. I used it to blackened all the exposed skin areas of my face, hands and wrists. I probably didn't need it on my hands because my gloves covered them up, but, I thought, there's always the unexpected chance that I may need to remove the gloves. I threw the charcoal into the fire and put my gloves back on. I still didn't feel cold, probably partly due to the lack of wind that couldn't penetrate this thick forest, even without the leaves on the branches. Also influential was the fact that I didn't have time to focus on the cold because my concentration was almost totally on survival.

It seemed like a Halloween kind of night, spooky, with the bare branches brushing against each other and acting like ghostly arms that were reaching skyward, as if reaching for and worshipping the moon.

I checked my watch again; 11:56 P.M., November 20th.

"Do not go gently into the night," I mumbled to myself. I couldn't remember the remainder of the poem, nor the author. It didn't matter. I sure wasn't going to recite it to the Gibsons. The words I remembered were the only words I needed to remember because as an ex-Marine, a loving and protecting father, and a human being who was in a life or death situation, I certainly had no intentions of accepting and going gently towards death. There would be nothing gentle about this night. Violence would dominate this night before it gave way to the radiant calmness of dawn. "Semper Fidelis," I thought and smiled. The Marine Corp. motto floated in my mind, as well as its meaning, "always faithful."

I was proud to have been a Marine; to fight for my country. I would have been proud to serve my country in any of the military branches. However, I wasn't proud of all the killing I performed, nor did I believe that U.S. fighting troops should have been sent to Vietnam especially if the political Rules of Engagement were going to prevent American soldiers from winning that war. The lives lost, the years wasted, and the billions of dollars squandered on a war that was ruled by politics and indecisiveness was, in my mind, unconscionable. That thought reminded me of the connection of those politicians with an idea expressed by Gerald Massey when he said, "They must find it difficult . . . those who have taken authority as truth, rather than truth as the authority." Unfortunately, cunning, deceitful political and military minds know that *authority* can manipulate the *truth*. This made me wonder what addendum Massey may have wanted to add to his often quoted words.

But, while in Nam, I did my job and tried to help my country and the democratic way of life. I'm a staunch believer in democracy, but I do make my share of errors. Once Sam and I had a political disagreement and she said to me: "You seem always clear about where you stand on issues, always self-assured, always certain, but you're not always right." It made me realize that "certainty" about something is often no more valid that an unsupported "opinion" about something. It also made me realize that I'm not as smart as I'd like to think I am.

I thought that my biggest internal conflict wasn't due to my feelings that the Vietnam War wasn't a *just* war for America to be involved in—though I had initially agreed with the war effort. My biggest conflict was focused right here in America, with Americans who treated our returning soldiers like dog shit on a sidewalk, harassed them spit on them as they spewed their hatred onto the soldiers and even called them "baby killers." Those soldiers went from hostile, life-threatening, dangerous action in Vietnam, to hostile mental and emotional pain at home. Many Vietnam Vets, even in their own home towns and neighborhoods, were subjected to verbal abuse, scornful looks and ostracism coming from repugnant strangers, and even more hurtfully, from friends and relatives. And as if that wasn't bad enough, the Vets were then abandoned by their own government and refused medical and emotional medical treatment.

I was one of the lucky ones to come home with only moderate depression and much bitterness for the way the Vietnam Vets were treated—the actress, Jane Fonda, was particularly vicious toward America's part in the war. She never lacked for a string of stinging insults about Vietnam Vets. Her unpatriotic and infamous trip to Hanoi demoralized American soldiers and American prisoners of war, but pleased the enemy greatly. She became known, with anger and bitterness, as Hanoi Jane. To this day, I can't help disliking that woman.

So many Veterans came home to so much worse, especially the amputees and the many other returning with serious physical injuries. I wished that my country and my fellow citizens had been as faithful to me and my fellow Vietnam Vets as we had been to them. My Vietnam buddies were the closest friends I ever had, and possibly, that I ever will have because those friendships were forged and hardened in the fires of combat; often in life or death combat.

I'm still glad that I passed-up the opportunity to join the Marine or Navy Special Forces groups. It wasn't that I disliked the Special Forces, per se, or disrespected the type of people involved in them—they deserve immense respect—I just didn't feel that it was the place for me. Actually, I didn't feel "special," that's all, though I had great faith, admiration and respect for those who were tough enough to make the grade and become members of our various superior Special Forces units. Luckily, for me, I'd have had to volunteer and then be approved in order to gain a chance to prove my skills and become a Special Forces member. But I didn't want to join, so I chose not to volunteer, though there was some pressure for me to do so. I made a lot of friends, saved many more lives than I took, and was proud to be an ordinary Marine Grunt, with ordinary Grunt friends. I'm not sure if I did the right thing by staying out of the Special Forces. At the time, I thought I was doing the right thing for me. But, as I said, I am very proud of the American Special Forces Units, especially their toughness, dedication and sacrifices.

I placed the last of the dry logs onto the fire and then on top of those logs I placed a couple pieces of green wood. Because they were green, they would burn slowly, dimly throughout the night, plus, they would create more smoke, which would help me use my planned subterfuge on the Gibsons. Then I circled the camp in an ever widening, silent-spiral, thinking, concentrating, letting my eyes and mind adjust to the night while trying not to look towards the fire which hindered night vision. Time to clear my mind and focus, to be self-assured, to be certain and to forget about what might be right or wrong. My task was survival, by any means, whether it was right or wrong in the view of civilized laws. For me and Grace, it was right to survive, so it couldn't be wrong to use any means, method or tool to kill Jake and Tom.

At a Marine combat school I'd learned, and perfected in the jungles of Nam, the technique of "unfocused viewing." That's where someone deliberately unfocuses their eyes so they can see a large, general area instead of focusing on one specific, small area at a time. This technique allows them, once they've perfected it, to detect almost any movement that occurs within their total field of vision, which is about 180 degrees, while their head remains stationary. Therefore, I started using this type of viewing, in spite of the darkness, because it afforded me a big advantage over an enemy who was using focused vision and, thus, had limited detection of movement due to his focusing on one object at a time or one small area at a time. For example, if you look into the night sky and try to focus on a faint star, it will disappear from your view, but if you unfocus your vision and look to either side of where you thought that star had been, you'll see that star again, and that's basically how "unfocused viewing" works. It has something to do with the "cones" and "rods" which are light-sensitive cells in the eye's retina. An added advantage, for me, was the fact that I'd been born with excellent night vision.

More useful, however, especially at night is the technique of "focused listening" which I also learned at that combat school. Focused listening enables someone to detect, locate and amplify sounds. As a matter of fact, it's like unfocused viewing in reverse. A person normally hear sounds that come at them from all directions. To focus-in on just one particular sound, all they have to do is place cupped hands behind their ears, or use one hand, if the other hand is holding a weapon, and push their ears slightly forward with theirr thumb and cupped fingers. It's the same action that you see a cat, dog and deer perform when they move their ears in order to get a better sense of direction from a particular sound that it's trying to focus on. Of course, you'll need to turn your head while cupping your ears in order to best zero-in on the particular sound that you want to listen to.

I didn't see or hear anything, yet, but I was certain that I would hear them soon. It was the same, nearly faultless feeling that I had in Nam when I detected the approaching enemy, even though they were a mile away—with Wolf's help—well out of my sight and hearing range. More likely than not, my acute senses, except the better-than-average night vision, can be attributed to Wolf.

About 12:30 A.M., November 21st—thanks to my watch, whose face could be lighted by pushing in the stem—I heard Wolf's low, warning growl, an indication that the enemy was detected, but that they were still far away. I had been walking around the outer periphery of the campsite so quietly that I couldn't even hear myself. My confidence got a boost. I was instinctively using the "ghost walk," which many hunters know about—though they may have a different name for it—and which I perfected during myriad night patrols in Nam. This is a technique that enables a soldier, or hunter, to walk so carefully and quietly that he seems to be a ghost, noiselessly floating over the ground. I guessed that Jake and Tom would know this maneuver, being woodsmen who frequently stalked game—but Wolf's senses were too keen to be fooled. It's an entirely different walk that takes much getting used to, but probably saved my life many times.

I circled past Grace one more time. She was still sleeping and well concealed.

My thoughts returned to the ghost walk. Most people are used to walking on flat, unobstructed ground, and thus, have developed a somewhat awkward and unnatural stride that is too noisy for silently approaching the enemy. On paved or smooth ground, where most of us usually walk, we step on the broad flatness of our footwear, with the heels of our shoes striking the pavement first, our bodies bent forward slightly, and our heads tipped downward. This type of carelessly, noisy walking can be heard very easily, from many yards away by anyone using the focused listening technique. Actually, it can be heard from a great distance by anyone not using the focused listening technique, which shows just how noisy a human's normal walking style is in the woods, where their feet constantly come into contact with rocks, loose dirt, twigs, branches, bushes, roots, dry leaves and other obstacles and debris.

Therefore, to be as quiet as possible, the ghost walk technique is necessary. During the ghost walk, I take a shorter, smoother step, and when I touch my foot to the ground, toes first, then I gently roll the pressure from the outside of my foot to the inside of my foot. while, at the same time, keeping my body and head straight. Thus, the ghost walk, instead of using the smaller calf muscles, uses the larger thigh muscles, as well as the buttock muscles. Furthermore, the ghost walk emphasizes the lifting of the legs rather than the sliding, or shuffling of the feet forward, thus having the ability to pass over obstacles instead of sliding into them. It's very similar to the American Indian style of stealth-walking, though, if wearing moccasins instead of boots or shoes, the excellent tactile sensations on all sides of the feet make you much more aware of where you can step silently and where you can not.

I could hear owls hooting and nocturnal scavengers searching for food. They didn't hear me. If they had, they would stop moving and stop making noise. As long as I heard these animal sounds, I knew Jake and Tom weren't close and, like I stated before, the ghost walk, or stealth-walking, wouldn't fool most animals, anyway, their sense of hearing being so much more sensitive than human hearing. Also, an animal's sense of smell, especially with the aid of the wind, is super sensitive compared to a human's sense of smell. If the wind is right, Wolf would be able to smell Jake and Tom from a couple of miles away. Many other animals can do the same thing. So, since I could still hear animal noises in my area, I knew that Jake and Tom weren't real close, yet. Wolf's growl would let me know when they were about half-a-mile away and that would be anywhere from 30 to 45 minutes of ghost walking..

The thought of the Gibsons being only a couple of miles away was unnerving, but only because of Grace being with me. I was limited in some of the things I could do. I couldn't be as offensively bold because of the necessity of protecting Grace. So at the start of the encounter, I had to act mostly defensively, then, if the opportunity presented itself, I could act offensively. A sudden surge of mingled emotions wrapped its muscular arms around me, squeezing me until I felt panic. I had to force myself to cut off the head of that emotional monster, killing it, then calming myself. I settled down by convincing myself that there was no cause to panic. I railed disapprovingly at myself for my constant mixture of emotions, then thought, "Shit! Maybe I am the wimp that they think I am." I was very capable of killing and willing to kill the enemy without hesitation or remorse. I distracted myself by focusing on thoughts of hand-to-hand combat techniques; what attacks may occur and how to counter them. Such thinking was like meditation; it took the edge off my nervousness.

Naturally, since I have the ghost walk perfected, I very seldom trip over rocks or tree roots that are protruding from the ground and, by keeping my body straight, instead of leaning forward, I posses much better balance. This enables me to move slowly, stop, or even change directions as smoothly and as quietly as a floating phantom. Furthermore, with my back and head straight, instead of leaning forward and looking downward, I can use the ghost walk while, at the same time, using the unfocused viewing technique which allows me to be much more alert to the movements, which occur in my 280 degrees range of vision, by steadily and slowly sweeping my head from shoulder to shoulder—where my eyes can look over and past each shoulder, thus allowing me to see much more than 180 degrees.

I paused to listen carefully. I still heard the nocturnal animals. I was about fifty feet from the campsite and decided not to go any farther, but rather, to circle back and await the enemy from dark concealment. The woods were pitch black, but my eyes had adjusted well. When I arrived, the campfire was burning low, almost to flameless, red coals. The sky had cleared, so now the crescent moon and the clear, starry sky offered some dim light. It was better to stay closer to camp and wait like an unseen shadow in the darkness. Darkness, like a best friend, put its arm around my shoulders and pulled me into the black shadow of its cloak.

I wondered if Jake and Tom would use the ghost walk. Then I wondered if they would use the "approachment" technique during the last hundred feet to the center of camp. If they used the approachment technique successfully, I may not hear them, but I would see them with my night vision. But even if this were not true, there was no way they'd fool the Roamin' Wolf. Wolf had been tracking them via smell from a couple of miles away, then by their smell and sounds from a mile away. Wolf would give me plenty of warning of how far away they were and the direction from which they were coming. Basically, the Gibsons were walking into a deadly trap, if all went as expected. The trouble is, I worriedly thought, that quite often things don't go as expected or as planned.

The "approachment" technique was a natural extension of the ghost walk, only much slower, more deliberate and controlled, and, basically, noiseless. The approachment technique, is used when you are trying to silently get extremely close to your enemy, or prey. This is how it should be done. You bend your back forward slightly, but keep your eyes on the enemy. Your upper arms should be bent in close to your ribcage and your hands should be folded in front of your chest or stomach area. If carrying a weapon you should follow the same procedure, trying to keep the weapon close to your body so that as few body appendages as possible are sticking out away from your torso. This makes your body outline less distinctive to the enemy, offering a better chance of not being visually detected.

However, you need to be very cautious, with this approachment technique, making sure to lift, not slide, your feet high in order to avoid any obstacles. Your balance should be so controlled that you can stop in mid-step, and freeze in that position until it's safe to move forward. Your feet need to be brought down very carefully and slowly by first touching the ground with the outside of the foot, near the toes, then gently rolling the pressure of your step to the inside and back before pressing your toes firmly onto the ground, or applying any weight to your step. Then you should relax your toes and try diligently to feel whatever may be under your foot and, if nothing potentially noisy is felt, apply more weight so you can get a better feel for what may be under your foot. However, if you feel an obstacle, you should lift your foot and set it down elsewhere, being careful to use the same technique. If no obstacle is felt, then you apply slow, steady pressure to your forward foot until your back foot naturally lifts off the ground. You wouldn't, however, slide your back foot forward due to the noise that this would make as the foot glides too close to the ground, possibly hitting various objects that lie on the surface, or are sticking-up above ground level. Each step should follow this procedure, being very slow and deliberate and even if no obstacle is felt under the foot, that foot is still pressed to the earth slowly so it can gently and quietly press any vegetation onto the ground. The Native Americans were experts at this stealth walking (ghost walking). Noise is one of a hunters primary enemies, so, ghost walking is a friend.

I could feel anxiety building within me, so I did some deep, controlled breathing that I learned while taking karate lessons. I also performed a self-hypnosis form of meditation that heightened my senses—Wolf growled, thinking that I had just done something unnecessary. When I finished, I felt better, more calm and much more confident. As I relaxed, I mentally raced through some martial arts combat techniques as well as combat knife fighting strategies. Actually, I didn't need to do this. Those techniques would come instinctively when I needed them, but the thought process helped keep me alert, so I continued further with thoughts of my knife-combat strategies.

The very first thing any potential knife fighter needs to know is that, if he's in a knife fight, with an experienced opponent, they are both going to get cut. It is extremely rare, no matter how good he is, or even if he's victorious, to have a knife fight end without getting cut—unless the opponent is lacking in training and experience, and even then the possibility of getting cut is high. It's simply the nature of close-combat knife-fighting. In knife combat, cuts are a "given." A knife fighter must simply expect and accept that fact and hope that the cuts he receives are only in non-lethal areas of his body. More than likely, it's the forearms that will get cut because the arms, by necessity, are in front of him and the knife-hand must extend outward, making it vulnerable, in order to strike the opponent. Plus, the forearm with the empty hand is often instinctively and reflexively used to block downward at waist level thrusts—not a good idea, but the conscious mind seldom has control over instinctive and reflexive muscle reactions. It takes much mental effort and physical practice to conquer those instinctive and reflexive actions. Unless the knife fighter is extremely quick with the thrust and flick of his blade, his forearm will almost always be vulnerable. Experienced knife fighters know and accept that they will get cut, that they will see their own blood and that the victor will be the person who inflicts the most serious cuts on his opponent, especially in the torso area. That's why very few civilians, and soldiers as well, are interested in learning knife combat skills—some of those basic skills I had already learned in my civilian martial arts classes. I learned more advanced techniques from the specialized, knife fighting, military instructors.

In a knife fight, holding the blade, cutting edge upward or downward, at waist level, is a matter of preference, depending on how you plan to use the knife and what your favorite techniques are—my preference is usually cutting edge downward, though, on rare occasions, depending on my opponent or my particular situation, I have held the knife cutting edge upward.

Putting the handle of the knife in the hand like a hammer and stabbing downward is normally a mistake because it limits you to downward strikes. It's much easier to counter a downward stab than an upward thrust. Also, by stabbing downward toward the upper torso you are much more likely to stab bones that will deflect the blade. Unless a man is extremely lucky, with the knife in the hammer position, stabbing a vital area, in his constantly moving opponent, is improbable—to be accomplished the knife would have to strike the neck area. So holding the blade low, cutting edge pointing upward, an experienced knife fighter can strike at the soft parts of the body, the groin, stomach and possibly the solar plexus area, where few bones can deflect his blade and he can find the soft, vulnerable flesh where the blade will penetrate easily and deeply. Of course, there is a time to aim for the boney head area since your opponent will probably have his back bent forward slightly. With his posture bent forward, you make a feint to stab or slash the stomach area, but when the opponent attempts to block your strike, you withdraw your knife hand with speed, raise the blade and slash across his forehead. This will send a flood of blood into his eyes, disrupting his vision. Instead of slashing the forehead, you can also poke into the throat or, perhaps, an eye. Slashes to the side of the neck, where the large veins and arteries lay is not advisable at the beginning stages of the fight. Slashes to the neck force you to reach too far, to extend your arm too much. Save this kind of strike for a weakened, slowed opponent in the later stages of a knife fight. The best areas, though at first it seems illogical, are the abdomen, solar plexus areas. From the waist upward, the higher you go, the more movement there is until you reach the head where the most movement of all occurs. More movement means more risk to you and less chance of striking your target. In the beginning, you target the opponent's abdomen area where he is most vulnerable. And if your opponent stabs downward or upward at you, he must extend his arm. In this case, don't retreat backward—It seems illogical, I know, but if you move backward you move away from the opponents arm and lose a good opportunity to slash that arm. Instead of moving backward, swiftly move right or left of his arm and slash it with as much force as you can. Try for the bicep because a deep cut to that muscle with render his arm partially or totally disabled. A more cautious choice, however, is to slash the forearm and wrist areas, although much less disabling. And some inane advise that one of my humorous instructors used to constantly joke about was that: *You should never take a knife to a gun fight. It dramatically increases your chances of getting seriously injured.* I chastised myself for the ill-timed attempt at humor, and focused on the present danger.

My coyote-skin footwear and coat might slightly hamper my mobility and flexibility, but, then again, so would Jake's and Tom's coats and, I thought, I'll bet they're wearing heavy, noisy boots that'll hamper their movements; make them less quick to react.

The throwing knife, which worked well in Nam, where very little clothing was worn, and when it was worn, it was very light and easily penetrated with any blade, wasn't likely to penetrate the Gibson's heavy, winter coats. To be useful at all, the throwing knife would have to be aimed at bare skin areas and that would be the neck and face areas. But head areas aren't a good area to aim at due to their boniness and curved shape, the bones being very hard surfaces to penetrate and the curved nature of the head usually causes knives to glance off of it. The only hope there is if you can make the knife penetrate one of the eye sockets, thus allowing the correct sized blade—thin, like a dagger—to enter the eye socket and penetrate deeply into the brain. However, this is not recommended because it basically requires the enemy to assist you in killing him. The eye socket is so small that it would be nearly impossible to hit with a thrown knife, even at a still target, let alone with a moving target. Also, a slim, dagger-like blade would have to be used because the boney eye socket would prevent a wide blade from penetrating into the brain—though the eye itself could certainly be penetrated. This eye penetration strategy is best used in close combat situations. So my throwing knife would probably not be useful to me, but one never knew what would be useful until the situation and circumstances presented themselves. I'd keep the throwing knife handy, the garrote, too.

That leaves the throat area and the back and sides of the neck to consider. These areas are excellent stealth-attack spots, at close quarters, but much too risky for a throwing knife, unless one has a tendency to believe in miracles. However, like the philosopher, David Hume, I didn't believe in miracles.

As I thought of the probable uselessness of the throwing knife, I pictured the dull, silver blade spinning threw the air. The image was so real that I thought I actually heard the gentle flutter of it, like a hummingbird's wings. It was that vision that reminded me that, for silent killing, when you don't want others to hear you, a throwing knife would be a very foolish weapon because even if you strike your target, he will probably still be able to yell and give a warning. Also, the blade may hit an obstacle before reaching the target and create a noise that will also warn the enemy. So, for silent killing, it's a regular, long-bladed, military style knife that's most useful. I would save the throwing knife for close quarters emergency use. Also, if, somehow my combat blade got dropped or lost, then the throwing knife could be substituted, even at close quarters.

I looked at my watch, 1:09 A.M. I was alert and as prepared as I'd ever be. I was used to waiting due to my Nam experiences. To kill the enemy only takes a short time, but waiting for him to approach your area, and then waiting longer for the right moment to stalk him can take a few hours. No, the waiting didn't bother me. But Grace's safety did. In Nam it was just my life at stake. Now there was something more valuable than my own life at stake, Grace's life. I wasn't some egotistical, maniacal fool who thought he was invincible. No one is invincible. It doesn't take a big mistake to get yourself killed. The biggest mistake I could make right now is to try to capture the Gibsons and bring them back for a trial. In this situation, that was a very foolish option. My choices were to kill or be killed.

I'll kill. Did choosing to kill make me uncivilized? Civilized and, supposedly, law-abiding people often hide behind their advanced culture, snobbish art, deceitful politics and hypocritical religions, then make laws that, quite often, do not dispense justice. Those are the real people to be feared. They are some of the meanest, cruelest inhabitants of the earth. They have high-tech disguises to cover up their murderous thoughts and actions. When unmasked, they can be much more dangerous that I am. They are the manipulators of their culture, religions, politics and laws so that these things can all work for their own benefit. Me? I'm not pretentious. Sure, I've killed for my country, during war, and I'll kill again to save Grace. So all the moralistic, ethical criticisms—more accurately and appropriately called "bullshit"—will have little effect on me. There was no law here and very little civilization, so "bullshit criticism" doesn't really bother me.

If, after Grace and I get back to civilization, some one questions my decision or motives, so be it. I will not risk Grace's life for anyone's laws, morals or ethics, and justice lay in my own hands while holding a combat knife, throwing knife, garrote, martial arts skills and a few traps in my fake campsite.

I climbed a large tree that had a fairly thick trunk and sturdy branches. I wanted to blend into the tree as well as I could. As simple as it sounds, hiding in a tree is good a strategy—a lesson I learned quickly from American and Vietnamese snipers—because man, as a hunter, almost always looks at the ground or straight ahead or side to side when hunting his prey. Even grouse and pheasants are initially spotted on the ground and not shot at until they are airborne. A hunter rarely, if ever, needs to look upward, unless he is hunting something with wings or something that lives in trees, as squirrels do. Therefore, without realizing it, man has trained himself to ignore the space above his head. This fact makes hiding in a tree an excellent choice, especially if Jake and Tom are aware of the focused listening and unfocused viewing techniques. I'll be above their normal viewing level and I doubt they'd expect that from me.

It would definitely be an uncomfortable wait, but that's the way it had to be. So I set my mind to the task. I was set and ready for action with my only obstacles to absolute confidence being my constantly nagging thoughts about Grace's safety. I desperately hoped that she wouldn't wake-up until the ugly deeds were done. How would she view me, if she witnessed me killing Jake and Tom Gibson? Would I lose her to emotional trauma? Would she then fear me? Would that cause her to emotionally and physically withdraw from me? Those possibilities bothered me much more than I wanted to admit. Even worse than *bothering* me, it was *distracting* me.

So I forced myself to concentrate even more. I eliminated the distracting thoughts from my mind, concentrating on Jake and Tom, karate and my fisted blade.

I scanned the area carefully and felt the blackness of the night engulf me, making me part of it. I was pleased with the feel and fit of it, like a black-clothed ninja, because that was an excellent, comfortable camouflage for a stealthy, unheard and unseen killer like me.

/.- -/../.-../.-../.-./../.-/- -/../.../.../..../././/..../.-/-./

Chapter 15

★★★★

Surprise

Darkness surrounds me, black as tar. Like osmosis, I could feel my body slowly absorbing it. Darkness is building up inside of me. The kind of darkness that is a precursor to extreme violence. A calm quietness surrounds me, like the inside of a century old tomb. But I feel no immediate danger, which is corroborated by Wolf's silence. There is turmoil embedded in the darkness that exists somewhere inside of me, like a rumbling, dark storm cloud preparing to shoot a bolt of lightening. I feel the coldness of it emanate from the canyon of darkness that's building inside of me. Out of that darkness I hear the ominous voice of the German philosopher, Nietzsche, telling me that: "When you look into the abyss, the abyss also looks into you." It's true; I can see it, feel it. But the dark abyss of death doesn't just *look* into you, it *bores* into the core of you, like a voracious worm in an apple. I felt it. The abyss is boring into my mind, steering me toward violence. It is wresting control from me, trying to dominate me. The abyss sprouted hands and arms that reached out and pulled me into it when I was in Vietnam. It was trying to do the same thing now. In Nam, I looked into that abyss and the abyss found a hesitant, originally unwilling, but talented companion. Gradually we embraced and I fed many dead bodies into its ravenous maw. It had a voracious hunger for death and was as insatiable as an astronomical Black Hole. Morality and goodness were dissolving within me. Wolf was howling and reverting back to his original wild nature. I was losing control and had to decide if I really wanted to lose control. It appeared that there would be two battles: one external battle with Jake and Tom, and a simultaneous internal battle with a past partner, the abyss.

Evil lies in all of us. Hopefully, goodness dominates. But when we look at each other, do we truly see an honest, objective assessment of our friends, relatives, strangers? I seriously doubt it. We only see superficially, what's on or close to the surface. We don't see into the hidden depths of those people. And, because of that, we all tend to underestimate the evil in individuals and society, just as we all tend to optimistically overestimate their goodness. We see their smiles, but never really see the rictus on the face of their personal abyss.

After Nam, my personal abyss lingered and I struggled to escape its poisonous fangs and razor sharp claws. Escaping unscathed, I knew, was impossible, but I thought I'd done it with only a few deep scars. That is, I thought I'd done it until the Gibsons intruded into my newly found, relatively peaceful, but sometimes depressed, life. Now that abyss opened, again, for me; welcomed me back into its deadly and blood saturated clutches. It stirred the dormant darkness within me, like long settled dust that's stirred by a violent wind. I felt the cloak of its darkness wrap itself around me like a shroud and a voice asking for acceptance. Once accepted, it would be activated and when activated it would be difficult to resist its power and ominous allure. Though a severe threat to civilized laws, the barbaric, lawless need for death of the abyss was exactly what I needed, and wanted. So, once again, I accepted it and welcomed its embrace.

*   *   *   *   *   *   *

It was nearly 2:30 A.M., November 20th, when I heard Wolf howl his warning. Then, about thirty-five minutes later I heard his close-by, faint growl. About the same time, the forest noises stopped, something the nocturnal animals heard made them quiet. I knew it wasn't the result of any noise that I had made. It could be that the animals sensed Wolf, but his growl was very low, plus his growls normally only occur within my head. No. It was the Gibsons arriving. I felt the malevolent force of their presence shortly after Wolf's warning. It was as if the air turned thick and foul, assaulting my senses and pressing its fetid weight upon my flesh.

Jake and Tom didn't know exactly where the camp would be. It was a few hours until dawn, and they were in a hurry to capture us while they were still under the cover of night. Because of this, I guessed they were walking hurriedly and the animals heard their somewhat hurried, somewhat careless movements, though I knew for a fact that it was extremely difficult to be quiet in the dark, with limited vision and the necessity to hurry your movements.

The moon was low in the sky and the tree branches blocked-out what little light it gave to the thick forest. It was like being in a cave, hard to see, but good for me. The darkness liked me and I liked it, a friend, a colleague that assisted my dark skills.

I soundlessly unsheathed my combat Ka-Bar knife and froze into position for a few minutes before I heard the soft crunch of frozen vegetation coming from almost directly east of me, over my right shoulder, as I faced north. The moisture on the ground froze as night time progressed, allowing me to hear faint crunching sounds. The noise was slightly prolonged, as if someone heavy was walking in a special way to avoid making any more noise than necessary. They must have sensed they were getting close or, perhaps, as I'd hoped, they saw the faint glint of the red coals, or smelled the wispy tendrils of smoke still rising from the slow-burning campfire. The campfire was doing what I had intended, being a beacon for them, like moths to a flame. Every muscle, except my diaphragm and eyes remained motionless.

A couple of minutes later, I heard a small twig snap, followed by the slightest noise of what sounded like clothing brushing against a bush, low branch, or tree truck. Those noises came from a northerly direction. Three, distinct noises; in all probability, human made. Wolf certainly wouldn't have made them. I thought about the squirrels I had encountered the day before, so I waited, just to be cautious.

I hadn't waited long when out of the shroud of night time blackness Tom approached from the north, performing his high-stepping, ghost walk. He came into view slowly, like some hellish wraith. His undarkened, oily, white face shone even though their was very little moon light, another careless mistake for a woodsman.

I didn't stare at Tom, however, because sometimes hunters have an acute sixth sense which tells them that they are being watched. It's a primordial reaction; part of some long-forgotten hunting and/or survival instinct.

Now I refocused my listening to the east of me. Jake was the heaviest of the two men, but he was also the quietest. I could sometimes hear the faint crunch of frozen weeds, but I never heard any twigs snap, or any rubbing clothing as he circled toward the south end of camp. I turned my head slowly northward, toward Tom. I could see him clearly now, a black shadow, that looked like a thick moving tree trunk. He was almost at the edge of our camp site, shotgun held close to his body at an angle that went from his right hand, on the butt near his right hip, and his left hand, on the pump action, with the barrel angled out past his left shoulder, the classic, right handed, "hunter's carry" position.

I returned my focus to Tom. It didn't surprise me to see him use the approachment technique as he came within range of the campfire. Nor did it surprise me that he slowly, quietly approached the tree that I was hiding in because it was strategically located for a good view of the entire camp site.

He walked directly under me, never once looking upward. I could have jumped down on top of him, slit his throat and it would be all over for him, right then and there. But, no, I thought, as I restrained myself from that mighty temptation. I was rewarded for my patience when Tom leaned his shotgun against the tree trunk, directly below my position. If I had jumped from the tree, I'd have made too much noise as I shifted my weight, preparing to jump, then even more noise as I landed on him. Then he may have made a startled noise before I could cut his throat. Those noises, and those actions would certainly be seen or heard by Jake. My primary weapon of surprise would be ruined, prematurely, and probably with grave consequences. It was better to wait and stick to the plan.

Tom quietly pulled out his large Bowie knife. He was doing just as I had predicted earlier. Know your enemy, I thought.

I was elated that Tom had rested his shotgun at the base of the tree, within my easy reach, when I jumped to the ground. Actually, I thought he'd hand it to Jake prior to pulling out his knife. This unplanned stoke of good luck encouraged me and hope became pregnant within me.

Where was Jake? I'd lost track of him. "God damn-it!" I thought, as I slowly looked from side to side, then back to Tom. No sign of Jake in the blackness of night. But right now I needed to concentrate on Tom.

As Tom approached the make-shift tent I could see his head-bobbing with confidence. I'm sure he felt that way as a result of seeing the sleeping bags and especially at the sight of seeing my boots—I had to take them off anyway, so I put them to good use—the toes pointing skyward. He'd think that we were both sleeping and, from my boots, he could tell exactly which side of the tent I was on. The boots happened to be on the side of the tent closest to him. To him it must have looked perfectly inviting. I couldn't see his face, but it must have had a huge, self-satisfied grin plastered on it. In his warped mind, he knew he had me in the perfect position for his favorite kind of attack.

I detected a very faint sound. I slowly turned my head as far as I could, not wanting to turn any other part of my body for fear that the movement might be seen. I could see Jake standing at the southern edge of our small camp clearing. Tom paused, turned to look at his father, and when Jake signaled, with a nod of his head, Tom stepped closer and closer to the tent. He held the big Bowie knife in a hammer grip, at head level, blade pointing downward, a power grip for plunging the knife deeply through the tent and deeply into the object that is inside the tent . . . me.

Jake and Tom could have both emptied their shotguns by firing simultaneously into the tent, but I was positive that they wouldn't do that. They'd both want me to die slowly, their revenge for my killing Lester. Slow, terrifying, knife torture was more their style. I knew them. I'd studied them; figured them out—which was not very difficult. They were in my mental grip. I could sense their thoughts and actions, though it was more difficult to do with Jake.

Tom looked at Jake, again, when he was only about ten feet from the side of the tent where my boots stuck out. Jake silently hand-signaled for Tom to attack by first placing his shotgun in his left hand. Then he pointed at the tent and raised his fisted right hand, as if it was holding a knife, then made repeated, downward stabbing motions. A huge, sadistic grin spread across his scruffy-bearded, bear-like face. It was the kind of grin that conveyed its intent in a split second.

They intended to maim me in order to incapacitate me. Then, I'll bet, they intended to torture my innocent eight year old daughter before my agonized eyes and mind, as I was wounded, bound and helpless. They would make the torture last all day, maybe two, if they could, in order to inflict as much misery, pain and agony as they could on the both of us. Then, when Grace was finally dead, they'd again avenge Lester's death by using their blades on me. They would, of course, cut my penis off, as I had done to Lester, only they wouldn't just cut it off quickly. I figured they'd cut it off ever so slowly, an eighth of an inch at a time as I writhed in the kind of torturous agony that only a very few terribly unlucky humans could ever know. Of course, that's just my guess, based on what I've seen of their mad, Cro-Magnon characteristics, mental sets, assumed polluted DNA helixes and vicious, sadistic, immoral attitudes and behaviors. They were mad dogs, carnivorous, blood-thirsty beasts in human form. I wouldn't surprise me at all if they were also fundamentalist, ultra-conservative fanatics in some branch of religious gibberish, also

No civilized laws would save Grace or me from their repugnant, bestial and maniacal behavior. No law out here but Darwin's Law: Survival-of-the-fittest, where might-is-right and the smartest, toughest and strongest survive. I had to kill them, the same way that a cop would shoot to kill a criminal that drew a gun on him. I'd either die or they'd die, as simple as that. I had no time to worry about civilized laws. The only law here was the law-of-the-jungle: kill or be killed. No hesitation. No remorse. No shame or guilt.

In my mind I saw dark, dead, disfigured faces with grotesque stares of horror: a scene from Nam. Thinking of the horrors that I saw in Nam, I wouldn't be surprised, if captured, if Jake and Tom attempted to make me eat each piece of my penis as part of their torture. If I wouldn't—or even if I did—they'd probably cut me up in order to disfigure me horribly, but not create enough blood loss to cause a quick death. They'd probably cut my ears, nose and lips off, as well as my fingers and toes. Then they'd clearly set them all on the ground in front of me, so I could see and agonize over what they were doing to me, pieces of me scattered along the ground. Of course, they wouldn't cut my eyes out because they want me to witness the horror of them dismantling my body, piece by piece. They'd want me to see, then feel the agony of my body being sliced up like luncheon meat at the local deli. No amount of pleading or begging would make any difference, it would only increase their pleasure. And if any of the cuts bled too profusely, they would simply cauterized the skin with a red-hot blade that had been stuck into the hot coals of a campfire. This would prevent my immediate death from loss of blood and enable them to torture me for hours, perhaps days. My task was to prevent this agony, especially for Grace. So, here and now, the laws of civilized man no longer applied.

The deathly silence was shattered as Tom screamed, maniacally, as he sprinted the last ten feet to the tent in a split second, then was airborne in a Superman-like leap. As he leaped towards my side of the tent, he was still screaming so loudly that the echo seemed to bounce off each and every tree. The intensity of the rage within his satanic scream sent a chill up my spine.

Time slowed for me as Tom appeared to float in the air, over the blanket-tent, his body stretched out to its full length, horizontally, with his right hand holding a Bowie knife in a downward, stabbing position. The weight of his body forced the blanket-tent to collapse easily, as planned. Then it was quiet and still for a few seconds. Tom's hand wasn't slashing and stabbing through the blanket where he thought my pinned body would be. Only a little movement came from his arm and then a low, weak, whimper came from the tent. Jake looked shocked, then walked, then ran to Tom to see what had happened.

Jake yelled as he was running, "Did yuh git 'im, son? Did yuh git the dirty bastard?" Jake stopped suddenly in front of the tent, staring at Tom as Tom's strong body struggled weakly on top of the collapsed tent. Jake stared, frozen in place by this totally unexpected sight, while the pleasant-feeling darkness grew inside of me and Wolf growled viciously.

Tom slowly rose, struggling to his knees with great effort, the blanket rising with him like an apron tied to him. He turned slowly toward his father. Tom's face appeared as white as fresh snow. He looked down at his chest, stomach and legs and saw the long, sharpened, sapling stakes that he had jumped onto, some of which were now protruding from both sides of his riddled body. On unsteady legs he looked at his dad and tried to speak. Like a fish out of water his mouth opened and closed, but all that came out was a spray of blood, bloody saliva and reddish foam. He was having great difficulty bending his neck to look downward because one of the stakes tore through his lower neck, under his Adam's Apple, possibly puncturing the jugular vein. The stake stuck out the back of his neck, just missing his spinal cord, or maybe deflected by it.

Jake's thick-boned jaw dropped to his chest, his eyes locked on his son's horrified, bug-eyed expression. Probably for the first time in his life, he didn't know what to do. Jake stood still, as if paralyzed and anchored to the ground.

My plan had worked and within my personal abyss there was a smile which was completely empty of the slightest guilt or remorse. I'd seen this kind of grotesque killing in Nam—the Viet Cong soldiers seemed to favor this type of "punji-stake" killing. But I viewed it as a mandatory job that had to be done ruthlessly and I was satisfied that I had accomplished the job successfully. Tom would be dead soon.

It was after Grace fell asleep that I had cut about two dozen, very sturdy sapling stakes, about one inch in diameter and two-feet long. I sharpened the thinner ends into points that were as sharp as spear points. I then sliced the sides of the points, at about a thirty degree angle, and pulled that slice out away from the sapling to make a barb, like a fish hook, a couple of inches from each of the sharpened ends—in Nam they were called punji-stakes that were usually found with the sharp end pointing upward from the bottom of a hidden pit that American soldiers would fall into—those punji-stakes were usually coated with animal or human feces to cause rapid, life-threatening infection. Thus, once a stake punctured the body, the barb would make it very difficult to get the stake out without further tearing the inner body tissue, muscle or organs that they came into contract with. I also held the sharpened tips of each stake in the fire for a short time, to harden them, and then set half the punji-stakes into narrow, four to six inches holes that I had bored into the nearly frozen ground with my rugged combat knife. I spread them out all along the area that my body would have been in, if I had been really sleeping there. None of the punji-stakes could be seen from the front of the tent—they were covered with a blanket. I placed the other stakes on Grace's side of the tent. I was certain that Jake would allow Tom to jump on top of me, like he had in the cabin when he had me trapped in the bunk bed, under a blanket. What I didn't know was if Jake would jump on the tent, too. At the time, I wondered if Jake would want to jump on my side and have Tom jump on Grace's side of the tent. I cursed the terrible vision I had of this really happening to Grace, but was greatly disappointed that Jake hadn't also jumped on the tent and been impaled on the punji-stakes with Tom.

Jake, in surprised shock, now stepped close to Tom, then pulled the woolen blanket off several punji-stake shafts to relieve the pain that the weight of the blanket was causing as it pulled down on the stakes that were embedded in Tom's staggering body. But once Jake removed the blanket he could see the full extent of the damage—Tom could not look downward due to the stake in his neck—and the horrified look that Jake gave Tom made Tom panic. His eyes bugged-out as he made croaking sounds while his mouth opened and closed in a futile effort to speak.

There were seven stakes in his body. One was through his neck, one went clear through each thigh, one penetrated the lower stomach-groin area, one in the upper abdomen and two in the chest. Some stakes probably punctured his arms, but the must have pulled out when Tom stood. The only stakes that didn't penetrate the body entirely were the ones sticking out of Tom's chest. The breast bones prevented deep penetration of the chest cavity. I also noticed that Tom's clothing was ripped in other areas where the stakes had ripped through the cloth, but not through any skin.

As Tom and Jake both stood frozen in preoccupied shock and horror, I returned my blade to its sheath and jumped down from the tree to grab Tom's shotgun. Jake barely heard me through the thick mental haze of his shock. But he did respond slowly by turning to look at me. I aimed the shotgun at his chest.

"Drop your shotgun, Jake. Do it very carefully," I said, through clenched teeth and pent-up anger.

Jake did as I said and uttered not a word, but his eyes were like bear traps aimed at my head. At this moment he wanted to rip my head off my shoulders and with his massive size and strength he could probably do it.

Tom started pulling feebly at the punji-stakes, but all that came out was an increased flow of blood. His body swayed on weak legs, fragile fingers trying to grip a stake. His coat, which wasn't thick enough to stop the penetration of the stakes, was stained with blood, the large stain looked black—in the dark, blood looks black. His hands slipped off the slick stake and his arms fell to his sides. Now I could see the blood flowing out of his coat sleeves, onto his hands and then drip from his fingertips. He stumbled as he grew weaker, his hands were greased with his own vital blood. He began shuffling his legs forward as he staggered toward his father. I wondered what it was that kept him on his feet, his body had taken tremendous punishment. I forbid myself any feeling of pity, shame, or remorse by mentally crushing them immediately. That kind of sympathetic crap and self-doubt would only get me and Grace killed. I knew that I should never pity someone I've had to kill because the pity I felt would freeze my instincts and reflexes, and get me killed, and the person trying to kill me would certainly feel no pity or sympathy for me as he laughs at my prostrate corpse. "Fight fire with fire and don't die stupidly," Wolf growled at me. After all my tough talk, however, I realized that though I had killed shame and remorse, I still felt pity for my enemy.

Tom looked at his father as if Jake could save him, do something to fix him, get him out of this situation, as Jake had probably always done before.

Tom couldn't talk with that punji-stake through his neck, and when he tried, again, to say something to his father, more frothy bubbles and bloody spray exited his open mouth—indicating lung damage. His mouth still tried to talk, but only opened and closed—not even a croaking sound could be made—as before, like a fish out of water. Tom's lips drooled red from the corners and down the sides of his chin. Slow but steady streams of blood flowed out of both nostrils. He walked towards Jake like Frankenstein's monster, stiff legged, arms outstretched. Then unconsciousness, from lose of blood, felled his body. His weight plunged forward, stiffly, driving his chest and head into the ground, causing the two chest punji-stakes, that had not completely penetrated this area before, to be forced completely through his chest and out his back. Jake, his actions still frozen in shock, couldn't catch Tom, but his—and mine—ears were working well, so we both heard the crunch of bones as the stakes drove completely through Tom's chest and out of his back. Those stake points must have been blunted as they passed through Tom's bony chest because they didn't penetrate through the back of his coat. As Tom lay face down on the ground, the two stakes made the back of his coat look like an inverted V-shape, like a miniature tent. He lay lifeless at his father's feet, although his body twitched convulsively with its final death spasms as if all his muscles were violently resisting giving up their young lives.

Big, vicious, cruel, tough, merciless Jake Gibson still couldn't move. The look of horror on his face could only have been duplicated, with heavy make-up, in a Stephen King movie. The realization that both his sons were dead paralyzed his mind and muscles.

Jake stared downward at Tom, then sucked air through his gapped teeth. As his shock thawed, he knelt, placed his shotgun on the ground, then he sluggishly stepped to his son, paying no heed to the shotgun that I had aimed at him. He looked up, then back at me, with heavy-lidded eyes that were as black as charred flesh in hell. Suddenly his eyes opened wide and the fiery inferno in them leaped from his eyes to scorch me. Then he refocused on Tom, removed his gloves and stroked the hair on the back of Tom's head. After a few seconds, he turned to look at me. He said, "Me boys. They both be dead now. Yuh kill't both me boys!"

Jake stood up slowly. He threw his hat aside and took off his heavy winter coat, bent over and spread the coat over the back of Tom's head and back. While still bent over Tom's body, Jake's lips moved silently, as if in mute prayer. The irony of that sight caused my eyes to bulge with disbelief. It appeared that even murderers, now-a-days, believed that their God is on their side, condoning their treacherous killings and, perhaps, even willing those acts of terrorism to occur. It was a sickening sight, I thought, to use the facade of religion to condone murder and other torturous and heinous acts of terror against the human body.

That irony sickened me. I had to swallow hard to keep the contents of my stomach from rushing up into and out of my mouth. The taste of sour bile lay in the back of my throat, nearly gagging me.

Beyond Jake a sleek whiteness took shape, as if out of a misty fog. Wolf appeared to me, making a warning growl, but a warning of what? Jake was no threat now, immobile and drowning in his own sincere grief. But Wolf always gave a warning of immediate danger and his growling continued. I was confused by it and was too slow translating it to the word "Grace."

I heard a twig snap behind me, catching me off guard. I turned to see Grace walking toward me. I screamed, "No, Grace! Go hide!"— Grace had awakened when Tom screamed as he attacked the tent. But before I could turn back to face Jake, he was only a yard away from me in a bent-over position, his back parallel to the ground like a charging lineman on a football team. His head and back went under the barrel of my shotgun and his massive head drove into my solar plexus with such force that I flew backwards and fell to the ground on my back. I bounced off of him and gasped for breath as I rose, with difficulty. I was dazed. Strange, I thought, that Jake didn't try to hold onto me as I went to the ground, even stranger that he didn't simply pick up his shotgun and shoot me. No, I thought, as my mind cleared He didn't want a quick death for me and that's why he didn't shoot me.

After the brutally jarring collision, Jake had rolled his body over, like an agile, full-grown bull and ran past me, using his momentum to spring to his feet and grab a left handful of Grace's hair—I heard her scream in terrorized surprise, fear and pain—and yanked her close to him. Somehow he managed to have his Bowie knife in his hand.

My mind screamed in terrible agony at the turn of events—I had had him covered with a shotgun. I had him dead in my sights. I should've pulled the trigger. I called myself the biggest fool alive, and silently screamed obscenities at my terrible foolishness; my damned carelessness.

"Don't freeze," I told myself. "Don't freeze. Think! Think!"

Jake grinned, sucked air through his teeth, again, and shouted with bitter hatred, "I never shoulda unnerest'mated ya, Boy, but now yuh fuckin' bastard, I'm gonna shows yuh how it feel ta has someone kill yur kin."

Quickly and roughly he pulled Grace off her feet as he yanked her head up by a fistful of hair and placed the blade so it lightly touched and cut the skin of her throat just enough to send two rivulets of blood streaking down her fragile and pale neck.

Grace began screaming from the pain. She grabbed at Jake's forearm for support as her feet dangled in the air.

"Think! God damn it, think!" I silently shrieked at myself.

Wolf had warned me and now Jake had turned the tables on me. I had underestimated him, too. Was I that much out of practice, that much out of shape and soft, compared to my Nam days? Stupid bastard, I called myself. Son of a bitch! I had him by the balls, helpless, and I let him get away. Damn-it to hell!

"Think! Think! Self-abusive, name-calling won't save Grace," I screamed at myself. Only I can . . . with courage and cunning from Roamin' Wolf. What to do, I thought. I must delay Jake in order to give myself time. I needed time . . . just a little, just enough to free Grace.

"Action! Action! God damn it!" I thought. "If not physical action, then verbal action, to gain time," I said as I removed my hat and coat to prepare for action—I had already removed my gloves earlier.

"We underestimated each other, Jake. You thought I was a helpless wimp, but if it weren't for your forethought in hiding those canoes in a different spot, we'd have beat you for sure." I put a pretend, confident smile on my face and grinned directly into his eyes—which was not easy.

I saw him slightly relieve the pressure on Grace's hair and neck as he let her feet touch the ground. Immediately, Grace could breath normally, so she tried to scream, but only a low, raspy sound passed over her lips. She started squirming and twisting again so Jake yanked her off the ground again and her dangling legs made her look like a marionette with Jake as her crazed puppeteer. Grace's legs were writhing, out of control, with herky-jerky spasms, her face a screaming, distorted picture of pain.

Jake replied, "An yuh never woulda find 'em, even though they be only a short way from where yuh sees us hide 'em. We covered 'em up wid branches an' such." But I gives yuh credit, Boy, fer havin' some gumption. Yuh fool us a couple times when we be trackin' yuh.

Smart, but not smart 'nough. Now if yuh wants ta really be smart, yuh takes them canoes, like we did, an' yuh sinks 'em in the water right next ta some big bushes that hangs out inta the lake. Then yuh ties the rope from each canoe ta the bottom branches of the bush so they be hidden un'er the bush where no one knows they be, exceptin' the person who hides 'em there. They be alumin canoes—he meant aluminum—so nothin' in the water goin' ta hurt 'em. Now let's be getting' away from all the bullshit, cause now yuh gonna sees yur kid die like I sees mine die."

Grace, whose face was in a painful rictus, again, started pulling with both hands at the arm that Jake held under her chin, as if she were trying to do chin-ups for exercise. Jake lowered her so her feet touched the ground again, probably because her squirming was making his balance become unstable.

Immediately, I said to Jake, with a convincingly false smile, "Jake, you don't look so tough to me. You're not really a mountain man, like your son's thought, are you? You're really just a puny . . . that means very small, Jake . . . a puny little hill-man, not a rugged mountain man. Just a dumb, ignorant, weak little hillbilly boy pretending to be a man. Look at you now, hiding behind a little girl. Did you hide behind your mommy's dresses, too? You look like such a damned sissy using a little girl to shield yourself. You must be really scared of me to do that, right? Hey, I know that you want to look as tough as Arnold Schwarzenegger, but really you're what Arnold would call a "girly-man," aren't you? Hey there, girly-man, come out and fight a real man. You want to prove how tough you are? Well, you certainly can't do it hiding behind a little girl, Mr. Girly-Man. The only person I ever saw hiding from a fight behind a little girl was a weak, little, sissy boy. Are you a weak, little sissy boy? You sure look like one."

Jake's eyes burned red with rage. I continued to provoke him. "I see you like a knife, girly-man, but you probably never fought a real man with a knife, sissy boy, so I can understand why I must really scare you. I can tell by your ugly face that I scare you, don't I, sissy boy? Hell, it's rather obvious that you're afraid of me, or you wouldn't be hiding behind the little girl. Man! That's really pathetic. Surely you can see that, too. Must scare you to admit it to yourself, though, huh? Of course it does. It's so obvious."

Jake's face contorted with rage. I continued, saying, "Damn! Must burn your ass to admit that a little guy like me is more of a real man than you are. How tough can a girly-man be when he has to hide behind a little girl to protect himself. Shit man! Look at you! You're a sissy full of bluff and bluster. Too bad your two sissy boys couldn't see you now." I pointed at him and laughed hilariously, then said, "You're really just a scared little boy, a girly-man pretending to be a tough, real man . If you think you're so tough, Jake, why not fight me, girly-man?" I sneered mockingly at him, then pursed my lips and made kissing noises as I pretended to be kissing him. "Such a pretty girly-man you are, too," I taunted. "I bet you like to kiss both boys and men, don't you?" Then I laughed as loud and as mockingly as I could.

Even the dim firelight and the moonlight couldn't hide the fact that Jake's face suddenly turned scarlet, as he sucked furiously through his teeth in anger. He yelled, "Yur dead, Boy. I'm gonna carve yur face up inta 'amburg, Shit Face, an' then I does the same wid yur girly. Yuh puts down dat shotgun an' we sees who be bedder and tougher wid a knife, an who be more a man."

"Sorry, pretty-boy, girly-man, no deal. I'll only put the shotgun down if you release the little girl who is protecting you from big, bad me. Then the fight will be a fair fight and you won't be a scared, girly-man hiding behind a little girl like a scared, little boy.

Jake was livid; his face radiating pure hatred. "Oh, sure, Asshole. I lets yur girl go an' yuh blows me away wid the shotgun. Besides, Boy, it be a fist fight I really wants wid ya. Changed my mind. Don't needs no knife to carve yuh up. I cut yuh up wid me fists. I lets 'er go if yuh agree to a fist fight. No weapon 'ceptin' bone and muscle. Deal, Wimp?"

When I paused to look at Grace's terrified eyes, Jake shouted loudly, "Oh! Now who be the girly-man? Yuh just be a wimp wid a big mouth."

"Deal!" I shouted, "If you let her get away from you," I growled at him as, my friend, the pale wolf prowled in the background of my mind.

Then swiftly he had Grace dangling off the ground, by her hair, again. She screamed. As she screamed, Jake tossed her away from him, like tossing a twig into the bushes, about ten feet to his right. He switched his Bowie knife from his left hand to his right hand and we looked at each other. Then he placed his knife into its sheath, on his right hip.

I pulled the shotgun in toward my chest, holding it tipped at an angle that ran between my right hip and my left shoulder, the "hunter's-carry" position. Then with my left hand I pumped the shotgun and the shells came flying out until none were left and the ground in front of me was littered with little red tubes. I pointed the shotgun into the air and pulled the trigger. The firing pin clicked, a clear indication that the shotgun had no more shells in it. Then I stood motionless, facing Jake.

When Jake paused, as if to realize that I was now unarmed and he could rush me and kill me with his knife. His right hand moved slowly towards his knife. Quickly, I said, "You're not both a coward and a girly-man, are you? The deal was between two men, right. The deal wasn't between me, the man, and you, the girly-man coward, right? The deal was no weapons, right? So why are you becoming a chicken and reaching for your knife?"

Jake grimaced, sucked air between his teeth, then grinned robustly as if he really thought he was going to win this battle, easily, and surely didn't need his knife.

His own shotgun was behind me, so he couldn't reach that without going through me. So, it was to be bones and muscle only. "OK," I thought, "let's dance." However, I wasn't stupid enough to believe that he wouldn't eventually have his knife in his hand.

I spoke to Grace. "Stay out of the way, Grace. Don't go near him again, and don't watch us. Don't watch us fight. Go hide." When she hesitated, I screamed at her, "Damn it, Grace! Go hide! Now!" She ran scared and crying from the killing field.

"Oh, Sweet Meat," Jake said, mockingly to me, "soon yur gonna be drinkin' yur own blood. That be for sure." He laughed demonically as he stepped cautiously toward me—and me toward him. He looked like a giant oak tree slowly moving forward, directly at me, long, thick limbs reaching for me, his body slightly angled forward like a huge, hungry grizzly bear reaching for food.

Wolf howled, loud and clear, but this time the howl didn't come from the outside, it came from within me, as if from deeply inside the abyss. I felt as if I had gnashing teeth, sharp claws, wily strength, and speed. Finally the Roman Wolfe had become the Roamin' Wolf. I heard myself growl just before I shouted, "Let's dance!"

It was difficult staying calm, confident, and in control. Roamin' Wolf lived for moments like this. Roamin' Wolf would go to places that would make Satan, himself, fart fire and shit brimstone bricks. Roamin' Wolf had already been to hell, a place called Nam, where he never once saw Satan bathing in the conflagration of napalm—the devil's reputation was all grand hyperbole. Satan is really just a red wimp, with a hot temper, looking for his little red wagon and his special, lacy and frilly-dressed dolly that's in it. Besides, even if he was real, the napalm in Nam was, most likely, a bit too hot for the devilish, horned bastard to handle.

Suddenly, and unexpectedly, I felt as if my finger nails were growing into claws and my canine teeth lengthened, while my nose (muzzle) and ears lengthened. I also felt itchy, as if hair (fur) was growing rapidly on my otherwise bare skin, and my coccyx tingled, as if it were extending outward, away from my body (tail) and improving my balance greatly.

/-.-/.-/-/...././.-/../-./././.- -./.-/.-../.-/- -../- -../- - -/.-../.-/

Chapter 16

★★★★

Night of the Wolfe

I REMAINED ALERT, BUT motionless, as Jake slowly and cautiously approached me. He had said that he wanted a fist fight, with the only weapons being bone and muscle. It seemed, at first, to be a tremendous advantage for him, but I accepted the challenge knowing that it placed Grace in a safe position, at least, temporarily.

I thought, Sure, just a fist fight, until things don't go his way—I hoped they wouldn't—then he'd opt for the knife, I was positive of that.

All my life I've faced an assortment of bullies, most of them with empty heads and large muscles, who think that pure strength will always dominate, always crush, always be victorious. Sometimes it was true, of course, but Jake was underestimating me, again, and I was so very thankful for that gift of egotistical and careless stupidity, as well as his habitual, over-confident arrogance.

As Jake approached me, what I saw was a bestial rube, dressed in layers of thick muscle. But I couldn't take him lightly, either, or I'd also be stupid and dead. Stupid and dead was definitely not good for Grace or me. I already saw, and thus knew, that he was extremely dangerous—I'd never fought someone quite as big and powerful before, but like most big brutes, layered with bulky muscles, he appeared to be slow. However, I knew that he'd present much more of a challenge than any average Vietnamese or Korean enemy. Jake was three times their size and weight. I knew I could never match his brute strength. The speed and precision of my physical combat skills, plus the ferocious and indomitable attitude of my inner Wolf, would have to counter his massive bulk, or Grace and I would perish.

Fist to fist, muscle power versus muscle power, I was no match for Jake. But Jake was in for the surprise. My mixed martial arts skills—from many different forms of martial arts styles—my Nam experiences, my killer instincts and speedy reflexes, my volcanic rage and, most importantly, the defense of Grace, would combine to defeat him, one way or another—though, in reality, I was not in nearly as good shape as I was before and during the war.

I've always accepted the fact that on any given day, anyone can be defeated, no matter how good he thinks he is and I'm no exception. But this day wasn't going to belong to Jake. It was to be "a day of Grace," but the "night of the Wolfe."

I also knew it wouldn't only be a battle of skill, but a battle of endurance—my endurance was questionable, but the rush of adrenaline would take care of that. Mountains of solid rock do not ever win the battle with and enduring and hostile wind. Mountains get worn away slowly, piece by piece as the wind carries grains of sand that wear away the surface of some huge monolith until, in time, that mountain has been leveled. Jake, the mountain, had to be, and would be, leveled. It wasn't the egotistical, bragging feeling of my super ego, either. It was a feeling of absolute necessity, supported by reasonable confidence in my combat skills. It was a strength, not of muscle, but a strength of character, embedded in confidence and wrapped in determination . . . something mysteriously and atypically spiritual, given to me by my spirit wolf who has a ferocious and feral will to survive at all costs. Rules? A fair fight? No. The only rule now is to survive by being victorious. A fair fight? In my experiences, fair fights are extremely rare, if by a "fair fight" one means that the combatants are equal in every way that's significant to the winning or losing of the fight. The concept of a "fair fight" is normally the rationalized, bullshit philosophy of a myopic adolescent. A fight to the death can never include the idea of "fairness" if you expect to survive. In this case, victory meant death for one of us. Life itself is often not fair, and you can bet that never in his long life has Jake ever entered a fair fight. His fights, certainly, were always stacked in his favor, always, or he wouldn't have entered into them.

I smelled a wild, ferocious, feral animal odor, a redolent musk of a Wolf. My body literally reeked of a wolf-like, primal determination to prevail, to pounce and claw and sink my teeth into flesh, to claw and shred the underbelly and to win the single most important battle of my life, of our lives, Grace and Sam and me.

To my surprise, Jake assumed a late nineteenth century boxing stance that I had only seen on old boxing newsreels. He looked like John L. Sullivan who was the heavyweight, bare-knuckle boxing champion. The urge was extreme, but I didn't laugh.

Jake's fists were held at face level, left arm bent half way, about two feet from his face; right arm bent half way about one foot from his face, with the thumb tips of both fists facing directly towards him. If his fists were opened in this position, both palms would be aimed at his face.

As he approached and arrived at a distance of about ten feet, I positioned myself into the Forward Guarding Stance, which is best suited for attacking an opponent, and can quickly be altered to the Back Stance which is primarily used for defense.

When using the Forward Guarding Stance, you face your opponent, looking straight ahead at him, shoulders at right angles to his position, but your legs are spread wide apart, about twice the width of your shoulders, in the opposite direction as the shoulders, i.e., a straight line from the back right ankle to the forward left ankle would point nearly straight at the opponent. The front (left) leg is bent slightly and carries between sixty and seventy percent of the body weight. Both heels are flat on the ground. The right fist is held near the right hip (palm up) and the left fist (thumb up) is held slightly out in front of your body, even with the shoulders, in a guarding position. When switching to the Back Stance you merely switch your body weight from one leg to the other, i.e., the rear, right leg assumes sixty to seventy percent of the body weight, while the forward, left leg assumes thirty to forty percent of the body weight. The right fist is still closed (palm up) and held near the right hip, as before, and the left hand is held out in front of you, at waist level, but now the left hand is open, fingers together and slightly bent (like a scoop), with the palm facing downward, toward the left toes.

Movement from these two stances, when covering short distances, like Jake and I were in now, is accomplished by sliding the front (left) foot forward about one to one and a half feet, and sliding the back (right) foot along behind as you maintain both your fighting stance and your body weight distributions for proper balance.

Jake was now within striking distance with his very long reach. He threw a stiff left jab which I expected and promptly blocked with a Forearm Block. He threw another left jab, but much harder and with the power to not only break, but shatter my nose or jaw, but I deflected that as well, in the same manner as before, but with a much more powerful Forearm Block—Jake looked surprised, perhaps by the power and unusual hardness of the block. Used correctly, a Forearm Block is a powerful blow to the fleshy underside of the opponent's left hand jabs, mainly because it's the bones in the top forearm that smash into the soft muscle and flesh that's on the underside of the opponents forearm as he jabs. It's a surprisingly punishing counter-attack to the typical jab used in most fist fights. The big difference is that the block isn't meant to just deflect the opponent's punch, it's meant to punish the arm of the opponent. Used correctly, it is both a block, or deflection, of the opponent's punch and, at the same time, a punch into the opponent's forearm, i.e., it's a very hard block that turns into a punishing punch.

Jake commenced talking as we circled each other, waiting for an opening. He said, "Both me boys thought yuh to be a tall, skinny wimp. An' even af'er yuh kill't Lester, Tom still said it be only dumb luck that let yuh do it. He swore fer certain that yuh would never be makin' it alive ta the lake."

Abruptly, trying to catch me off guard, he unleashed a left cross punch, then a right uppercut. But he telegraphed both punches with facial expressions and shoulder movement, so I leaned back away from him, feeling the rush of air from both fists as they passed by, about a foot in front of my face.

I made no reply to Jake, just concentrated on what I was doing and what he was trying to do to me.

Still trying to break my concentration, Jake continued, "Yuh know, Tom, he wan'ed ta fight yuh hisself, just ta prove he be right 'bout yuh bein' a wimp, an' then he wan'ed ta torture yur girly real slow so yuh can see 'er die an' yuh be almos' dead bein' sad. Then he say he would torture yuh nice an slow, jest fer more fun, 'til yuh be dead, too." Jake laughed loudly, but kept his intense gaze on me, as he continued to circled me. After a few steps he stated, in a half sarcastic, half curious voice, "That be some kine a Kung Fu standin' that yur doin'?" He spit, giggled, then smiled as a gob of brownish saliva ran down from the corner of his mouth.

When he realized that I wouldn't take the bait and engage him in conversation, he calmly said, "Me sons was good boys." Then, angrily, he shouted, "Yuh never shoulda kill't 'em 'cause now I cain't lets yuh outta 'ere, Boy! Or yur girly!"

I made a sudden feint by lunging forward at him, then pulled back, not intending to make contact. The feint shut him up and made him instinctively retreat.

"Tricky fucker," he mumbled, then spit at my feet.

I could see that he was getting frustrated by my non-responsiveness, as if he was sure that his continued talk would loosen my tongue. It would frustrate him and I wanted him frustrated. Frustration in your opponent is very good. It's a chain of thought: Frustration causes impatience, and impatience causes careless mistakes, while careless mistakes cause injury and enough injury causes defeat. Yep, let him talk, let his frustration build to a dangerous level and let it crack his veneer of invincibility. So I remained silent, focused and patient, just as if I were sparring with my sensei in the karate dojo.

"Me boys unnerest'mate you, by God. They sure did. Guess I done it too. That be why I'm gonna kill yuh quick, then take yur girly up ta me cabin and enjoy ass-fuckin' 'er, then cunt-fuckin' 'er, an' then makin' 'er suck on me till I comes in 'er mouth. How's that soun' ta yuh, Boy? Soun' damn fuckin' good ta me. An' I gonna do it till spring. Then when I be tired of it, I makes 'er dig 'er own grave. May take 'er a week, maybe two till it be done, yuh know." His smile was menacing and mocking. "But before she be taken that dirt-nap, I rapes 'er one last time, fer me boys, yuh know, 'specially fer little Lester."

Shit! My face was hot and flushed. I almost attacked him out of pure hatred and rage. I knew what he was trying to do, make me lose my concentration, become frustrated and make a foolish mistake, as I was doing to him. Even though I knew what he was trying to do, I still almost got careless by attacking him in anger. I had taken a step towards him, then stopped, calmed myself and thought, "He had nearly been successful goading me into making a careless mistake and that mistake could very well have been lethal. Think of saving Grace."

When Jake saw me pull back from his nearly successful taunting, he expressed disappointment, though it didn't take him long to continue his sadistic and mocking monologue. He displayed a disdainful grin, then laughter boomed from his cavernous mouth. He continued, "An' when the hole be deep 'nough, I ties 'er little hands ta 'er feet so she cain't stand up. That be when I drops 'er inta the hole, naked and strugglin' fer 'er life. Now there be a real Kodak moment, right Boy?" he screamed at me.

He was getting to me. My patience was running thin. It was my little girl that he was talking about. The rape, the torture, the burying alive? It quickly spread the ominous darkness within me. Murderous intent surged through my blood as if it were a searing chemical. I wanted to rip his heart out of his chest and bite a bloody chunk out of it while he watched me with his last few seconds of life.

"An' I don' wanna gag 'er. No siree. I wanna hear 'er screams. I sure be enjoyin' that, yes siree. She be screamin', while I enjoys listenin' ta 'er death music till the dirt I be shovelin' inta the grave be stuffin' 'er nose and mouth and she cain't scream no mo'. An' then I stops shoveling fer a little bit so's I can listen ta 'er choking and maybe gets ta see 'er jerking 'er head outta the dirt fer air, an' all the while she be chokin' ta death on the dirt-dinner that be up 'er nose and in 'er mouth. An' iffen she get 'er breath back, Boy, then I be shoveling' in more dirt till she be nice an dead. An' dat be me final revenge fer me two good boys. How that soun' ta yuh, Boy?" he screamed, again, as his bass voice exploded with maniacal laughter. The rage and bitter hatred in his eyes was unmistakable.

I was relieved that Grace could not hear any of Jake's foulness, as we continued to probe, feint and circle each other in a dance of death.

I remained mute, but his ugly, uncivilized, repugnant and torturous intentions were breaking my resolve. I was supposed to be frustrating him and not vice versa. I wanted to attack unrelentingly, but a commanding growl, inside of me, told me that I'd be playing right into his hands. Jake wanted me to lose control, just as my frustrating him was intended to make him lose his control. But the bastard knew exactly how a father would normally react to another man saying such things about his daughter. But if I lost control of my temper, body and strategy, I really would cause the deaths of Grace and me. My strategy should be like his strategy, to verbally assail his two maggot-brained sons.

I took deep breaths, in through the nose, then out through the mouth. I was exhaling the second breath when Jake bent down and rushed me, like a charging bull, in the same manner he had done before when he got hold of Grace. This time I side-stepped his rush and kicked his right knee so it buckled in toward his left knee. He stumbled to the ground, immediately whirled around on his knees to face me and got up slowly as he clenched his teeth and growled—Wolf growled back at him. It had to have been painful, but he just rubbed his knee and stared at me. His eyes squinted and his brow furrowed in frustration. I smiled when I noticed that he was favoring his left knee. "Problem with your knee?" I tauntingly asked.

Jake rushed me and threw a looping round-house, right hand, which I partially blocked with the Upward Cross defense—crossing both arms as they extend upward, over the head like the letter "X," However, the blow was so powerful that my arms slid against each other and Jake's fist deflected off the side of my chin. The blow still had enough power to knock me back a step, but I reacted quickly by stepping forward and violently kicked Jake's left kneecap with the heel of my right foot. I could feel the solid contact of bone colliding with bone. It was a powerful kick that hurt the both of us, though that certainly wasn't my intention. My heel felt numb as I backed out of his range. Jake lifted his left knee slightly and tried to rub the pain away as he glared at me.

"Yuh bastard!" Jake screamed in frustrated anger. "Yuh be payin' fer that, an' what yuh did ta me boys. That be a promise, yuh son of a bitch. Now fight fair. A fist fight. We had a deal."

"The deal was no other weapon except bone and muscle, and that's exactly what I'm using. You chose to use the bone and muscle of your chest, arms and fists and I choose to also use the bone and muscles of my legs and feet. I haven't broken our deal. Just listen to yourself whining like a cry-baby, little boy. You aren't going to do that infantile, girly-man act again, are you? And you talk of a *fair* fight? That's bullshit! I'll bet that you've never given anybody a *fair* chance in a fight." I glared at him as the dim moonlight cast shadows across his face, making him look like a Viking berserker.

I could see the pain on his contorted face. He rushed at me again, but more slowly because of his sore knees. And this time he wasn't bent over, but standing straight up, arms outstretched, hoping to capture me in a rib-breaking, bear-hug. I countered with a Side Kick to his solar plexus. Jake's weight was so great and his forward momentum so strong that I was knocked backward, off balance, falling to the ground on my back.

The side kick had, however, stopped Jake dead in his tracks, leaving him stunned and out of breath. But once he realized that I had been knocked to the ground, he rushed to grab me. Instinctively my left heel lashed out at Jake's right kneecap, quickly followed by my right heel driving up into his groin. A rush of air exploded from Jake's mouth as he bent over, staggered, then fell to his knees with both hands pressed against his groin. Quickly, I rolled away from him, sprang to my feet and circled him so my body was between him and Grace.

I glanced back in Grace's direction. Now I saw her, and heard her. She was watching the fight and crying hysterically. I never even heard her crying before now, due to my intense concentration on this life-and-death struggle. I yelled for Grace to go hide and not watch, but didn't have time to see if she had obeyed. I felt a strong twinge of guilt, but blocked-out further thoughts of Grace, as well as the guilt. If this battle isn't won, I thought, Grace will be dead instead of just crying hysterically. Guilt shouldn't have any power over me here.

I concentrated on Jake, who was rising from the ground and recovering from the blow to his groin. His breathing was ragged and strained.

I could feel the feral presence of Wolf. I could feel his strength and cunning. I even smelled Wolf, a musky, thick odor that blossomed within my nose. His feral odor was so thick in my nose that when I swallowed, I thought I could taste it. But it neither smelled badly nor tasted foul to me. It tasted and smelled right, appropriate, pleasant, natural and reassuring.

Jake stood before me, his pain subsiding. I watched him. I felt mentally alert, and my muscles seemed to actually ache for action, like a taut, coiled springs begging for release, or like a coiled rattler ready to strike.

Jake dropped his arms to his sides and stalked me, his squinting eyes trying to bore holes into me. I could feel the intensity of his hatred and his need to avenge his sons. But I certainly wouldn't run in fear of him, as so many other men must have done. I was going to topple this tower of muscle. It was life or death. Those were the only two choices I had and in choosing life for Grace and me, I also chose death for Jake. I must kill this savage mountain man. Then I thought, "I can't have survived Nam just so I could die here, in this bleak, cold, shadow-land of leafless trees and bare, nearly frozen ground, at the hands of a psychopath like Jake."

That thought angered me, but what angered me even more was the sudden realization that I had Jake down on the ground and I stupidly did nothing to end his reign of terror. It was definitely the wrong thing to have done—I had been looking toward Grace—and it indicated that I had lost my focus. I berated myself, intensely, then came to a quick decision as Jake slowly approached me.

I decided to stop playing defense and go on the offensive. I doubted that a powerful Front Kick—more powerful than the side kick that I already used—to Jake's face or solar plexus area would be feasible due to Jake's tree-like stature. So I faked a low Side Kick with my left foot and as Jake bent and leaned forward to try to catch my foot, I immediately withdrew it, stepped forward one step, leaped and delivered a Flying Side Kick, with my left foot, to the bridge of his nose. I heard a sound like that of a snapping, dry twig. It was the sound of his broken nose, and it was pleasant music to my ears—it was the wonderful sound of Chopin's Opus number 1 in B-flat minor.

His eyes watered profusely. Blood immediately streamed out of both nostrils, mixed with his streaming tears, then rushed to his upper lip, not even slowing down to follow the contour of his upper lip. Instead, the gush of blood and tears spilled over both lips, like water going over a cliff, then spilled onto his chin and steadily dripped off onto the ground.

Jake's hands, in an inverted "V" shape, covered his nose. His hands were smeared with blood. He looked stunned, his eyes showing alarm, and for the first time, I saw fear, something that must have been totally and incomprehensively foreign to him.

This time I didn't hesitate. I gathered all my strength, quickly switched to the Modified Horse Stance and delivered a powerful Round House Kick, with my right foot, to the left side of Jake's jaw. Again, there was that sound of a dry twig breaking, only this time it was the deeper sound of a thick branch breaking. Jake's jaw.

The kick was strong, with plenty of snap to it, but his jaw-bone broke for two reasons: first, it was a well-placed kick and, second, Jake was out of breath; his mouth was open as he gasped for air and an open mouth is weak, vulnerable. It breaks a lot easier than a closed, tightly clenched mouth. That's why boxers are taught to keep their mouths closed and only breath through their noses. Keeping the mouth clenched tightly makes the whole jaw area much stronger and less likely to be damaged. Jake stood there, stunned, unable to believe the damage that I had inflicted already. He stared at me, his confusion and disbelief obvious in his bloody, facial expression.

His body swayed, then collapsed straight downward, like the demolition of an old building that had dynamite charges strategically placed next to its basement support posts. When the dynamite is set off, and the support posts are blown away, the whole upper structure comes tumbling straight downward. That's how Jake collapsed.

Jake was lying on his left side, his left hand over his nose and mouth. I was moving in for the kill, a Heel Stomp to the right temple area, when I noticed his right hand reaching for his Bowie knife. A sadistic, vicious, demon like Jake would never think to select a rational option like surrendering. His life is controlled by a philosophy of extremes: life or death, all or none, pleasure or pain, his way of doing something or don't do it at all. He and his sons, I thought, were immoral, unethical, savage, mutant humans who see other people as tools to achieve their own personal, sadistic pleasures and satisfaction. Unfortunately, it was a victims pain that brought them pleasure and satisfaction. Now Jake was the victim and he was stunned and enraged by the unfamiliar feeling of being in pain, and losing a fight.

Before I could reach him, Jake stood up, his right hand clenched around the bone handle of his Bowie knife, his left hand supporting his jaw.

With my right hand I reached into my shirt for the inverted sheath located under my left armpit. I unsnapped the blade handle strap and the ten inch Ka-Bar combat knife dropped into my hand. Jake was puzzled by the location of my blade and how quickly I was able to grasp it. Then his eyes gave a look of grand surprise as he realized that I had been armed at the cabin and he didn't know it. He paused, with his mouth partially opened at an incorrect angle.

"Bad move," I said to Jake. "You should stick to muscle and bone, fists and feet."

"We see, yuh bastard. I'ma gonna gut yuh like a fish."

I smiled at him which enraged him even more.

* * * * * * *

In knife combat I was taught to use a natural grip, nothing fancy, simple is best, at least it is initially. With a natural grip, the blade handle rests naturally, comfortably and diagonally across my right palm. The butt of the blade handle can then rest on the mound of muscle and flesh that lies directly opposite the thumb. The four fingers wrap themselves comfortably under the handle with the thumb securing the grip as it passes over and around the top part of the handle, then coming into contact with the index finger. The blade is held slightly out in front of the body, at waist level, with the primary sharpened edge held downward—the first two inches of the top edge of my combat knife, from the point inward, are also sharpened.

Contrary to popular, belief, as depicted in movies and novels, the right thumb should not be pressed against the blade's finger guard for support. A sudden, powerful thrust, that suddenly hits a bone, could easily jam, sprain, or even break the thumb. Furthermore, with the thumb not wrapped tightly around the handle, the blade is much easier to dislodge from the other four fingers—try using a hammer without using your thumb and you'll get the idea of how insecure your grip is without the use of your thumb. Same thing with a combat knife.

With the blade held in this natural position, it's at a good angle for slashing or thrusting. This natural grip also offers the advantages of a full arm's length reach when slashing or thrusting. This natural grip also allows for a very securely held blade handle, due to the thumb and index fingers securely holding the forward-most part of the blade handle with the butt of the handle being tightly pressed into the mount of flesh and muscle opposite the thumb. With the blade handle held so securely, I can place my whole body weight into the thrust without the worry of losing my grip (Some knife fighters us a lanyard that's connected to the knife's butt area. The lanyard is a cord loop that can be tightened around the knife fighter's wrist so that his knife can be retrieved quickly if it slips or is pulled out of his hand.)

Also, since the first two inches from the point of my blade, across the top edge, opposite the full-length sharpened edge (also called a "false edge" because it's often not sharpened) was also razor-sharp, which, in effect, makes it a double-edged weapon. With this kind of blade, I can slash up and down, left and right, as well as thrust deeply into the opponent's mid-section.

In a knife fight, you need to move fast. You can't be locked into any set position; you can't stand flat-footed which sort of roots you to the ground and makes it difficult for you to react quickly. My knees were slightly bent as well as my torso. My legs were spread out about shoulders width, with my left foot slightly ahead of my right. Most of my weight was on the balls of my feet so I wasn't cemented to the ground, as I would be if most of my weight was on my heels (if most of your weight is on your heels, you are in serious danger of being caught flat-footed). My knife is gripped naturally in my right hand and my empty left hand is not extended out away from my body so it doesn't make a good target. Extending your empty left hand out to try to block the enemy's arm is an idiot's invitation to receive severed fingers or a deeply slashed forearm. The empty left hand is more correctly and safely held close to the body, out of harm's way, the same as one sees in sword-fighting.

Even with such little light, I could see that Jake's grip was so tight on his blade handle that all the knuckles of his hand were white, like lumps of miniature marshmallows. His mouth hung open with pink saliva trickling over his lips. With his left hand he carefully felt his jaw. When I saw him smile, I knew that I hadn't broken his jaw as I thought I had. The disappointment that I felt pissed me off, especially when Jake jerked his jaw and the joint popped back into place. But what he did next cheered me up.

Without taking his eyes off me he reached inside his mouth, felt around, picked something out and looked at it carefully. Then he threw one of his front teeth to the ground and made a move toward Grace, who was standing, in a seemingly catatonic state, by the tree that I had previously hidden in.

I sprang, cat-like, to cut him off and he stopped. I yelled to Grace, "Grace! Damn it! Get away from here. Quickly! Go!" I screamed angrily at her. "Find a place to hide! I don't want you to watch this!"

But she didn't move, just stared straight ahead. I yelled again, only turning my head ever so slightly toward her while keeping Jake in sight—he was pleased by Grace's immobility.

"Grace!" I shouted, again. "Listen to Daddy! Turn around and get away from here!"

I remained in a defensive martial arts stance.

As Grace lethargically responded, and turned to walk away, Jake howled heatedly, then shouted, "Are deal be off, boy. I di'n't know yuh be some fuckin' Kung Fu guy. But I gives yuh credit for foolin' me ag'in. Yuh sure be full a su'prises. This 'ere baby"—he held his blade in front of his face and stared at it—"be ten inches a razor sharp, cold, tough steel, an' I'm gonna gut yuh like I did my las' deer. I watch yur guts spill ta the groun' an' steam in the cold air." Yuh 'ear me, Boy? By God, I'm gonna enjoy seein' yur guts and blood splash on this here groun'."

It was a bit more difficult understanding him, now, because, even though his jaw was dislocated and then popped back into place, it still had to be sore and maybe starting to swell. Also, he may still have a cracked jaw bone even though the jaw popped back into place.

Jake grinned at me as best he could with a broken nose and a very sore jaw. He smiled and now I could see the gap left by his missing front tooth, as I thought, "Well, at least the low-life jerk won't be sucking air through there any more." Then I saw him take a deep breath and Wolf's warning growl rang loudly inside my head, a severe warning.

To me, a deep breath usually means the opponent is getting ready to attack and is filling his lungs once more just prior to his attack. With blade in hand I remained in the Modified Horse Stance. From this sideways position, by body offered only a small area for Jake to attack. I looked over my left shoulder at Jake and said, "Fear that man who fears not God." It was a quote from a guy with a foreign sounding name, something like "Kader."

Jake paused, as I thought he would, and delayed his attack. He looked puzzled and responded with, "What kine a shit yuh be talkin' 'bout now?"

He took another deep breath—Wolf growled more loudly this time—and attacked. He rushed me with his Bowie knife slashing the air into "Xs" in front of himself, at face level.

I anticipated part of his strategy. I anticipated that he'd try to use his bulk to bowl me over since I was so much lighter than he. So as soon as he came forward, I was going to kick into the knee or the groin area, whichever looked more susceptible to attack at that time . . . but tragedy struck me like a baseball bat as the coyote skin, that was tied around my right foot, snagged on a surface root, knocking me off balance.

I could feel the looseness of the coyote skin as I fell backwards. I pulled hard and was released from the inopportune snag.

Jake, seeing my vulnerability and his opportunity, rushed faster toward me, then slowed down as he saw me lift my back, supported by my left arm, and putting all my weight on my left hip and left elbow. I curled my left leg close to my buttocks, then lifted and bent my right leg for a possible strike—a martial arts ground defense position—as I did the last time I was on the ground. He'd already come at me once when I was on the ground and it turned out to be a painful experience for him. Undoubtedly, this thought made him pause in front of me and, as I faked a kick towards his leading knee, he stopped, backed up a step and prepared to use his blade to slash at my foot or leg if I tried to kick him in the knee again. But I never extended my right leg, as in an actual kick. I faked the kick, then withdrew it quickly. Then rapidly I pulled my leg back and bent it upward, together with my left leg. I was on my back, my knees up to my chest, as I threw both legs, in unison, up over my head so my weight was on my shoulders and neck. Sudden-like, I thrust my legs outward, in the opposite direction from Jake and using my hands like a gymnast, I flipped over onto my feet. The whole motion was like doing a backward somersault. It carried me away from Jake, and when I stood, I was already in position, facing him, and my blade was still gripped in my right hand.

A martial artist, familiar with weapons, especially bladed instruments, knows that his legs can be just as important in combat with blades as they are in unarmed combat. My leg reach could and did provide a relatively safe distance between my most vital areas and organs, and Jake's thrusts and slashes with his deadly blade. However, caution is of utmost importance, much more so than in unarmed combat, because a carelessly high kick may result in a slashed leg muscle, vein, or artery. I vastly decrease the odds of that happening by only using low kicks, never above the waist, not in a knife fight.

When kicking at an opponent's knife hand, at waist level, the leg and foot usually have the extra protection of whatever footwear is being worn. If leather boots are worn over the feet and a heavy jeans-type material is worn for pants, then this means added protection to the leg and foot area. Furthermore, cuts to the leg area, especially from the knee downward, are usually not serious because large veins and arteries are relatively few and minor, and the few major arteries that do exist are either well protected, behind bones, or not even known to most people. Most experienced blade fighters only know artery, vein and organ targets that exist from the waist upward. But this, by no means, is meant to minimize the caution needed in knife combat, because a slashed muscle will make a leg ineffective, which minimizes mobility which is a tremendous disadvantage. As I stated before, fast movements and fast reactions are extremely important in knife fighting. In most cases, a slashed muscle is more serious than a cut vein that produces a lot of blood. The bad affects of a cut muscle are felt immediately, whereas the bad effects of blood lose take longer to appear.

Actually, it's amazing how well the human body is designed to protect vital areas—with the exception of the groin area—even from razor-sharp weapons. The outer layer of skin is much tougher than most people give it credit for, then there's a layer of fat underneath the outer skin, and then there's a tough layer of connective tissue, called fascia, that covers or binds together body surfaces. Then, of course, there is the skeletal bones which are resistant to most blades of ordinary size and which seriously interfere with a blade's penetration into vital internal body organs (e.g. the ribs and breast bones).

Jake tried to circle around me. I didn't know his purpose and worried. I didn't know if he was just waiting for an opening in my defense or if he had his eyes on Grace, figuring that the best way to get me was to get to her. I glanced over my shoulder and saw Grace—she didn't hide like I told her to do. I screamed, "God damn it! Grace. Run! Hide!

Jake probably wished that he had never let her go. But using her as a shield now would be a humiliating thought for such a macho-man— that's why he let her go when I teased him, especially when I kept calling him a "girly-man." But he was losing this battle, so far, and I could see in his eyes that he wished he had never let me trick him into letting her go." If he got his hands on her again, he'd cut her throat.

I quickly turned my head to face Jake. Since my back was now facing towards Grace, I couldn't see her. I could only hope that she would go somewhere and hide like I had ordered her to do. The blackness of night, once away from the campfire pit, surrounded us like a curtain. If Grace would at least move a couple of steps into that darkness, where she couldn't be seen and couldn't see the fight.

Each time Jake tried to maneuver around me, I would fake a kick or a slashing or stabbing movement with my blade and he would get cautious and retreat. Then the thought occurred to me that he didn't seem to be in as much pain as he should be with a broken nose and a possible cracked jaw bone, one tooth missing, and the lower half of his face being caked with his own blood. I thought, "Jake must have a high threshold for pain." That pissed me off. All I could think of, now, was that this battle would probably be a drawn out and brutal struggle and, in the end, the one with the most stamina would prove to be the live victor or, put another way, whoever was the most careless would be the dead loser. I hoped an out of shape ex-Marine, like me, would still have enough stamina to best a tough and rugged woodsman who was injured and breathing heavily, but not grimacing in pain. "Why didn't he seem in pain?"

Jake had his knife tightly compressed in his right fist, with the blade edge-up, pointing towards the crotch of his thumb. From that position he could only attack the low areas of my body. And since his blade was edge-up, he would have to stab or slash low into me or slash upward at me with the up-turned edge of his blade.

Jake lunged forward to thrust his blade at my mid-section, but I side-stepped quickly to my left—his right—and saw his over-extended right arm shoot by me. I slashed downward into his right arm's biceps. Jake saw the slash coming and started quickly moving his right arm to the left. His maneuver caused my slash not to be as deep as I had hoped. He stepped back, put his left hand over his right biceps and when he pulled it away it was smeared with blood that looked black as watery tar. He looked at me and screamed with rage.

Suddenly, in a blur of motion, Jake, with one hand, flipped the blade over so the blade's cutting edge pointed toward the ground. I knew then that his next move would probably be to raise his right arm up over his head and slash downward at my face, neck and shoulder areas. I watched him closely.

Jake did raise his blade and just as his arm began its downward movement toward my head, I leaned my whole upper body backward, like a boxer slipping a punch, then waited for Jake's blade to slice the empty air in front of me. I was used to that move . . . unfortunately and to my utter surprise, it didn't go as I had expected. I felt the edge of Jake's blade strike my knife-hand forearm. The blow was hard enough to knock my arm downward so that my fisted knife was parallel with my right thigh.

Jake started to cheer in victory, but stopped himself after only a few words when he saw that I was still standing. His face showed tremendous awe and shock at the fact that my arm appeared to by uninjured, though the shirt I was wearing was slashed half way around my forearm.

When he saw me smile at him, he flew into a rage and, finally, carelessly attacked me by leaping forward and slashing at the side of my neck. Once again I leaned back, waiting for the arc of his arm to pass by me . . . but it didn't. Jake's knife slashed my left forearm, which was held near my belt. But no damage was done, but I realized right away that he'd had some serious training in knife combat techniques. Military, maybe? Self-taught? Now I was the one who was caught off guard and surprised.

Jake's face appeared monstrously furious, with his arm still slightly extended in front of him as he stood there with disbelieving eyes. I took immediate advantage and quickly leaned and shuffled my feet forward, latching onto his right wrist with my left hand. I immediately pulled his arm downward, forcing him off balance so he'd have to take a step forward, toward me. He was off balance, now, and his weapon hand was temporarily useless to him . . . I could have easily slit his throat . . . but I didn't and that inaction shocked me. Was the killer instinct in me gone, even in such a desperate situation? I felt panic slicing through me, like tiny razor blades in my blood. I wondered how I could possibly save Grace if I couldn't kill a piece of psychopathic vermin like Jake. "Such a terrible time for me to be morally hesitant," I thought. Silently, I screamed at myself, "There's no place for morality on the battlefield. Life or death situations don't lend themselves to moral dictates whether they are religious, social or political." I forced myself to act.

There must have been a lot of adrenalin along with that surge of panic because I suddenly let go of Jake's arm. Pulling his arm downward made his face come down to the level of my face. And as he looked at me, his right arm still down toward my knees, I gathered as much strength as I could and as Jake started to rise, I delivered a vicious left hand Fore-Knuckle Fist into his Adam's Apple followed immediately by a swift and vicious right elbow to the side of his face.

Jake dropped his knife, staggered, and with both hands he grabbed his neck as if he were choking himself. He couldn't draw air into his lungs and was trying desperately to inhale. His eyes watered profusely as his face turned blue. I kicked his blade aside, rushed into him for the kill, but rather than a straight thrust of my blade into his solar plexus area, then sideways, to the left, into his heart, followed by a quick withdrawal, and then a deep slash across the side and front of his neck, I found myself grabbing Jakes hair with my left hand, yanking his head downward while at the same time bringing my right knee swiftly upward. The resulting collision snapped his head backward. His eyes rolled upward, his long hair rose and fell over his face, then I noticed something white flew up over his head. Maybe another front tooth, I thought. I was correct, for when I looked at Jake's semiconscious body, lying on his back, I could see that both front teeth were missing . . . and my knee ached.

As Jake lay there on the ground (he was breathing now) I asked myself if I really needed to kill him. I had said that I did. I had said that I would. I had said that killing Jake was my only option. My mind filled with the sudden and terrible accusation that I really was a wimp. After all my spewed fighting philosophy, after all my tough talk and hard-core, survivalist oriented words and meaningless platitudes, it turns out that maybe I'm a fake, and that my bullshit façade isn't any more real or valid than that of my views about religion. I'm not as tough as I thought I was and the Gibsons were right, I am a wimp. Where the hell did my resolve go? In Nam there was a strong, tough, stealthy, and confident killer instinct in me. Where did that guy go? Where was the wolf in me now? My mind echoed with the sympathetic growls of Wolf, as I asked myself: "What am I now? Who am I now?"

I looked down at Jake and didn't know what to do. My indecision was really bad, a sign of weakness and, as I realized this, I was stunned even more. After a minute of stunned silence, staring at Jake's large, prostrate, unmoving body, I thought, "Perhaps I could tie his arms securely behind his back, find the canoes, make him ride in the second canoe, alone, while I towed it behind my lead canoe. That way I could bring him back to the jurisdiction of civilized laws. But suddenly a phrase exploded in my mind so fast that I thought it would give me a concussion from it's violence. The phrase? "A plethora of laws but a paucity of justice." If it's a quote, I don't know who said it.

/- -/.-/.-./-.-/-../.¦/-.../-.../../.¦/-./..¦/-.-./-.-/.- - -/.-/...¦/- - -/-./-.-.-/-.- -/.-../.¦/

Chapter 17

★★★★

Invictus

I STOOD ABOVE JAKE as he lay on his back, breathing heavily and semi-conscious. My breathing was heavy, also, as the sweat dripped off my forehead and off my chin. I looked at Jake's chest as it heaved with the effort of trying to furnish enough oxygen to keep his massive, muscular body in action. Again, I wondered where my killer instinct had gone. Wolf howled for action, yet I hesitated. Nam was "kill or be killed." Wasn't it the same now?

The pale Wolf appeared before me, like a misty, white apparition, his lips drawn tightly back to his gums, pointed teeth bared and glistening with saliva, as if giving me a serious rebuke. He was such a strong force within me. An alter ego? I hadn't killed in a long time. I'd hoped never to do it again. It's not something I could forget *how* to do. More appropriately, *should* I do it? Indecision. Wolf was the symbol of survival that resided in the primeval wilderness of my brain. But I no longer lived in that wilderness, where "survival of the fittest" dominated the fate of all sentient creatures. Shouldn't the "killer instinct" be tempered by reason? But, does reason have any value in a "life and death" struggle?

Wolf growled as his misty, white form solidified before me. I stroked his head and back. Touching him had a calming effect on both of us. Our rage subsided as unspoken messages traveled between us, like an electric current. Civility attempted to penetrate our bodies. It was a salve to my flesh, but an acid to Wolf's flesh. I sent him away and felt him vanish from under my stroking hand, unneeded now, unwanted now, and knowing it. But I knew that his lair wasn't very deep into my subconscious; he was always alert, watchful and there if I needed him, like a wild, untamed and cunning guardian.

I felt a subtle change occur within me. Sending Wolf back to his lair, in my subconscious, and deciding that it was unnecessary to kill, felt good, but was it correct? I had Grace to protect and if feeling *good* resulted in her injury, then I would castigate myself unmercifully. Feeling good was also a scary feeling because compassion can also be suicide in combat situations. I'd felt Wolf's presence since my early youth and there was very little compassion in him, except towards me, similar to an attack dog and his master. Wolf and I were in this tough life together. It was a symbiotic relationship; necessary for both of us; beneficial to both of us.

But seeing Jake lying there, helpless, brought some confidence back to me—a mongoose must feel similar triumph after defeating a deadly cobra. But I could feel Wolf's eyes on me, questioning my compassion and indecision, especially in this particular situation. I didn't blame Wolf at all. I was also questioning my thoughts, actions, reactions, indecisiveness; doubting myself. However, I felt confident knowing that if I needed Wolf, his energy, cunning and strength would surge into me, like adrenaline, immediately saturating my blood and highly stimulating both muscle and mind. And with Pale Wolf in me, there was little doubt of victory for me, though that was never a certainty. I had lost fights before. I'd lose some again. It's always a big mistake to think you'll win every fight, even with my skills.

This fight, though, I had to win or die trying. As in Nam, I would be "invictus," unconquered. With Wolf's ferocity inside of me, coupled with my martial arts skills, I could usually kill any man, regardless of color, creed or national origin. I'd be an equal opportunity destroyer, as long as I didn't get arrogant and over-confident. Perhaps, I thought, I already was being arrogant and over-confident. I wondered if a day would come when Wolf and I failed each other and Death, on its pale horse, came to claim both of us. Defeat was in the future for every man, like walking toward your own personal precipice. Indecision made that trip shorter.

I could feel Wolf stirring within me, knowing what I was thinking about him. In my mind, I almost always thought of Wolf anthropomorphically, i.e., as an animal with human qualities. I could see him grin, feel the warmth of his friendly eyes, sense his loyalty to me and even use words to communicate with him, though it was a matter of interpreting his growls. He understood my questioning thoughts about the necessity of killing—but disagreed with me about the need to kill Jake. Killing was necessary in Nam, I thought, but was it necessary now? When could I stop killing? Could that time start right now? Wolf's growl stated an emphatic "yes" in response to the first question and remained mute concerning the latter questions.

Unusual indecision caused me to lower my blade while looking at Jake's heaving chest and semi-conscious body. Wolf warned me that Jake only thought in terms of kill-or-be-killed, and that the risks of me allowing Jake to live were too great. I thought, "If any man ever deserved death, he did. Also, as long as he lived he'd want revenge, so for the rest of my life I'd be looking over my shoulder for him, knowing he's strike at my family because I killed his sons, then come after me to seek his version of justice. But should I be his judge, jury and executioner? And what would that turn me into? An amoral, vengeful, killer? And, more importantly, was Grace watching? What would she think of me if I killed Jake as he lay helpless?"

The human heart, I thought, is nestled between the lungs and protected by the breastbone and the rib cage. A person's heart is only about the size of his own clenched fist, and, even in adults, only weights about ten or twelve ounces. The bottom of the heart rests on the diaphragm. The heart, being basically a muscular, blood-pump, is similar to the carburetor of a car; smash it and the whole machine dies. Moral uncertainty prevented me from thrusting my blade's finely honed, ten inches of steel into the inverted "V" area located where the breastbone converges on the solar plexus. A deep, upward thrust, into the left chest area, would penetrate the diaphragm, as well as the heart, causing massive internal bleeding and sudden death, like stabbing a balloon full of water.

The unexpected, by definition, comes swiftly as a total surprise. So I cursed my own self-doubt and inaction as my right foot was being yanked out from under me. I staggered, then fell backward like a toppled tree. Jake had suddenly twisted his body far enough and fast enough to grab the coyote skin, that was now loosely wrapped around my right foot, yanked it up and threw me off balance. I landed heavily on my back. As the air rushed out of my lungs, I heard myself say, "Shit!" I instinctively rolled away from Jake's grasp. But when I got to my feet, facing Jake, my normally excellent reactions paused a second due to the realization that, during the fall, I had dropped my combat blade (I should have made a lanyard). I could hear Wolf's jaws snap in anger at me as I compounded that error by making the mistake of looking at the ground, in desperation and panic, searching for my knife . . . but taking my eyes off Jake.

Then, suddenly, Wolf howled loudly, sending a super-surge of adrenaline flowing through my body.

Jake reached around my chest to grab me in a face-to-face bear hug. Quickly, I reacted by bringing both my arms tightly into my body, elbows touching my sides and both fists clenched tightly at upper chest level, near the collarbone. Then, before Jake could apply extreme pressure, to pin my arms to my sides, both fists shot upward, like exploding cannon balls, toward Jake's chin. The fists rotated quickly from closed fists and palms-toward-me position, to an open-palms-toward-Jake position, with all my fingers up and slightly curved. My thumbs were tucked in close to the knuckles of my index fingers, forming a tight-fingered, crescent shape.

I could feel Jake's awesome, brute strength encircling my ribs as my Double Palm Heel tactic struck under his chin and snapped his head backward. His eyes rolled back and his face contorted into an awful grimace of pain as his arms lost their full measure of strength. He spit out fresh blood from biting his tongue

If I had my blade now, I would have been cutting deep gashes into both sides of Jake's Adam's Apple where the carotid arteries were superficial as they brought oxygenated blood, that was being pumped away from the heart, to the brain. Thus, bright-red, purified and oxygenated blood, that had already passed through the lungs, would have spurted out in a series of potent spurts, each spurt coinciding with a heartbeat. And not too many seconds later, Jake would have lost his strength as well as consciousness, and collapsed, dead on the spot. But my blade was gone, my mind screamed as it raced onto the alternatives. My right hand, almost instinctively tried to reach the throwing knife that was in its sheath, inside my collar, but the demands of struggling with Jake required both arms and I couldn't reach it. The knife was as useless as man's tits, at the moment.

Jake growled, in rage, through clenched teeth He strained to tighten his muscles, compressing my rib cage with such force that I knew soon he'd crack my ribs so forcefully as to possibly drive shards of ragged-edged, rib-bones into my lungs, probably puncturing and collapsing one, or both, lungs. That would mean that I would have difficulty breathing, with only one lung functioning, or not being able to breath at all, with both lungs punctured. Death would creep-up on me slowly during my last few seconds or minutes of breathless agony.

If that were to happen, I could vividly imagine the pleasure expressed on Jake's face as he stood over me, grinning sadistically, enjoying my last few seconds or minutes of slow suffocation. He'd be smiling at my body spasms, and upward rolling eyes. And his final pleasure would be seeing my open-eyed and glazed stare of death.

As these thoughts were going through my head I found myself giving a loud karate kiai—a fiercely loud shout from the lower abdomen which distracts or otherwise upsets an opponent and, psychologically, increases your own strength, courage and indomitable fighting spirit. At the same time as the kiai, both my hands had been removed from Jake's chin, raised to be level with the side of the head and each hand about two feet away from Jake's head.. My fingers were together—as they would be if you were clapping your hands—then brought simultaneously and swiftly crashing onto Jake's ears. The resulting pressure on the inners ears causes great pain, especially if the eardrums burst.

But Jake only shook his head slightly, shaking off the pain and continued to squeeze me until I thought my spine was about to touch my chest.

It was then that I heard the terrified screaming cries of emotional agony from Grace. She didn't run away and hide as I had ordered her to do. She was seeing me being squeezed to death in a muscular vise and, although I couldn't see her face, I knew that the agony and terror on it would make my frightening, demonic, facial gestures of pain, look angelic by comparison.

Grace's screams, plus the combined survival instincts of Wolf and I, overcame the crushing pain as I grabbed two hands full of Jake's long shaggy hair, pulled viciously with both arms until his head came close to my mouth, then bit into his large, broken nose with the full power of clenched teeth and jaw muscles. I locked my jaws—or was it Wolf's jaws?—tightly as I growled brutally, then pulled, yanked and twisted his nose, violently, up and down, back and forth, until the sounds of Jake's screaming drowned-out the sounds of Grace's screams. At the same time, I grabbed Jake's Adam's Apple with my right hand fingers. I squeezed and twisted it cruelly, burying my fingers deeply into and behind the soft flesh as I tried to rip it from his throat. Then, with my left hand, I poked the ball of my thumb fiercely into the socket of his right eyeball, pushing directly inward, toward his brain. I felt Jake's grip loosen immediately. He struggled and tried to shove me away from him, but, like a bulldog, I wouldn't release his nose from my clenched and locked together teeth. His screaming grew louder as I continued to yank my head ferociously back and forth, up and down, as I growled, with crazed effort, through my clenched teeth. With his powerful arms, he urgently shoved me away, but not having let go of his nose with my teeth, his actions only served to dislodge my thumb in his eye and my grip on his Adam' Apple. In his panic, though, his struggling was helping me to tear his nose from his face. The taste of his blood was thrilling. But soon the force of his shoving tore off his nose and caused me to stagger backward and fall to the ground, but I never took my eyes off his bloody, misshapen face.

The resulting blood, gore and milky-white bone sticking out from the center of his face made him look like an even more hideous monster than he already was.

Wolf had saved me again, saved me from my ridiculous hesitancy in following my warriors code. Why would I think I could behave in a civilized manner when my opponent was an uncivilized beast who fought by no rules, but his own, and with any means at his disposal? War isn't fair, it's planned, organized brutality. Personal combat is a war between individuals where being "fair" can't compete with the need to "survive." Wolf understood that instinctively and filled my body with his untamed ferociousness, the primal force for survival. There could be no mercy, no compassion, no morality, no debate, no hesitancy now. This battle could only end in death and I should've ended it when I had the chance to do it easily and quickly. Roamin' Wolf prowled inside of me as I finally realized that this was, unalterably, a "kill-or-be-killed" situation. I had no more thoughts of bringing him to justice. Jake or I would die in this mammoth struggle between opposing and unforgiving forces. I knew, unquestionably, that Jake had to die for Grace and I to survive this Adirondack ordeal. Only Jake's death could stop his maniacal, sociopathic juggernaut.

I was on my back, so I raised my knees to my chest, then arched my back and thrust my legs forward and quickly sprang to my feet to face Jake.

Jake was frozen in his tracks, touching the warm blood streaming down his face and gushing over his lips. Then his hands felt the empty space of raw flesh where his bulbous nose should have been, but instead, felt bone, cartilage, torn flesh and his own sticky blood. He looked at me without moving and in a temporary state of shock. Rage flashed like fireworks in his left eye as he rubbed his damaged right eye and his Adam's Apple.

I breathed deeply, through my nose, but had great difficulty with the almost unbearable pain that breathing created in my expanding ribs. I knew then that some ribs had been cracked, perhaps broken. I had difficulty catching my breath. I couldn't suck in enough air, as if there was a blockage in my airway. I opened my mouth widely, and as I tipped my head slightly downward, Jake's nose fell out and landed at my feet. It had been blocking the airway to my lungs. I sucked in huge amounts of air, enjoying the life-sustaining oxygen as if it were my favorite dessert.

I kept my eyes on Jake as I bent down slowly, picked up his nose, then raised my body in spite of the shooting circles of pain that burst around my rib cage.

Napoleon said that "Victory belongs to the most persevering." He was right and, through the study of karate, I knew that the ability to persevere and maintain a positive mental attitude was most often the difference between winning and losing and, sometimes, between life and death. I had frequently seen perseverance be the difference between a good karate student and a superb student, when, in fact, both students' skill levels and potential were very similar.

Roamin' Wolfe possessed the reins to my body and mind. I could hear him growling at Jake with the thrill of our struggle. Now he controlled my muscles and their actions.

I looked at the black lump of bloody gore that lay in my hand—in dim light, like moonlight, red blood looks black—and bored my eyes into Jake's eyes. Then I casually tossed the nose to him. Reflexively, Jake caught his nose. He stared at his amputated nose, then screamed at me with a bestial, maniacal rage that contorted his face into a mask of horror. He rushed towards me with heavy, plodding and weakened legs, while his powerful arms and hands reached out for me..

Under Wolf's confident guidance, I placed my left foot forward, legs about shoulder width apart and waited for him to get closer. I took a deep breath and just as he was within legs distance, but out of arms distance, I exhaled and my leg exploded with a vicious Front Kick to his solar plexus—a dangerously high kick because of the risk of Jake catching my leg. I snapped my foot back quickly, keeping it out of Jake's reach as he stopped in his tracks, gasping for air. I didn't bring my right leg all the way to the ground, though. Instead I brought the heel back to my groin area, then lashed out with another Front Kick to his groin, connecting solidly. Jake bent forward, grasping his groin. His body started to fall forward, toward me, so I quickly side-stepped to his right side, then thrust a right-foot Blade Kick—the outside edge of the right foot—into the side of his right knee, sending him crashing to the ground.

Jake slowly stood, then staggered on his wrenched knee with the frenzied look of a wounded grizzly bear who's ready to maim and kill. I could see past him. I could see Grace. She had her hands up to her mouth, which muffled the sound of her crying. There were vertical lines of reflected light on both her cheeks, twin streams of tears reflecting moonlight.

Suddenly I was aware that I was no longer between Grace and Jake, as I should have been. I hoped that Jake wouldn't realize my grave error, but as I looked at his maniacal grin I became deathly afraid that I was horribly wrong. And even worse was the feeling I had when Jake bent over quickly and picked up the large Bowie knife that I hadn't noticed. He stood, bellowing with ugly laughter, like an incoherent psychopath. Then he swiftly turned and limped toward Grace, slashing the night air in front of him as he approached my own flesh and blood.

I ran toward Jake, but, again, bad luck fell upon me like a boulder. The coyote skin, which was further pulled loose from around my right foot previously, when Jake grabbed it and tripped me, got snagged on something. I stumbled to the ground, losing precious time and, also, losing my chance to catch Jake. I rose to my left knee, then yanked my right knee upward, pulling the coyote skin free from its bindings around my right ankle. I sprang to my feet. Jake's body was directly between me and Grace so that I couldn't even see her, though I heard her screams of, "Daddy! Daddy! Help me!" penetrate my ears like hot daggers.

Panic reached out to grab me, but I resisted. When I saw that I couldn't reach Jake before he reached Grace, I had one option fueled by determination and rage. Like a lightening strike, my body was ablaze with motion. I reached for my throwing knife, grabbed it by the handle, yanked it upward, out of my collar sheath, then positioned it next to my right ear. I screamed at Jake to try to make him turn around so I could have a wide, clear shot into his chest or abdomen area. Jake didn't stop. The pain of my kick had worn off and he was limping faster. He was screaming insanely through a face full of blood and gore, badly cut lips, missing teeth, torn off nose, and cracked jaw.

The words of Machiavelli rang in my ears: "If injury has to be done to a man, it should be so severe that his vengeance need not be feared."

I shot my left leg forward—like a right-handed baseball pitcher—with both knees flexed. Like the baseball pitcher throwing a fast-ball to the catcher, I released the blade with my right arm fully extended, at ear level. I stopped my rapid arm motion with my empty fingers aimed at Jake's back.. Every remaining ounce of my energy went into that powerful throw, a throw that any major league pitcher would be proud to own for its accuracy and nearly one-hundred miles per hour speed. The silver blade sparkled with moonlight, like a small, shiny and deadly, missile. It took less than half of a second to reach that miscreant, juggernaut-of-terror, but that split-second felt like hours of agony to me as I sprinted towards Grace.

I immediately ran toward Jake who suddenly stopped about three strides in front of Grace. Grace was lying on the ground, curled up into a whimpering, fetal ball of fear. Jake's back arched upward and then backward as both his hands reached around to try to remove the blade which had penetrated six or seven inches into the area between his shoulder blades. I wished I could have severed his spine and stopped him in his tracks, but that was too much to hope for. The blade entered his back, to the right of his spinal column. As I continued to rush toward him I could hear his raspy breathing. By the sound of his breathing, I knew that the blade had punctured a lung.

Jake staggered a foot at a time towards Grace. I felt the garrote in my right hand—I don't recall reaching for it—when I was about ten feet from Jake, who was standing over Grace's fallen body. Jake had his right hand held level with his right shoulder, the blade sticking out of the bottom of his clenched fist, in a downward, stabbing position, toward Grace.

I was lucky to have reached Jake just as he began to stab downward at Grace—she was in shock; not aware of either of us. I lashed out brutally with my left heel into the back of his left knee, making him immediately collapse to his knees. The short wooden handles of the garrote were in my right hand, so I slammed them onto Jake's right wrist, numbing the nerves and causing the Bowie knife to fall from his grip. Then I reached across the front of his neck, garrote handles in my right hand, grabbed one handle of the garrote in my left hand and slipped the cord under his chin and around his neck. He surprised me by standing up, lifting me with him. I twisted his body violently to his left, away from Grace. Without letting go of the garrote, I spun my own body around 180 degrees, which placed our bodies back to back. This also had the effect of dragging him away from Grace. I could feel the heavy weight of his back pressing into my back.

I stagger-stepped a couple more steps away from Grace, bent my knees and dragged Jake's exhausted body downward. Off balance now, he collapsed entirely on top of me, just the way it's supposed to happen. My chest was on the ground with both my arms up near my right shoulder, both hands clenched around the garrote handles in a never-let-go grip of death. I pulled downward on each handle as Jake lay with his back on top of my back and the back of his neck on the back of my head. I could feel the tremendous pressure of his bulk as it pressed into my back. My body was also rocking back and forth due to the thrashing, flailing motion of Jake's arms and feet as he desperately tried to release himself from the chocking, flesh-severing force of the garrote. His thrashing movements drove my face into the nearly frozen ground as I pulled more tightly on the garrote handles. I felt Jake reaching over his shoulders to grab at the back of my head. He pulled my hair. That was all he could do. The advantage of this garroting technique is that the victim cannot reach your eyes, nose and mouth. He can only pull your hair, and that doesn't last long as he weakens rapidly.

Of course, part of the thrashing came from the garrote cutting off his air supply. Jake's fingers were now desperately, but hopelessly, digging into his own neck flesh to try to get a grip on the very strong, thinly braided strands of dental floss that were buried deeply into the flesh of his neck. Another cause of his thrashing was the tremendous pain of the throwing knife being driven deeper into his back, since we were positioned back to back—I felt the pain of the handle poking into my back as well, but, luckily, there was no point on the handle end of it. I strained against his body, again, and I could feel the garrote handles moving slightly down my chest an inch or two, as the strong, braided strands of dental floss cut more deeply into his throat. He made gagging and gurgling sounds as I continued to pull downward even harder, using every ounce of available strength. My arm, neck, chest and shoulder muscles literally burned with searing pain.

Jake's thrashing movements slowed as more blood flowed from the deep cut of the garrote and because he was out of air. His slick, hot blood flowed onto me. It felt like hot water as it poured from his neck, in a steady stream, onto the back of my neck and down the back and front of my shirt, then onto my hands and forearms. The blood warmed my chilled, exhausted body and, ironically, it felt good.

As I lay there, tightly pulling on the garrote handles, I thought, "When Jake's struggling completely stopped, I wouldn't let go of the garrote, for two reasons: first, although not likely, he could be feigning death—I saw this happen in Nam, with almost tragic results. Secondly, it's a certain sign of death to wait for the blood to stop flowing. A body that stops bleeding is a dead body because in order for blood to flow, the heart has to pump it. If the blood stops flowing, that means the heart has stopped pumping. When the heart stops, so does life. Dead bodies hold no lethal surprises, nor, unfortunately, do they hold their feces and urine.

I felt no movement from Jake, but didn't release the garrote.

A garrote, if something thin and strong is used, will sever the jugular vein and/or one or both of the carotid arteries. I kept the pressure taut on the garrote and expected the initial steady, heavy flow of blood. It was a good sign that the garrote was doing its job, I thought, though the thought seemed cold-blooded. Soon, after a few pints of blood spilled, the flow slackened. I loosened my grip then rolled on my left shoulder, thrusting my right shoulder upward, which forced Jake's body to roll away from Grace, chest down onto the ground. I twisted my body, got my feet under me, not letting go of the garrote, as a precaution, then sat on Jake's back. I placed the left garrote handle in my right hand, then reached around Jake's neck with my left hand fingers to feel for a pulse in his neck. No pulse.

My cramped right hand let go of the garrote and it fell to the ground.

I turned Jake onto his back, stood over him and stared at him as my lungs burned from exertion. I breathed quickly and deeply trying to catch my breath and slow my heart rate.

I studied Jake's face. His tongue had thickened, turned grayish and protruded from his mouth like a mouse halfway out of its hole. Jake's bulging eyes had the look of severe desperation and uncontrollable panic trapped within them. The whites of his eyes contained red spots and thin, red lines where the capillaries had broken and made the eyeball bleed. His anal sphincter muscles and urinary bladder muscles had relaxed and released so that his bowels and bladder emptied their foul contents. The air was redolent with the smell of shit mixed with urine, which was almost overpowering and nearly activated my gag reflex. I stepped over the pool of blood and urine (luckily the crap was trapped in his pants).

I kneeled in front of the trembling body and closed eyes of my shocked eight year old child who was, literally, nearly scared to death. Her knees where pulled tightly to her chest with her eyes buried into her thighs. She had her hands and arms covering her head and ears. She seemed frozen in that position and looked catatonic, though her body was shivering from the cold and paralyzing fear.

I must have looked like a maniac to her. Fortunately, she didn't notice me next to her. I slowly, carefully turned her head towards me. Her eyes opened but she wasn't exactly looking *at* me as much as she appeared to be looking *through* me, as if I was a window. She was off in some protective, psychological dreamland, where horrors, like she had just experienced, didn't exit and a blissful, amnesiac happiness dominated her thoughts. Maybe her mind took her to Neverland to be with Peter Pan. At this moment, that was a good thing.

I wiped my bloody hand on my pants, then gently picked up Grace. A grimace formed on my lips from the pain of my cracked or broken ribs. I carried Grace to the fire, set her down, then placed wood onto the still hot coals. When the fire flared up, I held Grace in my lap. She rested with her head against my chest. I couldn't tell if her eyes were open any longer or not. We sat quietly before the flames, feeling and absorbing the comfortable, soothing warmth.

I gently stroked Grace's hair and talked to her lovingly, each word being a gentle reminder that we were safe now and that we would be back to Mommy very soon. I whispered softly, my lips near her ear, telling her that the best thing that her Mommy and Daddy ever did was to have her; that she was our supreme accomplishment, which nothing else that we would do could ever surpass. I hugged her closely and kissed her cheek and forehead. I gently stroked her hair, then I sang her a song that I made-up when she was only three years old:

I love my little girl.
She has a little curl,
On top of her head,
She wears it to bed.
I love my little girl.
She is my special friend,
And that will never end.

I repeatedly whispered the song to her. I couldn't tell, at first, if she heard me singing, or even if she remembered the song. It sounded kind of silly, now. Certainly not something you'd sing to an eight year old girl. But when she was three and four years old, she'd frequently asked me to sing it to her. She seemed to find a strange and mysterious fascination with it, and the feeling of love that created it for her.

Slowly, I felt her bunched, taut muscles relax and knew then that she did remember the song and that the song was having a desirable, soothing and comforting effect on her.

I sat in a yoga position, with her on my lap, for almost an hour before her eyes closed and she drifted off to sleep. I laid her down on the ground, a little further away from the fire, for safety, then got the wool blankets and one sleeping bag. I moved her to the top of the sleeping bag, rolling the top portion of the bag down toward her head to serve as a pillow, then covered her with the two woolen blankets.

It was now a couple of hours before dawn. I didn't figure she would sleep too long, but I knew I wouldn't wake her no matter how long she slept. We would find the canoes and leave as soon as she awoke, but no sooner. She desperately needed the rest. Her body and mind had had too much to deal with, a brutal, merciless invasion of the mind that no child should have to experience. Who would've ever thought that I'd encounter Nam, once again, in the gorgeous Adirondacks of northeastern New York State, or that my child would also be dragged through this ordeal?

As Grace slept I unraveled the floss holding the coyote-skin moccasins and discarded both of them. I put my boots back on, after holding the openings upside-down over the fire to warm the insides. Then I searched for and found my combat knife, cleaned it, and placed it into its sheath—my father-in-law used to say; "If you take good care of your tools, they'll take good care of you, and last as long as you do."

I had a difficult time pulling the throwing blade out of Jake's back. The suction created by the wound, around the smooth steel, resisted my original attempts to pull it out of Jake, especially since only an inch of the handle was now protruding from his back and all I could grasp it with was bloody, slippery fingers. Finally, I had to use my Ka-Bar, Marine combat blade to enlarge the hole and pry it out. I wiped both blades off with dead grass and leaves, then placed them in their sheaths.

I dragged both bodies behind a nearby blow-down so Grace wouldn't see them when she awoke. It wasn't easy work with damaged ribs, especially now that the pain was much worse than in the midst of combat. The distracting ache had changed to severe pain now that the adrenalin had worn off. Nevertheless, I couldn't stop and pout about it. I had work to do before Grace woke up. I hoped that she wouldn't smell the bodies in the morning.

I prepared everything so we could leave quickly, shortly after Grace woke up. I sat near her, staring at her dirty, tear-stained face, wanting to comfort her and make her pain go away. I realized that she may need professional help to mentally heal. I hoped that *time* would also assist in healing her trauma.

I'd been lucky not to have gotten my forearms cut. It had never happened before. It worried and humbled me. The memory of my past advanced skill was sharper than my present skill. Sort of humiliating, in a way. I'd slowed down and while I did so, Jake was working with his knife skills regularly, I'd bet, and learning to perform newer, more modern knife fighting techniques. I was behind the times and almost paid dearly for it. Luckily for me I had the foresight to anticipate my being rusty and slower after being away from knife fighting for so long. Jake was much better than I thought he'd be, or I wasn't as good as all my bragging. I raised my right forearm in front of me to chest level. I looked at the long cut in my sleeve and as I did so, the cut cloth separated and my arm looked very rough and was as deep brown as tree bark. It was tree bark. Earlier I'd found two thick, curved pieces of bark and decided to use them to protect my forearms. I wrapped them with dental floss around each forearm and that's what had protected me from Jake's slashes onto both my forearms. Seldom does anyone leave a knife fight without being cut. I wasn't cut, but I was very lucky.

I took a restful break and ate gorp as I sat. In my thoughts I thanked Wolf for his part in getting us safely through this ominous ordeal. Then, with sadness, I ordered Wolf to hibernate within me and not surface unless another life-or-death, kill-or-be-killed situation arose. I had a peaceful feeling about this and spoke to Wolf, in my silent thoughts, of my deep appreciation. Wolf, then receded into the background of my mind, into a cave-like crevice of my brain, deeply inside that remote wilderness of gray matter.

Like an Indian spirit-wolf, I heard the howl of Wolf that said: "I will never knowingly do anything to harm you mentally or physically. I accept your decisions, my brother, for I am a protector. I will remain quiet, peaceful and dormant, like a volcano, but if there comes a time when you need me, you only need to call my name. I'll come and you'll have all my power and fury within you. Goodbye, my brother, my friend . . . until we meet again."

Now my own voice turned inward, to the core of me and replied, "Thank you, my protector, my brother, my friend, for you have helped save my life again, just as in Nam. I also thank you for saving the life of my daughter, our daughter. I shall be forever grateful to you and I am thankful that you realize that I can't lead a normal, healthy and peaceful family-life with you roaming freely and actively within me. You are indeed a warrior of great strength and cunning. The best warrior I have known and though you have learned some compassion, you have no place in a peaceful, civilized life. You are very wise to recognize this. To co-exist within me has created much rage, fury, hatred, bitterness and violence. By lying dormant within me, until your warrior abilities are again needed, you have shown yourself to have great honor and loyalty. I shall always honor and respect you. Goodbye, my brother, my friend, my protector . . . until we meet again."

Amidst the silence and darkness a white cloud floated in front of me, drifting slowly and, somehow, calling attention to the black writing written across its cottony white background. There were two lines of writing on the cloud. They said: *I Am the Master of My Fate*; *I Am the Captain of My Soul.* I recognized those lines from a poem by William Henley. The title of his poem is *Invictus*, which is Latin for "unconquered." I smiled inwardly with great satisfaction.

So, reluctantly, I, Roman Wolfe, have commanded my inner friend, Roamin' Wolf, to become dormant within me. I felt a great peacefulness within me. As the sun rose in the early morning of November 20th, I watched its rays reaching out into these Adirondack forests, much as the first Native Americans must have witnessed hundreds of years ago. And then, again, I thought about the final dialogue between Wolf and myself. I thought how much it sounded like two Indian brothers saying their final "goodbyes" to each other. I felt sadness at first, but then I felt even more at peace with myself.

I looked all around me and felt contented knowing that I received great comfort, in spite of our ordeal, in these forests, this "forever wild" Adirondack wilderness.

/.-../- - -/.-./../.-./.-/-./-./../-.- -/-.-./- - -/..-/-./-./-/-././-.- -/.-/-.../-..-/../../...

Chapter 18

★★★★

Homeward Bound

GRACE SLEPT AN HOUR past dawn. She missed the blossoming beauty of the gradually brightening eastern sky. As the sun rose above the horizon, it was a painter's brush, coloring the sky pink, then a reddish-orange that chased the darkness away from the earth, just as a campfire chases the darkness away from a campsite. The brilliant orb continued to rise slowly, like an arm rising in slow-motion; the arm saluting the world and welcoming the new day.

When Grace woke up, she was like the sun that made my day bright and warm. I smiled at her, then walked to the fire and put a few sticks on it. When I turned around, Grace rose into a sitting position, feet pulled back to her butt, knees close to her chest and both arms tightly wrapped around her knees. Then she released her knees and rubbed her eyes. She acted mentally sluggish, but that was normal immediately after awaking. She looked around the campsite suspiciously and I saw that suspicion suddenly turn to wide-eyed fear.

Rapidly, I exclaimed, "We are safe, Sweetheart. There's no more danger."

She didn't respond verbally, her forehead wrinkling in serious thought as she searched the area, again, her body immobile, just her head turning.

I was kneeling by the hot fire with my coat off. I rose from the fire and walked to her, then sat next to her. I put my arm around her shoulder and pulled her close to me. I still felt that primal urge to be alert, be cautious and to protect my child. I tried to relax as I stretched my legs towards the campfire. It took awhile for the warmth of the fire to penetrate my insulated boots and conquer the slight chill. Grace sat quietly, leaning her head against my ribs—her gentle contact caused only mild pain. Her breathing was normal, with streams of white mist forming as her warm breath came into contact with the cold air. The white mist rose a few inches then slowly disappeared, until her next exhalation, when the cycle started over again.

The sky was a chilly-gray, the kind of sky that normally brought snow. That worried me. I hoped that we'd only see flurries, at the worst. We still weren't safely at civilization's doorstep and snow, combined with strong winds and a drop in temperature, would make our last few miles extremely difficult. I thought about how lucky we were not to have had snow already, especially a blustery snow storm. That might have been fatal for Grace and I. I looked down at Grace's sleepy face, again, and smiled. I thought about how happy I was to have her safe and close to me. I gently kissed the top of her head and whispered, "Daddy loves you."

Grace looked up at me, smiled, then surprised me with a question that I didn't expect.

"Papa? Do you believe in heaven?" Grace said, startling me.

I paused, thinking whether or not I should postpone this conversation with her, like a parent wanting to postpone a serious talk about the *birds and the bees*. "No." I answered, laconically, but honestly.

"Is it because you don't believe in God?"

"Yes. You see, if there's no God, like I believe, then there's no heaven, since God is said to have created heaven. Also, I don't believe in Jesus, Satan, angels, miracles and things like that." I paused and thought of the famous quote by Stephen King, the author of many horror novels. He said, "The beauty of religious mania is that it has the power to explain everything. Once God is accepted as the first cause of everything which happens in the mortal world, nothing is left to chance and logic can be happily tossed out the window." I didn't tell the quote to Grace. It would raise more questions than answers and she wasn't intellectually mature enough. Actually, I didn't believe Grace was intellectually mature enough for any of this God/atheist discussion. I wondered why she was asking religious questions.

"Why don't you believe in God or heaven? I think angels are a nice thing." she said.

I'd rather talk to her about the birds and the bees. It would be easier. "Our world, all of existence can be proved with our senses and our brains, but our senses can't detect anything supernatural. As a matter of fact, all human knowledge is of the *natural* world that we all live in. We can't know about anything beyond our natural world. We can't even prove if there is anything more than a natural world. If it existed, it would be beyond our power to know about it. That's what *super-natural* means, knowledge or events that are beyond the natural world, beyond our everyday natural experiences, beyond our ability to know, examine and prove. If God exists and lives in the supernatural world, then he, she, or it is beyond our knowledge. Our innate intelligence— the intelligence that we are born with and that grows with a good education—also rebels against belief in Gods. Unfortunately, most of us are all thoroughly brainwashed into believing something that is entirely ridiculous and based on centuries of fantasy, exaggerated story-telling, and a huge number of personal interpretations. To me, belief in God simply makes no sense; it's as illogical as wasting all your life trying to fill a pot that has no bottom. To believe in God a person must constantly reject his own common sense behind a thick blanket of blind-faith and self-deception. Self-deception means that a person has to fool himself, Grace. A person like that must desperately want and need to believe in those unreasonable, unprovable ideas, stories, and concepts. That desperation or need allows them to forget about logic when dealing with anything religious. They need it so badly that they are willing to accept nonsense."

Grace ignored me, saying, "I understand a little. When you said 'God' you said 'he or she or it.' That's cool. Do you think that God could be a girl, if there was a God?"

"Why not. It's women that create life, right? Makes more sense that God would be a woman since women are the creators of human life."

"You also said 'it.' What's that mean?"

"Grace. It just means that, if there is a God, it doesn't necessarily have to be male of female, you know, a man or a woman. Perhaps God is just energy, a cloud of energy or, since the Earth could not survive without the sun, then maybe God is the sun."

"That's weird Papa. Isn't the bible proof that there's a God?"

"Is a comic-book about Spider-Man proof that a real, flesh and blood Spider-Man actually exists, and can perform his seemingly miraculous actions, in our real and natural world? Of course not. The bible is a book written by men who tell their fanciful stories of things they can't prove, things that they desire, things that they wish were true, but are not. It's their personal interpretation of events in history. Unfortunately, it's a history of self-deception, passed from grandfathers, to fathers to sons and daughters who then pass the mythical tales onto their own families. Do you think that loving, respectful sons and daughters are going to reject and rebel against something that their own parents strongly believe in? Of course not. Only a few very independent, very thoughtful people have the strength of character to do that. Today's modern bible had to be re-written because the God in the old bible was very mean, cruel, vengeful and, actually, to my mind, much worse than the humans that he is said to have created. That God tortured people and killed them unmercifully. When you get older and have had a chance to study some history of the world and the history of religions you'll learn, if you are a thinker, that no belief system, in the history of the world, has caused more unnecessary death than the belief in a God or Gods. America is said to have formed so that people could have religious freedom. Many famous people, back then were atheists, but the history books will never point that out." Those atheists weren't looking for 'freedom *of* religion,' they were looking for 'freedom *from* religion.' They wanted the freedom not to believe in a God, and not have to participate in religious fantasies because the idea of a God was unreasonable, illogical to them."

"So, if there was proof, then you would believe in God?" Grace asked.

"If there was *convincing proof,* that includes valid, proven facts and scientific evidence, I would believe, sure. A famous scientist named Carl Sagan once said, "Extraordinary claims require extraordinary evidence." Blind-faith, bibles and churches are not proof that there's a God any more than the claim that since horses, horse-care books and horse stables exit, there must be an all-powerful Horse-God who also exists. A Horse-God that provides food and shelter for horses. A Horse-God that demands certain good behaviors from all horses and if the Horse-God's demands aren't met, the bad horses will all go to the 'big corral, in the hottest dessert to spend eternity. Of course, the good horses would go to a pasture with plentiful food and water that has wonderful weather and be happy for all eternity. Eternity means for the rest of time, which may be billions of years, or never ending time.

"Papa? You're being funny."

"And that's exactly my point, Grace. What I just said sounds ridiculous, it sounds funny and unreasonable and, as you said before, weird. That's the way belief in God sounds to me. You know, Grace, I really think you should wait until you're older to explore these difficult ideas and concepts. You shouldn't just accept my beliefs without serious study, serious thinking and searching. Too many otherwise very rational parents pass on their illogical, blind-faith to their impressionable kids and after years of being saturated with false beliefs, the kids accept those false beliefs without much thought. I don't want you to feel that you have to believe like I do. You need to wait and make up your own mind, when you are an adult."

"I wish there was a heaven and angels. It's nice to think about."

"Yes, it is," I responded. "But bibles, especially the Christian bible, have been unquestionably and thoroughly wrong about so many things that can now be proven or disproven by science. The scientific theory of evolution offers overwhelming proof of how mankind and animals evolved on Earth over many millions of years. I think the Christian bible implies that humans have only been on earth between six and eight thousand years. The bible makes one heck of a big mistake there. There is overwhelmingly convincing proof that the earth has existed for millions of years and that our universe is billions of years old, and that humans have been on earth for about one hundred thousand years. So why would any logical, reasonable, astute person ever accept the bibles fairy-tales about going to heaven or hell when they die?" If religious beliefs can be so absolutely dead wrong about the beginnings of the universe, earth and man, then why can't those same religious beliefs be just as wrong about where we go after we die? or perhaps all those religious beliefs, themselves, especially unreasonable belief in a God, are wrong. Perhaps the Bible is simply a fairy tale that future generations took seriously?"—two thousand years from now, will Dr. Seuss's Grinch be an unquestioned, unquestionable God or Devil? Will the divine Dr. Seuss books be the Bibles of the future? Silently, I thought, "Gods certainly are fragile, falling like dominoes in the winds of reason."

"Have you always not believed in God, Daddy?"

"No. I was forced to go to church when I was a kid, but I didn't think seriously about God then. Back then God was like Santa Claus to me, only Santa came to our house, but we had to go to God's house, a church, Grace. After I reached adulthood, somewhere in my twenties or thirties, I studied, researched, thought many hours about it, over a period of many years, and finally decided that I couldn't believe in the existence of an extraordinary, supernatural power, like God, without extraordinary proof, and there was no extraordinary proof. I have never seen, heard of, or read about any extraordinary, objective proof, so I don't believe in God because I can't believe in non-sense. I really think that people, now-a-days, find religion less and less meaningful as those people become more and more educated and understand the truths of science and logical thought. The more they become thinkers, the less blind-faith appeals to them and they stop being unquestioning followers of myth and superstition. Science is one of educations sparkling gems and, in many ways, science is also the enemy of religion. Science teaches about the real world, the one that we all live in and can prove. So the more educated people are, the less need they have for preachers and the more need they have for teachers. Actually, knowledge is the enemy of religion's strongest tool, which is a blind, unreasoned faith in something super extraordinary, while offering no extraordinary, objective, and logical evidence."

"I think Mommy and Grandma and Grandpa believe in God, don't they? Everybody we know believes in God, I think."

"Yeah, I'm sure they do. It's something that they want to believe and they feel no need to question it or to have convincing, objective proof for it. It makes them feel good to believe and that's not entirely a bad thing . . . for them. Many people don't want to think about these very complex and frustrating ideas about religion. For those people it's just easier to believe in God, to accept what they inherit from their parents. There's something you should remember, though. Just because people believe and other people don't believe in God, that doesn't mean that they are good or bad because of it. Very religious people can be very good or very bad people, just as atheists can be very good or very bad people. Grace, normally I don't talk much about religion. It causes a lot of arguments and bad feelings. But if someone asks me about my religious *beliefs*, I tell them about my religious *disbeliefs*."

"What's that 'object' word mean?"

"You mean the word 'objective?'"

"Yeah, ob-jec-tive."

"Are you sure you want me to explain all this? It's kind of hard to understand most of what I'm telling you, isn't it?"

"Well . . . yeah, but I understand some of it and it's interesting. Tell me more."

"OK. The word 'objective' means that someone's thoughts are not biased or prejudiced and that those thoughts are based on provable facts and on evidence of those facts. An objective thought can be proved, it's not simply a 'blind faith,' opinion which is called 'subjective' because subjective thoughts are someone's personal and biased opinions or feelings that are not based on facts or evidence so that they can be proved."

"Papa? Is what you're saying objective or subjective?"

Wow! ..Surprised me. The kid's smart. "Well, Grace, those words have definitions that give those words meaning. By definition 'blind faith' is subjective because it's based on unproved, personal opinions. Since religious beliefs are all subjective, then the opinions of all religions and all religious people can not be proved. So those religious opinions have to be accepted on faith alone. But if no objective proof can be given or shown, then why should anyone waste time believing blind-faith opinions. In other words, no matter how much blind-faith your friends or relatives or teachers have, believing in something that can't be proved doesn't make sense. For me to believe something, it has to make sense to me. So to me, religion and blind-faith, religious beliefs are non-sense and that's why I'm an atheist."

"So an atheist is someone who doesn't believe in God, right?"

"Well, more accurately, an atheist is a person who doesn't believe in the *existence* of a God."

"Oh. I'm kind of confused now. Can I ask you more questions, sometime?"

"Sure. Anytime, unless your mom gets mad about me talking to you about it. I thought, mischievously, "If Grace talks to her mom about our discussion, I'll certainly catch hell—so to speak—from Sam. I'll just tell Sam that the devil made me do it.

There is something very special between fathers and their daughters. I knew for sure there was a special closeness between Grace and I as soon as she was placed in my arms immediately after she was born. I hope it will last until my death of old-age makes me leave her.

I felt Grace's head snuggle closer to my chest. I bent forward and reached toward the fire with my open hands, fingers spread apart and palms toward the fire, to soak up the warmth. I brought my warm hands to Grace's face, rubbing the warmth on her cheeks and neck like a healing salve. She gave a sigh of contentment, after which I did the same thing for myself. The warmth felt good as it penetrated the stubble of my beard and settled into my skin like a heated lotion. It was only then that I was aware that I hadn't shaved since the kidnapping. I must look like a wild man, I thought, as I ran my hand across the sandpaper stubble of hair.

I heard blue jays and chickadees greeting the morning, then the rat-a-tat tapping of a woodpecker somewhere in the distance. I thought I also heard a crow, or a raven, cawing. It was a faint sound, but it created a vision of a black feathered bird, with the sun's rays dancing on the blackness and then being absorbed by those charcoal black feathers. I imagined an ebony bird perched on top of a tall pine, swaying in the breeze as it surveyed the territory, like a king, from the top of his castle.

I felt the frozen ground under me and realized that in these last few days I hadn't really been too conscious of the weather, except for being thankful for no large accumulations of snow. The first inch of ground felt frozen. I guessed that the temperature was in the low twenties, or high teens, and as I exhaled, billows of white condensation, as if I were smoking, exited my mouth, rising a few inches into the air, then disappearing like a shy phantom.

I could imagine the lakes starting to freeze very soon; the ice crystals starting to spread out thinly from the shoreline, working their way towards the center of the lake, each day getting thicker and thicker.

That thought sent a shard of panic up my spine. Canoes are useless on an iced-over lake. The panic subsided when I realized that Long Lake probably didn't totally freeze over until mid-winter. We were out of danger from the Gibsons and could, if we had to, simply follow the shore of Long Lake southwestward, on foot. It would take us a few days longer to get back, but that was acceptable . . . if no snow storms arrived. The thought of a snowstorm or freezing rain still worried me, but, with concentrated effort, I kept my anxiety in check. There's always that little bit of doubt that keeps a person alert to alternatives. The Adirondacks certainly weren't famous for their lack of snow and below freezing weather. Somehow Grace and I would make it safely back to Sam.

My daydreams ended when Grace stirred against my ribs, and pain circled me as if I was wearing a hot belt around my chest. Grace had fallen asleep from days of being exhausted—one good night's sleep wouldn't make up for several days without much sleep. I held my hands toward the fire, again, getting them nice and toasty. Then I stoked her cheeks, again, with both warm hands and a contented smile spread across her face as she stretched her arms up around my neck. Suddenly, as if waking from a bad dream, she jerked herself up to her knees and looked directly in my eyes. She stared at me with frightened, wide-open eyes, then rapidly twisted her neck back and forth, looking nervously around the campsite area, again.

"Papa? I had a bad dream about you and that big guy fighting. It was scary."

I pulled her close to me and reassured her, again, saying, "Everything's all right, Sweetheart. There's nothing to worry about now. We're alone and safe. There's no more danger"—except, perhaps, for the weather, but I didn't want to mention that to her. "We'll be home soon," I added as I gently hugged her, and dealt with the rib pain with a concealed grimace and a silenced grunt.

She didn't speak. She hugged me back with the longest hug that I've ever had from her. For a few seconds I was afraid that she wouldn't let go, or even if I wanted her to let go. When she did let go, we stood up. She said, "Can we go home, now, Papa?" She didn't mention the Gibsons, but she did use the word "Papa." I was aware that she'd been using the word "Papa" more frequently than usual. Tears clouded my eyes and I felt chocked-up with happy emotion because I knew that she would be okay; that she would recover from this terrible ordeal.

"Sure," I said, clearing my throat, as I rose from the ground. I gave her some gorp to eat while I packed our sleeping bags and blankets and other supplies into and onto my backpack. She looked at the gorp with disinterest, wrinkling her nose and upper lip at it. She was bored with it, but she ate some anyway. I wish I could cook something hearty for her. Sam or Grandma would take care of that soon.

We sat by the fire until she ate her fill of gorp. The fire burned down to coals where the red colors changed in intensity, in a mesmerizing display, as the colors faded in and out, flickered, brightened, then faded again.

I had to put the fire out, but couldn't cover it with dirt since the upper ground was frozen. I grabbed my Ka-Bar knife and searched for some ground moss. I cut off thick slabs of it about the size of pot-holders. I carried them to the fire and placed them over the hot coals until they were entirely covered with a sizzling blanket of moss. The moisture hissed and steam rose from the hot, blanketed tomb. The steam disappeared into nothingness a few feet over the fire.

I checked my watch. It was 9:14 A.M., November 20th. I thought of Sam as I looked at the watch that she had bought for me the previous Christmas. I really missed her. I couldn't wait to see her, to touch her, and to see the look in her eyes when I brought our daughter back to her, physically safe and sound—I wasn't sure about the "mental" part yet.

I gazed back into the fading steam from the fire. I knew that Sam must be worried sick, even though, on the surface, she'd be telling everyone that I'd bring Grace back, safely, no matter what. I knew she'd never give up hope without seeing our bodies. I knew she'd have an unshakeable faith in me. She was a wonderfully smart woman who had a great knack for accurate hunches, instinct or intuition—whatever it was called. I thought, perhaps Rudyard Kipling was right when he said: "A woman's guess is much more accurate than a man's certainty."

But I also knew that Sam would be riddled with concealed doubt and anxiety, just as I had been, several times during this ordeal. But she wouldn't show that to the world, she'd only show a positive attitude of courage and hope. In private, however, she probably lived in a chamber of horrors, imagining all sorts of terrible conclusions. So we'd have to get home as soon as possible to end her private terror.

"Daddy? . . . Daddy?" Grace called as she tugged on my arm. I snapped out of my trance and smiled at her, then replied, "Yes, Sweetheart? What is it?"

"You were staring. You were just staring at the steam from the fire and you scared me."

"Sorry. It's okay, Grace," I stated, broadening my smile to calm her. "I was just daydreaming about how nice it'll be to get back home to Mommy and Grandma and Grandpa. Everything is okay now. Are you all set to go?"

She nodded her head affirmatively, put her left hand into my right hand and we walked unhurriedly toward the lake without looking back. I picked-up Jake's Bowie knife and stuck it into a tree so it could be easily seen by anyone who wanted to return for their bodies. The two bodies were lying out of sight behind a blow-down tree. I had pulled-out the punji stakes earlier so no one could get injured. We didn't look back, not even once. Nor did I feel the slightest stir from Wolf, although when I thought of him, my thoughts sobered and all daydreaming stopped.

It only took us about an hour to find the aluminum canoes. We had to search the low underbrush for the ropes that secured the canoes to the shore. Jake didn't mention the exact location, but I knew that they couldn't be too far from where we had camped, when we were all heading towards the cabin at Preston Ponds. Jake and Tom wouldn't have traveled far at night, and the short amount of time that they were gone from camp verified my assumption.

Actually, to be accurate, Grace is the one who found the ropes by getting on her hands and knees and crawling under bushes to locate them. And when she did locate them, she excitedly yelled, "Papa! Papa! Come here quick. I found them for you."

Sure enough, when I looked, she was pointing to the ropes that were tied to the bottom of a bush. You couldn't see the ropes if you were standing up, as I was, because the branches of the bush spread out at the top like a mushroom and, even bare of foliage, the ropes were difficult to spot, the dirty, tan-colored ropes blended in with the earth and the dead, brown-colored vegetation. I followed one of the ropes from the sunken canoes and pulled on it. That caused my ribs to feel like they were on fire as the pain traveled like a circle of intense electricity around my rib cage. The sunken canoe was, of course, extremely heavy and I had to pull the rope with all my strength. Grace saw me grimace, showed concern, then grabbed the rope and helped me pull. When I heard her cheery voice upon finding the ropes and when I saw her try to help me pull the rope, I was pleased to see that her attitude had turned positive, hopeful and excited.

We had to be extremely careful not to fall into the ice-cold water. I decided that the thing to do was to drag the canoe along the bottom, away from the large bush that concealed it, and which was in my way, as I tried to pull the canoe. There was a small clearing about ten feet to the left of the bush so Grace and I took a couple of steps to the left and pulled the rope, turning the canoe so it angled toward the clearing. Then we dragged it slowly, not trying to lift it, along the muddy, slippery bottom until the level of water inside the canoe was about level with the lake, and the front of the canoe, that the rope was attached to, was only in about a foot of water. Then we left it there, temporarily.

A person with the size and strength of Jake, using his knees as fulcrums and his powerful arms and back muscles as levers, would have been able to easily pull the canoe out of the lake, but I didn't have that kind of musculature. I also realized that I wouldn't have the strength, even without the painful rib injury, to pull the canoe out while standing on the uphill bank. I'd have to get into the shallow water to gain the leverage that I needed to get the canoe up the slightly inclined bank near the shore.

Grace asked, "Why are we stopping, Daddy?"

"Well, we need to build a fire, Sweetheart. Can you help me look for dry twigs and larger branches?"

"OK, but why do we need to build a fire? I'm not very cold, are you?"

"You see, Sweetheart, I don't have the strength to just yank the canoe out of the lake when it's full of water. So I have to wade into the cold water to push and pull at it so I can tip it to get as much water out of it as I can. That'll make it light enough for you and me to pull it the rest of the way out of the water. That means that my boots, pants and hands will get wet, and when they do, the cold air will make the water freeze. My skin will freeze and that'll be terribly dangerous because I won't be able to work or walk or get us out of this place. So the smart thing to do is to prepare for it. When I'm wet I can use the fire to get dry and warm quickly. Once my hands get cold and frozen, I probably wouldn't be able to build a fire. See what I mean?"

"That's smart, Daddy."

Grace certainly appeared to be rebounding much better, from this ordeal, than I'd expected. Perhaps she would even rebound better than I would. Only time would tell

After the fire was started and burning well I gave Grace the important job of tending to it, making it bigger by collecting and adding more wood and keeping a good supply of wood handy. She immediately searched the area for dry firewood.

While Grace tended to the fire, I went to the canoe, which was now only a couple feet from shore, where the ice-cold water was about a foot deep.

I was glad that I thought of giving Grace the job of tending to the fire because I didn't want her to help with the canoe for fear that she'd get wet and get severely frost bitten. I glanced over my shoulder at her and saw that she was tending to the fire responsibly and humming cheerfully. She was being very helpful. She was a really good kid.

I stepped into the water, hoping all the while that my boots were still weatherproof and not punctured or cracked. I paused but didn't feel any water seepage. So far, luck was on my side because my boots went up my calf far enough that no water went over the tops of them.

I grabbed the wet rope with gloved hands and pulled mightily. The strain racked my ribs with pain. I bent over in near agony, resting my hands on my thighs and breathed shallowly to ease the pain. When I stood and looked, I saw that the canoe had slid toward shore about a foot more. That almost made it worth the pain. Now the canoe was close enough to me so that I could grab the bow. I was thankful for the gloves because I certainly didn't want to touch the frigid aluminum with my bare flesh. I bent at the waist, then bent my knees and leaned back towards shore, pulling with all my strength, enduring the pain. I slipped and almost sat down in the water, but I twisted my body to my right and stuck my right arm out to brace my falling body—it must have looked like I was doing a one-arm push-up, like Stallone in the movie, *Rocky*. It worked and only my right hand, wrist and lower coat sleeve got wet. However, I had to immediately go to the fire and pull off my right glove to dry and warm both the glove and my hand and wrist, as well as to dry the lower part of my coat sleeve.

Grace held the wet glove high over the fire to dry, with a long stick poked into the middle finger to let it dry. The other fingers hung down limply as the middle finger stuck out. Grace had no idea how silly and obscene the glove looked, with that middle finger sticking up and all the other fingers bent down. It looked as if she was giving her final and parting obscene gesture to the Gibson clan and this remote wilderness.

I returned to the canoe when everything was dry. I was being very careful not to let water splash inside my boots, but as I rocked the canoe back and forth, splashing the water against the sides and over the top of the canoe, a large ripple of water sent a little water inside my left boot. It wasn't much water and probably was nothing dangerous, I hoped. It felt like only a trickle of water that would be very cold until my own body heat warmed it. As I emptied the canoe of water, I kept pulling it up the incline, a foot at a time, with Grace's help, toward the fire. It was 11:33 A.M. when the canoe was entirely out of the water. I had been wondering where the paddles were. I thought I was going to have to make a crude paddle from a tree branch, but knew that that wouldn't be necessary when I saw that both paddles had been lashed to the inside bottom of the canoe before it had been sunk. The same must be true of the other canoe, which I would leave in its watery grave—I thought about hauling Jake's and Tom's bodies back to civilization in the second canoe, to save them from the ravages of scavenger animals. I couldn't bury them in the frozen ground, so the second canoe confronted me with a matter of ethics. I guess I lacked strong ethics because I said to myself, "Screw them." I wasn't going to haul two dead and bloody bodies for Grace to see. Plus, carrying their bodies would exhaust me and further delay our return to Sam. Plus, with my injured ribs, it would be agonizing torture to try to carry them to the canoe. Right now it was better, I thought, to have them out of sight and out of mind. If anybody in civilization has any problems with my decision, screw them too. They can come back and retrieve the bodies themselves—a search and rescue party probably would do exactly that and Jake's Bowie knife would be a marker for them to find the bodies. Let them have the pleasure of that particular, gruesome job.

When the canoe was emptied of water, Grace and I dragged it to the fire. We tipped the canoe so that the inside was facing the fire so it could thoroughly dry. I moved the canoe every five minutes until the full length of it was dried. As we waited, Grace and I munched on some gorp—thank goodness for the gorp because it made it so that I didn't have to worry about food during our escape, though it had become very boring. I noticed that we had only one bag left and I was, again, grateful that I had taken all the bags instead of just a couple, as I had originally intended. The gorp provided all the extra calories we needed, and it stopped us from being weak from hunger. Even with the gorp, we were still a little weak and sore, of course, but it was mostly from exhaustion, not from lack of nourishment. We both were, however, getting quite bored and tired of the same tastes and textures of the gorp. We needed some meat and vegetables. Ahh, I thought, I could really go for Sam's hearty, meat and vegetable soup.

My mind started to wander. I recalled that when I had located Jake's and Tom's backpacks, on the fringe of our camp ground, I hadn't found any food in them. I wondered if, in their hurry to start after us, they either forgot to bring food, or they hadn't brought enough and ran out before they caught up to us. Perhaps they never expected it would take so long to catch up with us. They may have gone hungry for a couple of meals, not wanting to shoot any game because the sounds of their shotguns would give me a clue to their direction and an idea of about how far away they were. Nor would they want to take the time to stop and collect edible roots, or try to catch fish. So, I thought, they might have been weakened mentally and physically by the lack of food, when they finally caught up to us. If that was true, then I had more of an advantage, and more luck, than I thought I had.

So many things worked in our advantage. I knew that a lot of relatives and friends were probably praying for us, especially Sam and her parents. I didn't share their religious views but it was comforting thinking of them being concerned and know that we had intrinsic value to them. I concluded, as I almost always did, that our good luck was just that, "luck," which is the random occurrence of events and the positive results of those events. Luck wasn't a religious commodity, with a religious meaning. Luck was very personal and secular. In many cases, a person makes their own luck using goals and the persistence, motivation and perseverance to accomplish those goals, and along the way some unexpected, chance events occur that help him accomplish those goals. Sometimes luck is simply gratuitous and/or serendipitous.

Grace brought me back to reality. "The boat looks and feels dry, Daddy," Grace stated.

I snapped out of my trance and smiled as I saw Grace's bare hands pressed comfortably against the warm aluminum.

I checked the canoe, felt the inside in various places and replied, "Yep. It sure is, so let's get going, kiddo."

I used our cup to get us both drinking water from the lake, then filled the canteen, extinguished the fire with canteen water, then refilled it.

I unlashed the paddles from the bottom of the canoe, letting them lay there, put Grace into the canoe, with her sitting on top of one wool blanket, and the other blanket wrapped around her for warmth—I was chilled, but tried to put it out of my mind. I pushed the canoe into the water and climbed in it without getting wet. My weight made the bottom of the canoe drag a little on the shallow shore bottom, so I used one of the paddles like a pole to push us away from the shore. A couple of pushes later we were floating freely and headed southwest on Long Lake.

I sat in silence, amazed by the beauty of the Adirondacks in the late fall. I could feel their uniqueness and splendor. It made me feel comfortable and secure, like being under a warm, electric blanket on a chilly night. Then, I wondered if I'd ever return to see more of this Adirondack beauty. I felt that I would, but I also felt that it wouldn't be soon because deep wounds heal slowly and mental scars usually heal even more slowly than physical scars.

Aristotle said, "The physician heals, Nature makes well." So maybe in order to be fully well, Grace and I would have to return. And the truth is that that wasn't an unpleasant thought for me. Perhaps I would even become a 46'er, an Adirondack mountain climber who climbs all forty-six Adirondack mountain peaks that are over four-thousand feet high. I chuckled inwardly, thinking that I didn't know if I loved this place quite that much. Grace certainly didn't have any pleasant feelings about the Adirondacks, but maybe, with time, she'd change her mind.

Another quote, this one by Disraeli, came to mind. "There is no education like adversity," he said. It made me laugh inwardly, again, as I thought, "If Disraeli's quote is true, then Grace and I must have earned our doctorate degrees with our ordeal into and escape from this Adirondack wilderness."

I felt a surge of delight encompass my body. It seemed inappropriate, but still it was there. This venture had, indeed, strengthened me. Out of tragic adversity, there had grown, in me, and, hopefully in Grace, a self-confident strength that had drained from me after Nam. I felt as if I had been born again,—not in any religious sense—as if I had risen from the ashes of near destruction, like the Phoenix of Egyptian legends, a bird said to have lived five or six centuries, a bird who was consumed in a fire of its own making, and then rose in youthful splendor from its own ashes.

I felt a new outlook gaining a strong foothold in my mind. This new outlook was more hopeful, positive, forgiving and loving. I knew that, in time, Grace would also be better. I don't think the full extend of what we went through has hit her yet, the most brutal part being covered by a thin layer of amnesia, perhaps. I would be there to help Grace and Sam would be there for the both of us. I felt a spiritual warmth growing and glowing inside of me, not a religious spiritualism, but a spiritualism that seemed to emanate from nature itself. A spiritualism that Thoreau must have felt while living on Walden Pond, as if nature was a medicinal salve and was healing my mental torments about Vietnam.

Yes, I knew I would still need to visit my psychiatrist to iron out the last remaining wrinkles in my personal record of mental health, but at least I could now be hopeful, even certain, that all would be well for me and my family. Some day, I thought hopefully, we'd all return to this, or some similar Adirondack setting—maybe the Catskills Mountain area—and once again give thanks to whatever it was in nature and in this ordeal that helped me to heal. And for all this, I am thankful. However, it did seem to be ironic that having to kill in war brought on my problems, yet killing in self-defense, in the Adirondack Mountains, began the healing process much more so than a doctor's sometimes insipid talk, and a daily regimen of pills.

Being thankful reminded me of Thanksgiving and I was like a child at Christmas time thinking how wonderful it would be to spend time with my family and some relatives. I could envision the dinner table at my mother's-in-law and father's-in-law house. I could even smell the juicy turkey, taste the corn, cranberries, sweet potatoes, mashed potatoes with gravy and stuffing. I could smell the warm, freshly made rolls with golden butter melting on their doughy interior. I could see other relatives enjoying themselves with food and friendship and hear the friendly, warm, often humorous chatter at the dinner table. At this moment, all the world seemed wonderful and right to me.

I had to paddle to shore about an hour before nightfall and make camp. It was difficult getting to sleep. Grace and I talked excitedly about how nice it would be to get home and what we would do when we got there. We were like two children who couldn't get to sleep on Christmas Eve. Then there was silence. I noticed that Grace was staring up at the stars, in a contemplative mood. I wondered what she was thinking as I also stared into the starry, black dome. Then out of the darkness came a voice, Grace's very serious voice. She inquired, "Daddy. What if you are wrong about God?"

I was totally surprised, of course, and not really anxious to talk "religion" with her. I thought Grace might be too impressionable and I didn't want to corrupt her independent thought with my own opinions, which took years to form and solidify. Despite a fear of brainwashing my own daughter, I ventured into an uncomfortable and apprehensive answer. "Well, Grace, you know …Ah…that everyone of us is technically an atheist. We don't believe in all the past Gods from much older civilizations, which existed many thousands of years before the beginnings of Christianity, which started about two thousand years ago. Few people, if any at all, still believe in the ancient Greek and Roman Gods. The Greeks and Romans had a different God for almost everything in their lives. Earlier civilizations had many Gods, too, not just one God as in the Christian religion. Extremely few people, if any at all, still believe in these numerous and ancient Gods, so they are atheists concerning those Gods. A great majority of the world's population does not believe in the Christian God. They have their own God or Gods, which they also can not provide proof for, and they are atheists concerning the more modern Christian God. They don't appear to be harmed by their disbelief in the Christian God. I imagine that almost all of them would say that they are very happy with the lives that "their" God has given them. Furthermore, they would probably make a point of saying that "their" God is the true God, not "your" Christian God. I certainly don't believe that I've been harmed by being an atheist. I think my life has improved since I decided that I was an atheist. I definitely see the world, civilization and people a lot more honestly because valid and verifiable truth means a lot to me. And even if there really was some sort of God, I doubt that He/She/It would have such a rice-paper, brittle ego as to be offended by those who doubt His existence. After all, if there really is a God, then its His fault that He doesn't present Himself to the world. He doesn't have to work "in mysterious ways," He can prove Himself very easily, if He really exists. If God created everyone, and He gave all of us a free-will, that means that we truly make our own decisions and our actions are not determined by God, then how pitiful that God must be to allow people the freedom to deny His existence without proof, then punish those people for using their brains. Also, if God determines our actions, our destiny, then He has made each of us act as we do and that means that He made people deny His existence. *Shit. This is becoming way too involved and complex. I wish she hadn't asked me that question.* Um…you see, Grace, if there is a God and He already knows what we will do in the future, then we have no choice but to do what God already knows we will do. He can't be wrong about what

He knows, right? I can't change my mind and not do what God knows I'm going to do, can I? So, dear daughter, if I'm wrong about the non-existence of the Christian God, or any existent Gods at all, then I owe God a sincere apology and I will readily give it to Him if He will only present Himself to me and to the world, and simply quit acting like a childish magician who "works in mysterious ways." If I'm wrong, then I'll take the consequences, but I've played "Hide and Go Seek" with the idea of a God for too many years. Now when I say, "Ready or not, here I come," I come as an atheist. I have always found nothing, so now I'm convinced that when I say, "Ollie, Ollie in Free," the God, who supposedly hides himself from mankind, will not show up simply because He does not exist. Imagine, Grace, that perhaps one hundred or more years from now, people may view their modern Gods the same way that we view the ancient Gods, as ignorant creations of simple-minded people who were not as smart as us and who didn't know any better way to view and explain and understand the world they lived in.

"I'm sorry, Grace. I've probably said too much and didn't bring it down to an eight year old's level, right?"

"Right?" I repeated.

I looked at Grace. She was sound asleep. I guess that my explanation was so boring that it put her to sleep. I should write that speech on lemon-wet toilet paper, then squeeze the juice out of it, distill it to purify it, put it in very small bottles, call it "Heaven Scent," then get rich selling it as a "sleeping aid" and make millions of dollars from all the gullible God believers.

I yawned. Damn! I thought. I'm boring myself also. I closed my eyes.

I woke before daybreak, November 21st. I built up the fire, letting Grace catch a few more minutes of sleep. When I woke her up, we ate more gorp and to warm our inner bodies, I heated cold water in a cup, then sprinkled pine needles into the hot water to make pine tea. A cup of pine tea has about five times more vitamin C in it than a cup of orange juice, but it doesn't taste as good. We both drank half a cup. Then, I dowsed the fire with the remainder of the canteen of water and refilled it. We packed what little we had and dragged the canoe a few feet to the lake—my ribs hurt even more from all the paddling I did the day before, but I concealed it from Grace. I figured we'd arrive in civilization today, around noon, or at least early afternoon.

It seemed like a couple of months instead of a week since this ordeal started. Grace and I were both quiet, now, in spite of the fact that we were filled with excitement and anticipation. Grace's lips were constantly stretched into a smile, while her eyes sparkled with the joy that she was feeling. She didn't look tired, even though her face looked slightly emaciated.

She almost always looked forward, southwest, toward the end of Long Lake, toward civilization, toward her mom, relatives and friends. I found myself paddling faster for her sake, as tears of joy and pain trickled down my cheeks. I thought, "There will only be one moment that can match the joy of this particular moment, and that would be when Grace and I stood before Sam and we all cried joyfully together as we hugged each other tightly in a triple embrace." After that thought, I found myself paddling faster and faster, looking in the same direction as Grace and forcing myself to ignore the pain in my ribs.

The sun rose above the horizon's dark wall, but looked blurry from being distorted by my tears. The morning was warmer than I had expected it to be. I guessed the temperature was in the mid to high 20F range. I could feel the warmth under my coat created by my vigorous paddling. I removed my coat and hat and, to my surprise, I stayed very comfortable, as long as I paddled constantly. The fresh air, the happiness of being safe, and the anticipation of seeing Sam assuaged my rib pain.

"It's a nice day, Papa," Grace said, as she looked back at me with a broad smile; the sun reflecting off her pearly white teeth.

"Yes," I replied with a return smile, "it's a wonderfully clear, sunny day. Almost like Indian summer."

Then something stirred inside of me as if triggered by the word "Indian." Deep inside my brain, as if from a long lost cave, deep in some unknown, remote wilderness, Wolf growled and my interpretation of the meaning of the growl was, "You have done well, my brother and friend, for you are not only a master warrior, but you are becoming the master of your future. You should be very proud of your courage and strength." Then silence prevailed.

That was one of the few times that I was to hear Wolf's growl, in a peaceful situation. He was right though. I was proud of myself and Grace, too. I paddled through the water as it sparkled in the brilliant sunlight, content with myself, and very thankful for my good fortune.

As my arms strained against the oar to keep up a moderately fast pace, my mind drifted to the three dead bodies that I left behind. I didn't enjoy taking their lives. I was saddened by the fact that I had killed and that I could kill so quickly, so efficiently, so coldly and easily. But, I also thought, I really had no other safe choice . . . not a logical or sane choice anyway. The Gibsons left me no alternative, just like the VC. It was kill-or-be-killed, and I wouldn't allow Grace to be killed, at any cost, so long as I remained alive. I knew that I could never live with myself if I couldn't bring Grace home safely, at least physically safe. I thought I might as well be dead, myself, if I had allowed the Gibsons to injure, maim, or kill her.

So, in my eyes, it was all-or-nothing, kill-or-be-killed, probably the same conclusion that Jake came to, only for different reasons. Either I killed all of them or they killed us, and no laws of society, civilization, or religion could change that for me or them. Our survival depended on me being smarter, quicker, luckier and deadlier than the Gibsons. No mythical, mysterious hand from the sky would reach down to help. Way out here, the police couldn't assist me either. I killed the Gibsons because, by my standards, I had no other choice, and that conclusion rested easily and peacefully with me—though I'm certain it will not rest easily and peacefully with many others, especially the ones who can't or won't defend themselves and will whine and complain that it's someone else's duty to protect them.

But the sadness of killing in Vietnam and having to kill again here in the Adirondack Mountains in no way made me unable to kill again. I knew for certain that I could, and I would, if I knew that I had to. That declaration didn't rest well with me, though I accepted it as an unfortunate or fortunate fact of my life, depending on the situation and circumstances. I hoped, however, that I would never have to kill again. There's no glory in it; that's for sure. The glory of killing comes from movies, plus comic books, novels and other literature by the writers of fanciful hyperbole. If justifiable, killing may bring rewards, such as medals, but they're never worth the hours of lost sleep that comes from killing. It's important to remember that when you kill someone, you've changed the history of the world. That person may have done something exceptionally good that is now prevented by his death. Also, that person may have done things that are exceptionally bad, and now society is rewarded by his death. But one way or the other that person affects the world he/she lives in, and also affects everyone he/she comes into contact with and their actions within their society. If Abraham Lincoln had been assassinated prior to becoming president of the United States, would the history of America have been different? Of course it would have. One person's death can change history. That's one reason that makes life so precious and the taking-of-life sad and regrettable.

There is great evil in this world. I have witnessed some of it. Some men will automatically reject it, while others will welcome it and even embrace it, though most men are trapped in the middle. The men trapped in the middle are the ones who feel the most pain and regret for evil deeds that they have committed or evil deeds that they have witnessed. Their consciences are pulled, like a rubber band, between two great forces, sometimes pulled towards the light and sometimes pulled towards the darkness. They become skeptical and suspicious of their peers, political groups and governments. They become like me.

When I was in Nam, during private, solitary moments, prior to my night stalking, I came to the conclusion that every conscientious adult must have a Pandora's Box of guilt and shame, and every now and then those ghosts of guilt and shame escape to haunt them and bring abundant tears to their eyes. I have felt those tears and, if other adults are like me, those tears run down their cheeks like scalding lava down the side of a volcano. I think, however, that I'm worse than the average person because I've had to kill too often. So, out of necessity, I've mentally built a needed addition to my own personal Pandora's Box. It's a cellar for my deepest, darkest shame and guilt. I'm mostly a good person, I think, but there are some dark shadows lurking in some of the folds and crevices of my brain.

I brought myself back to reality. It was approaching mid-day and we hadn't come as far as I thought we could have come by this time. Apparently I made the mistake of thinking how long it took us when we traveled in the opposite direction with the Gibsons. But then, two people in each canoe were paddling and could make better time compared to a single person, weakened by the rigors of a life-and-death struggle and by painful ribs.   Furthermore, and more significantly, I was paddling against the flow of the lake and not with it like the Gibsons had done on the way to their cabin.

Thinking of the Gibsons made me think of the worst things about life, the cruel, perverted child predators and the misfit, demented criminals prowling amongst us. I wondered if the Gibsons, and all the other misfits in our society turned to crime and ugly deeds because of the hand they were dealt, or because of the way they played the hand that they were dealt.

I relaxed. No real hurry, if the weather stayed like it is now. And though my arms, ribs and back ached, my lips smiled happily as the sun's golden rays pleasingly washed over my face like the feel of a wet, warm washcloth.

I gazed at Grace and felt a proud and very pleasant warmth which encompassed my entire body, like a very personal aura that was even more pleasing and comforting than the warmth of the sun's golden rays upon my face.

/--/../-.-/./.-../-.- -/-./-../.-/-.-./....//.-/./.-/././-.-/./.-../../.-..//-.-/-.../-.- -/

Chapter 19

★★★★

Red Squirrel Days

I KEPT THE CANOE about thirty feet from the western shore of Long Lake in order to avoid shallow spots and protruding rocks. I would have liked to have been out in the middle of the lake, but, I reasoned, if something happened and the canoe overturned, Grace and I would both die of hypothermia. This way Grace and I would only have to swim a short distance in the frigid water to reach shore, then quickly build a fire. Also, being close to shore, near the tall trees, protected us from most of the cold wind that swept unimpeded across the middle of the lake.

However, even being as far from shore as we were could be extremely dangerous if the canoe overturned. Grace and I would be wet from head to toe and we would need a fire desperately. If the wax-head matches didn't work, we might even freeze to death, or develop sever frostbite, especially if it happened near a remote shoreline, as we were now..

I looked toward the eastern shore of the lake and saw two red squirrels chasing each other on the ground and then up the trunk of a tree. They leaped like acrobats jumping from limb to limb. Grace heard their chatter, too, and delighted in watching them play tag. I could imagine Grace thinking about her cat while watching the squirrels.

She must miss her black cat, Shadow, a lot, I thought. I detected no sadness on her face, just joy, that spread across her face like butter over warm toast. And as we both observed the squirrel's frolicsome and often hilarious movements, I thought, How wonderful it was for them to be so cheerful and full of play that they could so easily be victorious over the cold, dark gloom and danger within the nearby, almost impenetrable, evergreen and hard wood forest. They seemed to have the right attitude, so cheerful, so positive and energetic. I thought, "That's what I wanted to do, return to the "red squirrel days" of my youth when all seemed well because of my positive, cheerful, energetic and youthful attitudes about the world and the people in it, especially those who were close to me.

We had to strain to see them now, as we moved into the distance. I paddled a few more strokes and when I looked back, I couldn't see them any more, just as I had paddled through my life and couldn't see my own youth any more. All I could hear was the paddle dipping and splashing quietly in the water as I used a "J"-stroke so that I didn't have to paddle on both side of the canoe to keep it going parallel to the shore line.

Then another sound penetrated my senses deeply and pleasantly. Grace started singing a children's song, very softly, as she stared into the depth of the frigid, clear water, the canoe gliding, almost silently over it, like a glider on a current of air. I didn't know what the song was, but it had a very soothing effect on me, like that of peaceful meditation.

The canoe rocked as Grace leaned sideways to look into the water. I felt the canoe lean slightly and I reminded Grace not to lean too far or we'd tip over. She smiled and said, "OK."

She sang, then would hum, sometimes, indicating that she didn't remember all the words. But even her humming was like a chorus of angels singing to me. Grace's voice reminded me of Sam, who had a lovely singing voice. The sound of Grace's voice flooded me with pleasure, just as the memory of Sam's voice surrounded me with delight. It was an experience of auditory ecstasy. I stopped paddling and closed my eyes for a minute in order to soak-up the pure joy of the moment, soaking it up like a sponge, letting the sounds engulf, embrace and penetrate me.

Then I heard her mellifluous voice saying, "I think I can. I think I can." I knew that she was thinking of one of her favorite bedtime books, when she was younger, a book entitled, *The Little Engine That Could.* That reminded me of all the rhyming Dr. Seuss books that she loved so much, and that, in turn, made me thankful for those books that helped give her a very happy childhood, where fun, thrills and excitement were plentiful.

When I opened my eyes, Grace was smiling at me, as if she knew how good her voice made me feel. I studied her smile and wondered if it was more like mine or her mom's, or was it simply a pleasing combination? No words were spoken, they weren't needed. Our eyes talked to each other with perfect understanding. I returned her smile then puckered my lips, kissed my open palm, then blew across that palm, sending her an "air kiss." She mimicked my "air kiss" movements and sent me a kiss. We smiled at each other, again, then she turned toward the western shore of the lake to look into the nude, hibernating wilderness.

I saw her face reflected in the wavy water caused by the wake of the canoe. She was such a beautiful girl. I knew I was very lucky to be her "Papa." She was average height, slender, and athletic looking. Her reflection on the water reminded me of Snow White's appearance in the evil queen's mirror. It had a shine all its own, so full of character and warmth and sensitivity. Of course a face like that would make an evil queen jealous, but it made me very lucky, appreciative and proud. I contributed to her creation. She was my crowning life's achievement and my most valuable gift to the world. She made me happy.

She turned toward me, face suddenly serious, the smile gone. I looked back at her, concerned. A question lingered on her lips.

"Papa? You had to kill those bad men, didn't you? Or they would have killed you and me, right? Will you be in trouble now with the police?"

"Yes, Sweetheart, I did have to kill them to save our lives. And, no, I don't think I'll be in trouble with the police, although it's possible. The law says that I can kill a person if I believe he is trying to kill me or my family. But, Grace, many people won't like me because I killed those men, especially when they find out that I had to kill other men when I was in the war in Vietnam. It's not a good thing to kill, but sometimes there's a good reason for it. Protecting your life and the life of your child is a very good reason."

"I still love you Papa. You stopped them from killing me. I'm not mad at you and Momma won't be mad either," Grace said, thoughtfully.

The only words I could think of were, "Out of the mouths of babes." I didn't vocalize those words because Grace wouldn't understand them. Sometimes children speak very wisely, at a level much beyond their years.

I didn't know what to say to her or, more accurately, I didn't respond because I was chocked up with emotion.

I was staring at her; seeing her as if I was wearing blinders. I saw her smile brighten and her eyebrows and eyelids raise in a sign of joy. Then, in a suddenly, surprising tone of voice she said, "Daddy . . . Daddy, there's somebody coming toward us in a canoe." She pointed towards the oncoming canoe.

Though I heard her, my reaction was sluggish. I could see her excitement. She looked as if she wanted to jump for joy and start yelling and screaming, but she restrained herself when the canoe started rocking. She looked at me to give her the indication that she could yell and scream and wave her hands at our rescuers . . . if they were rescuers. She could hardly control herself as she stared at me with open-mouthed joy. I stared, used my open hands, over my eyes, to block the sun's glare off the water, then squinted my eyes to get a better look at the occupants of the rapidly approaching canoe. It contained two, adult male paddlers.

A distant and vague thought burned a path across my brain. I recalled a brief conversation between Jake, Tom and Lester while we were traveling from Chemung to the Adirondack mountains. They thought I was asleep. The focus of their conversation, if I remember correctly, was that they had some cousins in the Adirondack mountains that Tom and Lester hadn't seen in a few years and that, if time and circumstances permitted, Tom and Lester might get a chance to see them. I can imagine how "saintly" those relatives must be—the thorough study of all the religious saints must be a required course for all mental health professionals.

Out of my mouth came a yell that startled Grace enough to rock the canoe, again. "Get down in the bottom of the canoe, quickly!" I paddled vigorously on the right hand side of the canoe, turning it sharply to the left, to the shore. Then I paddled, on both sides of the canoe, to get maximum power and speed to get us to shore as quickly as possible.

"But, Daddy" . . . Grace began, hesitantly, as she knelt down in the bottom of the canoe. "What's the matter?" she asked, her face distorted in an expression of confusion.

I yelled, in a very severe voice, so she understood that I wanted immediate obedience to my command, "Lie down in the bottom of the canoe, now!" Then I said, "The two men in that canoe look like they might be cousins of the Gibsons, especially the big, bearded guy that's holding a rifle. Stay down low. We've got to get to shore. I think we're in danger!"

As I was yelling this explanation, I was desperately putting every ounce of remaining energy into the oar. I wondered how Jake's cousins knew where to find us. Did Jake have a radio transmitter hidden somewhere? He couldn't have. I saw no indication of a radio receiver/transmitter inside the cabin and no antenna outside the cabin. And if they were the Gibson's cousins, why wasn't that bearded son-of-a-bitch shooting at us from his canoe? Perhaps their canoe was rocking too much. He could still have us in his sights, especially if he was an excellent shot. But he didn't shoot. Why? Did they want us alive? We must reach shore and run, I thought, with a panicked and addled brain. I paddled furiously, picking up speed.

My mind was caught totally off guard. My mind was racing with unanswerable questions. My heart was pounding like a blacksmith's hammer. Full-fledged panic erupted within me as I heard myself say the words, "Wolf! Come!" Immediately I heard the growl of Roamin' Wolf and felt the almost immediate surge of additional adrenaline.

As I calmed down a bit, I asked myself, "How could I have been so stupid not to have picked up Jake's and Tom's shotguns and brought them with us." If we made it to shore, we'd have to try to lose them in the forest. I thought, "We're both tired and won't be able to travel fast or cunningly." I felt discouraged, but dismissed the feeling immediately. If they're good trackers, they'll be able to hunt us down easily. We won't have a head start, nor any of the other advantages that we used against Jake and Tom.

Jake's or Tom's shotgun would be a hell-of-a-lot better than two knives. A shotgun, even with slugs in it, would be a piss-poor match for a big caliber rifle, though. I thought, "Bring a knife to a gun fight and have a ring-side seat to watch yourself get killed." I really wasn't sure if it was a rifle, could be shotgun. If it was a shotgun, then that's why the bearded guy didn't shoot yet. He'd be out of range.

"Damn!" I shouted at myself as I continued to paddle powerfully. Those men were yelling, but I couldn't understand them. I didn't need to understand them. We needed to get into the woods where there was some protection. But still no shots were fired, which made me more convinced that the bearded guy had a shotgun, not a rifle. They're probably sadistic brutes, like Jake, I thought. "Son-of-a-bitch!" I screamed at myself, ignoring Grace. I thought, "They want to capture us alive. Or, perhaps, they wanted to get closer before they killed us. But why? It didn't make sense. No time for logic, E & E—escape and evade—was needed, immediately, just like I had to do so many times in Nam.

I glanced over my shoulder at their canoe and saw that the bearded man was waving his left arm as he held onto his long-gun with his right hand. The motion was rocking his canoe and his partner was holding tightly onto the sides. His partner didn't appear to have a weapon. Perhaps he had a concealed pistol. Then that man, too, started waving at us, with both arms. Are those bastards taunting me? I swore silently, gritting my teeth. They knew that our escape was almost hopeless and they were taunting with ultimate, sadistic pleasure. "Those rotten bastards," I thought with extreme anger.

Escalating panic bubbled up inside of me as the bow of our canoe dug into the sand and lacy looking ice that crept out of the shallow shoreline. I had been paddling so powerfully and was going so fast that the bow of the canoe cut through the ice and plowed a narrow furrow into the sand, depositing us well into the shore line so that when I jumped out, only the lower half of my boots got wet. I pulled the canoe ashore with one great heave that resulted in a tremendous circle of pain in my rib cage. I grabbed Grace, who was once again terrified, and ran to the tree line. Still no shots. They must be trackers, I thought, and not worried about us escaping. Jake had underestimated us like that, too. Maybe, just maybe, there was a shred of hope. I heard Wolf howl and clung to that fragile hope.

My mind flashed with an image of my white wolf and I was reassured by his presence. I couldn't give up; I wouldn't give up. My hopeful thoughts bolstered my confidence and made me realize that I had all the skills that I needed to defend Grace and me, and that panic was my enemy. So I shunned the panic, and the rib pain, that threatened to engulf me, mentally wrapping it into a shroud loaded with rocks and, in a vivid mental image, I sent it to the bottom of the lake.

As I stepped into the tree line and ducked down for cover, I heard it. It was the strangest damn thing to hear out in the wilderness. The shock of it almost bowled me over. Grace and I looked at each other, mystified by it. I felt haunted by the very sound of it. It made me dizzy, disoriented and unsure of just what the hell was going on here.

As I felt Wolf's strengths and fierceness swell within me, I took Grace deeper into the woods as the strangers' canoe landed. They got out and I looked at them over my shoulder. "Goddamnit!" I mumbled when I saw that the bearded guy did have a rifle. No doubt about that now. Mr. Beard was yelling a word over and over, like a loud, but slow, mantra from a praying Buddhist monk. The words echoed through the forest and into my confused head. Grace was tapping my leg, trying to tell me something, but the echo of Mr. Beard's words had me inescapably in their grip as the two men stood on the shore looking at me. Grace and I stared at them from just inside the forest's edge.

Grace was still tapping on my leg, trying to talk to me, insistently, but I didn't understand her. Then, again, I heard those strange words spoken by the strangers, but now, as my panic and anger subsided gradually, I started to understand those words.

"Roman? . . . Roman? . . . Roman! We want to help!" they repeated over and over. But they stretched out my name so it sounded like "Ro . . . man?"

I felt as if I was struck by lightening when I realized that my name was being called.

Grace hit me harder and got my attention. She was yelling, "Daddy! Daddy! I think they came to help us!" My mouth opened, my jaw dropped and the fog of confusion started to clear. Then, I picked up Grace and hugged her tightly. She put her arms around my neck and hugged me so tightly that I thought she'd break my neck. But the ultimate joy of being rescued numbed the neck pain, as well as the rib pain.

Then I turned suspicious again. Sure, they know my name, I thought. Was this a devious trick. "Be cautious," Wolf warned me. In a few seconds, Wolf spoke again, saying, "Be prepared, don't get caught off guard by a ruse." I saw the image of Wolf, which reinforced the notion that I needed to be cautious until I was absolutely sure about who these guys were.

My mind was clear and alert. I was thankful for Wolf's reminder, but caution was a survival instinct with me and Wolf since being exposed to the dangers of combat in Vietnam for thirteen very long months. I appreciated it, but didn't really need a reminder.

I got down on my knees, still hugging Grace, and whispered in her ear, "Let's be careful. I don't want to be tricked, OK? Stand behind me. I love you." Grace stood behind me and I turned my head to check. That's when I saw Wolf standing beside me.

As I stared at the strangers, I could feel the cold, deadly steel of both my throwing knife and my combat knife pressing against my body. A low growl from Wolf rumbled in my head, then, suddenly and instinctively, both knives were in my hands.

My hands had moved instinctively. I stared cautiously at the men with a heightened sense of smell, hearing and sight. My teeth felt tingly, as if they were elongating. The hairs on my arms felt as if they were growing, thickening and turning white. My fingernails seemed to lengthen into claws and I felt as if my body was being covered with fur. I blinked my eyes and held the eyelids closed for a second. When I opened them I was clear-headed and alert. I also saw Wolf, standing beside me, growling viciously—only I could hear it—at the two strangers. Then I looked at my body and there was no change. The feelings of wolfish-change had been inside my head, not external.

Though they were standing about fifty feet away, I could vividly see every button on their coats, one having been re-sewed with mismatched thread. The bearded man had three gray hairs in his beard, both men had brown eyes and one, or both of them were smokers, I could smell

burned tobacco. Looking at Mr. No-Beard, I could see that he was
the smoker. He had yellowish-brown stains on his right hand thumb,
index and middle fingers The thread on both their coats stood out
clearly as if under a microscope. Mr. No-Beard was nervously rubbing
his right hand index finger against his thumb, making a loud friction
noise. One of them had bad breath. I figured that it came from the
smoker, but I wasn't sure because they were about fifty feet away from
me. Those were the heightened senses of Wolf.

I felt as if a giant, powerful claw grabbed my pants leg and pulled
me. I glared down at the menacing power, but it was just Grace pulling
on my pants, my heightened senses tricking me. I saw that Grace
wanted to say something to me.

"Papa," Grace whispered with mature concern, "I think you're
scaring those men with your knives. Can you put them away now,
Papa? Please."

I looked down at my hands, vaguely aware that I was holding the
knives, threateningly, with the throwing knife raised to my ear. I stared
at the men. They looked friendly, non-threatening. Even the bearded
guy's rifle was held in a non-threatening position.

Still, I gave them an intentional, menacing stare, for the sake of
caution only, but they didn't know that. Mr. Beard seemed to know
what I was thinking, so he placed his rifle on the ground. I then stared
a Mr. No-Beard. Mr. Beard turned slightly and whispered to Mr.
No-Beard, then Mr. No-Beard raised the bottom of his winter coat and
removed a Colt, model 1911, .45 caliber pistol from his waist holster.
He set it on the ground next to the rifle. Both men showed me their
empty hands. Each had something shiny attached to their coats. The
sun's glare flashed off the metal so it was blurred. Badges?

We stood a moment staring at each other. I hoped that I looked
less menacing to them, especially now that I realized that the shiny
things were probably badges . . . police badges. Actually, they were
New York State Troopers.

Their peaceful actions and their badges convinced me that Grace
and I were safe, so I returned each knife to its sheath.

Grace and I looked like wild animals. Our clothes were torn and
filthy, our exposed flesh was dirty, my face and hands were covered
with black charcoal as well as mud, and our cheeks looked like they

had been scraped with a wire-brush. Cuts, scrapes, gashes and other minor wounds were plentiful. But we smiled as best we could and approached the two troopers.

As I approached them, my persona changed and Wolf retreated. "Holy shit! Finally. It's sure good to see you guys," I said excitedly, flashing them a big smile. "Thanks for coming, even if you are too late." I kept smiling to let them know that I felt no animosity toward them. Then I said, "I was trying to get away from you because I thought you were relatives of the Gibsons and that we were in danger, again."

I introduced Grace and myself—I was so relieved and wanting to talk that I didn't give the men a chance to give their names. Grace received admiring smiles from both men. We shook hands. We sat on a patch of dry ground and I gave them a quick summary of what had happened. Mr. Beard was an official Adirondack guide who had been deputized to assist Mr. No-Beard, the N.Y.S. Trooper. They informed me that they were part of many teams of guides and police officers that were searching for us.

My senses were still keen, but the hyper-sensitivity and the feeling of wolfish growth on my body was fading, now that the threat was gone. However, the muscles of my arms and legs still felt as if they were taut, steel cables that could hold up a ton of weight with little strain.

When I finished talking, they patted me and Grace on the back, the Trooper saying, "You sure you're both all right? I may be able to radio for a helicopter."

I looked at Grace and said, "Wha'daya think, Grace? Are we all right?"

"We are now, Papa," she said with a sly grin.

"Besides," I said, smiling at the Trooper, "where would the helicopter land?"

The Trooper looked all around the area, laughed, then said, "Point well taken. Our helicopter isn't able to land in water, that's for sure."

We all walked to our canoes as the Trooper, used a walkie-talkie to report that he and his guide had found us and were returning to base. It took him a few tries to convey the message through the static— transmitting and receiving was not good in the Adirondacks due to the thick growth of trees, hill, and mountains.

When this whole ordeal started, I wondered if the police would ever be able to rescue us. Actually, I didn't think they would be able to do it. I gave up on them. I guess it must have been as confusing for them as it was for us, kind of difficult to put all the pieces of the puzzle together. But, although they didn't rescue us—they *found* us, they didn't really *rescue* us—at least they were *trying* to find us.

We followed them in our canoe until we reached their destination on shore.

In another hour or so we were at the intersection of routes 30 and 28N, where the State Trooper took us to the local barracks to fill out an incident report. But first I called Sam at our home near Rochester. She wasn't there, so I called my in-law's home in Chemung. Sam answered the phone. Her voice was hesitant as if dreading bad news, but I savored the sound of her voice, which I had longed to hear for so long. "Hello," she said.

Very quickly, I said, "Hi Babe. Grace and I are safe and sound. We love you." I said it so quickly so that I could relieve the terrible anxiety that she must have been feeling..

There was a pause, a lingering silence, as if no one was there.

"Sam?" I said, questioningly, wondering if I had lost my connection with her.

Then there was screaming. She was happily screaming at the top of her lungs—and, as I remember, she had a very nice set of lungs. I heard her yelling, "I knew he'd so it!" to her mom an dad. Then, to me, "I knew you'd do it! I just knew you would! I just knew you would! I knew it! . . . I knew it!" Pause. The tone of her voice changed and became serious. "Where are you and Grace?" she asked, followed by more questions.

I blurted out the information quickly to answer her gush of questions. Her voice trembled as she asked those questions. I paused a couple times, when she started crying, to give her a chance to compose herself.

Then, "Let me talk to Grace. Let me talk to Grace, please," she said with a sniffle.

Grace talked to her mom as tears flowed down her cheeks.

When I took the phone back, I told Sam that we'd be home as soon as possible.

After I hung up the phone, I gave the information needed to fill out the Trooper's incident report.

While I was involved with the details of the incident report, a female Trooper occupied Grace's attention. I had to grin as I heard Grace talking to the Trooper because Grace was joking, saying things like, "Do you know that your bra is a booby trap?" and "You do know that Australian farts come from way-down-under, right?" and "You know why Chicago is called the Windy City? 'cause that's where the most windy farters live." The female Trooper had her hand over her mouth, trying not to laugh too hard and attract embarrassing attention from her fellow officers, but I could see that her eyes flashed like Fourth of July sparklers.

An even funnier thing was Grace telling the Trooper about a Pooka that she saw in the forest—Grace was teasing the Trooper now—and the trooper seemed fascinated with Grace's imaginative storytelling. I informed the Trooper that Grace and I had watched a James Stewart movie called *Harvey* a couple nights before the kidnapping. In the movie, Stewart's character, Elwood P. Dowd, is friends with an invisible Pooka—a six feet tall, friendly rabbit that follows Elwood P. Dowd around, keeping him company. This got Stewart's character in all kinds of comedic trouble that made the movie greatly entertaining.

When the reports were finally completed, Grace and I were driven by that same female State Trooper—at Grace's insistence, and my support of her insistence—on the six hour journey to my in-law's house in Chemung. On the way there, the Trooper told me about the tremendous confusion that caused long delays in tracking us down.

She told me that the local police and State Troopers searched the Elmira, Waverly and Chemung areas for a couple days before they found the "Annie button" in the Chemung hunting lodge because the button had fallen into a crack in the floor boards and just the tip of it could be seen when the police went back to check the hunting lodge more thoroughly. The roadblocks were between Elmira and Rochester, while we really drove off toward Binghamton on route 17 and then headed directly north on route 81.

No record of Jake Gibson's current whereabouts was found in the police computer files, so it took a couple days to scrape up that information from other sources. And once the police did find that Jake was an Adirondack guide, they had no idea where they should search in such a huge area. The Adirondack region encompasses millions of acres. Rescue teams were out everywhere, but it was like trying to find two particular fish in a huge lake.

"Then a big break came when one of Jake's drinking buddies, who was in a local police "holding cell" for being drunk and disorderly, told the police that while drunk one night, Jake mentioned a secret cabin that he and one of his sons had built way off in the Preston Ponds area of the Adirondacks. So, to make a long story short, the Trooper said, that that's why that Trooper and his guide were paddling along Long Lake, looking for any sign of us.

She also informed me that the two men in the canoe were just one scouting team and that they were to be followed by a dozen or more armed and specially trained troopers who would be assigned Adirondack guides. Another day, she said, and they probably would have rescued us from the Gibsons. "Another day," I thought, "and we'd have been dead." I didn't tell her that, though. I was too grateful to be safe and heading back to Sam.

The Trooper looked sideways at me as she drove. She had a curious grin, so I asked her what was on her mind. She said, "Trooper Dobbs is the name of the trooper that found you. I overheard him giving the other troopers a dangerous warning. I saw the warning's effect in their eyes, in their facial expressions and in their body language. Dobbs told the other Troopers that you scared the hell out of him, and the guide, named Gus, even though he was the one holding the rifle and you only had the two knives. Dobb's said that, from experience, he could tell from your posture and your eyes that you could be extremely dangerous. Damn! Ain't that funny. Dobbs'll really get teased about that. You look like a gentle soul to me. Wha'daya think about that, Mr. Wolfe?"

"Well . . . he must have gotten the wrong impression. When he found me I must have looked kind of wild and half crazy. I'm really just a pussy cat. But there's no need to tease Dobb's. You or the other Troopers probably would have felt the same way if you were the ones that found me looking wild, half crazy, filthy-looking and prepared to fling a throwing knife into you and/or cut your throat with a combat knife."

She stared at me and an uncomfortable silence filled the car, so I changed the subject and asked about the trooper that the Gibsons had wounded. I was told that he was out of danger; that he'd be fine in a few months. I didn't really want to know any more details. Maybe later I would. Right now, all I wanted was to get Grace and me back to Sam. I took a deep, refreshing breath, but still felt more tired than I have ever felt before, even in Nam.

Before I drifted off to sleep, I thought, "How wonderful it will be to be back in my classroom, as a teacher, to spend Thanksgiving with relatives and friends and, also, what an interesting tale I could tell my psychiatrist at our next appointment—maybe I'd make the story even more interesting with a spicy dash of hyperbole.

I wished that I had let Trooper Dobbs and Gus, the guide, introduce themselves. It was rude of me not to give them a chance to do so, but I was quite sure they'd forgive me, under the circumstances.

Total exhaustion hit me suddenly and I drifted off to sleep with the mesmerizing sound of the car's wheels humming in my ears. Grace was already asleep in the back seat. Peace at last.

A bump in the road jarred me awake near Syracuse. The car radio was on and the weatherman was talking excitedly about a big snowstorm that will be sweeping over northeastern New York State by morning. A couple of feet of snow was expected, along with very frigid winds. And an official snow warning was given for northern New York, especially south of the Great Lakes, and eastward to the Adirondack area which was liable to get hit the hardest. I took a deep breath and let the air out slowly through pursed lips. We had missed the storm by only a few hours. Luck had been on our side, very good luck.

I checked Grace. She was still sleeping soundly. My drowsy, heavy eyelids fluttered up and down, so I surrendered to the urge and drifted off to sleep, again. It was a deep sleep, filled with dreams of Sam and Grace, seeing relatives and friends and celebrating the Thanksgiving and Christmas holidays. Peace and relaxation for Grace and me, finally.

/-/- - -/-./-.- -/.-././-./././-...-/.-./.-/-/-./-..- - -/-./-.- -/./.-/....-/

Epilogue

FOR THE FOLLOWING FEW months my feelings vacillated between mild regret and sadness, to hopeful, optimistic joy, but I experienced no more severe depression.

My alter ego, Roamin' Wolf, remained dormant, as I had commanded, while I, Roman Wolfe, was physically healed and mentally improving. My doctor said that I was coming along extremely well, despite my stressful flashbacks of killing and visions of carnage in Vietnam, and in the Adirondack mountains. He felt that I was on my way to a good recovery which would enable me to lead a normal life. I thought I could feel those mental wounds healing and it was a good feeling, a hopeful feeling. Also, I could hear the optimism in the doctor's voice and see it in his facial expressions. Soon, he told me, I would be through with pills and doctor appointments. Needless to say, I was thrilled that my "shrink" had such a good mental prognosis for me. Physically, I was doing well, also. With the help of X-rays and my family doctor, my two cracked ribs healed in six weeks.

At one session the Doc and I talked about good versus evil, nature versus nurture and their effects on the human behaviors. But one thing that he said particularly became indelibly etched in my mind. He said, "We are all prisoners to our own identities, standing behind the metal bars of our own innate characteristics, surrounded by the concrete and steel walls of our limited knowledge, and at the mercy of our life's experiences. We are, in a sense, our own jailers." It made my stop and seriously think about how we all get to be who we are. Do unpredictable situations, circumstances, events and wise or unwise choices decide our fate? If there is a God, and everything happens in accordance with God's will (because He/She/It is all-powerful), then God causes both the good and bad that exists in this world. And if God is also said to be "all-good," then events that are bad, from a human point of view, must be good events, to God's way of thinking. Or, perhaps, God is not all-powerful and all-good, or our God delusion is just that, a delusion. Oh, well, I thought. What the hell do I know? I'm just a simple "born-again atheist" with a Rationalist and Empiricist frame of mind.

Much more importantly, Grace was doing well. Sam and I had been taking her to a child psychologist who helped her greatly. She no longer has to go to that psychologist because she has accepted and dealt with the ordeal very well, and in a remarkably short period of time. She rarely mentions the experience, and when she does mention it, she usually smiles and says, "We beat those bad guys, didn't we Papa?" I usually respond with, "We sure did, Sweetheart. They didn't stand a chance against us because we're an unbeatable team. You're the brains and I'm the muscle." She'd always laugh at that comment, usually while I was hugging her. And during the hug, when her head was adjacent to mine, I'd be silently thankful for my intense combat training and combat experiences, as well as thankful for the pale wolf, the Native American spirit wolf, who resided in the unexplored, psychological wilderness that lay in the crevices, indentations, folds, synapses and neurons of my brain.

During these times of thankfulness, I didn't feel Wolf stir within me, not even weakly; not even in whispers of subtle mental contact. Wolf agreed to remain dormant until I beckoned him, in an emergency. I realize that my relationship with this spirit wolf is anthropomorphic, but that's how I think of him: as a warrior in a wolf's body. Native Americans believed that spirit animals resided within some of them and the wolf was one of the most powerful and revered. If an Indian possessed a wolf spirit, it meant that he had "strong medicine," much power and courage. That may sound silly, but that's the way it is for me; that's how Wolf makes me feel. Luckily, I don't have to try to explain Wolf to anyone. I seriously thought of telling my psychiatrist, once, but I didn't feel like being committed to a mental hospital that day—I didn't have a "Get Out of the Crazy House Free coupon"—so I figured it would be very wise of me not to mention Wolf.

I returned to my teaching job, after the Christmas break, with mixed feelings. My students were excited. To them I had been on an incredibly exciting and amazing adventure. They wanted to know every detail—the boys, especially—and they wanted to know every terrible, scary and gory tidbit of information, in spite of all the radio, TV and newspaper accounts. They were disappointed when I wouldn't talk at length about some parts of the ordeal—I would've had parents asking for my immediate resignation because it may have scared their children. They'd be correct, of course, so I said as little as possible. However, I did find many of the parents' reactions toward me to be disturbing. Most of the parents were appalled when they found out that I had to kill to survive, and some were terrified to leave their children with someone who killed in Vietnam—my Vietnam war record had been exposed and glorified needlessly. But the kids? Hell they saw me as a hero and didn't feel threatened by me at all—and they had absolutely no need to fear me. But you can see how the controversy could affect my peace of mind and distract me from my job and family life. I thought that I dealt with it fairly well, but I must admit that many parents' behaviors towards me were very irritating and unnecessarily disrespectful and even irrational. But after the Adirondack ordeal, handling their doltish arrogance wasn't too difficult, just very disappointing.

I avoided hero worship and bragging. I wanted it all behind me. I simply wanted to move on with my family life and my teaching career. So, after the first week back to school, I stopped talking about the Adirondack ordeal with anyone at school: students, teachers, parents and other staff members. If questions were asked, I ignored them. If someone persisted questioning me, I said, "Excuse me," then walked away from them. Nor did I write about it or seek publicity. I wanted my family life and my career, not pretentious hero worship, gory glory and a constant invasion of my privacy. I didn't give radio or TV interviews, nor did I provide information for newspaper and magazine articles.

I'd been called a hero in Nam. It proved to be no great or satisfying honor. Heroes aren't supposed to be scared, yet I was. And look what I had to do to be called a hero, kill three men in the Adirondack mountains and kill many more in Vietnam. I knew what some parents and colleagues were thinking: "I don't want a 'killer' to be my child's teacher?" and "I don't want to work with a 'killer?'" I killed for my country. I killed to protect my family. I was satisfied with myself and tried to move on with my life, but it wasn't easy.

I hoped that my students' adult experiences with war and killing would always be contained in and limited to the fantasy world of toy soldiers, toy weapons, imaginary bullets and bombs and video games, as well as falsely glorified and entertainingly exaggerated accounts that are seen in pretentious movies and read about in books of ostentatious fiction. I hoped, for their sake, that they never had to experience the stark and brutal horrors of real war, the feel and smell of slick, red blood, the tremendous and unbearable pain of actual, serious combat wounds, to see or experience torn flesh, shattered bones and blown off limbs, or to stare into the abyss of death that is taking a friend's life, or to have to experience the ultimate horror, which is to plummet into that abyss themselves, as if pulled into that darkness by the fading light and life in a dying friend's eyes.

The smell of feces mixed with urine, when a dead body releases its contents, is another repulsive event. But much worse is the smell of a dead body left to putrefy and dissolve for a few days. That's the very worst sinus invading, eye watering, throat gagging, stomach churning, foul smell that there is on earth. There is absolutely nothing like it. No dead animal, no sort of decaying vegetation, no chemical, nothing natural or artificial can come close to the terribly shocking and sickeningly, foul smell of a neglected, dead, human body that's liquefying and engulfed in its own maggot-infested putrefaction and juices. Once you've smelled it, you'll never, ever forget it. It's the kind of experience that'll make you desperate to shower and wash your hair three times, then throw away the clothes that you were wearing, including your socks and shoes because that awful, horrendous smell seems permanently glued to you and all your clothing. I hoped that none of my students would ever have to experience, first hand, any of those terrible, life-altering and haunting experiences.

But, getting back to the topic of school, I have to admit that I was greatly surprised and saddened by the many condemning reactions of so many parents and teachers after they learned about my Adirondack ordeal and, also, to their unreasonable hostility and fear when they found out about my experiences in Nam. Luckily my principal was wonderful—her husband was a Vietnam combat veteran. She understood my situation, thank goodness, and helped me with the disheartening parental requests to immediately remove their children from my classroom. Apparently, some parents felt that killing in a war still made me a murderer, and killing in the Adirondacks, to survive, proved that I was still a murderer and unfit to be around children.

Did they really feel that their children were in mortal moral or physical danger being around a soldier who, during war time, killed the enemy in order to save the lives of himself and his friends and to fulfill his duty to his country? Did they really think that I had a logical choice not to kill Lester, Tom and Jake? For them, it was all too easy to judge, to criticize and condemn me when they'd never had a single experience that even remotely approximated my combat experiences, yet they were so quickly willing to condemn me with such stern vehemence and vigor. Perhaps they were the descendants of the original disgraceful, radical and fanatical Vietnam War protestors of the late 1960s and early 1970s. Well, I thought, at least they didn't attempt to spit on me or call me a baby killer.

Most parents didn't understand the inner torment that I had experienced, that I only killed because I had no other reasonable choice, that in Nam I only killed in defense of my fellow soldiers and myself and, in the Adirondacks, I killed in defense of my daughter and myself. Given the same circumstances, wouldn't they also kill to save their own children, to save their own lives? Furthermore, many parents didn't understand how I hurt emotionally and that the hurt cut deeply into me whenever I had to kill someone, even an enemy who was trying to kill me. Hell, I wouldn't hurt at all if I were a cold-blooded killer because I wouldn't have a conscience to make me feel guilty. I could see their condemnation of me in their eyes, their expressions and observe it in their behaviors. To some parents and teachers, I was still an unwelcomed murderer who would irrevocably taint their children and bring disgrace upon their school system.

They didn't, or wouldn't, try to understand that I wasn't a cold-blooded, maniacal, killing machine. I'm as human as anyone else. I have feelings like anyone else, I have regrets, I have doubts, insecurities, a conscience and other normal human characteristics and frailties. I was just a lot better trained and equipped to survive brutal, killing situations than most people are, just as a police officer is better equipped and trained to protect the public, himself and his family than the average citizen is. I won't roll over and die easily, not without a colossal struggle. Would any of them?. And if that struggle involves killing those who are trying to kill me or my loved ones, then so be it, it would be a kill-or-be-killed situation. That's not being cold-blooded or maniacal, or heartless, not in my book, anyway. It's simply the basic application of common sense, a very "human," and instinctive drive to survive, to stay alive, to preserve your life.

Then there were some of my colleagues, who previously had known nothing of my past until the newspapers informed them of my military, honorary medals and decorations, as well as the deeds that I had performed to earn them. The newspapers glorified my ability to kill with knives and martial arts skills, commando-style, and even let it be known that I probably killed many more VC (Viet Cong) and NVA (North Vietnam Army) in South Vietnam, compared to the Adirondacks killings, via silent stalking, at night, with a knife. I remember one unauthorized newspaper headline that stated: HERO SOLDIER KILLS MORE WITH KNIVES THAN WITH BULLETS. Thankfully, the various medias didn't find out about the garrote that I sometimes used.

During daylight hours, the Marine snipers were considered the deadliest beings on earth, by the VC. The VC had their own snipers, of course, but they didn't have the same high caliber excellent training, or superior weaponry—unless they had the superior Russian AK-47 rifle—so they usually weren't nearly as good as the Marine snipers. They had skills that were inferior to Marine snipers. That's not to say that the VC weren't feared. They certainly were feared, but not with the intensity that the VC feared the Marine snipers whose motto was "One shot. One kill," which the Marine snipers proved daily. It was a highly accurate motto that the VC couldn't match and it terrorized them.

But, as some newspapers went on to elaborate, only the American forces had such a man, sometimes known as "The Wolf," who stalked and silently killed the enemy at night with such stealth and deadly cunning that the VC and NVA offered an exorbitantly high bounty to anyone who could kill him and bring his severed head to the authorities. Supposedly, there were stories and rumors of VC and NVA soldiers seeing a white wolf when there were no native wolves in Vietnam. These sightings very often occurred the same night as many of the silent killing of their comrades The rumored sightings and tales of this white wolf absolutely terrified the VC, many of whom couldn't and wouldn't sleep all night—which was very good for American soldiers because without sleep the VC and NVA were tired and often careless. Being tired and careless got many of them killed before they could kill Americans. At night, with a combat blade and martial arts techniques, including the sometimes use of a garrote, I horrified and haunted the minds of the enemy. Wolf and I owned the night. We kept the enemy on *edge*, literally speaking.

Interestingly enough, some newspapers even dug up the fact that, in 1973, a murderer named Robert Garrow hid from the law in the Adirondack mountains area after killing two people with a knife. Needless to say, the comparisons that were made were tantamount to yellow journalism at its very worst. It was mostly shoddy journalism and sensationalism, but millions of Americans love that kind of crap. It's usually exhibited next to the check-out clerks in grocery stores, and sells quickly to the persistently naïve, thoroughly bored and extremely gullible type of person. Sometimes this kind of journalistic dung even gets into the regular city newspapers, but with much less detail and space.

I chuckled when I thought of the irony of the phrase, "The pen is mightier than the sword." The newspapers certainly were killing me with ink, though, I suppose, they thought they were making me a "hero." Perhaps they mistakenly thought that I'd be forever grateful with their self-serving, hyperbolic tales. I refused their offers to interview me, so I guess they had to make up some of the manure that they were printing, making the stories much more interesting, for the hopelessly credulous and also making their newspapers sell quickly and in large amounts. Of course, we should all know that it's the *dollar* not the *truth* that's of utmost importance. And the issues of privacy, accuracy and fairness are, for the most part, non-issues.

Anyway, that's how the newspapers portrayed me, as an unstoppable killing machine, like a robot or android, minus any feelings, except those needed to kill and kill again. Next, I half expected them to make a "paper coffin" for me, then bury me in their files when they'd finished glorifying some of my more accurate deeds. But, I guess it could have been worse. That was no satisfaction, however, because with further thought I realized that almost any situation could be worse than it was. No comfort for me there.

With all that hyperbole and lies, no wonder some of my colleagues, as well as some parents, grew cold and scared in my presence. I felt like a leper each time I walked into the teachers' lunch room and saw heads turn to look at me, then suddenly turn downward to stare at their food in total silence. That reaction was, of course, the exact opposite of the hurried and friendly chatter that had been going on as I entered the room.

Then, after I sat down, I could feel the heat of staring eyes on my neck. The heat of those stares, I imagined, were like alien laser-beams probing me. Sometimes the stares felt like worms crawling up my back and neck. I hoped, of course, that time would repair any distrust or fear that parents and colleagues had of me. But, in all fairness, I should mention that there were many who didn't treat me like that. There were some understanding colleagues. They were a great comfort to me during those somewhat sad months of mental discomfort and rejection.

My principal's Vietnam veteran husband called me. It was great to talk to someone who had something in common with some of my experiences. We talked often and became good friends. Actually, if something was bothering me, I preferred to talk to him, rather that my "shrink" because of our common Vietnam experiences and shared memories of places and things that we had both seen, though we were unaware of each other when we were both in Vietnam.

In the last few months I had also become very interested in the Adirondack Forest Preserve. I voraciously read books, booklets, manuals, maps and magazine articles about he Adirondack mountain area, all its mountains, rivers, forests, lakes, ponds, bogs, marshes, animals and even some tourist attractions. I plan to vacation there a week or two during the summer break from school, and this time I'm sure that I'll enjoy every day that I'm there. I may have to go alone, if Grace and Sam choose not to go. I'll do some mountain climbing, hiking the trails, fishing and canoeing. I think I'll stay away from Long Lake and the Preston Ponds area. No use dredging-up bad memories that should stay buried.

The beauty of the Adirondack mountains doesn't make a person their willing prisoner so much as it makes them not want to request amnesty or to seek parole. The Adirondack mountains area makes a person want to be its prisoner, voluntarily trapped in beauty that comes in many forms. The area is like a friendly jailer whom few want to run from.

*   *   *   *   *   *   *

Christmas was coming, a time for peace, friendship and good deeds, though I didn't believe in that holiday in any religious sense.

One night when Sam and Grace were asleep, I got out of bed quietly so as not to wake up Sam. Silently I walked into the living room and sat in the darkness with only the moon shining through the picture window to provide light. Big flakes of snow floated out of the dark sky like miniature parachutes that were landing silently on the ground. There was no breeze and a quietness prevailed that I found comforting.

I sat down and wondered what had awakened me. Must have been a dream. I tend not to remember my dreams. Perhaps they are disturbing dreams and forgetting was a defensive mechanism. I didn't know what it was, but I did know that I felt uncomfortable about something.

I sat in my recliner chair, tipped back slightly and watched the floating snow flakes build up, layer after layer until the grass was covered with a white, fluffy blanket.

Then, for some unknown reason, thoughts of a Native American story burst into my mind, like someone suddenly jumping out of a closet to scare me. My thoughts were of an elder Indian who was teaching a boy who was approaching manhood. The elder Indian told the boy that there are two wolves living in every man, one good and one bad. These wolves, the elder said, are constantly fighting as a child grows towards manhood. Eventually one wolf will win the struggle and be dominant. That victorious wolf will determine the primary character and behaviors of the young Indian throughout the remainder of his life. The boy is puzzled by the words of the wise elder of his tribe, so the boy only pauses briefly before he asks the elder, "Grandfather? How do you know which wolf wins?" The wise elder looks deeply into the boys eyes and gives a simple answer: "The wolf that always wins is the one that you decide to give the most food," he tells the boy. The boy asks for an explanation, but the elder stands and walks away from the boy.

Inside my mind there's only one Wolf, but, like a coin, there are two sides to him. It's my job to feed him much more good than bad. It's not an easy job. I hope I don't falter.

I watched the snow get deeper. I looked at the moon and it reminded me of a cut fingernail or a cuticle. The wind picked up and the snow started drifting, just as I was drifting off to sleep.

My last thought was of the time that Grace and I arrived home from our ordeal in the Adirondacks. I stripped off my clothes and took a shower immediately. I asked Sam to throw away everything that I had been wearing in the Adirondacks. She picked up my clothes off the bathroom floor and stared at the insides of my shirt and pants, then said, "Roman? What's all this white hair that's inside your pants and shirt?"

/../.-/- -/.-/.-./.-/-/../- - -/-./.-/.-../../...//-/